Coming soon:

SATAN HALL

CARROLL JOHN DALY

BLACK MASK

Matthew Moring
Editor

Keith Alan Deutsch
Editor Emeritus

Subrights & Permissions

For Reprints:
media@blackmaskmagazine.com

For Back Issues:
*Please visit
www.blackmaskmagazine.com.*

BLACK MASK (Vol. 37, No. 2), Spring 2018. Published semiannually by Black Mask. Annual subscription $29.90 in the U.S.A. and possessions, $59.80 elsewhere payable in advance in U.S. funds. Subscription orders and correspondence regarding subscriptions should be sent to P.O. Box 835, Norwood MA 02062-0835. © 2018 by Steeger Properties, LLC, all rights reserved. Black Mask is a Registed Trademark of Steeger Properties, LLC. The stories in this magazine are all fictitious, and any resemblance between the characters in them and actual persons is completely coincidental. Reproduction or use, in any manner, of editorial or pictorial content without express written permission is prohibited. Submissions must be accompanied by a self-addressed stamp envelope. The publisher assumes no responsibility for unsolicited manuscripts or artwork. POSTMASTER: Send changes to *Black Mask*, P.O. Box 835, Norwood MA 02062-0835. Printed in the U.S.A.

Behind The Mask

ISSUE NUMBER four of the revived *Black Mask* is here!

This time out, we've included five ALL-NEW hard-boiled yarns—written by a quintet of promising new authors. Please let us know what you think of their stories: we're planning on including new material in futures as well if the response is good.

In addition to these new yarns, we've included several classic pulp stories by some of the best authors of the pulp era.

Oh, and our cover is a rare treat: it's an unpublished, vintage *Black Mask* cover from the 1940s! Lunnon was the primary cover illustrator for *Black Mask* during Fanny Ellsworth's era. It's suspected it was intended as the May 1940 cover, but *Black Mask* was sold to Popular Publications and the title underwent a drastic makeover: Lunnon's cover illustration no longer fit the style of the magazine. We're glad to present it here to adorn an issue of *Black Mask*… its original intention.

Look for another issue of *Black Mask* in the summer.

"The Lookalike Killer," "Claire's Wasn't," "The Isle of the Dolls," and "Just Another Job, That Doesn't Pay Very Well" appear here for the first time. "The Griffin's Living Death" originally appeared in *Detective Fiction Weekly* (March 16, 1935). "The Unholy Crew" originally appeared in *Detective Tales* (February 1938). "Swamp Fetish" originally appeared in *Jungle Stories* (Win 1949/50). "The White Peril" originally appeared in *North•West Stories* (1st January 1926). "Spy Against Europe" originally appeared in *Argosy* (February 23 1935).

CONTENTS

THE LOOKALIKE KILLER

by Robb T. White

"OU AWAKE?"

"What time is it?"

"Time to get your lazy ass out of bed and start making me some money!"

When Ron DeVine called me for a job, it was like that. Never "Good morning, Mister Jarvi. Would you be available for some work today?"

DeVine was the founder of his law firm, DeVine, Sufritta, and Nelson, which comprised as slick a trio of lawyers as you'll find this side of the Mississippi, at least in our humble bedroom suburb of Cleveland. Th biggest law firm in Northtown, DeVine's advertised on Cleveland stations featuring a perky dyed blonde in a sparkly angel costume; their catchphrase played off Ron's surname: *In need of divine intervention? Call us! We're the DeVine Law Firm at your service!*—sung by a barbershop quartet, in white gowns with those tinfoil halos. It came on so often it burrowed into your neocortex. People in town hummed the cornpone lyrics.

The barbershop quartet was Mark Sufritta's brainchild. "Sore-feet" was the trio's ace trial lawyer with a luxuriant helmet of gray, coiffed hair; he connected me with Ron. I've known him since high school. He's a demon for attaching himself like a cockleburr to the prosecution's weakest point, and it's amazing how often it works with that one knuckleheaded juror who thinks holding out against a conviction despite a mountain of evidence meticulously accumulated against Sorefeet's client is a mandate from on high—Mark's syrupy closing statements practically promise the hold-out a guaranteed place in heaven. Jake Nelson, an ex-jock with a busted nose, handles tort cases and does any small-potatoes estate work. But every big-money case falls into the lap of Ron "Nino" DeVine, Esquire.

Much as I hate that gravely-voiced call, I wasn't doing so much business from my Northtown office in the harbor I could afford to be choosy. Being a one-man operation, it behooves me to roll out of bed, hit the shower, slam my system with two cups of black coffee and hie me to yon faux-Tudor office on Lake Avenue to do the master's bidding. DeVine's was a few notches above the ambulance-chasing firm it had started out as, and they paid well. Moreover, a word in the right ears from DeVine to his Cleveland connections could jolt my own business out of the doldrums.

As if I needed another reason, I was getting weary of following errant spouses from one freeway motel rendezvous to the other.

Some work I did for DeVine's was downright sleazy, some could be described as dangerous. None of it left goodwill in my wake when I turned in the reports. Some ex-wives in town despise me on sight after I'd assisted their husbands. The fact I worked as hard gathering evidence for wives to leave their husbands shorn of a sizeable portion of their earthly goods made little difference. My plate glass window has been shot out twice, my car vandalized, and one client's ex took special umbrage at my zeal in her behalf and is currently doing three-to-five in the Lake Erie Correctional for attempting to hire a hit man to arrange my premature death in as gruesome a manner as said hitman could accomplish. Fortunately, that hit man was an undercover sheriff's deputy.

Rich people are smart but not always in the ways of crime. However, you'd think by now everybody had the same memo that jails everywhere tape all calls in and out. The defendant's resorting to pig-Latin from the county hoosegow didn't fool anybody. During *voire dire* when "uck-fay that umbag-scay up" was translated for the jury, some laughed aloud. Sufritta told me when he and the prosecutor were in Judge Mangold's chambers before trial started, the judge gave out a yip or a bark of laughter at the pig Latin ruse. Northtown's "Hanging Judge of the Criminal Courts" isn't known for humor. "You see I'm not laughing, Mark," I told him outside the trial room.

Thirty minutes later, I was sitting across Ron's gleaming desk watching him give me that lawyer's appraisal, a stare to remind me I served at his pleasure. I gazed over his desk, big enough that a sequoia must have been sacrificed for it; it was cluttered with Newton's cradles and pendulum balls, those executive toys people display. In Ron's case, his stacks of briefs and client files obscured much of the space.

I'd asked him why he didn't want the name of his lawyer-client on my report.

"Because we're a brotherhood, shamus. You guys, *sheesh*, you private eyes would knock your mother over if she happened to be standing on a dime."

I said, "I can't be very effective if I'm working in the dark."

"Don't be dumb, Ray. No all-night surveillance dressed like a wino in an alley or crawling through hedges to peek into people's bedroom windows. This is easy-peasey."

I found it ironic that all the window-peeping, filthy-alley-lurking, and belly-crawling I'd done had been at his behest for his clients. If you've ever seen the derelict buildings and crime-ridden streets of East Cleveland, you'd appreciate that.

"It doesn't sound easy to me," I argued.

"Trust me, it is."

When a lawyer says to you, "Trust me," watch out.

"I don't know—"

"Ray, let me spell it out for you. The client's reputation is what matters here. You know what that means, right? You're in business. Word gets out some *schmucko* is embezzling funds, they're done around here."

I hardly thought Northtown qualified as the legal mecca of Northeastern Ohio. He saw the skeptical look on my face.

"I'm talking about Cleveland, Jarvi, where the action is."

Action means only one thing in Nino's lexicon. Justice? Truth? Those are quibbles for dullard law-school professors to wrangle over like some theologian in the Middle Ages arguing about how many angels could dance on the head of a pin. DeVine once told me *Share and share alike* was the absolute worst expression to come out of Blackstone's Law Commentaries since the Magna Carta. If a lawyer carried that silly notion on his pennant into trial combat, Ron said, he or she deserved the annihilation sure to follow. If it didn't involve spreadsheets with billable hours, it didn't exist. Next to *Make me some money*, *Get me some of that green* was his favorite saying.

Still, I had my doubts about the easy part. DeVine was a go-between for an in-house private investigation into a big Cleveland firm's finances. Using a Northtown law firm was a way to keep a lid on potential gossip from being leaked. If someone over there in the KeyBank building off the Memorial Shoreway was running a scam on Boone & Fuqua, it could ruin its glossy, white-shoe reputation.

Both Lisa Boone and Thomas Fuqua were among Cleveland's elite in law and social circles both. Lisa Boone was especially well connected to city politics and the upper levels of its social strata. I liked Tom. I'd met him on occasion and seen him on the news involving cases that weren't high profile. He was the firm's workhorse and biggest moneymaker. I liked him because he did *pro bono* work that helped defendants that needed a break to keep the law's machinery from crushing them. DeVine, on the other hand, was an ex-seminarian who had gone over to the dark side; he enjoyed pointing out *misericordia* was medieval Latin for "merciful" but *misericorde* meant a sharp-pointed dagger used for delivering the death stroke.

"I need more details," I said; "you say you want a report in three weeks, tops."

"Can't be helped," DeVine said, wrinkling his brow as if in sympathy with my dilemma. "The firm's audit is coming up. It'll be too late to plug a leak after that. Besides, Lisa wouldn't say—exactly," he replied.

"What the hell does that mean, she won't say *exactly?*"

"She thinks it's possible Tommy might be involved."

Thinks? I can't investigate properly on the strength of a partner's suspicion. Besides, I don't have the access I'd need to get deep inside an operation like that. You need a bigger outfit for this job, more personnel. I know some Cleveland investigators and you can afford them—"

"Ray, shut up and listen to me. You do way too much thinking for a gumshoe with a high-school diploma. You're a foot soldier—no, a mercenary—in the never-ending battle against the forces of darkness. You just need to do what your commanding officer tells you. Period."

It wasn't worth arguing with DeVine. I could have mentioned how many thousands of lowly foot soldiers perished charging machine-gun nests for no battlefield advantage on some nitwit commander's orders between Gallipoli and the Battle of the Somme in 1916 alone. It wouldn't change his mind or his attitude. We

both knew I needed the money. A *fait accompli*, as Ron had said to me in the past whenever he wanted to end all discussion over my objections. He's a walking French dictionary who improves my vocabulary all the time.

ALICIA BOWMAN, the office manager at Boone & Fuqua, met me at Riccardelli's on the pier off Ninth Street. I'm a fiend for Italian food and it was a rare opportunity to goose the bill to DeVine with some pasta primavera. She looked like one of those prim TV school marms from a black-and-white era western. *Prim* might not be the right word. Her ash-blonde hair was swept back and finished off in a braid. Every hair front and back knew its assigned place, even those tiny frizzy ones surrounding her pretty, oval face.

"I hope this isn't taking you away from your work, Miss Bowman," I said.

"No, it's my regular lunch hour," she replied.

She studied the wine list. All those varieties of mashed grape make no impression on me; my DNA had been stamped with a preference for malt whisky. I forebear on the job, mostly.

"Alicia—"

"Miss Bowman, if you don't mind."

"Of course, apologies. Miss Bowman, I know that Lisa Boone has taken you into her confidence, so I'll be blunt. You have access to the financial records, every transaction, and every lawyer in the firm has to submit work to you for and processing or to be passed on to one of the junior partners."

She looked impatient while I summarized her job description. I threw in a fake detail here and there to see if she'd react or correct me, but her façade never cracked excerpt for a scrape of her fork across the plate of mussels she seemed uninterested in.

"I'm stating the obvious, "I said, "but has there been any discrepancy in procedure or protocol in the firm that caught your attention in the last few weeks or so? Something… unorthodox?"

She stared at me for a long moment. "Unorthodox," she said, repeating my big-word-of-the-day.

"No, nothing like that. Everything's completely normal."

She had agreed to meet me at the bar when I called the firm. I described the blue suit I would be wearing. A light rain fell when she showed up wearing a stylish fawn poncho, which she kept on until we were shown our table. Her blouse was sheer, an odd combination with the black bra beneath, I thought, but a man with a single blue suit to his name ought never to speak of fashion *faux pas*, one of my borrowed terms from Ron. Odder still was the flouncy ruff at her neck and the thin silver cross hanging down her chest. All I could think of was *Jesus dangles in the valley*. When she leaned forward over her plate, the outline of the cups strained against the fabric. I admit to gawking at women, but on the job, I make sure I pay attention to how they use their bodies around me whatever they're saying. Alicia was pitching me fast balls of modesty in business attire but mixing in some tricky off-speed pitches to exploit a male's infantile attraction to a woman's breasts. Granted, it was subtle, hardly a Burly-Q performance, but it bothered me at the time. Ron had told me Lisa thought highly of her assistant, a divorced woman and single mother of two. Alicia had been hired over more qualified women with associate degrees, he said. Alicia Bowman's job was to coordinate the flow of business all day in a busy, prestigious law firm, so she was no clerical drudge assigned to shuffle papers, make coffee, and smile at stupid lawyer jokes. That made her a vector for any shenanigans or dodgy deals. Alicia's signature on documents was critical. Of course, that pointed the arrow of guilt right at her.

I made her my first contact for that reason. I'd cleared it with Tom Fuqua at Ron's suggestion. It was Tom, Ron told me, who first alerted Lisa to the possibility of malfeasance. Two weeks ago, he'd bumped into a guy from Price Waterhouse, who did the firm's accounting. They were having drinks at the bar in the trendy Warehouse district. This guy told Tom all was not kosher with the books and there could be "some surprises" in the forthcoming audit.

I looked back longingly at her unfinished plate of mussels destined for the waste bucket, paid the bill and left a tip. As the parking valet brought my dinged-up heap out front, I opened the door for her, but she refused my offer of a ride back to the firm, saying she had a small errand to run first. The valet waved a taxi over.

Why waste a moment trying to distract me? The answer could be either of two possibilities: First, I was deluded about her mixed signals—the body language going in opposite directions. Second, she was trying to distract me for a reason. I could still afford a couple databases that let go a little deeper on her than what Ron told me, but I saw nothing amiss. No criminal record, a speeding ticket on Superior two years ago, but not a whit of financial problems.

I cursed DeVine under my breath as I drove up Ninth behind her taxi. Maybe I'd spooked her, and she was bolting for Cleveland-Hopkins for a flight to the Caribbean with bags of stolen cash. Boone & Fuqua made DeVine's tort cases look like chump change. Their fancy website lauded credentials from Ivy League law schools and touted several "seven-figure judgments" involving faulty stents, surgical nets, or other kinds of product malfeasance.

I like to play the clown to see if I can shake loose a reaction when I do interviews, so I'd asked Alicia what it must be like to see court orders for massive payouts passing through her hands with all those zeroes behind the numbers: "Millions for the firm's lawyers to divvy up like pigeons diving on a spilled bag of peanuts." I didn't miss the downward curl of her lips; she cut her eyes to her plate as if those mussels suddenly looked yummy. That's when the upper-body movements began in earnest.

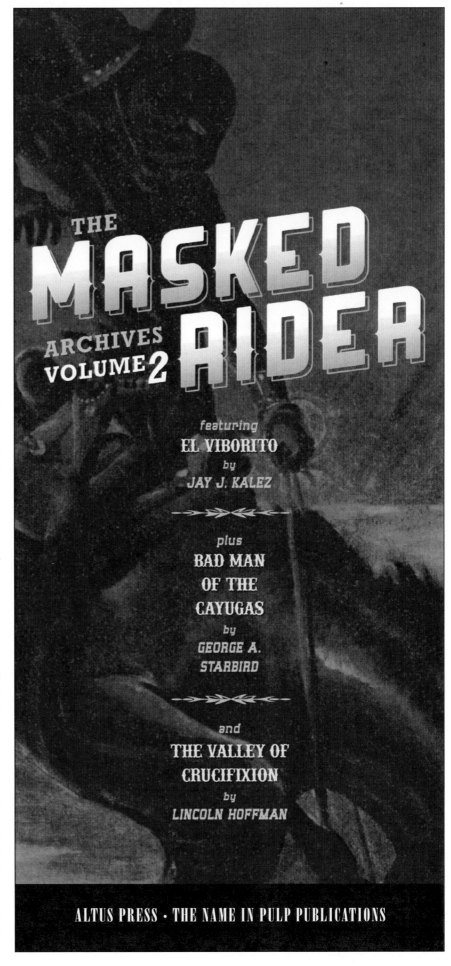

THE MASKED RIDER

ARCHIVES VOLUME 2

featuring

EL VIBORITO

by

JAY J. KALEZ

plus

BAD MAN OF THE CAYUGAS

by

GEORGE A. STARBIRD

and

THE VALLEY OF CRUCIFIXION

by

LINCOLN HOFFMAN

ALTUS PRESS · THE NAME IN PULP PUBLICATIONS

I'm not attractive to women, by and large; they don't flirt with me.

The gods who control private investigators enjoy watching us endure hours of boring surveillance. Occasionally, they cut me a break. Alicia made it easy. Her taxi jumped off Ninth to the innerbelt and blew past Progressive Field and swung right, weaving between the orange barrels, to hop onto Interstate 71. Nine miles later, I sat at the light for short-term parking as she was getting out and paying the driver in front of the airport Marriott. For a while, I thought that Caribbean escape was happening in front of my eyes.

It cost me twenty dollars and a nudge from a plausible story to get her room number from a motel maid pushing a laundry cart on the second floor. An ideal place for surveillance with transients coming and going all day as anonymously as any concourse a hundred yards across the parking lot.

I knew I couldn't be so lucky as to believe she was blowing town and making my work a one-day miracle. It could be a lover's tryst, nothing more. Except that she'd bypassed a half-dozen first-class hotels downtown and a couple dozen freeway motels to get here.

Tom Fuqua appeared at the opposite end of the lobby two hours later. He looked intent through my camera lens, which I'd stuck through a crack in the stairwell door. I had him full-face and profile before he rapped on her door. It opened almost immediately. Before it closed behind him, I heard the murmur of voices from a TV set playing. Now it was "hurry up and wait," the lonely p.i.'s credo once more in effect.

Naturally, my thinking fell into those grooves of marital infidelity. Most wives who hire me don't need the *in flagrante delicto* proof, as DeVine likes to say, of their cheating men, fortunately. Those aren't easy to get from a high-rise balcony. Just the fact that he's *there* with *her* does it. I've had only one case in my career where the wife refused to believe her husband was unfaithful because the lying cheater concocted a terrific story to explain the motel away and she bought it. I had to take her to small claims to get paid. They're still married, and he's still cheating on her.

Alicia left the room a half-hour later wearing that poncho. That didn't jibe with my experience. Even for a world-record quickie, something wasn't right. Sometimes the man will leave a few minutes after for appearance's sake—or in case someone like me happens to be in the vicinity with a telephoto lens. About five minutes later, I watched Alicia come back down the corridor. Her stride was different from before. This time, she took longer strides, seemed more purposeful in her walk. Her face was obscured with the hood over it, but I'd already snapped her leaving in profile. She rapped on the door three times, as before, and it opened to admit her.

Twenty minutes later, they were still inside. Then the door opened and she left again. The same purposeful walk. A woman's walk is dictated by her pelvis; every man knows that. Alicia's high can gave her a distinctive walk. I know that sounds terribly sexist, but as I said, I stay sober and alert on the job.

I was mulling over my confusion when a different maid passed down the hallway with a key ring on her belt. I left my hiding place in the stairwell and approached her. I said I'd accidentally left my shoes under the bed but had already checked out and just came upstairs to fetch them. When she looked uncertain, I put a crisp ten in her palm to help her decide in my favor.

She opened the door and stood in the doorway to make sure I wasn't going to steal anything. The TV set was still on. Ellen DeGeneres was dancing with some aging Hollywood celebrity while the audience clapped and danced in place. The beds were made, a bit mussed at the foot of the first bed where they'd been sitting.

There were shoes there, all right, and they were under the second bed. The trouble was that they were still attached to Tom Fuqua's feet. He lay behind the bed with a bullet hole in his otherwise immaculate white shite shirt and a surprised look on his face. When I turned around, the maid was gone.

The gods, like lawyers, also love to lead us private eyes on. *Here,* they say, *this one's a piece of cake. Follow the woman, see her lover show up. Snap the two of them, presto, finite, you're done and now able to reap your handsome fee from Ron DeVine, Esq.…*

It was a long day well into the afternoon spent being grilled by detectives on scene and then back at the police station on Lakefront, where I made a full statement and volunteered for a polygraph. The lead cop wanted to be sure I was on the up-and-up. Cops like private eyes like dogs like fleas. He said to me, "This will help out later if it goes to court and you get called to testify. You know how lawyers can be."

"Oh yes," I agreed; "I do know how lawyers can be."

DEVINE HAD steam whistling through his ears when he saw me the next morning.

"You screwed up royally, Jarvi, and I mean good."

"I fail to see how doing what you asked me to do—"

"Does the word *discreet* have any meaning in your vocabulary at all?"

We went around and round like that for a while—a couple playground kids arguing in the sandbox about whose toy truck wrecked whose castle.

Fifteen minutes later, he calmed down. I wasn't off the hook yet. I had to endure his lawyerly "summation" of the damage my ineptness had caused. The *Plain Dealer* devoted considerable space and a large type font on the front page. Not that big next to an alien space invasion of Earth but big enough. DeVine tapped the paper on his desk several times for emphasis, especially whenever he referenced Lisa Boone's name.

"She tore me a new asshole on the phone this morning," he said.

"You can blame me," I said.

"I did," he replied. "Do you think that matters? Even the mayor's dodging reporters at city hall."

"I didn't shoot Fuqua," I reminded him.

"You might as well have," he fumed.

No matter what I said to placate, I was pushing his buttons, so I got up to leave.

"Where are you going?"

"I thought we were done."

"*Undone*, not *done*!" DeVine exclaimed.

"What are you talking about?"

"You started this clusterfuck," Ron said; "you're going to have to finish it."

My jaw dropped. It's no cliché when people say that.

"You're not—are you telling me you want to keep me on the case?"

"Not me," he huffed. "Lisa Boone insists you remain on it."

"Why would she want me after… yesterday."

"How many times do I have to tell you? Stop thinking, Jarvi. Follow orders." He looked exhausted. "I told Lisa I wouldn't personally touch you again with a barge pole."

"Can I include this meeting as part of the fee?"

"Get out of my office, shamus."

He waved his hand idly back and forth as if I were a pesky fly that wouldn't cease bothering him.

In a way, that's what I was. Small payback for the insults DeVine had been heaping on me all morning.

THE CLEVELAND detective who had me polygraphed shut me down when I asked about the case. I tried several reporters on the *Plain Dealer* with whom I had a passing relationship. I couldn't pick up any scuttlebutt. When I'd hung out my p.i. shingle, I put away my ego. You have to get used to being treated like an Ethiopian domestic servant in Kuwait City if you want to get results.

I returned to my office after a meat loaf sandwich and a beer for lunch. The message on my recorder rattled me—her voice. I had to play it twice.

"Hello, Mister Jarvi, this is Alicia Bowman. I'd like to speak to you. Will you be at your desk later? I'll call back."

Sometimes the gods can't make up their minds whether to toss me a bone or toss me deeper into the latrine pit.

She called at seven that night. You couldn't tell from her voice she was wanted for questioning in a notorious murder or that the paper's implication of "a recent investigation into misappropriate funds at Boone & Fuqua" had smeared her reputation in the court of public opinion. She spoke in the same bland monotone as when I'd asked her how she liked her mussels at Riccardelli's.

"You should turn yourself in," I said.

"I can't," she said.

"Look, the cops go easier on you if you cooperate. Maybe there's an explanation why you had to shoot—"

"I didn't kill him."

That bored tone was gone, finally. Her voice quavered.

"What—what did you say?"

"I didn't shoot Tom," she repeated. "He was alive when I left the room."

"You better explain," I said.

Crazy just got crazier. "Alicia"—*to hell with the formality*, I thought—"do you have any idea what trouble you're in right now?"

"I can't talk right now. Someone's following me."

"Where are you? Just tell me that much," I pleaded.

"No," she said and this time she put real snap into the word. "I don't know you from Adam. I don't know if I can trust you. You could be setting me up."

"You called me, remember? I don't know how I can prove to you I'm not setting you up."

"I want it on the record," she said. The cold voice back in control.

Work for a lawyer and you start talking and thinking like them.

She agreed to come to my office and I'd record her statement for the cops. I told her I'd have a deputy sheriff, a friend of mine, there so he could escort her to authorities. I didn't know if I believed her claim of innocence. Once bit, twice shy, as they say. Every minute that passed after I hung up and did not call the police was another step toward an obstruction charge or possibly worse—accessory after the fact. She wasn't my client. I had no loyalty to her.

I drank a few whiskeys too many that night. I tend to reward myself for minor accomplishments, and I considered garnering a fat fee from DeVine's just that; it's a lifelong failing I've paid for often enough but it seems the bible is right about certain dogs returning to their vomit. I woke at two-fifteen, looking at my clock's bright-red digits, and sat bolt upright in bed. The first word out of my mouth was: "Shit."

Stupid, stupid.…Why didn't I think it through I stead of salivating over my money?

I thought of calling every freeway motel between the Rock-n-Roll Hall of Fame and the airport's Marriott on the off-chance she might have used her real name. With every cop in every muster room between Cleveland and Columbus having her photo and description, her car's description and license plate, that would have been a sheer waste of time. Cops would already have hit every friend, family member, acquaintance, and lawyer in the building by now. Motels and hotels would take longer if she'd used an alias, but they'd get to her eventually.

Make it through the night, Alicia, I prayed. I cursed myself for not thinking like a lawyer—like Lisa Boone.

Alicia was found off the Painesville exit from I 90 three blocks from her sister's house on Johnnycake Road in a parking lot. Her kids were staying there. Maybe that's how she was lured or the person who had been following her wasn't paranoia. A cruiser finishing up his graveyard shift saw her SUV with the engine running and was concerned the driver might have succumbed to carbon monoxide; it was lead poisoning from a small-caliber weapon. Alicia was slumped over with a bullet hole in her head. A two-shot derringer with fancy scrollwork issued to her was found on the floorboard with one of its two chambers empty. The autopsy said the slug rattled around in her brain, turning it into mush, before coming to rest against the skin of her scalp on the other side. The vehicle was leased to Boone

& Fuqua. Lisa was known to drive it more than anyone.

I told my theory to detectives. They were skeptical. I told it to Northtown cops, too, and wrote to the Ninth District State's Attorney General. I even went to my best contacts at the *PD* with it. Their lawyer said *absolutely not*, the paper would be sued for libel if my story was printed.

"You have no evidence, Mister Jarvi."

"I have photos of Alicia leaving that motel room on two occasions."

"Yes, we know. Wearing a poncho, you said."

"It's Alicia the first time. The second time is Lisa Boone," I insisted.

"Your images are too blurred to tell that, Mister Jarvi. Weren't you shooting through the crack of a door at the end of a hallway? Your photos add more weight to the case against Alicia Bowman, and if you can't prove Ms. Boone was already in the motel, what good are they?"

He was right. Lisa Boone had an airtight alibi on the day and at the time her partner was murdered. Not one person at the Marriott remembered anyone resembling Lisa Boone by name or description, although there were plenty of vague descriptions of other women. Cops said all the names for that day checked out and no one had booked the room in advance. The lobby had no record of anyone except Alicia Bowman registered for that room and she was identified by several staff.

"I'm afraid that's it, Mister Jarvi," the lawyer told me, "unless you can put her in that room."

I HAD another lawyer giving me similar advice, only more colorfully and with more Anglo-Saxon terms used than his usual lawyerly Latin. I was angry because he was so pleased with himself. He even told me he was feeling "chipper." I suspected the check from Boone & Fuqua carried a fatter bonus than I knew, and it was one not likely to be shared.

"Are you out of your fucking mind? You better sit on that whackjob theory until the pigs eat your brother," Ron DeVine said.

It was the second or third variation on that theme in the last fifteen minutes. The only constant in his invective was me in my lonely grave, in my casket, or drooling in some nursing home. I had to ask him what "shuffling off the mortal coil" meant, one of his more colorful figures for the time when it would be all right for me to release my theory again.

"Shakespeare, *Hamlet*—I think. Christ, didn't you get a high school diploma?"

"I took a lot of shop classes," I said.

"It figures," he said. "Wait, it's *Macbeth*, maybe. But who gives a shit? The point is this. Keep your overheated notions about that particular female under your hat, Raymond."

He was still gloating because his firm got off unscathed. That's all that mattered.

"No harm, no foul, right, Ron?"

My sarcasm blew right past him, a leaf in a gale.

"Nothing paints like mud, Ray. You were in way over your head."

"Who put me there, Ron?"

"Not me," he sniffed in disdain as if I'd passed gas in his *sanctum sanctorum*, another of his pet expressions.

"She had four patsies, including you," I said, weary of my failure to persuade even the man who sent me on that doomed mission. "All of us were playing a role, working in our turns like pieces of clockwork."

"Kiss my ass—how do you figure?"

"Alicia was a goner from the moment she signed off on those phony documents Lisa gave her—who else? Boone showed them at private parties, like some corrupt Tupperware party, fishing for investors to rip off. She never attempted to embezzle a single dime, Ron, don't you see?"

"Why isn't there a record then? No one's seen them," he retorted. He'd argue with the devil if it suited his purpose.

"Alicia never made copies," I said. "Why would she? She thought Lisa was her friend as well as her boss."

"She left a mark on you, too, didn't she? I always thought Lisa had a thing for her, you know? Neither one married, no guys in the picture. Hey, don't look at me like that. Two gorgeous women, who cares?"

"I didn't like Alicia," I said and felt bad having to admit it. "But we patsies recognize a—a complicity in one another."

DeVine scoffed. "The word you're struggling for is 'affinity.' "

"I was strongly advised by the lead detective to stop calling Cleveland PD. He told me no judge would sign off on a search warrant based on hearsay."

"That's true."

One motel clerk recalled a series of questions from the woman in that room asking about flights and long-term parking, but he could not recognize a voice recording of Lisa Boone as that voice. I gave Cleveland homicide credit for going that far in checking out my accusation.

"She had to be left as the guilty one after Fuqua was killed in the motel."

"Move on dot org, Raymond, for *Chrissake!* You can't explain how Lisa got there in what you wittily call her Alicia-disguise, can you?"

"Why short-change your esteemed colleague on a minor detail? She could have been dressed as a maid or a tourist before she changed to look like Alicia. Fuqua wouldn't have noticed right up to the moment she put the gun to his ear. Once Fuqua was dead and Alicia suspected, she had to make sure she could get to her in time. She probably used her sister as bait."

"Why *you*, if I may interject a minor wrench into your elegant theory?"

"I'll get to that," I said, "but the main thing is she's eliminated the two people who can implicate her in a crime, destroy her career, everything she's worked for, including the firm's reputation. If they're gone, Alicia blamed, she's clean."

"Not altogether," DeVine said. "There are those headlines, which aren't going away anytime soon."

"A calculated risk," I conceded. "She'll come through it. She's too well connected.

With Fuqua gone, her percentage goes up a big jump, right? Besides the way rich assholes stick together, she'll probably have a lawyer pal set up a Go-Fund-Me for her. Money calls to money."

"So speaks Northtown's working-class philosopher," Ron jibed.

Now I was sure the bonus check from Lisa Boone must have been sweeter than I first thought.

"I'll get to the part where I'm a dupe," I said. "But first I have a question for you. What did you tell Lisa Boone about me? It's been stuck in my craw she'd jump over a couple dozen hot-shot private eyes and big-name firms to want me on the case."

"I told her you were competent," Ron said.

"That's all? Competent?"

"I might have said you were new to the game, which is true. I mean, you haven't put in much time on this private-eye gig of yours, am I right?"

"Go on," I said.

"I told her you were dogged on a case but that you had—well, disadvantages."

Jesus Christ, it sounded like a line from a Hannibal Lecter film.

"What disadvantages?"

"You believe people too easily. You trust them. You take a first impression as valid coin until you get hit over the head with reality."

"What else?"

"I said you were lonely." He shrugged. "She asked about your personal life. What was I to do, man? I said you hadn't dated a woman in two years."

The prick. But he was right. It was three years. Three years, six months, two days, and a few hours since my wife had left me for another man. Lisa Boone wanted to know if I was vulnerable. She was fishing for a man a woman could mislead without difficulty.

"Did she ask if I needed the money?"

Coming Soon: THE ADVENTURES OF
BELLOW BILL

Ron shrugged again. *Affirmative*, it might as well have said.

Pigeon-holed, trussed up for market, and gift-wrapped by a clever, sociopathic woman who just happened to be one of the top lawyers in the city.

"What make you think I was duped?" Ron asked me on my way out the door.

"She knew you were a small-town piker. You'd be bound to know somebody like me," I said and closed the office door on his gaping expression. Maybe that's a wrong word, too.

YOU NEVER want to admire evil. It leaves a stain on you that doesn't wash off. I waited several weeks after the story died down, slipped away to the back pages, grew ever smaller until it finally disappeared. More sensational crimes replaced it. Embezzlement and murder had to compete with too much nowadays.

Bits of Lisa Boone's eulogy of Fuqua were cited in the Sunday paper's obit, and the memorial brochures spotlighted her glowing, anguished tribute to her "friend, partner, and mentor." I remember shivering when I read that. Imagine standing at the lectern in the funeral home gazing out among the sad faces of Tom Fuqua's wife, children, colleagues, and friends and waxing eloquent over his untimely death when that little voice inside your head is cheering you on while you pile up the phony platitudes for the very man you put in that casket just a few feet from where you're standing. It wasn't my expensive database for running deep financial audits on people that led me to it; it was the society pages in the Sunday *Plain Dealer*, dated six months earlier. Lisa Boone owned a small island in the Turks and Caicos. I made a call to a real estate office in Bermuda and enquired about purchasing land for a client. The woman I spoke to gave me an estimated cost of twelve to thirteen million for a private island.

I'll never look at a group of women chatting in an office setting and feel the same. I did get a look at Lisa Boone in the flesh. I was all the way to Memorial Shoreway just past the MLK overpass when I realized I didn't have a clue in my head what I was going to say to her. I wasn't even sure I could get past her secretary to see her for one thing. I could see a security guard throwing me to the floor and cuffing my hands behind my back. How hard is it to claim someone's a stalker? Maybe I qualified as a disgruntled employee, too, once removed. I knew I couldn't count on Ron

DeVine for a character reference if things got dicey.

I rode the elevator still unsure what I planned to say to her.

The Office Manager placard on the desk caught my eye at once. She had a desk in Lisa Boone's outer office where Alicia Bowman used to sit; she was a twenty-something brunette, cordial, with that receptionist voice you have to practice to get right: friendly but efficient, inviting but not open to untoward confidences. She startled me at first because she bore an uncanny resemblance to Alicia except for the dark chestnut hair that fell evenly down to her shoulders.

"May I see Ms. Boone?"

"Do you have an appointment, sir?"

She dropped her voice a little at the "sir" unlike the California lilt you tend to hear everywhere from young women who lack access to the levers of power. My one blue suitcoat and navy-blue tie didn't qualify as a power suit obviously. I looked down; my shoes were another disappointment.

My luck, however, changed just then—or else the gods thought I was worthy of a little "closure," another lawyer word I despised.

Lisa Boone came out of her office wafting a heady perfume in her wake. Her lips and nails were a matching carmine. She was a stunning, attractive woman in her forties, every inch the professional woman. Our eyes locked for a moment and then she looked down at her secretary and placed a manila file folder in front of her, one hand lightly touching her manager's shoulder. It was an intimate gesture in front of a stranger.

"Have that back to me at three, Sandra, hon," she said.

Sandra was all smiles and unconscious twitches, fluttering her hair but also—I could not help noticing—causing a slight temblor of movement in the fabric of Sandra's blouse. She was, like Alicia, bosomy, if that word isn't too archaic. Her blouse rippled again when she adjusted herself back around at her desk. Her boss obviously was a woman to be pleased. Lisa was high-hipped, full-breasted, and walked with purpose. Before the door shut behind her, I glimpsed a print of an island scene of palm fronds waving offshore, white sand sparkling in the sunshine, and turquoise water. Two shapely women wearing shades and skimping bikinis walked along the shoreline with colored drinks in their hands.

I thought once again of that determined stride from the Marriott motel. A moment's grim satisfaction.

Sandra said something to me, but I was already walking away. I had nothing to say. I rode down in the elevator, not thinking of anything but seeing a trio of women's faces revolving in my mind's eye like one of those kiddie kaleidoscopes at Toys-R-Us.

Alicia Bowman and Lisa's new office manager were practically sisters in looks. Lisa herself could have passed for one or the other despite the age difference; they were so much alike in facial features and body type to one another I wanted to laugh out loud—or maybe sob. Seeing one, you thought of the others. No wonder the motel staff didn't recognize Lisa that day. Once Alicia showed up, she was the only one in the room. Maybe Alicia had been picked out of the pile of applications on a hunch that her similarity would someday become useful. I imagined Lisa dyeing her hair to look like Alicia's shade and Alicia being pleased at the compliment her boss showed in adopting her color.

As Ron said more than once, my conspiracy theory has a lot of parts and anybody can ramrod one piece to fit the other.

I drank a little more back home in Northtown that night. I tried to put my mind into Lisa Boone's, but it wasn't possible. I didn't think Sandra, the new office manager, was in danger. Lisa Boone wasn't stupid. Looking like them was a way of possessing them, I thought. Once you possessed them, you could do what you wanted with them. You owned them. Maybe Lisa Boone's psychology was understood in some diagnostic manual shrinks kept on their office shelves. But it occurred to me I was a loose end. Cleveland's bigger than Northtown by far, but people gossip there, too. She'd have heard of me shooting my mouth off about my theory whether she recognized me in that glimpse from my office visit. Lisa Boone left nothing to chance like a burglar casing a house. The fact that I'm no one to give credence to makes me an acceptable risk, I suppose—until the day it doesn't.

Lisa Boone was an orb weaver who built slowly and with great care. Ever watch a spider roll a fly in a cocoon for eating later? I never told DeVine, but his Shakespeare quip stung me. I went to the library and checked out a copy of *King Lear*. There's a passage I've memorized:

As flies to wanton boys are we to th' gods.
They kill us for their sport.

He knew a lot about human nature, Shakespeare did, but he should have included—*and girls*—in that first line.

CLAIRE'S WASN'T

by Jonathan Sheppard

IT WAS a wet night outside, the rain coming down hard on the hot pavement so it sounded like bacon fat sizzling in a frying pan. It was a hell of a night to be out in.

Fortunately, I wasn't out in it.

No, I was holed up in what had become my favorite place in the whole wide world, an Irish pub on a dead-end street called Loughlin's. I sat bellied-up to the bar with my coat hung over the back of the stool and my hat pushed back on my head, drinking beer because I didn't have enough money for twelve-year-old scotch.

I was looking for something that night. Anything. A bar fight to spill me out into the alley and the rain. A friend to pick up the tab for a few of my drinks. An easy lay with a girl too drunk to know better. Or too sympathetic to know better. The only thing I wasn't looking for was what I saw.

I saw it when I got up from the bar and carried my drink over to the window to look out at the street, the wet pavement lit sporadically by the flickering neon signs in the window of Loughlin's. Signs that flashed the bar's name with a big green shamrock at the end, and two brands of domestic beer.

Across the street, half a block down, was the little store-front where I used to have an office. A tall woman in a purple raincoat stood in front of it in the driving rain, looking at where the letters of my name had been scraped off the door glass. I couldn't see her face from where I stood, just the purple of her coat and the rich chocolate brown of her hair. She hunched her shoulders up, trying to keep the chill of the rain out of her bones, and she glanced around nervously.

I stepped into the doorway, a few inches from where the rain poured down in front of me, and I yelled over the roar of the rain.

"Claire?"

Her head turned and she looked towards me. She didn't move. Neither did I, for a moment, until I saw what she didn't.

I turned back, slamming my beer down on the bar, grabbing a fistful of the bartender's sweater as I leaned across.

"You still got that old thumb-buster of yours behind the bar, Terry?"

He just looked at me.

"Hand it over," I said. "Right now."

"Trouble?" he asked. His hands went under the bar.

"No, but I think there will be in a minute."

I glanced back through the window, and the rain, at the girl standing there, and at the car that was rolling slowly up the street.

She cringed, thinking I was aiming at her, and stumbled back against the wall of the building. Only then, turning, did she see what I saw: the two men climbing out of the car that had rolled quietly up the street behind her. They wore long coats and hats, and each of them was carrying a shotgun.

I started shooting then.

My first shot missed to the right and hit the tire of their car, flattening it. I cursed and got a two-handed grip on the gun and aimed more carefully and fired again. The one on the left, on the passenger side of the car, folded up around the bullet that took him a little above the belt. Slammed back against the car and didn't move.

The shotgun boomed. The other one, the driver, was firing from the hip as he advanced towards me. He pumped, fired again, and shotgun pellets bounced off the pavement not more than three feet from me.

She screamed, then.

He wheeled instinctively towards her.

I sent my last four his way, as fast as I could pull the trigger. One smashed into a headlight on the car. One hit the bumper. And two hit him in the side, under the arm. He dropped on the sidewalk like a ton of bricks.

Claire was flattened against the side of the building, near what had been my door, shaking. I walked over to her, put my hand on her shoulder.

"Claire?" I said. "Claire, it's me. It's Jim."

Her wide eyes moved over until she was looking into mine.

"Jim…" she said quietly.

"Come on," I said. "Come with me."

With one arm around her and the other still holding the .38, we ran through the rain back into the warmth and light and Gaelic music of Loughlin's Pub.

I SWUNG the old .38 around on my hand and offered it back to Tim.

"Keep it," he said.

I looked at him.

"I don't have a permit for it and you just killed two men with it, Jim. Keep it."

I tucked the .38 in my belt and grabbed my coat off the back of the stool.

Terry's hands came up from behind the bar. In one of them, an old Smith & Wesson with a four-inch barrel. In the other, a few shiny cartridges. I grabbed them, swinging the cylinder out, pushing the cartridges in as fast as my fingers would work. I fumbled and dropped one, kept loading as I stepped out into the rain. Snapped the gun closed and thumbed the hammer back, dropping the few spare shells into my hip pocket.

Down the street she turned towards me, still not seeing what I saw.

She called my name, and it seemed like a shot, a sound that filled the whole world and zipped across the space between us to tear a bloody ragged hole through me and stop my heart. I motioned for her to move, and lifted the Smith's sights to my eye-line.

"I'll call the fuzz," Terry said.

I looked at him.

"Not yet."

I guess he saw it in my eyes, or heard it in my voice. But it comes to the same thing. He put the phone back in it's cradle without dialing, and stood there without moving. He knew.

Claire clung to my side, vibrating. I didn't need to look at her face to know that she was terrified.

"Come on," I said. "Upstairs."

We went back to the old payphone by the pool table, and ducked through the door next to it. Went up the narrow steep steps there to the second floor. I had a room over the bar. It was small, but it was cheap, and I liked it. Well, more or less.

I sat Claire down on the chair in the little kitchenette, and locked and double-bolted the door. I got a towel from the bathroom and handed it to her to dry herself with. She sat there with it clutched in her hands.

"Jim…" she said in a shaky voice.

I went to one knee in front of her, laying the .38 on the table beside me so I could take her hands.

"Claire, it's okay," I said quietly. I kissed her cheek, cold and wet from the rain. It didn't matter—it was still the best thing that had happened to me in a long, long time. "You're okay. You're with me. I won't let anyone hurt you. All right?"

She nodded, but she was still shaking.

"I'm… I'm…."

"It doesn't matter," I told her. "I've got questions but they can wait. In the meantime, let's get the hell out of here, what d'you say? Get out of the city for the night."

I went into my bedroom, which constituted three quarters of the little hole-in-the-wall apartment, and dragged my old Army foot-locker out from under the bed. I got the key from the sock-drawer and unlocked it.

My Colt Defender was right where I'd left it, wrapped in an old towel stained with gun-oil. I racked the slide and it locked back, crisp. I slid a clip into the magazine and watched the slide pop forward. Grabbed the two spare clips and the box of .45's that had been wrapped up with it. I put them on the table and then reloaded the .38 with the shells from my hip pocket. I took Claire's sopping wet coat from her, handed her my old leather jacket. She climbed into it without a word, hugged it around her.

I gathered up my guns and my girl and got the hell out of there.

ON THE freeway up through the hills, headed out of the city, I took my eyes off the road and looked at her, slumped in the seat beside me. Her dark eyes watched me.

So beautiful. And so long gone. I'd been certain I'd never see her again, and it had almost killed me. I'd stopped working. Lost my PI licence. Tried for a while to medicate the pain with cheap booze and cheap women. It hadn't worked. There wasn't anyone else for me. Claire was my first, my last, my only.

It had been a long time.

I thought about it, turning back the pages of the calendar in my head.

It had been almost four years.

The last time I'd heard her voice, it had been a cold rainy night just like this one….

I'D BEEN on the trail of a couple of real bastards, the Murphy Brothers. Danny, the older, had got the drop on me with an old leather sap. Gave me a good crack on the head, took my cash and my iron and left me bleeding face-down in a garage. I'd managed

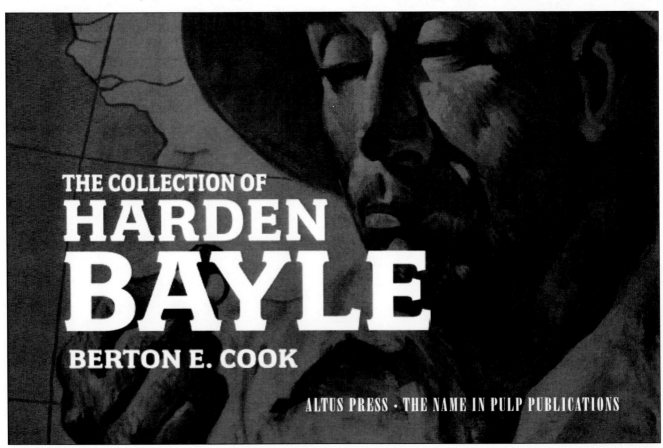

THE COLLECTION OF
HARDEN BAYLE
BERTON E. COOK

ALTUS PRESS · THE NAME IN PULP PUBLICATIONS

to get myself on my feet and got to a phone and called Claire at the office, told her to get in the car and bring me my spare gun and meet me out on the main road.

"OK, Jim, I'm coming," she'd said. "I'm coming now. You be careful. Keep your head down."

Those were the last words I heard her say. Nothing romantic or profound. Keep your head down.

And I had. I'd waited in the dark near a payphone on the side of the highway all night. I'd gotten wet and cold and shivered and waited for her.

And she hadn't come.

It wasn't the first time a woman let me down. It wasn't even the fiftieth. But I'd never thought Claire would. Not her. She was different. She was my student, my partner, a cute kid with a sharp mind, I had a diamond in the rough and all I had to do was chip away a little bit of shale. I'd turned her into a hardnosed op like me.

I thought I knew everything about her.

Then, a few days before she didn't show, she'd told me that maybe we could be more than partners. And then she'd kissed me, out of the blue. That'd been the sign. I should have seen it, I should have known that maybe there were other things about her I hadn't realized. But all the blood was rushing in the wrong direction just then.

I should have seen it.

WHEN WE turned off the main road and the tires crunched onto the gravel, she sat up straighter in her seat and looked around. I wasn't sure if she'd been asleep or just deep in thought. And I didn't care, for the moment. There would be plenty of time for questions when we got where we were going.

"Where are we?" she asked.

"My Uncle Barry's cottage," I told her.

"You never mentioned an Uncle Barry," she said.

"He died at Omaha Beach, when I was a little boy," I explained. Like his brother, my father, had.

I stopped the car at the end of the lane, maybe fifty yards from the house. Turned off the engine. I started to climb out.

"Jim, I'm scared," she said.

I got out and went around to her side, opened the door. She clung tightly to my arm, pressing herself against my side. Not that I minded at all. Claire's a nice thing to have pressing up against you.

"Here," I said. I took the bartender's .38 from my pocket and handed it to her. Five of the six chambers were loaded, and the hammer was down on the empty one. "Hold onto this for me." I figured having the piece might make her feel a little safer.

We started up towards the house.

I wasn't sure what I was expecting, but it wasn't what I got. I got the unexpected. The only thing I wasn't expecting was what I was looking for.

It was that kind of night.

THE LIGHTS were already on in the old cottage. A couple of old coal-oil lamps in the kitchen. And two men were in the house. When they heard the car they opened the door and came outside and stood in the rain to welcome us.

Seamus, the younger brother, was scarred badly along the right side of his jaw and under his ear. I knew that because of the lamp-light, and because I was the one that'd fired the shot that did the damage. He smiled with the part of his mouth that still worked.

Danny, the elder, looked much the same as he always had. A little thinner, and with a mustache now, but the same. Both of them stood in front of the house, waiting for us.

I heard two clicks in front of me. And then, a moment later, I heard one behind me. Felt something cold and iron pressing against my neck just a little above my coat collar.

"Shitbirds," I said, by way of greeting. I nodded to them politely.

"Jimmy-boy," Seamus said. "Jimmy, Jimmy, Jimmy. Long time no see."

He smiled and waved to me. The hand he waved with had a 9mm in it. Then his eyes shifted to Claire, and they changed. I saw what was in his eyes for her, and I recognized it, because I'd felt it myself.

"Come 'ere, love," he said, and she did, stepping out from behind me, lowering the bartender's revolver. She kissed Seamus's scars and handed him the .38.

"Missed you," she said to him quietly.

"Aye," he said. "Well, there'll be no more of that."

Seamus pointed his two guns at me, and Danny his.

I ignored them and looked at Claire.

"Claire?," I asked. "Baby?"

Her eyes were cold and hard when she looked at me now. I didn't want to see her like that. I wished I could forget it even as I stared at it.

"Sorry, Jimmy," she said quietly. Then she put her head down and went and stood in the doorway of the cottage. All three of us watched her go.

And then we looked at each other, and time seemed to slow down and stop, and all there was left in the world was rain and dark and bullets.

THERE WERE two of them, and they already had their guns aimed at me. I was twenty feet away from them in the dark, and my .45 was under my coat. But what the hell? I was game. I'd been pretty good, once upon a time.

A nine-second eternity later, I stood over them with the empty .45 in my trembling right hand, the slide locked open. My mouth was dry and my shirt was wet. I felt the wet place on my left side, and my hand came away red. There was a lot of red, more than the rain could dilute.

I didn't have long, and I knew it.

I hobbled over to where Claire stood in the doorway, the .38 in her hand hanging down at her side. I stumbled and fell to my knees in front of her. She was all that there was. She filled the world in front of me. My Claire, lost and come back to me.

She saw the question in my eyes and answered it before I could ask.

"I loved him," she said. "I loved him from the moment I set eyes on him. When you first sent me to tail him…."

I didn't know what to say.

"I'm sorry, Jim," she said wistfully. "I really am."

She raised the .38 and aimed it at my heart.

Instinctively I raised my .45 and pointed it at her face, the most beautiful face I've ever seen. I pulled the trigger. My gun clicked. It was empty.

Claire's wasn't.

THE ISLE OF THE DOLLS

by Richard Billingsley

ETH FELT like she was just waking up. It was nighttime and the air was cool on her skin. She heard the cries of the night creatures along the wide lazy river. Beth tried to look ahead but it was the dark of the moon. They drifted along, the boat was pushed as much by the slow current as by the tiny chugging outboard engine. What was this called? She remembered the term from her childhood, a johnboat. That's what her daddy called it. A wooden johnboat. Tommy was the pilot of their means of escape.

She suddenly and violently remembered the robbery gone wrong. The shots, the screams, the confusion. Three people dead. She couldn't believe what she saw in her head. She was lost in this, what did they call it? A fugue state. Thinking about what just happened she no longer paid attention to what was going on right now.

Tommy patted her shoulder and pointed ahead to a black mass. Beth could make out that the river flowed on both sides of an island with trees clumped in the middle. Tommy stopped the engine. There was the clunk of the engine tilted out of the water. Then she heard and felt the crunch of gravel, the scrape of sand. The johnboat stopped on the shore, Tommy roughly pushed her out.

She walked on unsteady legs in high heels onto the pebbled uneven ground. Ahead of them she could make out a small house or cabin or shack among a stand of trees. All around the shack were knee high thin weedy grasses. The breeze stopped here. The air was still, silent. On the lea side of the river bank, a cougar watched them. Overhead an owl chased some stray bats. But here were no insects, and she could intuit it, no snakes. No other animals.

Beth faltered. She had trouble walking on the loose ground in her heels. She fell back against Tommy, her little black dress riding up over her thighs. She felt the metal lump in his pocket with her hip. His .38 special. It was still warm. He pushed her forward. Tommy looked around the shack for what she didn't know.

Beth said, "You come here before?"

"Never." Tommy opened the door to the shack. He pulled Beth inside. He ignited his flashlight and shone it around the small cabin. There was a sturdy support beam in the middle of the single room. There was a cookstove off to the right. An old chair to the left. Shelves line the walls stuffed with dolls. All kinds of dolls. Their eyes wide open, seeing everything. Mouths open about to form words. Grotesque smiles on their painted faces. The dolls dominate the room.

Beth, "This creeps me out."

Tommy was silent. He walked forward and moved some dolls aside. There was a sound like an exhalation of breath. Beth involuntarily stepped back. Tommy quick as a flash stepped up and pulled her back in.

"Why do we have to be in here?" Beth's fear came out in her voice.

"The fuzz got infrared in their whirly birds. If we stay in here they won't pick us up."

"You really think the cops will use helicopters to look for us?"

"You don't know so you gotta figure they will."

"They'll see your light."

Tommy spun around and looked at Beth like he was going to slap her. She held up her hands in surrender, like she will be quiet now. Tommy turned around one more time and surveyed the room.

"It'll be alright in here."

Shock! One of the dolls lit up. Beth was paralyzed with fear. Tommy yelled at it. "What the fuck, you little fucker!"

The doll went dark.

Beth only heard the sound of their breathing. But she could tell they weren't alone.

Tommy, nervous as a cat turned to her, "I want you to sit down."

"No. Why would I do that?"

Tommy unconsciously held the gun on her. Then he dug himself and put it back in his coat pocket. "Stay put."

Beth backed up until she hit a shelf full of dolls. She looked at the dolls wide eyed, "What now?"

Tommy yelled at her, "I don't know! Why am I supposed to know everything?" He caught himself. He walked back and forth

in what seemed to Beth an unsuccessful attempt to calm down.

Beth, "Can't you sit?" She expected Tommy to shout at her again. Maybe he would hit her.

Instead he answered quietly, "I don't know how we will get out of this." There was a pause, "The dolls creep me out too."

They were silent. The only noise comes from the fish jumping in the river, the sound of gently running water, the cry of the distant cougar, the flap of wings, their breathing.

Tommy looked out the window. "I can't see anything." Beth: "I saw the boat." Tommy: "I oughta go out there and hide the goddamn boat." But he didn't move.

Beth, "There is no place to hide it."

Tommy, "I'll sink it."

Beth, "You can't! How will we get off the island?"

Tommy grabbed her and held her hands behind her. "I won't try to run away!" He jerked her hands and arms behind the support beam in the middle of the room. Beth felt the rope dig into the flesh of her wrists.

"That hurts!"

"Shut up!"

Tommy picked up his light and took the .38 out of his pocket. He went out the door. Beth sat miserably in the middle of the room. She could tell he was walking around the shore of the small island. She saw the light come come back around. A shaft of flashlight came through the window and lit up the face of a clown doll. The clown doll grinned deliriously at her.

Beth could hear Tommy as he with struggled to shove the boat off the shore. She thought that the boat was hung up on something, a root maybe. It was like he fought the boat to push it out in the water. Beth didn't like the way the clown doll looked at her. She took a chance and screamed.

He ran back inside the shack. He looked like he was going to slap her. Or shoot her. "What the hell is wrong now?"

"That dddddoll. Talks to me."

"Which doll?"

"The clown doll." Tommy can't find it. "Up there."

"I don't know where up there is!"

"If I were untied I'd point it out for you."

"That's it. You want to be untied. Well, you ain't. I'm leaving you here all night." Tommy went outside.

Beth felt the rope cutting off circulation to her hands. She feared they would turn black like she saw on that one kid on her street that time. Beth looked up at the clown doll. "He used a what? A sheet bend?" Her fingers fumbled with the knot. She found the end of the rope. All she could do was pull at it with her fingers. "I pull it here?" Did that thing just nod at her?

Beth kept working at pulling the knot and untie her hands. The clown doll kept looking at her as though to egg her on. She tried one more time. The knot gave a little. One more tug and she pulled her hands free of the rope. She exhaled as she brought her arms around in front of her. She rubbed her wrists to get the circulation going again. She looked sullenly out the door toward….

Tommy grunted as he pushed the boat. It moved a foot or so. Tommy turned and said, "Who is it?" He listened.

Beth saw Tommy stride back to the shack. She put her hands behind her back as Tommy entered and shined a flashlight all around the single room. "Who said that?" Beth was quiet while Tommy looked at each and every doll. He said to her, "Did any of these things talk?"

"No." She said it like he was stupid for asking.

"I mean like with a little tape recorder in their head."

"No."

"I heard someone talking. There's someone else out here."

Beth watched him go out the door. She wanted to warn him that the flashlight would attract attention. Now another doll, this one a baby doll begins to giggle. Beth looked at it, "Oh yeah, I want attention."

Tommy came back inside. He looked at the baby doll. It jiggled as it giggled. "Shut that damn thing off."

It was like he remembered that Beth couldn't. He yanked doll up and turned it around looking for the on/off switch. Frustrated he ripped open the back. "Goddamn!"

Frightened Beth said, "What?"

Tommy showed her the empty back of the doll. "No batteries!"

"Then how?"

That's when the doll stopped giggling and moving. Tommy threw it out the door. It seemed to Beth that the other dolls started to frown.

By now Tommy was out in the strand of trees waving his flashlight this way and that.

Another doll, a stuffed sock monkey, caught Beth's attention. "There's a what buried outside the door." A breeze blew through the window and the sock monkey swayed. Then the doll turned on its hook. "In back of the shack. Okay, but I'll just use it to draw attention." Beth untied her feet. She stood up and brushed herself off.

She looked outside again. She saw Tommy try to sink the boat. It kept floating back to the surface.

Satisfied that he was busy, Beth crept out the door. She walked around to the back and dug furiously into the sand. The sock monkey doll said something about a gun buried out here. When she didn't find it, she dug in a larger circle. It had to be here. It had to be. He would be back any minute. Still no…. He won't be fooled by her holding her arms behind her back. Even in the dark, he will know. The sand and the grit built under her fingernails. This is going to take too long.

And it did.

Beth felt the firm grip of Tommy's hand on her the back of her neck.

"Just what the hell did you think you were doing?"

"I'm, I'm looking for something."

He pulled her roughly, "Get up."

She walked in a crouch back into the shack. First thing, each doll seemed to stare at her. Second thing, he pushed her to her knees.

"What were you looking for?"

"I'm scared Tommy. Real scared."

"So am I!"

"You shot all them people!"

Tommy's look burned into her. This was deep anger. Abiding hatred. This is how someone looks before they say to hell with it and shoot someone.

Beth whined and cried, "You cut loose! On three people!"

Tommy, "Cops ain't people."

"You shot that little old man!"

"What? Are you high?"

"I saw it!"

Tommy kneeled down before her. He said, "I didn't shoot that old man." Tommy was gentle as though he tried to explain something and support her at the same time.

BETH FELT Tommy's trouser leg against her bare leg. "You're wet from playing with the boat."

"I gotta get out there and fix that."

Tommy got up and started to walk out the door.

Beth, "How do we get off the island?"

Tommy stopped and sighed.

Beth continued, "You know they are going to open the gates? That means the river will rise. Maybe even enough to cover the island. Don't you care what happens to us?"

Tommy said in a whisper she could hardly hear, "First time in years. The rains. They're

going to do it this morning."

"Let's just go. We'll make it on the lam."

"No we won't. I can't run anymore."

Beth exploded, "Well I can! They won't get me!"

Tommy looked at her like he couldn't believe her.

There was a sound on the river. The sound of an aircraft engine.

Tommy knelt by her again and put his finger to his lips.

Beth felt exasperated, "What?"

Tommy clamped his hand over her mouth. "They can hear you." He mimed the words, *Super sensitive mics.*

The engine sound got closer then passed over their heads.

Beth said, "Whirly birds." Beth wanted to live. She thought she could make a deal with the fuzz and let him hang. He was going to kill her anyway. He was so close. She smashed her forehead into his nose. Tommy fell back screaming in pain. The fuzz wouldn't need a sensitive mic to hear him out on the river.

Tommy held his nose and flopped around trying to raise up on one elbow while he dug his 38 out of his pocket. Beth launched at him and they wrestled on the dirty floor underneath the gaze of the haunted dolls. Tommy was stronger and got Beth down the ground.

To which she laughed. "Come on, baby, we got this! We still have fun."

"No."

"Yeah, let's have a little fun. Then we can breeze outta here."

Tommy got up off her. The way he held the gun on her she knew he would do it.

Tommy tied her to the post again. Beth heard the dolls say something to her. "When they open the gates, how high will the water rise?"

"Don't worry about it." He finished tying her hands.

He moved to her feet. As he cinched the knot, she thought why he was tying her down. "This is it for us isn't it?"

"Hey Doll, one thing ends, another begins."

Beth frowned at him, "Bullshit."

Tommy stood and brushed his trousers off. "Whatever, I'm going out and sink that boat."

"You know…." Beth let the rest of her sentence hang there. Tommy stopped at the door. Her intended effect. "The river isn't that deep. I could walk across on the riverbed."

He was antsy like he was in a hurry.

"There's the current. Water's up to your chin. And you ain't a swimmer. I don't have time to debate this with you."

He left her alone with the dolls. She looked at them. Stared at each of them in the face. "What now? He's right about the river and I can't swim." But now the dolls were silent. In anger Beth strained against her ropes. She felt around with her fingers. The knot was different this time. She couldn't tell what kind it was like the last time and the dolls weren't talking. Tommy walked out and Beth was alone in the darkness with silence. As the airless night enveloped her, her memory came to her. She sat there and worked on the knots while she was assaulted with unbidden images from her painful past. Her bastard father, her brothers. The dead baby. He looked at her, while she sat in the forest, with dead doll's eyes. Familiar eyes. She remembered crying as she buried him. Then decided she was never so happy to bury someone as she was him. The coldness and hardness within her was born then. She found the buried guns at her father's hunting shack. One of her brothers was drawing disability from his injuries. The others….

The memories came back to Beth. Now she remembered everything. The knot fell off her hands. How did that happen? She was aware of the dolls through the darkness.

From outside Tommy shouted, "Yeah!" Beth though he must have sunk the boat. She thought what to hit him with as he came back inside. The clown doll, her friend, indicated that the microwave oven would work.

Next thing, Tommy came looking down expecting to see her on the floor. "They opened the gates."

Beth swung the microwave with all her might. She saw Tommy on the ground, covered in sand. The 38 knocked out of his hands fell on the sandy floor. She grabbed it before he could react. Tommy was still conscious. He looked up at the dolls. At her. She grinned at him.

"This is like a film noir. And you know what happens in film noir?"

Tommy's eyes filled with tears. "It's always the doll."

Beth felt the pressure of the trigger pull. She saw Tommy's brains splatter all over the shack's tiny room. But she didn't hear the explosion for the laughter of the dolls.

Somewhere north of them, the flood gates opened, the water cascaded down, and the river began to rise. 👓

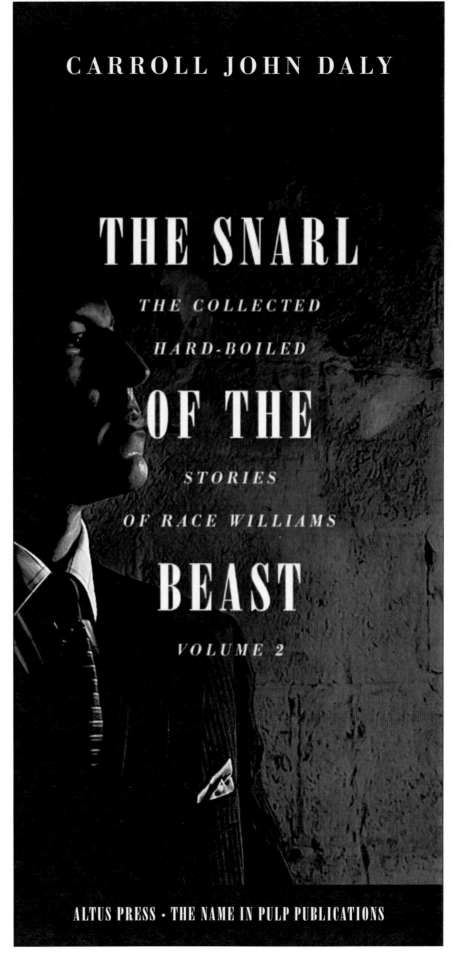

CARROLL JOHN DALY

THE SNARL

THE COLLECTED

HARD-BOILED

OF THE

STORIES

OF RACE WILLIAMS

BEAST

VOLUME 2

ALTUS PRESS · THE NAME IN PULP PUBLICATIONS

JUST ANOTHER JOB, THAT DOESN'T PAY VERY WELL

by J.D. Graves

WHEN I first heard the rumor—just like you—I didn't believe it. I thought it was some sick joke. I didn't laugh the first or second time, but the third? I had to chuckle… too bizarre not too. I started thinking—maybe all this buzz is true. Dallas's another planet from here… and Jersey? Another galaxy—but naturally—they all knew about Tony before we did." Andrew shook his head with disgust. The three mugs who shared his air just ignored him. They'd done so ever since he arrived late at Uncle's BBQ and delivered the package. No one wanted to talk about the six flowers in the vase on the table.

Andrew's jaw dropped like an attic door, "Black pansies… don't you see what this means? It's a message. He could've sent us anything. Roses or violets or Japanese Peace Lilies, but no—Big Jake sends us a special order of black pansies. This is bad. Really bad! The Don knows—THAT FACT alone should prickle your short and curlies."

A collective silence screamed back. If the Uncle's crew wasn't on board with him after the flower delivery, then Andrew knew he'd stepped across the wrong line in the sand. He found this fact more upsetting than all those familiar milk carton faces. Andrew couldn't understand the crew's quiet acceptance. It couldn't be for something as common as loyalty. Could it? In this business, loyalty was the only currency a fella could bank on… it never dipped in value. Of course, it was always hard to cash out when a friend suddenly lost a bullet in your skull.

"I mean don't get me wrong," Andrew said, walking back his dissatisfaction. "I understand… or at least I'm trying too. Hell, I lost my sister in this whole deal. But you don't fall apart—and if you do—you don't rebuild yourself into something you're not. You keep your private life out of business—I know it's hard to keep a secret, especially when Tony's got something like this… This! Burdening his soul—righteous jackass!"

"Do you hear yourself talking Hoss?" Freddie broke their silence. His round dough-face jiggled. Tonight, he'd stuffed himself in chinos and a too small pearl snap. His bolo tethered his fat head to his neck. Freddie looked kneaded and tossed beyond reason, "Who the hell do you think you are—calling the boss names?

You want Petey knowing what you're saying about his brother?"

Andrew's heart squeezed, "Oh hell no! Do any of us want what I'm saying getting out? This is between us and the flowers!"

Nobody moved.

"We still gotta go around acting like the beat goes on," Andrew said. "If anyone steps out of line, then Petey'll know. Ask Texas Dan about that… *if* you can find that fruitcake."

"I heard they found his head at least," Freddie said. "His body? No clue." Then he formed a triangle with his sausage fingers and gently aimed them at Andrew, "Damn shame, don't you think Hoss?"

A bead of sweat formed at Andrew's temple. He didn't like how Freddie's pork rolls lingered on him. He swallowed hard and responded slowly, "There's worse things in this world than a head without a body, Freddie."

Andrew reached into his coat pocket. The crew eyed him cautiously. Fat Freddie and Ricky Sant'Angelo, who dressed like an undertaker, and Arnie Marino, who tried the hardest to fit in with the locals. Arnie hoped you'd confuse him with James Dean in Giant. Not that he'd seen the movie, only the poster.

Andrew cautiously pretended not to notice their shifting glances and retrieved his lucky handkerchief. The one his sister, Emilia, gave him before his first communion. The one with strawberries sewn into the corners. As Andrew held it, a queer notion crossed his mind. Even though there existed two decades and three thousand miles between then and now—for a second he could still smell Emilia's perfume.

Instantly, Andrew was nine years old again. Not long before the family moved west to Texas. The withered and shaky hands of the priest wove over the boy. This old relic warbled archaic words, between the snaps and clicks of the photographer's camera. Mom had hired Aunt Patty, Emilia's Godmother, to commemorate Andrew's rite of passage. She moved in and out of his peripheral, snapping Polaroids. Somewhere there's a trunk with all of Aunt Patty's pictures of cousins, uncles and aunts showering Andrew with love and praise. Some pressed quarters into his hand…but it was Big Jake Viti, who made the biggest impression. The Don pulled his Godson aside, "You're on your way Andy. You've achieved the age of reason. Now listen close. There's two paths you can go down. Whichever you choose, remember this… it was you that made that choice."

The Don pressed an envelope into Andrew's young hand. Dutifully, the boy repeated his father's instructed words. With a tiny voice, Andrew mumbled, "Thank you for coming and celebrating this event with me."

Big Jake laughed heartily and mussed Andrew's hair, "You remember what I told ya." He pointed at the envelope before moving on, "There's always more, from where that came from."

Afterwards, Andrew opened it and found five crisp pictures of Andrew Jackson. He'd never held so much money at one time. Had the choice made itself that day?

Suddenly, the envelope disappeared. The family reunion disappeared. Even Emilia's perfume—replaced now by the pungent smell of moldering onions.

Andrew pressed Emilia's handkerchief to his forehead and wiped. Then returned it home, above his heart. Andrew sighed, "You grow up thinking the world's like a tomato. They start out small and green. Then they turn red and get picked. Some go into the salsa. Some go into sauces. Some make ketchup or get canned or wither

on the vines. But don't none of them suddenly become fruits!"

The fellas stirred. Freddie ceased twiddling his fingers. Arnie peeked out from under his hat. Ricky's one eyebrow raised, "Tomato's already a fruit." Ricky coughed a smoker's laugh, "Besides Tony's no fruit. He still likes chicks!" The eyebrow pitched a ramp and turned to the others, "Am I right?"

Again, nobody responded. Ricky nervously lit a Marlboro. He puffed and stuck his shaking lighter hand in his suit pocket. Andrew showed Ricky his palms, "I mean it takes a lot of bravery to do what Tony did—I'm not saying he don't have a set of eggs on him this big—" Andrew's arms stretched wide. "I mean no one's saying that—" Andrew's shadow darkened the red-checked tablecloth. His heart beat in his throat, "No one's saying anything good or bad, and that's what worries me. You don't drop a bombshell on our business associates without—you know—some blow back!"

"Keep your voice down," Arnie drawled from under his Stetson and the fellas agreed. Arnie's cowboy hat tilted back, "This is not the time or place, to forget yourself."

Their blank faces were grim totems. At that moment, Andrew felt like every rearview mirror dog he'd ever seen cross a highway—it was only a matter of time. Surely, Andrew thought, there still existed a way to get safely across the road.

Arnie's hat tilted downward again. He leaned back with his Justin's, red and polished like Satan's smile, propped on the table. Andrew couldn't believe they'd all drank Tony's Kool-Aid. Who knew? Maybe they were closeted freaks too.

Like a condemned man hoping to talk himself free of the noose. Andrew couldn't help his word vomit. He heard himself say, "For crying out loud! What would Tony Senior do if he were still with us, God rest his soul. Would he hunker down here in East Texas? Would he hide behind the pine trees, blending in with the rednecks, hoping it'll all blow over? Hell no! He'd've straightened Junior by now—forced him to understand that death's a part of life. You keep yourself together when you lose someone close to you!"

Freddie grunted, "Are you done yet Hoss?"

"It don't matter," Andrew said, "no one's listening anyway."

"The hell they ain't," Arnie's Stetson tilted upwards again. "Don't you know the boss probably had this placed bugged?"

Andrew squinted and whispered, "I don't care. I'd say the same thing if he was standing right in front of me."

"Don't lie," Arnie said. "You're candy ass would put a cork in it."

"I'd say it… I swear to St. Christopher."

"Could you do your swearing someplace else?" Ricky asked with clenched teeth. He'd lit a fresh cigarette with the butt of the old. The smoke drifted around him like all seven rings of hell.

"Who made you head of the class, Rick?" Andrew asked, "You think I'm dumb enough to be absent when Tony calls roll tonight?"

Ricky's cigarette ember glowed in the gloom. "Do us all a favor then…."

Andrew knew better than to turn his back on his friends. Slowly, Andrew moved to a far corner. He bumped against a wooden booth and sat.

The fellas and the flowers looked like a postcard. Ricky mournfully glanced through the smoke at Andrew. Freddie re-tightened his bolo. Arnie crossed and re-crossed his boots on the table. A framed picture of quiet menace, but the three guineas were just playing dress up. Luckily for them, most locals mistook them for Mexicans.

It was what it was.

Andrew reached towards the window blinds and pinched them slightly open. The sun set fast behind the parking lot's pines. It painted the twilight blood red. Nothing moved except for the automatic lights, which buzzed on hot. Andrew removed his fingers and the outside world disappeared. He wished the inside would disappear too. He surveyed the dining room. A strange familiar clash of cultures. Uncle's hadn't changed much from when Tony Senior ran it. The building had once been a Pizzeria. The walls still owned Leaning Towers and Venice canals and other touristy stuff—except Tony Senior had added street signs and rusty farm equipment—you know, give the dive a rustic feel.

Why an Italian-American from Jersey would forgo his native cuisine for smoked meats, Andrew didn't know. But he figured it had something to do with fitting in—like hiding in plain sight. Barbeque joints were a dime a dozen in the thick East Texas woods. Not that Uncle's ever sold much. The staff, whom the Spano's employed, mainly operated the back-door business—but the front's where Andrew got his start.

In the beginning, Andrew ran the register. An easy enough gig, since customers rarely came back for a second meal. The brisket tasted sandpaper dry even slathered in brown ketchup. However, every now and then some old heifer would bring up her plate of potato salad and point, "There's something in my food!"

Andrew nodded, "Yes ma'am there certainly is…."

Andrew would dutifully take her plate and fish out a stolen diamond ring or spent shell casing or that one time—a human tooth. That was the first time Andrew saw someone killed. One of the cooks went out to apologize and invited that lucky woman to inspect the kitchen. She accepted his offer, only to be choked to death with a cold link of sausages. On that particular day, had the choice made itself?

After that, Andrew earned promotion. He tended the empty smoker while the others handled deliveries. Every week Big Jake's tractor-trailer's unloaded buckets of potato salad and slabs of beef. You didn't touch a thing until Tony Senior had finished his inventory. Amongst the restaurant's perishables were usually bags of Mexican weed, illegal handguns, stolen jewelry, or anything else that could be sold at black market prices.

Andrew's eyes stopped near the register. On the wall, amongst framed photos of sponsored little league teams, rested a plaque Tony Senior installed. It celebrated ten years in the restaurant business—righteous jackass.

After Tony Senior passed, the Spano brothers attempted to legitimize. They'd hired a real cook and staff. They also hired Andrew's sister Emilia to spruce up the decor. Why wouldn't they? Everyone loved Emilia. She'd been voted homecoming queen as well as Miss Pig-n-poke County, or whatever the rednecks called their fair. However, she never got very far with the Spano's gig, since Tony kept distracting her. Nobody batted an eye when they ended up married a year later. God's a cruel joker since Emilia never got around to decorating the restaurant or the house Tony had bought her.

A chill shot through Andrew. He looked up and shuddered. A forgotten remnant of the old pizzeria clung overhead. Plastic grapevines wove throughout this part of the rafters. Their fruits dangled overhead like gallows dummies—

Everything happened faster than the rodeo's main event. Petey bucked through the front door, like a bull clearing his cowboy. He thrashed around the frightened clowns, "Don't tell me he ain't here yet?"

Arnie hid his red boots while Ricky distracted Petey, "He'll be here any minute—Chico called, said they were leaving Mt. Pleasant about twenty minutes ago."

Petey nose flared and his breath steamed, "Okay. We got a little damage control to manage. Nothing's wrong though. He's still my brother. The good lord and St. Michael knows I love him. WE love him! You with me?"

All the fellas agreed.

Petey stamped the floor for traction and avoided eye contact, "She got sick… he took care of her…. Okay! He had to watch his wife go through something tougher than anything I could imagine. I mean cancer's a damn shame. If anything—He's just lost the plot. He needs a little vacation—you know—to get his head straight. Then everything will go back to normal—" Petey halted mid rant and pointed at the table. "What the hell are those doing here!"

Freddie sighed, "Andrew says they're black pansies."

"You think you're funny bringing them here, Andrew?" Petey asked.

"It's no joke. They arrived this afternoon," Andrew said and found the card in his pocket. He crossed back to the table and slid the card towards Petey. "Special rush delivery from Jake Viti, himself."

Petey screamed and sent the vase of flowers crashing against the cash register. When he turned back to the crew, his eyes burned crazily, "What I need to know—right now's simple—anyone else getting any messages?!"

Petey screamed this so loud his mug went red. He stood there seeing stars, before finally spilling into a chair at the table. His hands found his temples and rubbed.

At first no one answered. Finally, Ricky lit another square and said, "Maybe not hearing something's a good thing. Probably less to worry about."

Petey laughed. A shrill, high cackle, "Just because you schmo's haven't heard nothing doesn't mean I haven't."

Fat Freddie perked up, "Who you talking to Hoss?"

Petey flung the package on the table. The crew leaned forward as Freddie unwrapped it. After Freddie had smoothed back the paper—a collective groan cut the air. Uncle's BBQ felt smaller. The plastic grapes hung lower. Andrew felt like he'd suffocate.

Freddie held up the six flowerless stems. "What's this supposed to mean?"

Petey's eyes rolled like two wet marbles, "It's not good—he wants Tony to step aside or else."

Arnie's Stetson reared, "Or else what?"

"One of us gets a half-dozen black pansies and I get the other half—without the heads." Petey laughed again. "With a message as clear as that—I wouldn't rule anything out. Big Jake's put us on notice."

The room erupted with gasps and excuses.

Petey waved his arms, "If we stick together! Listen! All we gotta do's stick together and defend ourselves from whatever's coming and… eventually the Don will have to accept it."

"Surely Don Viti don't want us all dead?" Ricky asked.

"That don't seem reasonable," Arnie said.

Fat Freddie asked, "He's willing to start a war over this?"

Petey growled, "I ain't turning my back on my brother for that meatball! Is that understood? No one makes a move from inside do you hear me?"

Again, they all nodded. What else could they do?

Petey stood with such force the chair fell back, "Now I am willing to democratically nominate myself to take over as Interim boss. We are not replacing him… Tony's still in charge—he's just not making any more decisions—or being seen in public. Not until he's fixed!"

Ricky leaned forward and scissored his fingers, "You mean." His hands snip-snipped.

Petey groaned, "No you schmuck! Tony ain't losing his thing…I don't care what he says, or how much worse this gets. Okay! Big Jake'll just have to see it our way, you know how the Don gets—especially when he's given bad news!" Something compelled Petey to add, "Not that this is necessarily bad news. I'm not saying that! We all know I love my brother! WE ALL LOVE MY BROTHER!"

All agreed.

The front door chimed a warning bell. Chico's in first and held it open for Andrew's former brother-in-law. To hear about a thing's different than actually seeing it with your own two eyes.

Tony entered.

The first thing Andrew noticed… for crying out loud—Tony's mini-skirt fit like it was painted on—you could count the wrinkles on his little Tony. At least that was the worst of it. Despite the ruffled blouse, black bra and blonde wig—it's still Tony Spano—sort've. His mascaraed eyes cut steel through the room. He'd smeared base make-up into the edges of his moustache and his eye shadow clashed with his ensemble—but he didn't act like no queer or nothing. Andrew felt a pang of discomfort in his gut. Could it be pity? Or disgust?

Petey immediately screwed up his courage, "We gotta talk Tony. In light of everything, we took a vote. I'm sorry but we all think it'd be best if you took a break awhile… just until things settle—"

Tony Spano stepped towards his little brother, cooler than your puppy's nose, "Don't be cute, Little Pete. There was no vote."

"The hell there wasn't! I'm taking over! We decided!"

Tony clucked his tongue, "I'm disappointed in you, brother."

"Disappointed in me? Who's got the nerve to be disappointed in who here?"

Tony clapped both of Petey's ears between his hands. Tony's red press-on claws dug in to his brother's black hair. Tony seethed, "You expect me to believe that my guys voted against me?" Tony brought Petey's nose to his own. "I know for a fact they wouldn't do that in a million years. I don't know what you're trying to pull here, but—I'll accept your apology!"

Petey whimpered and grabbed at his brother's wrists. Tony wouldn't let go, "Say it Petey!"

"I-I-I-"

"Say it—and all will be forgiven."

Petey whimpered.

"Say—I'm sorry for trying to tear our family apart—say it!"

Petey struggled, but it was no use against Tony's bulging—gossamer sleeved—biceps. Tony shook Petey's twig so hard and fast that whatever response Andrew heard was pitched high and shaky. Tony let him go, and Petey crumpled the length of his brother's black stockings and three-inch stilettos. Tony reduced Petey to a calf cowering beneath its momma. He kept bleating, "I'm sorry," over and over again.

Tony looked down with peculiar interest. He reached towards Petey. Andrew thought he'd throw-up at this bizarre sideshow of brotherly love. Petey, all red faced and sobbing—eagerly awaited his brother's forgiving touch—but instead, Tony stooped, then stood holding one of the discarded black pansies. Tony examined it closely. Twisting and turning the thing between his fingers. Without ceremony, he slipped its stem into his blonde wig, over his ear. He turned to the rest of the crew and posed. With a completely straight face, Tony said, "Fellas I want to thank all of you for coming. Your loyalty will be rewarded once the dust settles. Allow me to address the three-hundred-pound gorilla in the room. As you are definitely aware by now, Jake Viti has declared war on our outfit."

Arnie's hat rustled and he blurted out, "Outfit? He should see what you're wearing now."

"What was that?" Tony asked flatter than your first girlfriend. Arnie quieted. "No really?" Tony's eyes glazed over, "What did you just say to me?"

Arnie, slow as the sunrise, tilted his Stetson, "I'm sorry Tony I-I-I didn't mean nothing by it—it's just that…it slipped out."

The shot rang loud in everyone's ears. Arnie gripped his stomach and bent backwards out of the chair. He hung there like a puppet stuck in its strings, but amazingly his Stetson stayed on. The gun smoke burned in Andrew's nose. Suddenly Andrew turned—instinctively towards Arnie—and punched him in the face. Arnie dropped all the way down. Ricky and Andrew's heavy boots stomped the cockroach. He wasn't proud of it, but for the first time in days, Andrew thought—things felt relatively normal.

Tony holstered his piece and Andrew wondered, where the hell he'd hidden it. After all, the boss wasn't leaving much to their imaginations. Tony casually scrunched the back of his blonde wing and shook it out daintily—just like a lady—and calmly said, "Anybody else feel the same as this insect?"

No one squirmed. Tony demanded the traitor be removed. Andrew and Ricky pulled a table cloth down. The poor soul groaned as they drug him towards the men's room. A thin smear of red followed them inside.

The men's room, no more than a glorified closet with a sink and commode, stank like hell. They dropped old Arnie on the linoleum and finally the Stetson rolled free. Arnie, the frightened goose, squawked.

"Shut up Arnie, ya dumb puke," Ricky's eyebrow darted. "As far as I'm concerned you brought this on yourself."

Arnie cried for water and Andrew ran the tap.

Ricky's cigarette bounced between his teeth, "What the hell are you doing Andrew?"

"Come on Rick," Andrew said, "He's dying."

"Well he should've kept his dumb mouth shut. We both did."

Andrew ignored him and found a crusty cup in the trash can. He filled it and knelt beside Arnie and tried to help him drink, but Arnie's constant blubbering just made a mess.

Ricky shook his head, "Ain't no cure for gut shot. Best thing—let him die with some dignity."

"There's dignity in this stink hole?"

"Does it matter? Leave him be," Rick said. "Besides it was his fault."

"You're okay with all this?" Andrew asked amazed, "You probably think that circus freak-show's Arnie's fault too huh?"

"I'm just saying, there's a clear reason Arnie's the one bleeding to death in the john and we're not—"

"You buy into all this nonsense?" Andrew asked.

The cigarette bounced once more and Ricky lit it. He fished another smoke out the pack, "Arnie. You wanna smoke?"

Arnie writhed on the floor, "Water!"

Ricky kicked him, "Pipe down! You want them coming in here and finishing you off? The least you can do's die like a man. Ah nice…!"

"What's wrong?"

"Look at this," Rick said and hiked his trouser leg, "he got blood on my shoe."

"Quit kicking him and it wouldn't be there."

"Water!" Arnie groaned.

Rick picked up the crusty cup from the floor—filled it with water—then flung it at Arnie's face, "There's ya water ya dumb puke. If you don't quit your belly aching, I'll put a fresh one in your ear."

"Go on and do it!" Arnie screamed.

Andrew covered his ears and looked away. The percussion echoed off the walls. When he turned back, Ricky was kneeling beside Arnie. He waved his gun through the thick smoke floating from the dead man's skull.

"You still ain't answered me," Andrew said.

"You really gotta ask?" Rick exhaled, "You got better options?"

"It's started a war," Andrew knelt and fanned away the cloud. "Now the Spano's expect everyone to fall in line—I can't get behind this—not one hundred percent. I think they've both lost their damn minds."

Ricky squinted, "What are you saying?"

"You know what we have to do."

"No way," Ricky nodded, "you thinking ambush style?"

"For Tony? Yeah," Andrew said, "but what about Petey? And the other two? They ain't gonna let it happen without a fight."

"Whaddaya suggest?"

Andrew smiled, "We go in one at a time. Someone stays in here as back-up. When you hear the execution come out blazing."

Rick's unibrow pitched a roof over his dark eyes, "So who's going first?"

Andrew suggested they flip for it.

"You got a quarter?"

"No… you?"

"Hell no…" Ricky thought on it, "What about paper, rock, scissors."

"Sure," Andrew said, "on three?"

Ricky stamped out his Marlboro. Next thing Andrew knew they'd squared off over Arnie's body, pumping their fists in hand.

"One… two… three…."

They shot.

Ricky sighed with relief, since paper always covered rock.

"Alright, alright," Andrew said, "But you'd better be ready for Petey when I waste Tony."

Ricky checked the chamber on his forty-five, "Don't sweat it. Hey…." Ricky said as Andrew moved to the door. "…do ya think the Don'll offer us a reward for putting an end to all this?"

"I have no doubt about it," Andrew said and left him to it. He emerged from that stink hole thankful he'd lost. Andrew knew it went without saying that his plan would

end up getting them both killed. If he could halve that number early then—there was nothing else to do about it.

THE DINING room was a ghost town. Andrew followed the muffled sound of voices towards the kitchen. The gang had gathered around the close circuit TV's. With their backs turned, Andrew had a good view of his old friend, the back door. He quickly calculated the odds.

Andrew hoped his math was off.

"T-T-Tony," Andrew said, "I-I-I gota talk to you about Ricky."

Tony withered into a crone when Andrew spilled the beans. He found himself begging Tony to not shoot the messenger.

"I came to you in good faith and loyalty. If we can't be open with each other—then we don't stand a chance against Big Jake."

"That's all we need," Tony growled. "Don Viti wants us to unravel. Well I ain't falling to pieces. Not after he said such awful things about me… to everyone!"

Tony started to tear up, but choked it back instead. His former brother-in-law looked Andrew dead in the eyes, "Don't you think I look pretty?"

Andrew didn't miss a beat, "You'd've been a very handsome woman if you'd been born with the right parts, Tony. I'm sure you and my sister would've had gorgeous babies."

Tears ruined Tony's mascara, "Thank you Andrew! I'm glad I still got good people like you. You're a stand-up guy… always have been. Emilia would've wanted you by my side for this…."

"What about Ricky?" Petey asked sheepishly. "How do you want that handled?"

"I don't care just get it over with," Tony looked to Petey with knives in his eyes. "Do I gotta do everything?"

Without saying a word, Petey and Chico checked their guns and headed towards the dining room. Andrew's clock ticked. Tony and Fat Freddie stared at the grainy black and white monitors. It showed the four corners of Uncle's BBQ—as well as the parking lot. Andrew paced around waiting for the sound of gunshots. But they never came. He only heard the impotent silence. He went to the back door and gave it a tug. The heavy metal creaked open an inch. Okay, Andrew told himself, at least I still got a way out. He pulled out his lucky handkerchief and pressed it to his nose. He couldn't smell a thing.

Suddenly, Freddie percolated, "What the hell was that Hoss?"

"Where?" Tony asked frantically. Freddie pointed a fat finger, "There in the parking lot!"

Andrew crept behind them just in time to see something move across the screen.

Tony yelled. "They're armed to the teeth!"

Then Andrew heard it—as sweet as Frank sings—a muffled Pop! Pop! Pop!

Again, Andrew's choice made itself.

Andrew lifted his m1911. The blast deafened. Tony's blonde wig flew off. Freddie's face sprayed red. A wet look of shock. Instinct told Freddie to draw his hog. But he hesitated—as if he really had a choice. But he was too slow. Andrew quickly backed out of the office—the kitchen—he reached the back door and pulled—

God tells the funniest jokes.

The outside chain rattled but held firm. The three-inch gap mocked Andrew. Not even enough to stick his foot through. He yanked again on the door, but the chain and its padlock stayed true. Outside, the stench of the nearby dumpsters wafted in, as well as an off-target bullet. KAA-TANG! Andrew slammed it shut, slid to the floor. A few more rounds peppered the metal as he felt the trap snapping around him.

Everything elongated. Petey arrived in slow motion. Confusion replaced his rage once he eyeballed Tony—Petey crouched and gathered his dead brother. From the backdoor, Andrew watched the monitors over their heads.

He watched them come—like army ants— wave after wave, ready to strip flesh from bones. The ants scattered across the bloody screens. The front door exploded open—

They say, life's what happens when you make other plans—Death too apparently. She's waiting just ahead of you. Arms out stretched and ready. No matter how fast you run, she'll double back and beat you to it. She's warm. She's beautiful. She's here now as we speak. But even she can't break that primal bond between brothers. It's a special thing. She had no choice but to take everyone.

Petey clutched Tony and wailed like a new widow, all mouth, tongue and gnashing teeth. Peter Alphonse Spano refused to let his brother go, even as the bullets ripped through Uncle's BBQ—both of them—righteous jackasses. ∞

WICKED, WICKED RAIN

by Brian Townsley

SONNY HAYNES sat in the Starlite Diner in the spring of 1951 and stared out the window at the night as the endless rain carried on, vandalistic and angry. He sipped his coffee. Lefty Frizzell sang "If You've Got the Money, Honey" on the juke, and could barely be heard above the biblical downpour flooding the desert outside.

Sonny was waiting here on a man—well, of course, there would be more than one man, but the only one of import was a Mr. Saul Bernstein, who also happened to be a relatively successful Hol-

lywood director. Mr. Bernstein was 'missing,' and certain people in Los Angeles needed him returned sooner than later. And, he was told, the situation was *delicate*. And while Sonny Haynes was generally not someone who would spring to mind when the word *delicate* was brought up, he was beginning to build a bit of a reputation for handling the types of situations people associated with that word.

His hat lay crown down on the table, drops of rainwater circling the brim and dripping onto the plastic tabletop. It was designed to look like wood, the tabletop, with grains running lengthwise and adorned with red and yellow ketchup and mustard dispensers, salt and pepper shakers, and napkins. His waitress was like a girl

you grew up next to and believed to be pretty and then you grew older and left town and gained experience in all things mundane and eccentric and returned home to realize she was quite mundane herself. And there is both wisdom and sadness in that. Sonny smiled to her and raised his cup an inch as a gesture for a refill.

"Everything here okay, sir?" she asked, as she poured the steaming coffee into his mug. Her name tag said Josie. Sonny placed her at maybe 25.

"Everything is just fine here, Ms. Josie. Glad to be out of the rain," Sonny answered, and raised his glass again at her, this time as a salute.

"Okay then. You let me know if you'll be wanting any dinner," she said, and glanced out the window at the darkness and rainfall. "My mama woulda called this here rain a reckoning, somethin' brought down by God hisself to cleanse those things that need cleansin." She paused. "But then, mama was always findin' biblical meanin' in things that just seemed like things, to me, you know?" She scrunched her nose and raised her shoulders together at once as if a question had been asked to which she did not know the answer and looked at Sonny as if perhaps he had meanings for things, too.

"Well. Folks are going to find meaning when they need meaning in things," he answered, and winked, sipping his coffee.

"'Course, my mama was crazy as an outhouse rat sometimes too, so who knows?" she said, and laughed quickly afterwards, collecting herself at once. "Well, lookit me, carryin' on."

"It's just fine, Josie. Bring me some French fries. I think the meaning in the rain for me is that I need some French fries," Sonny said.

She placed the coffee onto the table and wrote something on her menu ticket and said, "French fries, comin' up." With that she picked the coffee carafe back up and gave Sonny one more glance, and he saw her look at his neck and the inkwork there, then embarrassedly back into his face and hurry off.

The diner had a western motif, as most things did out here, with a horseshoe above the door and a wallpaper of spurs and horse profiles. Faux-wood tables. Faux-wood vinyl stools at the counter. There were only three other people in the place at the moment, an elderly couple near the door in a booth and a gentleman sitting at the counter, finishing a chicken-fried steak covered in gravy and drinking a soda. He was perhaps Indian, though Sonny couldn't be sure. The couple were white-haired and the man wore a gray western shirt, slacks, and boots. The lady had her hair cut short and wore a navy blue dress trimmed in white. Sonny sipped his coffee. The jukebox began "I'm Movin' On" by Hank Snow, and the rain continued its onslaught outside.

THE FRIES were overcooked with burnt nubs and ends but truth be told Sonny liked that type more than any other so he dipped them in the mustard pooled on the plate and tried not to look at the door any more than necessary. He motioned again to Josie to fill his cup and knew now that regardless of what happened throughout the rest of the evening he may never sleep again, such was the amount of caffeine he had consumed.

The diner had gone silent and Sonny wasn't sure how long it had been that way. He stood and hatted himself and walked to the juke. He dropped a dime for two plays and chose *Moanin' the Blues* by Hank Williams, and then searched the titles for something he hadn't heard. He settled on *Mercury Blues* by K.C. Johnson for the second song and walked to his seat in expectation. His coffee mug had been filled again and was steaming. He removed his hat and placed it on the table. Hank began crooning the tune and Sonny stared for a moment at the congealed yellow grease on the plate and the lack of French fries. Such things undone. He looked at the clock on the wall, felt unconsciously for the .45 he carried in a shoulder holster. It was still there. His imaginary friend hadn't taken it, yet. He sipped the steaming coffee and realized that he had to piss something fierce. It was no wonder, he figured. Four cups of coffee and 40+ years will do that to a man. He didn't want to leave, either. Find his mark, Bernstein, out here sitting with whatever model of greaseball Chicago had come up with for the New Year. But still. He stared at the coffee, unhappy with it now.

The record finished and was replaced with all manner of efficiency and the stacking of vinyl. *Mercury Blues* began on the juke and the tune was a traditional blues song that featured a Mercury, as Sonny had hoped that it would. He sipped his coffee and smiled as the bell rung above the front door, and three men entered the diner. The first and last were large men, both in black suits and fedoras and arrived in the diner ducking and dodging as if the rain were ignorant to the pugilistic arts. The man between them was a good six inches shorter than either, and more narrow by half; if they were 250 lbs, he was 150, soaking wet. Which he was. He had not been given a hat to wear and wiped his bald head and face vigorously as he entered. Sonny looked away in recognition.

The men hung their dripping coats on the rack near the door and left their hats on. They ushered the man before them like a child, and laid stakes at a booth near the front entrance and stuck Saul Bernstein on the window side as the two sat across from one another. Sonny still had to pee, badly now, but tried to focus. Josie came over to the men and they ordered coffee. They didn't allow Saul to order, Sonny observed. *Mercury Blues* finished and Sonny noted with a small sadness that he had missed the end of the song. He would have to remedy that in time. He liked that song, he decided.

A FEW minutes later Sonny saw with an immense amount of relief that one of the lugs had stood and started towards the restroom. Sonny counted to twenty and followed. He approached the door with his hand under his coat, only to push the door open and find an unused urinal. The greaseball had taken the stall, and if his feet were any indication, he wasn't draining the weasel. Sonny took to the porcelain and unzipped and released a torrent of rented coffee that seemed to continue longer than there was liquid consumed. Finally he zipped up and walked to the sink, looking in the mirror at the stall. The lug was still in there, grunting away. He took note of his escape route. There was a small window in the wall, but it would be a piece of work to get through that. He smiled quickly at the thought of shooting a man in the stall and then getting stuck in the window, his bottom half scissoring in impotence as the authorities arrived.

He pulled the switchblade from his pocket and released the blade there as he coughed and turned quickly and slammed open the stall door with his left palm and drove the knife into the man's chest until it went no further. The man grunted once and shuddered and fumbled awkwardly at Sonny's arms. Sonny pulled the knife out then and drove it upward into the man's chin, the blade exiting through the cheek. Sonny grabbed the man by the hair and looked at him. He was perhaps 35, black hair, slicked back.

Chubby but not fat. Dead, now. And nary a sound. Sonny pulled loose the weapon and saw it exit the man's cheek obscenely and wiped the blade on some toilet paper he wadded and pocketed the knife. He then ran his hands down the man's sides and first keys with a Cadillac keychain, which he pocketed. Then lower still and there a piece, a .38, removed and placed in the backside of Sonny's waistband. No taped up drop, serial removed, to be found at the ankle. Sonny shrugged. They weren't worried, apparently. The man was bleeding mostly downward into the toilet water, so that worked well. Sonny flushed once and turned in the tight stall, two elephants in a phone booth, and tried to lock the latch but he had busted it. So much for secrecy. He wadded some toilet paper near the top of the stall doorjamb to keep it in place after he had exited and walked out of the bathroom. He realized with no small amount of irony the regularity with which he seemed to be killing people in bathrooms. Life and death in the shitter—not exactly the stuff of Chandler, he thought.

Sonny guessed that he had probably five minutes, to be safe. There were very few folks in the place, the old couple had since left, so there was really only the guy at the counter or one of the cooks that would enter the men's bathroom anytime soon, but he also realized the guy wasn't just going to sit on the pot and bleed into the toilet all night either. The next man that entered, whether in 30 seconds or 15 minutes, was going to find himself a mess. So, he figured, he had better get to work.

HE GRABBED his hat off of his table and slid into the booth opposite the huge meatball and the small jew.

"Alright, big boy, this is how this is gonna work," he said, before either of them could react. The mobster's facial expressions morphed quickly from surprise to confusion to anger, none of them making him look any smarter. Saul Bernstein, on the other hand, just looked terrified. He had sparse and wiry grayblack hair popping out on his scalp and his eyebrows were made of the same stuff and were bushy and wild. His eyes were small and kind; his nose was wide with large nostrils. Sonny noted that the jukebox had gone quiet again.

"You've got a gun pointed this instant at your twig and berries," he said to the man across from him. "As far as I see it, you've got two options—1. You can do exactly

as I say, and you'll live. I promise that. Although you will end up in the trunk of your car in the rain. But you'll live. 2. You can either try to take out myself or Mr. Bernstein there, most likely with the pistol from your shoulder holster on your left there-," he motioned with his left hand to that shoulder in case he didn't yet have a handle on left and right, "—and never be able to piss normally again."

"Wha—" the man began, more grunt than speech, before pausing, as if the situation were simply moving too quickly for comprehension.

"Yeeeeeesss," Sonny answered, in mock condescension, "gun. Your dick. Go bye-bye." He paused then, winked at Saul, and continued: "Your partner is taking a huge dump in there," he motioned to the bathroom, "so we're not going to wait for him."

The greaseball seemed to have composed himself, finally. "Look here, circus freak, I ain't giving you nothing. You—"

"Circus freak?" Sonny interrupted. "Because of the tattoos? That's very clever. I knew you were using that big brain up there for something during all of this. You're supposed to be professionals, right?" Sonny waited briefly for an answer.

Receiving none, he continued: "Your boy in there is bleeding from multiple holes into the toilet. If anybody in this room, *right here*," and he lowered his voice to a whisper, though no less audible, and all three of the men briefly looked around the diner, taking stock of the numbers, "*any* of them, finds him while we are sitting here, you are dead. *I will paint the walls here.* So really, we're playing a game of truth or dare—with a clock. You do as I say, right now, or we bullshit here, and somebody eventually walks into that bathroom. And then all hell breaks loose—and I'm the devil."

The man across from Sonny looked like he needed directions for his next move. The guy on the shitter must have been the brains of the operation, Sonny hoped. Saul had broken out in small beads of sweat on his forehead, and his eyes moved quickly from one man to the other. Josie appeared suddenly at the edge of the table.

"Anything I can get you all here?" She asked, before looking at the greaseball and adding "Your food should be out in just a sec."

"You know what, Josie?" Sonny said, keeping his eyes leveled on the men across from him, "These guys are old friends of mine—we haven't caught up in years. Do

me a favor and pack that food up to go." Sonny looked up and her and smiled, for just an instant.

"Mmmkay," she said, sounding confused.

"And you know what?" He continued. "This gentleman here has offered to pay my bill, as well. So he'll just go ahead and clear both bills up now."

"Well," she remarked, "that's awful nice of you." She patted the man on the shoulder to show how nice it was.

"I know," Sonny answered. "I mean, it's not like I had to put a gun to him or anything. He just offered—for old time's sake." Sonny slapped the tabletop with his left hand in a show of appreciation, and both men across from him flinched.

Josie took out both tickets and placed them on the table. "I'll go back and bag up your meals."

"K, hon. When you come back we'll have the bills set," Sonny answered as she walked off.

The man glowered at Sonny, although there was more than a small sense of shame and fear in there as well. Something unrecognizable. He began to reach into his left coat pocket.

"Anything comes out of that coat besides your wallet and you have no penis," Sonny said.

The man removed his wallet and removed a twenty from the billfold.

"Put it on top of the checks," Sonny said. "Leave all of it for Josie. She's a nice kid."

The man did as he was told, and Josie returned with a brown paper bag folded once horizontally along the top. "Here you go, guys." She left the bag on the table and swept up the cash and checks.

"Keep the change," Sonny said. "And you have a nice night, Josie."

"Well, thank you kindly, boys. You try to stay dry now," she answered, and paused, looking puzzled. "Did the other gentleman who was here leave?"

Sonny smiled at her. "Oh, that was Eugene. He's a little crazy in the head sometimes. I'm not sure where he's gone off to. He always did like the rain though."

SONNY ORCHESTRATED the lug leaving, to Saul leaving, to him following out of the restaurant and the ropes of rain in wait. They walked until Sonny told them to stop. Their shoes were all near ankledeep in puddle and it was difficult to hear. They stood there in the parking lot, the three of them, like the first family.

"Take off your hat, and place it on Mr. Bernstein's head there," Sonny shouted, and motioned with the gun in his hand.

The lug looked at him as if he had not heard, then nodded. The diner shone like a lighthouse in the allover darkness that the rain and night had colluded to.

THE RESTAURANT windows were only some 50 feet away but looked like another world entire given the weather and the night and the large man lifted the soaking hat off of his head and plopped it softly onto the dome of the small man beside him.

"Good man," Sonny said. "Now, where's your car?" He asked, loudly.

Each of their shoes were stuck in the muddy deluge at this point. The lug looked around for a second, then pointed at a Caddy not 30 feet distant.

"Okay," Sonny said, "now reach in your jacket and pull out the gun. *Slowly.* Then drop it in the mud. Mr. Bernstein, when he does that, I want you to pick it up and hand it to me. Can you do that?"

"I can do that," Saul answered, and his voice sounded more assured than Sonny would have given him credit for.

The big man in the suit sighed and reached into his jacket and pulled on the butt of his pistol and removed it with two fingers, dangled it once in the air to show it, and dropped it into the mud. It made a palpable splat upon landing. Saul bent carefully near the man, picked up the gun with an amount of caution you might give a feral animal, and walked it to Sonny. If he had any sense of what he should do with the gun, it did not show. He handed it over and Sonny placed it into his overcoat pocket.

They walked to the Caddy and Sonny had the man unlock the trunk and get in. He felt for a drop near the ankle, and, upon finding none, stood back and looked at the large man prostrate in the trunk.

"You shouldn't be doing this," the man said, above the din of rain. "It'll come back."

"Yeah," Sonny answered. "I know. It always does. Everybody pays."

He looked up then at the rain for a moment and sighed, then sideways at Saul, who looked back at him without expression. The light from the diner showed one side of his face and most everything else in darkness.

"What's your name, soldier?" Sonny asked.

"Frank," the lug answered without hesitation.

"Alright, Frank. You were cooperative tonight. Thanks for that. So you get to live, like I said." He snapped his wrist down quickly then, slapping the gunbutt hard against the man's face. The sound spoke of viscera and bone amidst the rainfall and the man grunted twice and exhaled.

"Sorry about that. That was a favor, though. If your boys found you, and without even a scratch? Like you just gave it up? So hey, you're welcome," Sonny said, shrugged, and slammed the trunk down, leaving the man in darkness as the rain beat incessantly as on a tin roof in the Tennessee home Sonny believed himself rid of. He smiled at this, and walked with Saul to the Merc that would ferry them westward toward the city of angels.

Chapter 2

THEY DROVE west on the 10 in the rain. Neither man spoke. Sonny rolled his window down and threw the Cadillac keys into the night at one point.

They stopped in a town called Banning and looked for a motel there. On a frontage road they ran across the Hi-Line Motel in neon, VACANCY rimmed in red across the bottom. Sonny stopped the car a block away and killed the lights. The windshield wipers continued their monotonous uniformity, carrying hopelessly on.

"Okay," he started, "here's the deal. I am not the bad guy here. I am taking you back to Los Angeles for a friend—he is, I think, someone you know well. In return for bringing you back, I am getting something very important *from* him." Sonny looked at Saul then, the shadows and bars of light horizontal. "I'm telling you this because I want you to know that this is a job for me, and an important one. If I were in your shoes, I'd wonder what the fuck is going on." Sonny paused then, unsure of what to say next.

"S-so you're taking me back to LA?" Saul asked, with a brief stutter. Disbelief spread across his features in the halflight.

"Yes."

Saul exhaled then, loudly, and put his head into his hands. He raised his face and looked at Sonny, at once pleading and incredulous.

"YES," Sonny said, again, and nodded.

"Thank you," Saul said. It was dark and the rain was loud but Sonny was pretty sure he saw tears that rimmed the man's eyes.

"Don't thank me yet. Thank me when I drop you off. Thank me when I'm driving away. Right now, we're going to crash in a motel room. Tomorrow morning, we're going to LA. By tomorrow afternoon, you'll be seeing your family again. But that's only if you do *exactly* as I say. Got it?" Sonny asked. The man nodded.

The Hi-Line office was empty as the two men entered, but contained a universe of pamphlets and postcards in a metal case that held them all. Sonny and Saul dripped onto the carpet and removed their hats. Sonny secretly wished that he could shake himself dry like a dog. He pulled some pamphlets from the assortment and spread them on the counter to read as they waited, his hands dripping water onto the colored paper, distorting and reshaping the message. They advertised tours of western movie sets, movie star's escapes in the Palm Springs area!, and hiking and trails in the Joshua Tree National Forest. He finally rang the bell loudly when no one arrived.

"I'ma comin'," came from a back room, in a high voice, at once old and strong. A lady arrived around a corner with blue curlers in her hair and a cigarette dangling from her lips. Sonny placed her at 70, but she may have been 90. She was five feet tall at best. She shuffled behind the counter and looked up at the two of them with creased eyes.

"So, you want a room at the Hi-Line, do ya? Want to get out of this rain?" She looked at the two of them then, and ashed her cigarette into the glass tray on the counter. "And I suppose you realize that it's damn late out, and you're gettin' an old lady up from her bed?" She was throwing questions at them pell-mell, but neither of them expected that they were required to answer. They were right.

"I know men like you," she continued. "and they're called *men*." She laughed at her own joke and inhaled her cigarette anew. "Selfish and hopeless, like the rest," she said, as she exhaled. Then she looked at them as if seeing them for the first time. "One room, or two?"

THE ROOM contained two double beds and a nightstand, adorned with an attendant lamp, between them. The carpet was brown, and the artwork contained desert scenes. The two men sat across from one another, each to each, on his own bed.

Sonny had removed his jacket and collared shirt and sat in his A-shirt and trousers with a Lucky Strike behind his ear. Saul, after some time in the bathroom, had emerged with a towel around his shoulders and his pants still on. His socks, shirt, and jacket hung on the shower curtain rod.

"Be straight with me," Saul said, as he sat. His face had lost much of its stress, and Sonny saw in it a mirth and boyish impishness that had been vacant earlier in the evening. "What is this whole deal? Is this what you do?" Sonny saw Saul looking over his tattooed neck and shoulders, the inkwork loosed upon his arms, hands, fingers.

Sonny caught eyes with him then and did not answer for several seconds. Saul dropped his eyes and shook his head, as if realizing he had perhaps overstepped his bounds. Whatever decision Sonny had been making in his silence, he finally made it and put out an arm to show the small man that everything was fine.

"I do jobs for people. I protect them. I pick them up. Sometimes, I do more than that. But this job is different," Sonny said.

"How is this different? And that guy, back there, the one in the car, what's gonna happen to him? And, I mean, the other guy…" he said, and didn't finish.

"The guy in the car will be fine. He'll get found tonight, or more likely tomorrow morning. He'll be cold and wet and in more trouble with the spaghettiheads that hired him than anything I did." Sonny smiled at this. "The other guy was found last night. I stuck a knife through his face. Look, the situation was this: Dealing with one greaseball is pretty easy, most of the time. They don't get paid for thinking much. But dealing with two—that changes the odds quite a bit. Plus, I had to piss. So I took one out of the equation. After that, you saw how easy that was. Anyone could do it," Sonny said. He grabbed a toothpick from his wallet and began to pick at his teeth.

Saul took this in and it was quite clear from the look on his face that he did not believe that 'anyone could have done it' though he did not reply.

"Oh, I forgot," Sonny started, pulling the toothpick from between two of his bottom teeth, "you asked why. No, I don't go around rescuing guys just 'cause somebody needs rescuing. I got bills too. But I got a call from an old partner in Vegas a week ago. Me and my daughter, she's a bit of a poker shark, and so we had to get outta town anyways, and I get this call with a deal. See…." He stopped here, thinking he had already told far too much of the evolution of the thing but knew also there was no chance he was

stopping now. Plus, Sonny had to admit, as he looked at the man across from him, he liked the little guy. So, cards on the table and all that, he figured. If it didn't work out, maybe the guy helps him out down the road. Or it all goes to shit. C'est la vie, what will be, and all that nonsense.

"I used to be a guy on the force. LA. I'm investigating Cohen, my wife gets killed, and I'm the suspect. It was all a mess. So," he paused here, flipped the Lucky Strike into his mouth and lit it with a match he struck on the nightstand, "I'm not exactly welcome company in the City of Angels with my old peers, if you get my drift."

"You're a wanted man," Saul said quickly, showing he had been following along quite nicely.

"That's one way of putting it," Sonny said.

Saul smiled at this. "Is there another way?" He asked.

"Look, little jewish director…" Sonny said, and wagged his finger at him. He smiled then, and realized that yes, there was something in this guy he liked. He exhaled a lungful of smoke at the popcorn ceiling.

"So, what's the deal you got?" Saul asked. "And," he looked at the door quickly, "what's to keep three more guys from busting down the door tonight?"

Sonny took a drag from his smoke, exhaled, and waited for the cloud to dissipate before answering: "The deal is I give you back to the studio head, untouched and ready to go into your next picture, and D.A. Simpson gets off my back." He mashed the remainder of the cigarette into the glass ashtray on the nightstand.

"Ahhhh," Saul said. "You get LA back."

"Yup."

"You want your old job back?" Saul asked.

Sonny spit out a laugh then, a staccato burst of something he barely recognized. Then: "No. No, I don't want it back, I don't expect they'd ask, and I wouldn't take it if they did. Very, very done with that group." He paused a moment. "Plus, I like what I do. A lot more freedom."

"As for more goons," he continued, "they had no idea I'd be there. No idea where we are. Probably haven't even found Frank yet, and whether they've gotten the word on the other lug, I doubt that as well. In a day or two, somebody associated with Cohen is gonna lose their shit. But for now, we're good." Sonny smiled, not so much at Saul but for the admission itself, and lay back on his bed. "And," he continued, "if they do, I've got something for them,"

and he motioned to his .45, and the two .38's that lay on the bed next to him. He lit another cigarette and exhaled toward the ceiling.

"Ever had any thought of acting?" Saul asked.

"No," Sonny said, quickly. He didn't look at Saul when he said it, as he was still staring at the ceiling and the smoke negotiating the nooks and crannies of the ceiling. "I make fun of actors. I don't act."

"My next film," Saul barreled forward while getting underneath the covers of his bed, "is being filmed out this way, mostly in 29 Palms. It's a western. If you ever want to get on the set, let me know."

Sonny said nothing to this, and turned out the lamp. Saul wasn't sure if he had even heard him, but lay back and watched as the embertip of Sonny's cigarette sat suspended in the darkness atop his lips.

THE RAIN was a light mist in the morning as Sonny stood next to the Merc. Saul emerged from the room and walked to the office with the room key. When he returned, he looked at Sonny over the hood.

"Ready?" Sonny asked.

Saul looked himself over once, at his dirty clothes he had worn for a week straight and put his hands out once, then ran them over his wiry and unruly hair. "I guess," he said.

The 10 west was littered with puddles from the night before and the windshield wipers continued working on the dusting that remained as they moved towards Los Angeles. The radio was tuned to a jazz station and neither man talked much. At one point, Sonny turned the volume down and asked: "What did the wops want from you anyways?"

"I dunno. Some guy, close to Cohen I guess, some Capo, he wanted his daughter in the picture. He sends her to me. Girl couldn't act sick if she had a cold. I said no way. They said, think again. I said, I got sick just from thinking of it. Next thing I know, I'm getting picked up in a car I don't recognize." The two men looked at each other and Saul shrugged his shoulders. Sonny laughed out loud.

"You regret it now?" He asked, when he had finished.

"Not if it means she's not gonna be in my film," Saul answered, and looked out the window. Sonny laughed again and turned the radio back up. Saul Bernstein was one stubborn bastard. 〜👓〜

MURANIA PRESS

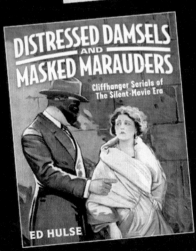

Covering a Century of Adventure, Mystery and Melodrama in American Popular Culture!

The award-winning *Blood 'n' Thunder* explores the long-forgotten byways of America's cultural landscape: its vehicles of popular fiction, beginning with story papers of the mid 19th century that evolved over the next hundred years into dime novels, nickel weeklies, pulp magazines and, finally, paperback originals of the mid 20th century. *Blood 'n' Thunder* also covers such derivative and complementary storytelling forms as gaslight-era stage melodrama, feature-length and serialized motion pictures, and Old-Time Radio programs steeped in adventure and mystery.

Launched in 2002, Murania's flagship publication features contributions from knowledgeable fans, pop-culture historians and members of academia. Their essays and articles are carefully sourced and thoroughly researched, but written with fannish affection and enthusiasm for the subject matter. There's nothing dry or stodgy about *Blood 'n' Thunder* — how could there be, with a title like that?

The "Classic Pulp Reprints" line has established its own niche in an overcrowded field. Other pulp-reprint publishers specialize in the works of fan favorites and the adventures of popular series characters. Murania Press shines light anew on isolated, long-forgotten yarns by some of the field's most prolific and influential wordsmiths, including Gordon Young, J. Allan Dunn, and H. Bedford-Jones, to name just a few.

Other Murania Press books focus narrowly on subjects covered broadly in the pages of *Blood 'n' Thunder*. For example, *Distressed Damsels and Masked Marauders* presents a comprehensive history of cliffhanger serials of the silent-movie era. The upcoming *Riders of Gower Gulch* documents the production of "B" Westerns by scrappy independent producers operating along Hollywood's fabled Poverty Row. You can count on these and future Murania Press works to maintain our long-established standards of excellence in writing and reportage.

MURANIAPRESS.COM

MURANIA PRESS

THE GRIFFIN'S LIVING DEATH

by J. Allan Dunn

ALTHOUGH TIME was the one thing he could not afford to waste, Gordon Manning did not use the police siren allotted to him by the department. He did not dare in any way to make his progress conspicuous, despite the fact that he had made arrangements for a quick and secret shift from his own to another car, before he got out of the city.

For the first time it began to look as if the use of his peculiar type of agents to close in on the Griffin, to discover the secret lair of that homicidal mad monster, were about to be crowned with at least some measure of success.

But Manning was well aware that he himself might be under the constant surveillance of the Griffin's own men, and they would work as mysteriously, be as much under cover and hard to distinguish as Manning's own private corps.

One slip might spoil everything. At any moment that evil genius might become suspicious. It was hard to cope with the swift changes of an eccentric but brilliant mind.

It was best to strike the moment the iron became tolerably warm, rather than wait until it was hot and glowing.

For long, weary weeks, Manning had been receiving the reports of his unprofessional but efficient spies. It had seemed hopeless work, while every now and then the Griffin struck sometimes with warning, sometimes without.

When he warned, it was because of a belief in his own invincibility, the belief that the stars were in favorable aspect for the success of his crimes. Such warnings were intended to strike terror to the soul of the victim and those who loved him—or her. To fray the steady, strong nerves of Manning, always attuned to the thrill of evil, the expectation of hearing the Griffin's mocking voice announce a new murder of some one the world badly needed; or receiving a letter to that effect in the Griffin's characteristic writing, signed by his scarlet seal—scarlet as fresh-spilled blood, and stamped with his symbol.

NOW MANNING was on his way, summoned to a rendezvous

where one of his men waited to point out the trail to the Griffin's den.

Such a job had been like the assembling of a mammoth jigsaw puzzle, handicapped by an intricate and confusing design, and the fact that the pieces had to be picked up here and there, scraps that seemed impossible to weave into the answer.

For weeks Manning had been plotting circles and triangles within which he would gradually narrow the limits of the neighborhood where the Griffin had his aerie.

That lair, Manning had concluded, was within fifty miles of City Hall, New York. That was a territory that included three States in its scope. None knew better than Manning how many places it held that were still rural, remote from the general lines of travel.

Radio and telephone may link up a house with civilization; a mile of dirt road and a lack of street lighting keeps it a place apart. The rapidly increasing mixture of cosmopolitan population, in both city and country, breaks up the old neighborliness.

Manning believed the lair was north, from the beginning; probably somewhere in Putnam, Dutchess or Rockland Counties, with the last doubtful. New Jersey had the handicap of too easily checked tunnels or slow-moving ferries. Long Island was not hard

to scout and Manning had dismissed it before his first clews began to point to the north. Connecticut was, of course, a possibility.

But this tip, from one of his own agents, swung the needle of suspicion steadily north. There were hamlets in Putnam and Duchess where woods were still thick about them, railroads well away. They had been the centers for farmers before most of the farms went back to sumach and thornapple. Now they had dwindled to a disconsolate general store or so. The mills no longer ran; deserted houses stood about, reached only by wood roads. Houses that dated back to the days before George Washington wooed Mary Philipse at Philipse Manor, near Carmel, in Putnam County, and was refused.

There are, believe it or not, forgotten villages within that radius, where the main attraction for the winter is The Swiss Bell Ringer, playing the *Blue Danube Waltz.*

In such a place the Griffin lurked.

MANNING WOVE his way through traffic expertly. Near the bridge that must take him out of Manhattan, he swung off the street into a garage. He stepped swiftly from his roadster into the closed van of a dyeing and cleaning establishment, and was driven off immediately to another garage, where he transferred again to another roadster, of different make and color from his own, but equally as powerful.

He had used this method of throwing off possible espionage before. He had no reason to think that he had been followed, even to the first garage; but precaution was paramount if the Griffin was going to be caught. Nothing would be learned at the garage. They knew who he was—Gordon Manning, special-service agent, commissioned to eliminate the Griffin.

Manning had brought him in once, and the clumsy law, working on medieval procedure, had called the Griffin mad, legally irresponsible for his hideous crimes. They had locked him up in Dannemora, and the Griffin had not stayed there long.

Next time—this time, Manning prayed it might be as he sped along the parkway—Manning was going to assume responsibility. If he closed in and the Griffin gave him the excuse, as no doubt he would, Manning meant to bring back a dead monster, eliminated beyond all recall.

Manning's present method, continued steadily, aside from the events furnished by some new crime of the Griffin, was similar to that of the old bee-hunters who roamed the prairies, catching bees as they went, letting them escape, marking their lines of flight.

Where those lines converged there would be their prize, a dead limb of some tree, dripping with luscious honey.

Manning's "bees" were the cars in which the Griffin, or his agents, escaped from the scenes of horror. Many times those cars were the same machine, and carried the Griffin. It was a long-hooded sedan of the most expensive make. It was black, shining with the rich luster of enamel. Many rich men had cars like it, and it was not easy to distinguish.

It seemed certain that the Griffin had a more powerful engine than the one originally sold with that make. He had left Manning's fast roadster behind, more than once. There was no doubt that the license number was frequently changed, that it could be shifted automatically as the car sped along.

The flight of these "bees" was of course broken by the very nature of the routes taken by the cars, by the odds of a deliberately twisted course; yet, little by little, they had converged to what should be a common center.

And Manning had established, within the narrowing area of his search, both key men and field men.

He had picked them from all ages. Some were learned and others could not spell properly. They had no headquarters; only few of them came in contact with each other.

Now he was bound for a key man, a good mechanic who had been glad to be placed in charge of a roadside garage and machine shop. There was not much trade, but the profits were all his, aside from the salary Manning paid him and the prospects of bonuses. Manning got a public telephone booth installed in the garage, which brought Farrell close to village gossip.

It was through Farrell, and a field man, Bishop, that Manning was making this play. His agents made themselves known to be in good standing with each other by the use of code words, changed every three days. A man not in possession of the last word was to be considered untrustworthy.

Though he picked carefully, paid well, and knew them grateful, Manning was careful. It was not that he mistrusted them so much, as his knowledge of human nature. The Griffin had unlimited means. He could offer a sum to a man that would, after months of poverty and distress, tempt him beyond his powers. Or he could threaten, he could strike. Once let him suspect one of Manning's spies and he would surely either bribe the man to be a traitor, or make away with him.

Chapter 2

FARRELL WAS thirty-odd, unmarried, ambitious and straightforward. As garageman he did not play a hard rôle.

Bishop was over fifty. A man who had had much and seen it swept away. His wife was dead, his children scattered, all their prospects sunk in the depression.

But he had spirit in him yet. He had at one time in his youth been an actor, playing character parts. Money left him, and the breakdown of stock and repertoire companies by the movies had led him to business successes that the crash of '29 had ruined.

He could still act. It was Bishop who had reported, through Farrell, the present lead. He had seen the Griffin's car four times within the past two weeks. Its appearance in that neighborhood was like the hot scent of a fox to a wise hound.

Bishop posed as a down-and-outer, begging odd jobs, slouching about the fields. Sometimes he was a mushroom picker, with a few mushrooms in his worn basket. He trailed from farm to farm, and house to house, choosing hours when the Griffin's car was least likely to be on the road, mostly after dark.

He too picked up gossip and he compiled a sort of record, as did other field men, of the people in that vicinity, and how they lived. That was not easy. Many were of foreign birth, close-mouthed, especially to derelicts; many spoke only broken Americanese.

There were houses here and there that had been restored, or partly restored, from Colonial days. Some of these were vacant these hard times; others had caretakers of various kinds, often poor relatives, who shut the door in the face of any rover.

Manning analyzed these descriptions, set aside the most likely. In this locale, patrolled by Bishop, there was an ancient house that had fallen, with its family, upon evil days. Once it had been the stately manor house of a King's Grant, now it stood in a few forlorn acres, unpainted and decrepit. There were first growth trees, some dying, others blighted chestnuts, about a melancholy mere that had known more than one suicide. There was a private graveyard, with the stones tilted, the mounds heaved or fallen in, the inscriptions hardly to be read.

The natives called it haunted, not the only one on Manning's list. A surly man and his bitter-faced wife lived there, keeping to themselves, buying cheap and scanty supplies.

For the Griffin, such a place might be a perfect camouflage, if it provided certain conveniences. Such as a site for the laboratories where the Griffin kept his nameless slaves at work for him.

They too were derelicts, like Manning's men; but these slaves had sinned against the law, escaped from its penalties, and the Griffin held them in thrall through knowledge of their guilt. Most of them had been in high rank in the professions from which they had been banished.

MANNING TURNED off the State highway, through the forgotten and almost abandoned village, over a bridge and by a broken dam. The dirt road was poorly kept, the taxes raised in such a section were small and highway commissioners and supervisors ignored the byways.

Stone walls crumbled, hedges grew rank, fields lay overgrown with weeds and brush. Old red barns sagged, farmhouses stood forlorn on the hills, untenanted. The ditches were clogged. Once in a while he saw gaunt cows, trying to keep alive in worn-out pastures.

Poverty reigned, with neglect. The only merit to the district in the eyes of travelers lay in the fact that here was a short cut to the bridge across the Hudson, if the weather were good.

There was an unused schoolhouse, no better than a shack. The children were picked up and taken to a central school. Gardens were neglected, save for a few, poor vegetables. He passed few cars and those were relics, chattering and staggering along, keeping together by a miracle, a prayer, and baling wire. Few people.

This was called Cow Hollow. Less than fifty miles from New York, sinking yearly into worse condition. Gnarled orchards strove to bear a little bitter, wormy fruit, not worth the picking.

Manning stopped at Farrell's garage. He did all the business there was in the neighborhood, largely because he seemed inclined to give credit. Most of those who hung him up for gasoline or repairs on one of their rattletraps considered him a sucker.

He came out, and Manning ordered oil, not wanting to mix his own ethyl with the gas Farrell handled. The oil *was* his own brand, kept for such a time by Farrell.

There was nobody about. Farrell could talk freely.

"Bishop gave me the new code word yesterday," he said. "Before I telephoned through to you. He's seen that car three times this week, including yesterday. It comes through between three and three forty-five in the afternoon."

Manning glanced at his wrist watch. It was two forty-seven.

"He knows it's the same car," Farrell went on, "though it has a different number each time, because its been in a smash some time, and it's got a new rear fender on the right side. They did a good enough job putting it on, but it hugs the chassis a bit. I noticed that the time it stopped here and asked was this the right road to the bridge. That was a stall. They saw me outside and wanted to ask questions of me, see? I told 'em what you said for me to say."

Manning nodded. Farrell was a good man.

"So I tipped Bishop off. You only notice this when the car's passing you. They saw me looking at it but they didn't know why. I only really saw the chauffeur. He had a sour puss, looked like it was cut out of a turnip. The one in the back might have been the Griffin. The blinds were drawn and I could just see there was someone. I told 'em I didn't expect to see such a fine car out here and he said it was because of the short cut."

"Been by here since?" asked Manning.

"No. They must come in over Grimm's hill. But they swing in to the road where Bishop sees 'em. They can turn off that to get to the bridge, though it's not the best way. Still, folks often get mixed up on the short cut. If you don't turn off the road it leads to the place they call Manor House, the spooky dump you know about. Used to go on through to the river, I guess, but now the road peters out beyond the graveyard. Nobody uses it."

"Where shall I find Bishop?" asked Manning.

"You can turn in at Three Elm Farm. Nobody living there now. Only two elms left. You can see 'em plain from this road. They're by the farmhouse. No gate, and rough going, but you can make it. Cut right across the farm behind the house, down an old cow lane to where the mailbox used to be. Just the post there now. There's some trees and scrub where you can park out of sight if you want

to. The fence is down along the Manor House road. Bishop'll be loafing round there to tell you if the car has passed or not.

"And he'll show you yesterday's tire tracks. It rained yesterday morning. If they ain't changed 'em. I doubt it. They're the regular tires for that car, and the rubber's new. Unless they figured you had spotted the car, otherwise they'd likely keep 'em on."

"Good man," said Manning. He looked at his watch again. "I'll be going." He handed Farrell a twenty-dollar bill. "Bonus," he said.

IT WAS two minutes before three. With luck, he would get in touch with Bishop before the car passed. But luck, he knew, was too often with the Griffin.

For some reason the Griffin had been making regular trips. And that meant deviltry.

It began to look as if the Manor House might be the lair. Three Elm Farm was not the place. The shutters hung crazily, the chimneys were tumbling down; there was not the track of tire or hoof, or even the pads of a roaming, hungry dog upon the place.

Manning drove down the cow lane, came to some street choked with wild grapevine. He was above the Manor House road, but hidden from it.

He braked, hesitant. To his left, a man shambled dejectedly along, using a stick, a basket like a fisherman's creel upon his back. A tramp, a mushroom picker—Bishop.

To the right, he saw a car advancing, a long, black car. It came on at a good fifty miles an hour, its weight—and the skill of the driver—seeming to ignore the inequalities of the dirt road. Now and then it swerved, or swayed a little, but it held a fair course.

It neared the shambling figure, which moved towards the ditch, humble and insignificant.

Suddenly Manning threw off his brakes, snatched a heavy automatic from a side pocket, and went rocketing down the slope. He made a beeline for where the fence was broken, distant from where a path had once led to the mailbox.

He dodged sumach, thornapples, plunged through a thicket, surged through second growth and saplings that made his passage a minor miracle. The gun was tucked under his thigh. He risked a blowout every second, but he trod hard on the gas. Now he could not see the road and every pulse-beat seemed to tick off the fatal message—that he would arrive too late.

The Griffin had been ahead of schedule, if there *was* a schedule. Bishop had been faithfully ahead of time. He was to pay for that faithfulness with a hideous death.

Perhaps the Griffin had suspected or merely disliked his presence on that road. It would take little for that monster to get rid of anything he deemed the slightest nuisance.

Manning had seen a thing that would have seemed unbelievable to any one not acquainted with the Griffin.

AS THE long car sped, it suddenly accumulated pace. A weird, incredible figure, like some nightmare fantasy, like a shattered gargoyle plucked from an age-old cathedral, swung to the running board. It clung there, legless, one apelike arm through the open window.

The lonely landscape held no other living things. The rushing car—Bishop—Manning, thundering, bounding down the slope, avoiding disaster by split-seconds.

Only a flock of somber crows cawed through the air, witnesses of Death, striking fiendishly.

It was Al, the legless freak bought by the Griffin from a traveling circus, a deaf mute with an atrophied soul and brain, corrupted by his new master.

In its free hand the freak held something that looked like a lance, or a sharpened pole. The big car raced, charging, hemming in Bishop against the fallen fence and the hedge that backed it.

The young trees blotted that out for Manning. He had all he could do to avoid them. He could not. His running board and fenders struck them, dented and crumpled. A buried snag tore a tire and he barely escaped collision with a stump. He held on, lurching on a rim, his arms and wrists wrenched.

He crashed through the tangled fence, smashed rotten rider poles, plunged into the ditch, skidding to the road, twisting and turning on the surface, still slimy with yesterday's rain.

He wound up with his back bumper bent against a fallen stone wall on the far side, leaped out, gun in hand.

The black car was out of sight.

Something lay twisted in the opposite ditch. A body thrust through and through with a lance, writhing in the last, convulsive agonies of death, bloody and distorted.

Manning stood over Bishop—what had been Bishop. He had seen death in many shapes but none worse than this. For a moment his blood ran cold.

Bishop was impaled upon a stake six feet long. It had been armed with a point of wrought iron, now clotted with crimson.

Al had held that lance, or had flung it. The latter was more probable. The car, with its tremendous speed, perhaps seventy miles or more at the moment, had provided the frightful impetus that had taken Bishop off his feet, as the spear sheared through belly and backbone until half of it stuck out behind; left him like an impaled beetle, squirming and gasping as he died.

The tire tracks were plain in the road. But here was the dead man, and Manning's car was stranded with a jammed brake, a bent axle, a blown tire and twisted steering gear.

The body that had been Bishop gasped its last breath.

The cawing crows came wheeling back, as if they saw or scented carrion. And Manning stood gun in hand, powerless.

Chatper 3

AL, THE deaf mute, legless freak, squatted on a square hassock in a corner of the Griffin's private chamber. There was no morality in him. Killing was a delight, the instinct implanted in him as it is in some epileptics who commit homicide instead of having convulsions.

And now this abnormity, whose clothing was sprinkled with the blood that spurted from poor Bishop as the car rushed past, was enjoying his reward with complacency. He squatted on his legless trunk, with an all-day-sucker thrust into his mouth, blissfully absorbing it.

When Al had been in the museum of the circus, he had put on an exhibition of shooting arrows, hurling lances and flinging knives. It was this performance that had helped decide the Griffin to buy off the freak.

This afternoon he had made use of Al's accomplishments, staging it to suit his own love of the bizarre, adding the force and fury of the speeding car.

The Griffin had not been definitely suspicious of Bishop, nor of Farrell, but it had struck him that the lonely neighborhood had rather suddenly acquired an increase of population. He had noticed Bishop several times. He might be tramp or mushroom picker or he might be a spy. The fact he was an interloper on territory the Griffin reserved for himself, the merest thought that he might be scouting for Manning or the police, sufficed for his warranty of death.

The Griffin, seated in comfort in his car, had watched the killing with the sadistic delight of a Nero. Human lives meant no more to him than those of the guinea pigs, rats and mice used by scientists in their researches. But the Griffin experimented for no cause but his own. He was indeed like Nero, who encouraged Locusta, the poisoner, by providing her with slaves on which to experiment.

Now the Griffin sat gloating behind his carven desk as Al guzzled his sweet. The Griffin's features were screened by the mask of thin material that looked like goldbeater's skin, like the skin of a snake just before shedding. He looked like some ancient conception of Mephisto. The mask twitched to his grimace as he recalled the dying contortions of Bishop—who might or might not have been a spy.

He sucked at the amber mouthpiece of a hookah pipe, and the bubbles danced in the rose-scented water that cooled the smoke. The bowl burned to ashes and the Griffin rose, and began to pace up and down his chamber. He was clad in a long black robe of heavy silk brocaded with cabalistic designs. A sable skullcap was on his head.

There had been amber as well as hasheesh in the pipe, and now the fumes of the former gained ascendancy. From some unseen source music sounded in a barbaric strain of drums and cymbals, of pipes and stringed instruments.

THE GRIFFIN seemed to talk to the freak, with whom he could actually communicate only by signs; but the mad monster was really talking loud. Boasting to himself, loving the sound of his voice, the proclamation of his intentions.

"It was well done, Al," he said. "It was nobly done. He leaped and fell, like one smitten by the shaft of a centaur. Though you are far from that. But it was a good play.

"It has been in my mind that there are too many new and strange faces that follow me about. Gordon Manning on the trail. The fool! Does he think to trap me again and send me to that madhouse. Ha! Forewarned is forearmed, Al. He who strikes first strikes shrewdest. So—we shall strike. Manning shall be the victim. Long ago I promised him an unusual death. And he shall have one. This very day it is perfected. And, by Ahriman and Abaddon, not all the hosts of heaven, not all the fiends of hell shall save him!"

A bronze disk supported between pillars suddenly boomed sonorously. It was the signal that Griffin had been expecting. In the wall a space was suddenly revealed, the entrance to a lift that the Griffin entered, forbidding Al to follow by a gesture. The hidden door closed, the lift descended, going to the cellars of the old manor, now enlarged and converted into laboratories where the Griffin's evil genii worked his perverted will.

Left alone, Al sulked, then sucked at his candy. He set it aside and swung himself on his palms to the desk. He looked around, like a mischievous ape, at once curious and fearful. The booming of the gong made certain impressions upon his atrophied sense. He knew that it summoned the Griffin, that it announced events.

He balanced his torso with one arm, reached up the other hand and touched timidly the disk. Out of it there came a spurt and crackle of blue sparks and tiny lightnings. The shock of the discharge stung through the freak, bowled him over, his arms numb, his ugly face convulsed as he gave vent to a hideous, bestial cry that he sought to stifle by stuffing one sluggish hand into his mouth.

He rolled to his hassock and lay there while his flesh seemed stabbed with pins and needles. His God, the omnipotent, all seeing, ever present Griffin, had punished him for his sin. Al was cured of meddling. The more so as he had seen his Master touch and tap the plaque without harm; not knowing the Griffin had thrown a switch before he left the chamber.

Al moaned, with uncouth noises, drooling and gabbling. At last, finding himself recovered, he retrieved his sweet, and squatted once more on the hassock, educated and subdued.

BELOW, THE Griffin stalked through cemented corridors just high enough for him to pass without bowing, and came to a central crypt. This was his theater—like the theater of a hospital. Here things were dissected, inanimate objects assembled, demonstrations made. A man awaited him, more like a robot than a human being. He wore an overall of yellow on which was painted, back and front, the numerals 67. His face was the hue of beeswax, bloodless, expressionless. His lips were without hue; the only color showed in his eyes, intensely blue, blazing behind lenses that enlarged them, made them goggle, glow with something akin to insanity.

Innumerable wrinkles radiated about his eyes and mouth. He was entirely bald. His shaggy eyebrows were white. But there was still a restrained vigor about him. Number Sixty-Seven had been a famous chemist, a toxicologist who had mixed up his subtle poisons with his own cosmos.

The Griffin had snatched him from the chaos that resulted. Here was a slave after his own evil heart. He had made a pawn of the other, rescued him from the death penalty to transfer him to a hideous servitude only mitigated by the fact that Sixty-Seven was given apparatus and allowed to use his alembics in experiments. The Griffin consulted him, and Sixty-Seven knew well enough why.

There had been a time when despair came to him, followed by a measure of resignation; of late he had been restless. This last task had pleased him, strengthened the perversion of spirit that he had gradually accumulated, as if partaking of the Griffin's unholy nature through association.

It was the Griffin himself who had suggested the source of the present experiment. Sixty-Seven had perfected it.

There were two draped figures on narrow tables. One sheeted form was quite still, yet not entirely rigid. There was something about it that suggested life was not extinct. The other covering moved slightly as if the unmistakable body beneath it breathed. Now and then there were twitchings.

The Griffin frowned at this and Sixty-Seven spoke swiftly. "This is the example in which the toxin was first used upon a human subject. It proved not to be sufficiently concentrated. You told me you did not mind how many subjects I used from the numbers you supplied me."

"True, so long as you succeeded. Those men have passed their utility to me. But why show me a failure?"

"I shall show you also a perfect success. I thought that you might like to see both phases. The first man will ultimately die. He has suffered frightful torments. He is now anaesthetized by pain. He can bear no more."

SIXTY-SEVEN STRIPPED off the coarse shroud. The body of the "subject" was emaciated—the Griffin did not feed his slaves too munificently—but it was also horribly swollen. It looked like something badly stuffed. The limbs were shapeless and blotched, the veins like black cord, twisted and coiled. The lips were drawn back, and the teeth showed between the bloodless gums like those of a skull. Only the blood-specked white of his eyes showed. They seemed to be staring inwards.

"This is after twenty hours," said Sixty-Seven. "I doubt if I could save him, even if I had prepared an anti-toxin. No one else could. They could never determine the toxin. There are no known tests for it."

"He looks as if he had been bitten by a snake," said the Griffin. "Let us see the other one."

Sixty-Seven covered the blotched man, whose body still twitched to the pain engendered by the toxin, though the worn-out consciousness no longer registered.

There were no such terrible stigmata on the second body that lay exposed and nude. The eyes were open but fixed.

They did not respond to touch or movement, but there was a horror manifest in the distended pupils, the narrowed irises.

Like the first, this body was ill nourished, but it showed no sign of violence, or of agony, beyond the haunting horror in the immobile orbs. The breath misted the mirror Sixty-Seven placed to the slightly parted lips and the chest rose and fell almost imperceptibly. The limbs were plastic, the flesh seemed normal but it was cold as that of a cadaver.

Sixty-Seven thrust a lancet into the nearer arm. No blood followed the withdrawal.

"The heart has ceased to beat, the arterial system is idle. This is after twelve hours. It is a perfect state of suspended animation. He will be dead, to all intents and purposes, within another hour. But there will be no decay. Not for many weeks. He is embalmed alive. While alive."

The Griffin frowned again.

"It is good," he said, "but not all I had hoped. He will die too soon."

"I can modify the toxin so that the subject will not lose consciousness, as this one nearly has, for days, for a week, perhaps more."

"Good. And the brain?"

"The subconscious cerebration will cease, but he will know he is alive. Until life—as we term it—finally passes, he will be able to think, he will remember, he will imagine the future."

The Griffin chuckled. He tapped Sixty-Seven on his shoulder, leaned on him and began to shake with ghoulish laughter.

"It is excellent," he cried at last. "I was not sure when you showed me the two which I might choose, after all. The torment or the peace, with perfect understanding. I select the latter. The living death. The torture in the brain. I shall bring you your subject soon. And then, Sixty-Seven, name your reward."

The magnified blue eyes flamed behind the lenses. "You mean—whatever I wish?"

"I have said so," replied the Griffin magnificently.

"Freedom, that is what I want. I want the sun, I want to mingle again with men—and women."

"Strange talk for a scientist. Yet you wizards are often very human. It was a question of women that brought you here, I remember. Would have taken you to the chair, if I had not intervened. If I gave you freedom you are apt to land there yet."

"Who would know me?" Sixty-Seven burst out bitterly. "Look at me, forty in years, seventy in appearance. Old enough, in seeming, to be my own father. But young enough to want to use my life. I could leave the country. I could...."

The Griffin checked him. "You shall have your freedom," he said. "Complete and absolute. After you have done this thing for me."

He turned away. Sixty-Seven gazed at him with an expression hard to interpret.

"What shall be done with these?" he asked. "The first will corrupt before long."

"Dispose of it. Have the other set aside for observation. Interesting things may be done with living death, if only for exhibition, and an object lesson."

"And I shall be free?"

"You have my promise, after you have served my purpose."

Sixty-Seven stared after the Griffin's departing figure. His lips moved as he muttered silently.

"Freedom, complete and absolute! I have his word."

The Griffin had disappeared. From the stone passage there came a chuckle. The low roof echoed it.

Chapter 4

GORDON MANNING, in the study of his house at Pelham Manor after dinner, preparing to enjoy a cheroot and a liqueur, was not surprised when Mizu, his Japanese butler, brought in a letter, instead of the Eau-de-vie de Dantzig.

One might never be surprised at a madman's whimsies, murderous though they were. The Griffin had struck the day before, though Al's hand had held the lethal weapon. The sight of blood, of death, had whetted the monster's appetite perhaps; or he might be merely boasting, not knowing Manning had seen the crime.

The letter was in the usual gray envelope of thick, hand-made paper. Manning could see it had been sealed with a scarlet *affiche,* an oval stamped with a demi-griffin in relief. The address was in purple.

How it had been delivered did not much matter, he thought, a trifle wearily. The Griffin was not to be so easily traced. He listened to Mizu's half apologetic explanation.

"The berring, verree, ritter ring, but I hear. I put on chain, open ritter bit. This retter come through, prease excuse."

"Excuse what, Mizu?"

"Excuse I no rook. You terr me be carefur. I pick up this, shut door."

"That's all right, Mizu. Bring in the liqueur."

Manning broke the seal, glanced almost casually at the few lines. Whatever this might be, he had already prepared a counter-stroke.

Farrell had taken his damaged car back to the garage, taken along Bishop's body, from which Manning had wrenched the lance.

Police regulations did not count where Manning was concerned with the Griffin. The medical-examiner could be dispensed with in his capacity of being the first to arrive on the scene. And the local authorities would be subordinate to those Manning summoned.

He wanted to fade out of the picture for the time. There had been no other witnesses but the crows. The tracks of the black sedan were still there, not to be traced immediately.

The Griffin was wanton enough in his slayings but there must have been some suspicion behind this one. He would be alert to watch for any follow up, though Manning doubted if he would

return, in person or by an agent, to the scene of his crime.

That was, Manning fancied, perilously close to his lair. The Manor House must be investigated if, as Manning felt they did, the tire tracks led there. But it was best to let the Griffin think he had definitely succeeded. His madness must be growing for him to be this reckless. It was his swollen ego, inevitably leading him on to what he might consider a sort of divine immunity, granted to him, the appointed servant of the stars.

Manning had prepared the net to be drawn. He had consulted with the commissioner, made plans that would be put in motion at midnight. Then Manning, in his own roadster, would join the picked New York detail at Farmers' Mills. The commissioner would be there in person.

IT WAS a few minutes after eight. Manning drew the straw from his cheroot, lit it carefully, inhaled the first fragrant pull before he read.

MY DEAR MANNING:

This notifies you of my next elimination. But not of the date. You must puzzle that out. Briefly, I am tired of you. You do not play the game properly. You move pieces in ways the rules do not permit. You have won a game or two, but I no longer propose to lose.

I am sweeping the board, so far as you are concerned. You no longer amuse me. The name of my next "victim," as the papers style it, is Gordon Manning.

In this the stars are with me. Put your affairs in order, Manning, for you are about to die. And, as I promised, I have designed for you a demise both fitting and unique.

For the last time, for you, I sign myself.

The signature was a sketch of a griffin, excellently drawn above a blob of crimson wax.

It was not really news to Manning. He knew the Griffin had many times tried to kill him. This would be a special and concentrated attempt, but it did not disturb him. He was striking first.

The tire-tracks had been followed that afternoon, closely enough to know they led to the manor, beyond which there was no road. The Griffin had been traced to his lair. The place would be surrounded. Manning had heard the short speech the commissioner had made to his subordinates.

"The man who shoots and kills the Griffin will be promoted. He will be praised by the whole nation. The Griffin is to be treated like a mad dog. Major Manning will have charge of the detail, and I shall be along."

Mizu came with the square bottle, where flecks of gold danced in the liqueur he poured into the tubelike glass.

"Prease, I hope nothing wrong," he said anxiously.

"Nothing wrong, everything very right, Mizu."

Manning let the slick potion glide down his throat. He drank silently to the confusion of the Griffin, to his death. The world would breathe easier. This insane, satanic monster had disrupted social and financial circles, had destroyed the most worthy. His demise would be the resurrection of public confidence. While such a fiend stalked free, the very stability of government was threatened.

He picked up the letter again. The gray paper had changed color, or seemed to. So with the ink. The writing was no longer firm. Everything was fading.

And Mizu was standing, watching.

Manning fought with the lethargy that surged upon him. He

forced his tongue to speak, his will to function, while swift thought rocketed through his brain.

The Griffin had not named the hour. He had not *meant* to give enough grace to Manning to "put affairs in order." He had designed a "unique death!" This was not it. It was only the preliminary. After all, the Griffin had struck first.

"Mizu," said Manning with his stumbling tongue, his thickening speech he strove to make distinct, "what have you done? What did you put in this drink?"

He looked at Mizu in a haze that grew denser. He heard Mizu's voice, mocking.

"Mister Manning, I verree sorree, but my honoraber nation not rike your American nation. You try keep us verree down. Pretty soon we fight. Pretty soon we take. Me, I am officer on staff of Imperiar councir. Here I am butrer, but rearry major. Pretty soon generar, I think. I rike money to back Japan. My famiry not rich. Money arways good for man with ambition. The one who sent that retter give prenty money to me and Yamato. Now we prenty rich. *Sodiska.*"

The final sentences faded out like shadows in the sun. Mizu, and Yamato, smitten by dreams of grandeur, even as the Griffin, had betrayed him.

Manning slumped in his chair.

ALL WAS blurred until he felt himself reviving. The rim of a glass was between his lips. A man stroked his throat, inducing swallowing. He gulped, involuntarily, and his head cleared. But there was no vigor to his limbs.

He looked up into the masked face of the Griffin, gloating behind the screening skin, his eyes glittering through slits.

"False move, Manning. You thought you were a roving pawn, moving across the board to where you could move, as the queen moves, and close the game. But I castled. It is checkmate. Now I'll tell you what I am going to do with you."

Manning wondered what the time was. Not much more than ten o'clock. Two hours until midnight. They would wait for him at Farmers Mills, delay indefinitely. Meanwhile—he was lying on a table in a crypt with cemented walls. He could not move. He was bound, hand and foot, and the drug still gripped him, though the effect was passing.

He saw the Griffin, robed in sable, masked with a leprous film. He twisted his neck painfully and saw Al, the freak, squatting like a creature in an obscene nightmare. Two figures in overalls, with numbers painted on them. One number was Sixty-Seven. The man was bald, pallid, wrinkled, with weird, mad, blue eyes back of powerful lenses. This one felt his pulse, nodded.

"I'll tell you about the fitting death I have devised for you," said the Griffin. "You have the distinction of being the first to experience it. You know, of course, of the Hymenoptera—the stinging and social insects. Bees, wasps, hornets, ants. In your travels you must have encountered them. Some of them, most of them, are carnivorous, cannibalistic. They feed their young and themselves upon the bodies of their victims which they sting into paralysis. That venom has the rare, antiseptic faculty of being able to preserve the meat they drag into their larders.

"Another case of the spider and the fly. I had a notion that you meant to come into my parlor, Manning, but I have forestalled that, and brought you here. Taking an advantage of the misunderstanding between Japan and America, of the perhaps inflated ideas of certain Japanese loyalists, who are overeager for a final adjustment.

"Bees have stung men to death. The digger-wasps possess a vicious venom. They belong to the genus Sphex. The *pepsis femoratus* stores its burrows with the great tarantula spiders, highly poisonous themselves, but less agile. As *you* have been less agile. Sometimes they kill, mostly they reduce their prey to a state of immobility. That is the method I have adopted, concentrating their venom with the expert aid of number Sixty-Seven, here present, who will now inject you with the toxin.

"I shall leave you a living corpse, Manning. Even if you were found, you could not be restored. Your brain will function for a few days, as you recount your sins, your follies, your stupidity in pitting yourself against the Griffin.

"The Zodiac declares that this is the time when the heavenly powers desert you. I am going to place you in the mortuary of this manor, in an empty coffin, from which I have strewn the bones that thought they claimed it. Later, I may arrange to have you found, exhibited, living but dead, until corruption slowly decays you.

"In the meantime, since you may have been too active, and be traced too soon, I am departing. For some time I have sought and found a better place for my righteous activities. But you"—the Griffin's mask quivered with the intensity of his hate—"*you* will no longer irk me. You will cease to exist, save as your brain knows you are doomed, like an envenomed larva. Inject him, Sixty-Seven."

Manning saw the bloodless countenance bending over him, felt the prick of a needle in his arm.

"You will stay here," the Griffin ordered his slave, "while I conduct the final preparations for leaving. Then you shall be freed. Manning, you have made your last move. The game is over."

MANNING WAITED for the paralysis to set in. A light burned low in the ceiling of the crypt. It was shadowed by the figure of Sixty-Seven, who bent over him.

"You are his enemy, the man who seeks to destroy him? You are Gordon Manning?" whispered Sixty-Seven.

Manning nodded. The blue eyes were glaring down. How did this serf know of Manning? As if he read the thought, the other answered.

"He told me who you were. His enemy—and mine. You represent the law. Now you are helpless. Never mind who I am—or was. If I free you, if I help to deliver him to you, will you help me?"

Manning made no compromise, though it was not his own plight he considered. Whoever this Sixty-Seven might be, might have done, he was an angel compared with the Griffin.

"What do you want?" he asked.

"I need money. I need clothes. Then I can escape. I did not inject you with the real venom. I will release you. We can both get away."

"I've got money with me," said Manning. "I'll change clothes with you. I don't know who you are, how you came under the Griffin's power. But we want *him* more than you. Do you know what time it is?"

"Night. But what day, what week or month, even what year, I cannot tell. Only let me go free."

"We'll change clothes," said Manning, "but how do you get out of here? As for the time, I've got a wrist watch."

"There is no ventilating system," said Sixty-Seven, "but I have studied the drafts. There is a way to the open. I have seen him and that unhallowed freak of his pass out, and smelled free air. If he

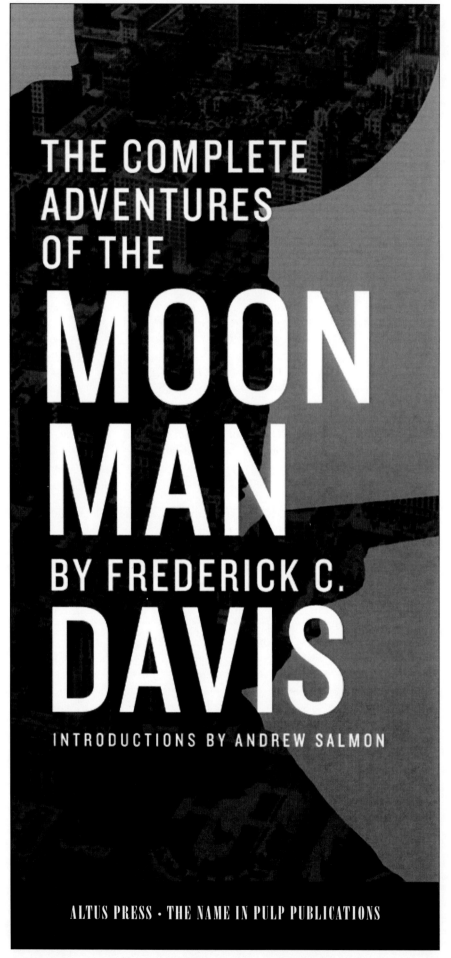

THE COMPLETE
ADVENTURES
OF THE
MOON
MAN
BY FREDERICK C.
DAVIS

INTRODUCTIONS BY ANDREW SALMON

ALTUS PRESS · THE NAME IN PULP PUBLICATIONS

leaves he will not bother with us who live underground. We are all condemned. We cannot tell who he is or where he goes. It's eleven-fifty, by your watch."

In ten minutes the commissioner would be assembling his forces, seven miles away. How long he would wait for Manning was hard to say.

Sixty-Seven severed Manning's bonds with a scalpel. They changed clothes swiftly, crept out to a corridor.

"The exit is this way," said Sixty-Seven. "I can feel the air. Do you want to come with me? I have freed you. There is an elevator to his quarters."

"It will be an automatic," said Manning, "I'll go with you. I suppose I'm compounding a felony in this."

"Listen," said Sixty-Seven. "I killed her. I admit that. She deserved it. When I'm away, it won't be where they'll extradite me. I'll write the truth. Not about this. But I'll give proof that she betrayed me. And, take this."

He pressed a small metal case into Manning's hand.

"This is the hypo, charged with the wasp venom. You may need it. Stick it into that fiend, if you get the chance."

IT SEEMED to Manning a fitting instrument, but he doubted if he would have the luck to use it. The place was a labyrinth. It was quiet enough. The Griffin was above, making his getaway. His slaves were asleep below, or seeking surcease.

Sixty-Seven, strange in Manning's clothes, his bald head topped by Manning's own hat, wetted a finger, held it up.

"The air current blows this way," he said. "We can trace it."

It seemed to Manning that hours and miles passed by in the dank silence of the passages. None accosted them. The Griffin believed him inanimate. But he might return at last, to give Sixty-Seven his freedom. For the slave had known what the Griffin meant by that. Those who served the Griffin were no longer useful to him once they achieved his purposes. The Griffin never repeated his methods. And, if this slave destroyed his greatest enemy, he would in turn be blotted out. Or left to his fate. The Griffin's word held more than one meaning.

The cold air-current guided them along the corridors. They came at last to a high grating where a figure stood on guard. Sixty-Seven stood back, and Manning, in the garb of Sixty-Seven, the numerals on his overall the clearest thing in the dim light, moved on.

"I've orders to set a body in the mortuary," said Manning, in a muffled voice.

"Well, I've had no orders," said the other surlily. He did not wear an overall. Manning saw he was belted, with a gun in a holster.

"Look at this," he said, and thrust forward his half closed hand.

The other stooped, and Manning's fist caught him in a swift uppercut to the jaw. As the man swayed, Manning hit him again and let him slide to the floor. He took his gun, searched him, found keys. One of them fitted the lock to the grating. Manning opened it, and there was a rush behind him. Sixty-Seven, who was Sixty-Seven no longer, was in full flight.

Manning bent over the guard. He was a typical thug, a hood. He snorted through his nose, knocked out. Manning bound his arms behind him, with his own belt, tied his feet together with the laces on his shoes, left him lying. He would stay out for a while.

The grating had closed off a mortuary. The inside bulb showed vaguely shelved caskets, others on the floor, broken and empty.

Here the dead, forgotten, owners of the manor had been set in their last sleep. Here the Griffin had meant to store Manning.

Ex-Sixty-Seven was scrabbling at another grille.

"Get me out of here," he said. "Let me out."

Manning sorted the keys, found one that clicked back the wards. There was moonlight outside, a medley of tilted head-stones. Sixty-Seven was gone, vanished in the night.

He turned towards the house and saw the only light vanish. He heard the whir of a motor, and ran through the graveyard towards the front of the manor. Its back was to the cemetery. There was a sort of lane between tall trees.

GUN IN hand, Manning reached the driveway in front of the house. The moon glinted on the high varnish of a big car. Its headlights were turned on. It began to move, to gather speed, making for an exit.

Yet the graveyard faced the highway. Manning now knew that the Griffin had restored an oldtime road, that he had a perfect getaway. There was but the one

car. He might have already transported his slaves. Or he might have left them, knowing they could not betray more than was already known, as he fled to his new retreat. Doubtless the caretaker and his wife had gone already. The big house was dark.

Manning shot at the car, aiming low for the tires. He was groggy and his aim was none too good. He realized that, as the car winked its red tail-light at him derisively before it vanished.

He had emptied the weapon. He was powerless. The Griffin had escaped.

But the Griffin had thought Manning left to a living death, and Manning was still very thoroughly alive, if helpless for the moment.

Something whimpered, leaped out of tall weeds, launched for Manning's throat. Hands clawed at him, at his windpipe. The fury of the attack bore him backwards. He tripped over a bush.

It was Al. The Griffin had discovered his meddling, had discarded him. Mute and unhearing, the freak could disclose nothing, knew little. But he was still faithful, like a dog that has been kicked, but still knows only one master.

He knew that this man had fired at the car, had tried to stop the exit of the God, his Master. Al was in a frenzy of fear and rage. His Master might come back, forgive him, if he found he had killed this man he grappled. This side of the house was in shadow. Al did not see the numerals on the overall. His dull senses blended to only one idea—to slay.

He slavered as he wriggled his torso on Manning's chest, his powerful fingers sinking deep. His thumb was compressing the jugular vein, the fingers of the other hand on the vagus nerve.

Manning, hardly over the drug Mizu had given him, strove with failing strength to release that deadly grip, knew that he could not. In his fall he had lost the emptied gun but he groped for it in the dirt, hoping to use it as a club.

With every slowing beat of his labored pulse he was losing energy. He tried to roll uppermost but the freak clung like a bloated leech.

Something prodded Manning's leg, halfway

between hip and knee. A last, flaming flash of comprehension came to him. It was something in the outside extra pocket of the overall, used by mechanics for a rule, by Sixty-Seven for other purposes.

He clawed at Al's face and nostrils, got half a gasp of air, a temporary release upon his throbbing blood vessels, before the freak clamped down again.

His fingers closed upon the metal case, opened it, found the needle, jerked the plunger.

His brain seemed flooded with burning blood, the whole world reeled about him as he jabbed the needle into Al's neck, thrust it home.

THERE WERE lights all about him. Headlights, spotlights, moving flashlights. A police surgeon was kneeling beside him, saying something about a pulmotor.

Manning heard himself speaking faintly and hoarsely, felt his voice rasping his raw throat.

"Never mind that," he said. "Let me up. Give me a drink."

The liquor seared his gullet, but it revived him. He gulped air. Saw the commissioner in a sort of halo of intermingled rays.

"We waited an hour, then came on," said the Head of the Police. "Rounded up a bunch of beggars in the basement, but there was no sign of the Griffin. Then we found you in the bushes, with this Coney Island exhibit. What did you do to him?"

"What did he do to me?" Manning echoed wryly, gingerly feeling his neck. "I gave him the same dose the Griffin meant for me. And, if he spoke the truth, the freak will be well out of it all. He won't even know what it's all about, with what he has for a brain. They should have chloroformed him when he was born. The Griffin's got away. But it will upset him a bit when he finds out I'm still in the game."

"That's all that counts, with me," said the commissioner.

"Thanks," said Manning grimly. "But I think I'd be willing to pass out, if I knew the Griffin was ahead of me. Or with me. It's likely to come to that, some day, and, if it does, I'll be content."

THE UNHOLY CREW

by Paul Ernst

"HERE IS some one in this audience with murder on his mind." The hundreds of people in the Kensington City Playhouse gasped as if icy water had been thrown on them at these words of the figure on the stage, who was billed as Anton Karlu, mental telepathist.

Karlu was an exotic figure; six feet six inches tall, thin and muscular as a stretched wire, with greenish eyes and prematurely snow-white hair. Till now, he had given an excellent, if standard, mind-reading performance. Blindfolded, with a black hood over his head, he had called out objects held up wordlessly by his assistant. He had answered unspoken questions. It seemed the real McCoy in thought-reading, since no word of any kind passed between him and his assistant that might be construed as a code.

A mystifying and entertaining act—until he now made his shocking announcement.

"There is some one in this audience with murder on his mind," he repeated.

The audience was stone still, following that. Karlu's assistant, a squat giant less than five feet three inches tall but weighing two hundred pounds, all iron slabs of muscle, stood motionless in one of the aisles. The men and women in the crowd stared at the tall, taut mind reader on the stage.

And then Karlu went on, amid a feverish rustle of excitement, hysteria and skepticism.

"Murder has just been committed by a man in this audience. He is thinking of the place where it was committed. He is trying not to think of it, but can't help himself. And some of the picture I am getting, very weakly…"

"Nuts," some one said. "He's faking. It's just a smart gag—"

"*Silence,* please!" Karlu's voice cracked out. His fists clenched in concentration. "I see a man's body, in a sort of crypt. I see a house, old, almost deserted looking. It is a large house, in a large lawn, so it must be on the outskirts of town. And now, ladies and gentlemen, I begin to see the killer. Very faintly, for a person does not think clearly of his own appearance. The murderer is a man

with a body as warped as his soul. A small man, I shall describe him, feature by feature—"

Instantly and dramatically the playhouse was plunged into darkness. A woman screamed. Somewhere a man shouted in excitement. Karlu's voice sounded imperatively, "Lock the doors! Don't let that man get away—"

Those seated in the first row heard a swish, and a sharp thud. Then Karlu's voice, *"Lights!"*

Steps sounded in the wings. There was a click as a switch plunged home. The house was flooded with light again.

Karlu still stood by his straight-backed chair. On the floor under the chair was a long knife, with its point broken where it had hit the wood of the chair instead of Karlu's flesh.

Karlu's assistant, tagged by the curious name, Answer, was running down the aisle like a lumbering bear. Incoherent sounds came from his size-nineteen throat as he sprang ferociously to the side of his threatened master. As he ran, his big head turned from side to side as though he would smell out the man who had thrown the knife.

"It's no use, Answer," Karlu said quietly. "The killer has gotten away now… Ladies and gentlemen, with your kind permission I shall let this conclude my act. There may be more knives thrown."

Karlu bowed and stalked to the wings, eyes as green as an enraged panther's. The squat giant, Answer, trotted behind him. There was no applause from the audience—only a wild babble. The theater manager came up, chattering like a terrified ape.

"I thought you were just another vaudeville performer with a clever act. But you can *read* minds! You were about to describe the real killer and he got frightened, slipped back to the switchbox, turned out the light, and tried to kill you to shut you up. And when I booked you, I thought you were just another trickster—"

Karlu brushed past him and went to his dressing-room with the faithful Answer following on heavy, stumpy legs. He was saying something, but the mind reader wasn't listening. Karlu was thinking of that narrow escape from death.

SLIM, DARK, dainty, the girl who knocked at Karlu's dressing-room door and came in when Answer opened it, was as lovely as a porcelain doll. But her cheeks were blanched with fear as she said wildly, "That murder you detected in some one's mind tonight—it was the murder of my uncle! I am sure of it! You must help me… Please!"

Karlu's greenish eyes bored coolly into her dark ones.

"The house you described is the house I live in," she panted. "I live there with my Uncle Caleb Valley, who owns a small newspaper in Kensington City. I'm sure it was his body you saw in that murderer's mind!"

Karlu sighed and looked at Answer. The five foot giant stared back with eyes that were cunning as are an animal's. Answer shrugged. Karlu leaned down a little from his great height so that his thin, taut face was nearer the girl's.

"My dear," he said, "that business on the stage was just an act. I wouldn't tell you, save that you are so upset. I do that on opening night in every town I play. I stop at the end of my performance, suddenly announce that there is a murderer in the house, after which the lights go out."

The girl stared bewilderedly, almost pathetically.

"An act? It couldn't be! You described the house—"

"In every town there are houses answering to my vague description."

"But the objects you described as your assistant took hold of them! Surely that was mind reading. No word was spoken."

Karlu smiled a little.

"Objects held up in an audience are usually the same. Ring, pen, knife, glasses, watch. Answer and I have a time-code. He shuffles his feet when he takes hold of an object, and shuffles them again when I should describe it. My ears are keen. If a second passes, the object is a watch. Two seconds between shuffles means a knife. And so on. As for unspoken questions I answer—some one may have thought them, or they may not have been thought at all. Usually they are such general questions that they must apply to somebody in the crowd. The tricks of the trade. But don't give me away," he added with another smile.

The girl shook her sleek dark head. "Just an act… The announcement, the darkness… But was the knife thrown at you part of the act?"

Karlu's eyes took on their icy green flame again. "It was not," he said crisply.

The girl caught at his arm. "Doesn't that mean that you must have struck fire with your act? In that audience there must really have been a killer. With a man and house like you described in mind! Do you know yourself how much of your act may be regular stage pretense, and how much may be real? There is such a thing as telepathy, you know."

"There is," nodded Karlu. "But I don't think of that much, though I am as sensitive to it as any one." He shrugged. "I may have uncovered a murderer by mistake, but that's all it can amount to. It can't have anything to do with your uncle, or his house. That part was pure rigmarole."

The girl was staring luminously, fearfully at him.

"I believe there's a connection. I—I'm sure of it. Will you come home with me now? I'm afraid—"

"Of course," said Karlu. "Though it is incredible that we will find anything wrong…"

KARLU'S GREENISH eyes expressed no emotion as he approached the girl's home, but behind them he was thoughtful. He might really have had this house in mind when he spoke. It was large, of ancient frame, in a big lawn that was not too well kept. He had to remind himself that there must be a dozen homes like this in Kensington City, in order to fight down the little eerie feeling that tingled his spine.

"Pardon the look of the place," the girl—her name was Adrian Valley—said tremulously. "My uncle doesn't make much out of his newspaper. In fact he's rather badly in debt. We can't afford much help."

Karlu nodded absently. He was thinking the forbidden thought: How much was there to mind reading, the simulation of which provided him his handsome living? Often he had startled himself with such a close guess that, it would seem, it simply must be sheer thought transference. But in this case… A dead man in this place? Nonsense!

Adrian opened the front door. And to Karlu's brain, keen by any standards, whether or not it could read the minds of others, came a vague intuition of disaster.

A light shone from one of the doors opening off the front hall. He followed the girl to it. It was a library, and it was empty.

A moment Karlu stood on the threshold, staring at a big desk with paper on it.

"Call him," he said sharply.

With her lips whitening a little, Adrian raised her voice. "Uncle Caleb!"

There was no answer anywhere.

"I'm sure he was going to stay home tonight… *Uncle Caleb!*" Only echoes replied.

"The basement," said Karlu, voice harsh and bleak.

They went downstairs. Adrian led the way; but Karlu needed no leadership. He seemed to know where he was going as if he had been there before.

In the cellar, light from an unshaded bulb shone on a door to one side. Karlu strode there. He opened it, and looked into a small room, like a crypt. And like a crypt, the room contained that for which crypts are built.

Adrian screamed, high and shrill, and burst past the mind reader. She ran to the sprawled body on the floor, and knelt down beside it.

"Uncle Caleb! Uncle Caleb!"

Karlu stared at the body. It was that of a man in late middle age, small, thin. It lay face down and red trickled from the chest where a knife pierced the heart.

Karlu drew a deep breath and stood there, high head held down so that his white hair cleared the low ceiling. He had described murder and the murder setting. And behold. Here in just such a setting—was murder…

Chapter 2

THE KENSINGTON City police chief glared at Karlu. "You're in this up to your neck! You describe a murder exactly—and a little later we find you beside the body!"

Karlu stared back out of greenish eyes. He had confessed to the girl how little of his act was genuine. He had no intention of confessing that to this man. Nor was he confessing something else known to few—that he was a criminologist of some note. As such, he found the chief's vehemence perplexing.

"You think I killed Valley and told of it on the stage?"

"I think you went on the stage with murder in mind. You started to give a fake description of a murderer, to throw suspicion off you, and then went ahead with the killing."

"I'm a stranger to Kensington City," retorted Karlu, green eyes emotionless. "I have no friends or enemies here."

"You seem friendly enough with the dead man's niece," blustered the chief.

"You actually think I killed Valley—with the girl right beside me and looking on?" demanded Karlu.

"I think you're guilty as hell, mister," snapped the chief, avoiding Karlu's eyes "And you're staying behind bars from now on."

Karlu stared steadily at the chief. More than once he had used his reputation for mind reading in his role as criminologist as well as actor. It was a powerful weapon. He used it now.

"You have strange and confused thoughts, my friend," he said. "I cannot read them very clearly. But a few facts come through."

He combined his keen brain, fine observation, and logic, in that approximation of mind reading that had convinced more than one university professor that he really could read every thought in a man's head.

"You have an idea who the killer is, and you are deliberately protecting him." That was for the man's blustering, shifty vehemence: "You know why Valley was killed: To shut him up!" Adrian had told him her uncle was a poor man, and had no close woman friends. With mercenary and passional motives ruled out, a desire to silence the man remained as the sole murder motive.

"This murder goes deep into the social fabric of the entire city. It is only part of some bigger menace." Of course! It takes a lot of money—or fear—to bribe a police chief as Karlu was betting this one was bribed. Also there was the Kensington City Prosecuting Attorney. He had just been in here, acting as vehement about hanging the murder on the telepathist as the police chief himself.

Karlu couldn't dream what he had stumbled into. But he knew it must be powerful, complicated, dangerous. The case against him was so thin that he had laughed when they arrested him. He was laughing no longer. Strange things can be done to justice when unscrupulous high city officials are against you.

"Well," he said harshly, "those are your thoughts."

"They're your hot-air ideas, not mine," blustered the chief, moistening his lips. "I'm only concerned with seeing justice done. And because I am, you're going to a cell." He sneered. "Unless you can raise twenty thousand dollars bail at two in the morning!"

"Let me put in a phone call to New York," said Karlu, who could have raised five times that if he'd had to. "And when I'm out," he added quietly, "you can expect things to happen. It strikes me there's a setup in this city requiring my kind of service—the work of a mind reader."

The chief sneered again, but in his eyes was fear.

KARLU, CRIMINOLOGIST, telepathist, green-eyed figure of mystery, walked back toward Caleb Valley's home in the early morning. His white, silky hair was bare; he never wore a hat. Beside him waddled Answer.

Two strange figures, they made. But as they neared the Valley home, a stranger one approached them.

A little hunchback, with a sly, clever face, swung toward them. He walked with a half-hop like an ape, peering up toward their faces. As he passed them—he spoke.

"If you know what's good for you, you'll get out of town at once."

Karlu whirled and his long arms shot out. He caught the twisted little man by the shoulders.

"Who are you? Why had I better leave town?"

"What are you talking about?" snarled the hunchback. "I didn't say anything to you. Let me go or I'll call a cop."

Karlu released him. There was nothing else to do.

"Him throw knife last night," said Answer suddenly. The squat mountain of muscle got his grammer mixed, sometimes.

"How do you know that?" demanded Karlu.

"The knife was thrown in the dark. That little man has cat eyes. Slits for pupils. He can see in the dark."

"You're jumping at conclusions" shrugged Karlu. "But at that, you may be right…"

Another man was walking toward them in the early morning light. He was as odd as the hunchback; thin as a skeleton, with a head that looked as big as a pumpkin. His eyes were immense, dull, staring. The bulge of the forehead told of cretinism. He looked like an overgrown ventriloquist's dummy.

"Get out of town right away," he half-whispered, as he minced past them.

A third man was coming down the walk, like something out of a bad dream. He was without legs, hitching his torso along on brawny arms.

"Leave Kensington City and you may live a while longer," he snarled, as he passed them.

Again Karlu whirled. But the cripple was ready for him. He turned too, and thrust out a tin cup and pencils.

"Buy my pencils, Mister?" he whined, as a typical beggar whines "Buy my pencils…"

Karlu turned back toward the Valley home. But as the beggar rounded the corner behind them he said to Answer, "Follow him. Keep either him, or one of the other two, in sight, and see where they go. Quickly!"

Answer stumped back grimly along the walk. Karlu knocked at the door of the Valley home. Adrian was at a friend's home, but a cop was there, on guard. The cop opened the door.

"I'd like to look around a bit," said Karlu.

The cop's jaw squared.

"Nope. Chief's orders. Nobody gets in here."

KARLU STARED at the man, with his eyes filming a bit as if with terrific concentration. The cop knew of his reputation. He began to look uneasy.

"You know I read thoughts, don't you?" Karlu said.

"I know you're supposed to," snapped the cop. "But that's bologny, of course."

"Would you like me to tell you what act of yours, last year, you'd like to forget—and can't?"

The cop swallowed. "Nuts! You can't read—"

"That's it," said Karlu. "Now you're thinking harder of it. I get the picture clearly. It was a pretty rotten thing you did wasn't it? Would you like me to tell the newspapers?"

The cop shifted as if his feet hurt. Karlu smiled cryptically.

"I'd like to get in this house. If that were allowed, I'd forget everything."

"Well," mumbled the cop, "if you'll make it snappy…"

He stepped aside. Karlu walked down the hall to the library, wondering, without much interest, what it was the cop had done last year that he was so ashamed of. It didn't matter. It was a rare man who didn't have something on his conscience done within the twelve-month.

Karlu went to the desk in the library. He had a picture of two things in mind from the night before. One was a stack of paper on the desk. The other was the cardboard back of a tablet of paper in the wastebasket. It was on the latter that he pinned his hopes. If the final sheet of paper in the tablet had been written on before the cardboard was thrown away…

He took it from the basket, and nodded as he saw faint indentations on it. He rubbed a pencil lightly over the indentations. Fragmentary words stood out.

Publicity for… crawling horror… menace that holds… —ton City in dreadfu—… like a grasping monster…

As Karlu had deduced, Valley had been writing something when he was killed last night. He had been exposing some peril. The "menace that" held "Kensington City in dreadful" bondage (?) "like a grasping monster." And he had been struck down to keep that exposure out of his newspaper.

The door suddenly burst open. Karlu whirled from his study of the tablet-back. Answer was backing into the room, hands in the air, snarls coming from his lips.

Over the broad, squat body of his assistant, Karlu saw for one instant a face demoniac in its murderous fury. It was pitted with smallpox, broken-nosed, scarred, like the face of a devil. The man had a gun, which was the reason for Answer's snarling retreat. Karlu reached for a heavy brass inkwell, but before he could grasp it, the door was smashed shut, and bolted.

Answer turned, eyes red points of murder.

"They make me fool! I follow man with no legs. He met man with pumpkin head and the hunchback; and this man with gun. I listen from behind a tree. They say something about a girl. Then they catch me. I get one hand on Pumpkin-Head for a second when we get back to house. Then the man with the broken nose backed me in here with the gun."

KARLU WAS staring at Answer, thinking, thinking. Locked in here by a heavy oak door. But—why? And where was the cop? Well, no matter about the cop. It seemed stupid merely to lock them in the library. There was a window, and they were on the ground floor. It would seem that all they had to do to get away was to step out the window to the lawn and walk off.

He went to the window. The early morning sun was streaming in. There were three huge maple trees about fifty yards from the house in this direction, casting a tracery of shadows before them.

Karlu raised the window a foot—and immediately found out why the window was not as simple a way of exit as it had seemed to be!

There was a faint *thikkk*, barely to be heard, as a silenced gun spoke from somewhere in the direction of the maple trees, and a ragged small hole appeared in the window glass not six inches from Karlu's white head.

He dodged back into the room, and peered out more cautiously. The silenced gun spat again, and once more a slug came within a few inches of his head. Somewhere in one of the maples there was a man who could shoot like a fiend. It was certain death to try to get out that window.

Answer had his big round head back. He was sniffing, as an animal sniffs, with flaring nostrils.

"Smoke," he said gutturally. "There is a fire in this house."

Karlu smelled it then, too. And an instant later his preternaturally keen ears caught the sinister crackling sound of fire just blazing up in a roaring advance.

"By God, they mean to burn us alive in here! That's why they're not shooting us if they can avoid it—they don't want bullet holes to spell murder in charred corpses!"

Karlu went to the door, with Answer padding ponderously after him. He looked at the door. Oak, two-inches thick. You could break a heavy chair to bits against it without hurting it. He tapped the partition

wall. It was of solid brick, in this old, well-built place, instead of the flimsy lath and plaster used on more modern construction.

He looked at the lock. It was an outside, box-lock, held by half a dozen screws. Karlu nodded. Those screw-holes, in a regular pattern in the wood, were a weak point. He pointed to the door-knob.

"Pull," he said to Answer.

The little giant grunted something that might have been an assent. He took hold of the door-knob with both hands, and then slowly worked his feet up the doorjamb till they were almost even with his hands. In that position, a thick loop of solid, straining muscle, feet braced against door-jamb and iron hands locked around the knob, he pulled.

Karlu folded a thick rug and put it under Answer's body, so he wouldn't hurt himself when he fell. For he knew he presently would fall, with the knob in his hands. When Answer pulled, something had to give.

The enormous shoulders of the squat giant writhed and heaved. There was a tearing crack, and Answer fell on his back on the folded rug. He got to his feet with the lock of the door in his hands. It had torn out through the wood, following the screw-holes and chisel-marks that had weakened the oak slab a little.

Karlu reached through the orifice resulting, and shot the bolt back on the other side. They walked into the hall.

The hall and stairway were an inferno of flame. Answer coughed and put his head down. Karlu went with him to the front door.

Before they got there, he stumbled against a body in the smoke. He bent down. It was the body of the pumpkin-headed man. But his head was facing the wrong way on his neck. Hideously reversed. Answer had said he got one hand on his throat for a second or two…

Still nearer the door there was another body. In this one lay the answer to Karlu's query of what had prevented the cop from interfering when Answer was marched into the hallway at the point of a gun. The cop was dead, that was why. He lay in shadow near the wall with his head smashed in.

Karlu opened the front door. Flame and smoke whooshed toward it as air rushed out. The shots had come from the left side of the house.

"To the right," Karlu snapped, "and run fast!"

They sprang onto the porch, vaulted the right railing, and raced in zigzags across the lawn. Around them zipped muted slugs, like deadly hornets. But none struck them as they zigzagged to safety, away from the blazing house.

Chapter 3

KARLU'S LEAN height loomed over the three men in the office of the chief of police. He faced again the thin, dry prosecuting attorney, and the pudgy chief. The third man, paunchy, with a great seal ring on his thick left hand, was the mayor of Kensington City. And there was veiled terror in the mayor's eyes as well as in the eyes of the other two!

"You're a disturbing influence in Kensington City, Mr. Karlu," the mayor said. "We don't want men like you here. You have heard the attorney's offer. Leave town, and we will quash the murder charge."

"You're late with your warning," Karlu said. "Before I was locked in that burning house, three men warned me to get out of town. One was a hunchback, one had no legs, and one was a skeleton of a man with a huge head."

Karlu thought he saw the terror leap higher in the eyes of the three men; and he wondered afresh what menace the city could hold that could snare even these high officials.

"You forget I am out on twenty thousand dollars bail," he went on. "I'm not going to jump that and forfeit it."

"We'll take care of that," said the attorney eagerly. "There will be no forfeiture."

"I'm under contract with the Kensington City Playhouse," said Karlu. "I can't break my contract."

"I'll talk to the theater manager," the mayor said, his seal ring flashing as he spread his hands. "You won't be reported to the Actor's Equity or have any trouble whatever."

"Would you gentlemen mind telling me why you are so very anxious to have me leave town?" Karlu asked.

The three looked at each other. Finally the mayor spoke. "We've told you. Whether or not you're guilty of Caleb Valley's death, you're a bad influence. Murder seems to follow you around—"

His voice died at the expression in Karlu's eyes. They were filming as if with great concentration.

"Shall I tell *you* why I am to leave town?" Karlu said, speaking as though almost in a trance. "I can read it plainly in your minds.

It is because I am a new proposition to certain powerful crooks here. Crooks who killed Valley, murdered that policeman, and then tried to burn me and my assistant alive. They fear me. They are afraid that a telepathist could discover things no ordinary investigator could. So they want me to leave before I find out too much. And you three are actually trying to help them! You, too, want me away from here before something horrible is exposed."

"You're mad—" began the mayor, half rising.

Karlu stood straight and tall and still, staring with deadly intensity into His Honor's fear-sheened eyes.

"Your thoughts are *very* interesting," he said. "I can understand why you three should want me to leave at once."

"Nonsense!" blustered the mayor. "There is no such thing as thought reading! Your claims are preposterous!"

"Shall I tell you what I read in your mind?"

"No, *no!*" The mayor rose all the way to his feet this time. He fought for control. "You won't leave town?"

"Naturally not," said Karlu. "I have a murder charge against me to face—and beat. Good morning, gentlemen."

He left the office. Behind him three men stared at each other with pallid faces. Karlu's icy smile returned as he shut the door behind them.

Mental telepathist! What a powerful weapon a reputation for mind reading was in the hands of a criminologist! Surprising how the great majority of people wilted into apprehensive lumps at the fear that the secret recesses of their brains were suddenly accessible.

A great weapon. But a dangerous one too. For some bizarre power in this city so feared that weapon that they wanted to kill or chase away the man who owned it. They had tried once by fire. They would try again in some other way, he knew, and that shortly.

But as he joined Answer at the street door, his taut, immobile face would have revealed to no one his sure knowledge that death was leaning close.

THE LIMOUSINE waiting at the curb a few doors from police headquarters, was a fifteen-thousand-dollar job. The girl at the wheel was recognizable to Karlu. He had seen her face in society columns in many newspapers.

She beckoned to the telepathist. And in

her blue eyes he saw the identical fear he had seen in the eyes of the three important men he had just left!

Karlu walked to the curb, with Answer waddling beside him, squat and ponderous.

"You are Mr. Karlu, the telepathist?" the girl said.

"Yes," said Karlu.

The girl clutched at his arm.

"I must talk to you. It is about the murder you read in some one's brain last night. But I must see you alone."

"I'll see you at the hotel, Answer," Karlu said.

Answer looked suspiciously at the girl, then at Karlu. The look in his master's greenish eyes demanded obedience. The squat giant stumped away. Karlu got into the car, and the girl started off.

"My name—" she began, as they pulled from the curb.

"Your name is Rinehart," Karlu said.

"Oh… You know who I am? I'm glad. Then you know you have nothing to fear from me."

Karlu stared at the profile of this daughter of wealth, and said nothing. A person bearing a name like hers *should* be above suspicion. But—

"I was seated just behind a man who acted very suspiciously last night when you told the audience that it held some one with murder in his mind," the girl said. They had gone about six blocks, now. She turned down a sidestreet. "He seemed astounded when you said what you did, and—"

Strong arms jammed a blanket down over Karlu's head from behind. He smelled chloroform, and struggled blindly. But the fumes clogged his nostrils. He slumped far down in the seat, and the girl drove the car on, apparently making no effort to seek help; apparently satisfied with developments…

That was the last he knew. The next was—voices.

"No, you fool, we can't kill him yet. We must find out what he knows and who he may have told it to."

"Bah! He doesn't know anything. Unless he really is a mind reader, which is ridiculous. *We* know that the death of Valley came, *after* his vaudeville act. *We* know, if no one else does, that the murder was the result of his stage stunt, done afterward to use that stunt as a screen. He knows nothing."

"His act at the Playhouse last night was impressive. We must be sure before we put him out of the way."

"Boris shouldn't have tried to kill him

last night. Still less should he have missed when he did decide to try!"

"Easier to frame a dead man than a living one…"

Karlu began to be afflicted with the nausea that follows chloroform. But he fought it down. He wanted to hear more. Three voices had uttered the words, one of them a woman's.

The woman said suddenly, "He is listening to us!"

"But he hasn't moved—"

"For a moment his breathing was different."

Karlu opened his eyes, since it was useless to pretend unconsciousness any longer. He gasped at his surroundings.

He was in a room fully fifty feet square, high-ceilinged, with a pseudo-holy air like that of a church devoted to blasphemous practices. The furnishings were Oriental. Divans dotted the floor, draped in silk on which were embroidered figures of Pan, the satyr god. In place of chairs, high cushions were scattered on the thick rugs.

STANDING AROUND Karlu were five people. Two were the man with no legs, and the hunchback. The other three were a big paunchy man with a mask over his face, another a man who might have stepped from a circus sideshow because he had hair all over his face including his nose, and—the woman Karlu had heard.

Karlu's greenish eyes dwelt longest on the woman. She was the most compelling person there. She was nearly six feet tall, and slim to emaciation. Her eyes were black and dull. Her sinuous body was sheathed in dead black as tight as her own dead-white skin. On the front of the black sheath was a ragged red marking. Karlu finally recognized it: It duplicated the marking on the poisonous black widow spider.

"So, mind reader," the woman said. "You are awake."

Her voice was as harsh as a peacock's cry—and as oddly seductive.

"I am awake," Karlu said evenly.

"You have heard us talking?"

"I do not need to hear men talking," he evaded.

The woman's lips were a red gash in her white face. "Ah, you read thoughts, of course. A marvelous gift."

"One which you would like to possess, Black Widow."

The woman laughed. The sound was chilling. "To show you how little I believe in your 'gift'," she said. "I would be willing

to turn you loose. But these others fear to do that. They would like to be sure you know nothing. Though as I have told them, if you were a mind reader you wouldn't be here at all. You would have read the thoughts of your charming chauffeur, and at the danger in them you would not have stepped into her car."

Karlu's frosty smile appeared. He had flexed his long arms and found them bound tightly; but no uneasiness appeared on his triangular face.

"The easiest way to find those who hide in the night," he observed, "is to allow yourself to be 'captured' and led to them. Indeed, carried to them! It was obliging of you."

The little hunchback squealed out a sudden curse, and whipped out a long knife which was a mate to the one broken against Karlu's chair the night before. The paunchy big man in the mask raised his clenched fist. A seal ring glittered on his finger as he did so.

The woman's harsh voice stopped them. "Fools. He draws you out like children. I tell you he knows nothing—can no more read minds than I can."

"For once in your life, Duchess," Karlu said, "you may be wrong. You'll pardon my calling you Duchess? It seems appropriate. The Duchess of Death. But, as I have said, you may be wrong about my thought-reading abilities."

She sneered at him. "If you should convince us of your ability, you would sign your own death warrant."

"A gentleman must tell the truth," Karlu shrugged sardonically. "Let's see how little I know."

His greenish eyes went to the bitter, weak face of the hunchback; the masked countenance of the paunchy man; the hairy countenance of the dog-faced man; the blazing eyes of the legless cripple; the dead-white, repulsively handsome face of the woman.

"Last night at the Playhouse, one of you saw my act. In that man's mind I read murder so strongly that I thought it had already been committed. I told about it. The man, at first startled at having his plan exposed, later decided to turn to advantage my mistake of thinking the crime already achieved. He decided to kill Valley at once and implicate me. He turned out the lights, threw the knife, and raced from the theater thinking he had thrown the knife true and would have a dead man to frame as murder goat.

"Immediately after his murder, he

learned that I was alive, and had been forced by circumstances into the case. He and the rest of you became alarmed at what I might discover by reading men's thoughts. Hence my capture. The man, by the way—is that one." Karlu nodded toward the hunchback.

The little man squealed another curse. Only the quick move of the paunchy, masked man kept him from plunging his blade into Karlu's heart.

"Kill him!" the hunchback panted.

"Not yet," the woman's raucous voice coolly cut across his hysteria. She turned to Karlu. "If you know so much, tell us why Valley was killed."

"To keep him from printing an editorial he was writing," Karlu said promptly. "The article would have told why you have this city—even the mayor and prosecuting attorney and chief of police—in your power."

Even the woman looked taken aback at that. The skepticism faded a little from her dull black eyes.

"He'll have to die," said the paunchy man harshly.

"Yes," nodded the woman. "But there is another who must go with him. One to whom he has almost certainly told too much. When we get that one here, we'll attend to both."

"*After* we have pried from them a confession of what others they may have spoken to!" said the dog-faced man, speaking for the first time.

"Yes. We must make sure of that first."

The words were like a death knell in the great room.

Chapter 4

COLD SWEAT stood out on Karlu's bound body as he worked at his bonds. "There is one other who must go with him. One to whom he has almost certainly told too much. As soon as we get that one we shall tend to both." They could only have been talking about Adrian Valley.

And while they were out seeking her, he was helplessly bound in here with the dog-faced man watching him.

Karlu stopped straining at his bonds, as the man turned to look at him. Then Karlu heard a woman's scream come faintly from somewhere through sound-proofed walls. The shriek was freighted with suffering. And it was followed by barely audible, shrieked words.

"I can't stand it! And I won't! Not any

more. I'm going to tell! No matter what you do—I'm going to tell—"

The shriek ended with appalling suddenness. Just died, sharply, terribly, as a flame is extinguished by water.

The door of the great, exotic room in which Karlu lay, suddenly opened. The woman with the mark of the black spider on her breast stood in the threshold.

"Watch him more closely than ever, Veese," she said imperiously to Karlu's freakish guard. "There is something now for which he must take the blame. He must not escape."

The hair-faced man nodded, almost indifferently. The door closed: Karlu was left with this new reassurance that death was all he had to look forward to. But he had other ideas…

He stared at his ghastly guard, and worked his bound hands stealthily behind his back. Before, he had tried to hide his movements from the hair-faced man. Now he made them apparent. Then, suddenly, he stopped, and lay very still on the divan.

It was good acting. One would have sworn Karlu had worked his hands a bit loose at last, and had at once stopped moving lest the guard get suspicious.

Which, naturally, made the guard very suspicious indeed.

The hair-faced man walked warily toward Karlu, gun in his hand. Cautiously, he felt under Karlu's bulk, gun muzzle jammed to Karlu's side. But the telepathist's hands were still securely bound.

The dog-faced man grunted, straightened up and turned away.

And Karlu's bound legs shot out like a catapult!

It was all he had played for—to get his guard within reach of his long legs. And he had won. His heels cracked the man's skull as a club cracks a ripe melon. The guard pitched forward on his face without another sound or move.

Karlu wormed to his body. With his hands behind him, he fumbled through his guard's pockets. There was a knife.

Very shortly Karlu crept to the door of the huge, Arabian Nights' room with the hair-faced man's .38 in his hand. These warped, freakish people! This curious place he was in! They still spelled nothing coherent to him. Nothing, that is, but murder…

He opened the door onto a long hall, stepped out, and crept toward a door at the end which he hoped led to the outside world. But as he got to the door next to the one he'd just left, he heard steps ahead. He jumped into the nearest doorway as the man with the satanic, pock-marked face stepped to the outer door and stood in the attitude of a guard.

Karlu glanced around the room he was in, but saw no enemies. It was empty of life. Empty of *life*…

In a corner of the place, which was fitted out as an elaborate office, next to a huge safe, he saw a woman's body. He hurried toward it, past a big walnut desk. A corpse…

Young and hardly more than a girl, she lay on the floor with red congealing slowly around a narrow slit in her breast leading to the heart. More of the hunchback's work.

Karlu's lips thinned. This was the woman he had heard screaming. The one who had vowed to "tell everything." She had been killed to keep her from talking.

He tiptoed to the walnut desk. There was nothing significant in the drawers. He saw a tiny crack in the back where there should have been no crack. His long deft fingers felt over the near-by surface, there was a click, and a section of the back hinged out.

There was something in the opening… pictures. Three of them. Karlu's eyebrows went up as he stared at them.

THE THREE pictures were of three women, with most of the hellish gang he had seen here. Two of the women were fairly young and good-looking. The third was middle-aged and homely. But all were the same in one respect.

Each of the three had been photographed among the gang of repulsive freaks in an attitude that would have drawn gasps had they been made public!

With his green eyes blazing, Karlu stared at the pictures. He saw, then, that one of the younger women was the well-known debutante who had driven him there. The wealthy girl in the limousine, with the terror in her eyes, whom no one would conceivably have suspected of being concerned with anything criminal. Many things were beginning to click into place in Karlu's mind, now. His gaze went toward the big safe beside which the dead girl lay. Were the negatives of the pictures in there? Along with many other negatives, perhaps?

Women photographed with freaks. Did the mayor have a young wife, perhaps? The police chief a daughter? The prosecuting attorney a young sister? Karlu started toward the safe, and then stopped abruptly. The door of the office was starting to open.

He leaped toward it, and to one side. It opened all the way, hiding his body, then closed.

With her dull black eyes wide as the eyes of a startled leopard, the tall woman in black stared at Karlu. Her lips parted a little.

Karlu shoved the gun forward.

"If you cry out," he said in a low, even tone, "you'll be shot."

The woman stared at the greenish eyes. In them she saw a remnant of fury at the death of the girl by the safe; dregs of disgust at the pictures in the secret desk panel. She knew the tall mind reader meant his lowspoken words. Her lips closed again.

"Go to the safe," Karlu said.

The woman's body stiffened with anger and apprehension.

"Why?" she demanded, voice carefully low.

"You're going to open it, Black Widow. I have an idea that in it lies an explanation for the way you and your crowd have got control of this city."

"I refuse to open it," said the woman, eyes like black stones.

Karlu smiled a little. It was a glacial grimace.

"Sorry to have missed my chivalry. But I repeat, if you don't follow orders, you'll be shot. And I'll aim for the heart." His finger whitened just a little over the trigger.

The woman went to the safe. She was not trembling. Her eyes were calm. There was something almost admirable in her composure. Her fingers touched the combination knob.

"Go on, open it."

In the face of the gun she turned away from the safe, stared up at him.

"Look here. Why do you fight me?"

"That's a nice question. You are trying to kill me, and then frame me with the murder of that girl in the corner. Should I take that without a fight?"

THE WOMAN shrugged. Her shoulders moved voluptuously. She was a person to take a man's breath, with her exotic sinuous body.

"We had intended doing that to you. The plan would be different now. A man who could get out of that next room, in spite of bonds and an armed guard, is too brilliant to kill."

"Open the safe, at once."

Still the woman defied the gun. She moved a little closer, swaying like a long-stemmed flower. Her firm round breasts slid a little under the tight sheath of her black dress, revealing all the outlines of their mature perfection.

"You and I together could rule this city," she said, lips parting just a little. "I have wanted a man I could look up to, both in actual height and in mentality. You, my friend, seem to be that man. We *would* make a couple!"

Karlu stared just a moment at her almost unwholesomely graceful body, offered to him without reservations. At least six feet tall, she was, and slender as a white birch. While he was half a foot taller than that and straight as stretched wire. Yes, they would make a couple…

"Once more," he said steadily, "open the safe. Do it before I finish counting ten. If you're trying to pass time in the hope that the man you left to guard me will raise an alarm, you're wasting your hopes."

"You killed Veese?" said the woman.

"I think so," said Karlu. "One…"

As he began his slow counting, the woman stared at his greenish eyes.

"Two…"

She cursed like a man, and turned to the safe. Karlu watched the knob move, slowly counting his time limit as he did so. He interrupted at seven to say, "Better not make mistakes. If you miss the proper figure at some stage, and the safe doesn't open, there'll be no second chances. I will pull the trigger at the count of ten. Eight…"

The woman straightened a little. With her black eyes flaming dull fire, she pulled at the safe door. It started to open. And, almost as if its opening controlled the door of the room, that burst open too!

Karlu whirled toward it. Pock-Marks stood there, with his mouth agape with surprise. Karlu's gun came up—and a flying harpy caught him from behind, so that he couldn't move.

Once, Karlu's gun spoke. But he could not aim. The bullet crashed the wall three feet from Pock-Marks' head. And then the man was on him, swinging his clubbed gun an instant before Karlu could get free. For a second time, the tall telepathist sank into unconsciousness.

Chapter 5

THE SOUND of his name, repeated over and over, wildly, brought Karlu slowly back to consciousness. He was still in the elaborate office. And there was a girl lying by the safe. But the girl was not the one that had been there before. She was not dead. It was

from her lips that his name kept coming. She was very much alive, straining agonizedly at heavy cord that held her.

Adrian Valley. Karlu's teeth set hard. "How did they get you?"

"I was still at my friend's house," said Adrian, keeping her white lips from hysterically trembling by a great effort of will. "They phoned me there—some one of them. It was your voice I heard—or seemed to hear. They told me to come at once to my uncle's house because you had made a very important discovery. There was a black sedan there, with drawn curtains at the windows. I got to it, looking ahead at what the fire had left of Uncle Caleb's house, and that's all I can tell. Next moment something was drawn down over my head, and I smelled chloroform…"

Karlu started to nod, and stopped as the movement increased the throbbing in his head. One broken exclamation came from Adrian's lips before she could resume her rigid self-control.

"Why are we here, anyway?" she said. "What is all this? Why was Uncle Caleb killed? What do they want with us?"

Karlu stared speculatively at her. Fragile looking as a porcelain doll, she was. Pathetically small and helpless seeming here in this sybaritic den. But a glance into the deep dark velvet of her eyes showed that she could take it.

"It's wholesale blackmail," he said. "An old game, but with a slightly new angle. You have seen the type of people composing this gang?"

She nodded, with all her small body shuddering. "Yes. Monsters!"

"FOR A purpose," said Karlu coolly, "girls and women belonging to families of wealth or power in Kensington City are caught by this crew. They are doped, and then photographed here in this degenerate-looking place with members of this mad gang all around them. You can imagine how they would be photographed—and how repulsive the result would be with the pictured freaks. Publicity for those pictures would be worse for a woman than any death.

"I've no doubt the gang has dozens of pictures. In some cases, I suppose, the men of the family don't know of them, and the women pay thousands monthly to keep them in ignorance. In other cases, apparently, the husband, brother or father has been deliberately shown them, so that they too would come under the power of

the gang. A man would do anything rather than let such a picture be published of one of his women!

"This must have been going on for a long time. The gang has felt secure because, even if something did slip now and then, the officials of the city are afraid to prosecute them. They could crush down any obstacle that rose against them. One such obstacle was your uncle, Caleb Valley. He had found them out, some way, and was about to print an editorial against them in his paper. It would have been the end of the gang. So they killed him—and tried to take advantage of what seemed to be favorable circumstances to pin the murder on me."

Adrian Valley drew a deep breath.

"But why do they hold us now? Why haven't we been killed already?"

Karlu chuckled.

"Because of my supernatural powers of mind reading. They are convinced I do all that I'm supposed to do. They think that, with my ability to read men's thoughts, I have found them out. Well, I have now, even though I hadn't before. They want to drag from us, before we die, just what I know, what I may have told you, and, what is most important of all, if I have let slip anything damaging to some outside source."

"So?" said Adrian.

Again Karlu let her have it.

"So they may use rather unique means to get a full 'confession' from us."

"But we have nothing to confess…" Adrian stopped. "Then it's a quick death, if they find that out, and a slow one if we can't convince them that nobody else has been told what you know," she summed up slowly.

"I'm afraid you have hit it precisely."

The door opened. In came all the ugly, freak crew they had seen so far, with the woman at their head. Only the hair-faced man, Veese, was absent.

THE TWO had been taken back to the Arabian Nights' room in which most of the pictures Karlu had seen had been taken. He and Adrian lay, bound, side by side, on one of the broader divans now. The woman with the markings of the black widow spider, bent over Karlu.

"A while ago," she said, "in the other room, I made you an offer. Work with me, and your life will be spared. You thought I was saying that before just to delay opening the safe. But now I have you utterly in hand again. And I repeat the offer: Work with me, and we can have this entire city as our personal property. I can use intelligence like yours."

Karlu stared up at her out of baffling greenish eyes.

"You seem to forget there are two of us here. If I accepted your offer, what would happen to Adrian Valley?"

The tall woman moved her sinuous shoulders. "She will have to be silenced just the same."

"You are wrong, Duchess. I tell you now that she shall not die. Nor shall I."

The woman drew back a little at the green blaze in his eyes. Bound as he was, with that silk-white hair of his in virile disorder over his lean, tight face, he looked indomitable.

"You *have* communicated with some one about us, then," she said in a low, vibrant tone. "Who?"

Karlu smiled.

Her long-fingered hand cracked across his cheek. "Who? I *will* be told!"

"Your thoughts tell me whom you fear," Karlu said, with no expression in his face. His cheek slowly reddened where it had been struck, and paled again. "You're afraid I've gotten in touch with—the United States Government. They're interested in kidnaping. And you have committed kidnaping, at least technically, many times in getting your victims to this room. Drugged, all of them, weren't they?"

"Did you tell the government?" The woman's voice had no allure in it now. It was raucous and unlovely.

"Let the girl go and I'll tell you."

The woman Karlu had called "Duchess of Death," laughed. The sound was discordant, murderous.

"You'll talk. Rugger, do you like her?"

The little hunchback drew near the divan with avid eagerness in his bitter face. He touched her throat, drew his little, dry fingers down her whiteness. Karlu fought his bonds. He *had* to get free…

"Claymoore, do you think she is beautiful?"

THE LEGLESS man hunched to the divan and stared with bold eyes at Adrian Valley's miniature loveliness. His hairy paw went out. There was sweat on Karlu's forehead.

"These two can persuade your little friend to do almost anything, I think, from the look in her eyes," the tall woman taunted. "All right. Claymoore, Rugger, you can have her—"

"Wait!" Karlu's voice cracked out. "I'll talk. And you've got to believe me. I have told no one what I know against you. That is the truth, so help me. Adrian Valley knows nothing."

The woman's red, red lips writhed in a sneer in her dead-white face. "You lie. Rugger, Claymoore, go ahead."

"Wait! Wait—" Karlu said hoarsely, as the little hunchback and the legless man between them got the girl from the divan. They paid no attention to the telepathist. But they could not carry her. The paunchy man in the mask laughed a little. He came forward and helped them.

Karlu's lips opened to lie, to tell them anything, if he could delay a little the actions of the legless man and the hunchback. The look in Adrian's eyes made him sick.

For a second time, in this place, he lay bound. But this second time they had not tied the cords so tight at his wrists and ankles. There was a little slack at his wrists. The slack would have done an ordinary man no good. but Karlu's hands and wrists were typical of the rest of his limbs: wiry and thin, flowing in tapered suppleness. His long, thin hands, when narrowed as hard as he could compress them, were very little thicker than his steely wrists.

He had worked at the infinitesimal slack in the cord till he had his hands half free. Now, he let them bear off the girl without trying any more to stop them. All eyes were on her—and that was what Karlu wanted for a little while.

There was a massive hook in the near wall. With the paunchy man helping them, the two deformed creatures got Adrian's arms up so that the cord binding her wrists slipped over the hook. She hung there, too paralyzed even to scream, with her dark hair hanging half over her white face, and her eyes enormous.

"Are you ready to talk?" said the woman, glancing at Karlu.

The mind reader stopped twisting his arms while her eyes were on him. "No," he said.

The Black Widow shrugged and turned away from him.

The hunchback laughed with the laughter of a woman—or a she-fiend. His little, dry-looking hand went up. The fingers hooked in the curve of Adrian's dress at the throat. He pulled.

"By George, she *is* beautiful," said the paunchy man, seal ring glittering on his hand as it went up to his masked face.

THE TATTERS of Adrian's dress hung from her slim, firm waist. She screamed at last. The paunchy man stared quickly at the tall woman.

"It's all right," said the woman. "You know how we tested this place after the sound-proofing. She can scream as hard as she likes, and no one outside can hear."

The hunchback's repulsive little hand went out again.

"Wait!" said Karlu in a tired tone. "I'll talk."

"Stop, Rugger," the woman said calmly. She turned toward Karlu. "Whom did you tell about us?"

"You guessed right," said Karlu, lying because the truth was useless here. "The Federal Bureau."

The paunchy man swore through his mask. The hunchback squealed his rage, with the girl forgotten, and whirled with that ever-ready, venomous blade of his in his hand. The legless man hunched toward Karlu on bowed arms. Only Pock-Marks remained stolid.

They were all around him, now. The tall woman, leader as always, bent low over him, with her eyes flaming into his.

"You actually gave information to the Federal Bureau of Investigation?" she hissed. "You die for that! Rugger, use your knife—"

That was all she had a chance to say. For at that moment Karlu's supposedly bound arms flashed up. They went around her in a deadly embrace, and held her close as a living shield.

Rugger was yelling shrilly while he strove to use his knife—and could not. The paunchy man had a gun in his hand. But it was impossible for him to shoot without getting his mistress.

The woman's head went down and her teeth flashed as she tried to sink them in Karlu's straining wrist. He increased his hold. Her head snapped back up in agony.

"Oh, my God! Stop! You're breaking me… in two! Stop—"

The woman's struggles were weaker. Karlu risked holding her with one long arm while his left hand roved down her body. He found what he had thought he might: a small but bulky obstruction on the inner side of her right thigh.

At that, the paunchy man cursed, and gambled a shot.

Something that felt like a branding iron creased Karlu's left forearm, but he only swung his burden a little more squarely between him and the masked man, and explored the hard lump. He raised the black sheath of a dress calmly. There was a little holster strapped to the Black Widow's

long tapering thigh. And in it there was a .25 automatic.

"Kill him!" squealed the hunchback to the paunchy man. "We can't let him get out of here. We'll all go to the chair. The hell with her! *Kill him!*"

The paunchy man's hand went up. But in his assumption that Karlu's embrace of his living shield was only a temporary victory, and that a man with his feet still bound and with three enemies around him in a locked room could not possibly escape, he had delayed too long.

His gun whirled from his fingers as Karlu squeezed the trigger of the .25. The paunchy man looked at the bleeding wreck of his hand for a second, and then cried out in a strangled, shrill falsetto. The hunchback leaped, knife flashing down as he did so. The blade grazed the throat of the panting woman in Karlu's iron embrace. Blood welled in a ruler line from the cut—and spouted from the deeper wound the hunchback succeeded in making in Karlu's right shoulder.

The greenish eyes blazed death. But it had to be put off for an instant. Pock-Marks, also disregarding the life of the woman in black, was firing emotionlessly, with the roar of his automatic sounding like double thunder in the room.

Karlu got him through the abdomen— and then the door quivered to a ponderous impact.

Rugger whirled toward it. Pock-Marks did not. He sank to the floor, clutching at his belly.

The door shivered again, then burst open, trailing from one hinge. Answer came in, eyes flaming, blood welling from a deep gash in his head. With murder in his eyes, he started toward the hunchback.

"Let him live, Answer," said Karlu. "I'll keep him covered… How did *you* get here?"

"You did not come to the hotel for too long," said Answer. "I got afraid. I go to Miss Valley to see if she know where you drive with that other girl. I see her leave for uncle's house, and see car take her away. I follow. Maybe they take me to you. They did. But one struck me from behind as I crawl up on this house. I get better, and hear shooting in here."

Karlu sighed. "Well, you've got a lot more brains than most people give you credit for, Answer. Hurry! Get Miss Valley down from

the hook, and then go to the next room. It's a kind of office. There's a phone on the desk. Get police headquarters while I untie my feet and tend to Miss Valley."

THE MAYOR, the chief of police and the prosecuting attorney avoided Karlu's gaze as he towered over them in the chief's office. The contents of the blackmailing gang's safe had been taken, and every picture and negative burned. Among them had been three that the chief himself touched matches to, while the perspiring mayor and attorney watched, with the chronic terror fading slowly from their eyes as the things went up in smoke.

But they realized that Karlu knew what had been in those damning pictures. And they did not look at him now. But there was no more bluster in their voices.

"Justice will be done," said the mayor. "The three of them will go to the chair for the murder of Valley, and the patrolman on guard at Valley's house, later, and the woman we found in their house on the outskirts of town where you were held."

"The heavy-set man who went masked," said Karlu, feeling at the bandaged knife wound high up on his right shoulder. "Related to you, isn't he?"

"My half-brother," said the mayor heavily.

"I thought as much. He wore a seal ring that was identical with yours."

"My mother gave one to each of us when we were twenty-one," said the mayor. "But no matter. He'll pay the penalty just the same." He swallowed. "Thanks to you."

"Then I'm not as undesirable as you thought me yesterday?" said Karlu, a shade maliciously.

The three men looked at each other, and raw color showed in their faces.

The chief cleared his throat. "You've done Kensington City a great service. I wish—"

"Sorry," Karlu cut in. "I couldn't stay here and work for the Kensington City police force no matter how attractive the salary."

The chief stared. "How did you know I was going to ask that?"

Karlu smiled. And if his smile was at the thought of the confession he had made to Adrian Valley in the Playhouse dressing-room, at least these three officials didn't know it.

"You forget," he said, "that I make my living—because I can read men's thoughts."

SWAMP FETISH

by Dan Cushman

HE FOOTPRINT was not more than an hour old. Gongomed, the *capito* boy, had found it pressed in muck where the footpath sloped down through bush ebonies to enter the swamp, and now he was on one knee, pointing to it after the fashion of Congo natives, with his scar-enlarged lower lip.

"You see, O *bwana m'kumbwa?*" He asked the one-armed white man who walked up from his place at the rear of the safari. "You see track? *Bondele* shoe. White man, like-so. You see?—he fall down. Maybe tired. Maybe *fobwa.*"

The one-armed white man stood for a while, looking at the footprint, then he grinned, twisting one side of his ugly, Irish face.

"Maybe tired like *capito* boy."

"Me not tired! *Kay-abba!* Behold, *bwana!*" Gongomed pointed down the footway of sapling poles that bridged the swamp's bottomless muck. Here and there were marks showing where the man had staggered off. "You see, *bwana?* More tired as *capito* boy."

The white man nodded and took time to dig a long, blue-paper cigarette from his pocket and light it. He inhaled and let smoke drift from his nostrils. The tobacco was strong Egyptian leaf cured

with date wine and gum hashish. It had a soothing effect on nerves that had been frayed by long travel through the heat of late dry season. After inhaling three or four times, the lines of the white man's face could be seen to soften a trifle.

HE WAS shorter, broader than the average of his race. His age, thirty-five, or maybe a couple of years more. His accent stamped him an American, but he'd been long in the country. His face was broad, as ugly as an idol from Bangkok, and about the same hue from tropical sun. He wore brown shorts, half-boots, a tan shirt and a sun helmet in need of pipeclaying. He had only one arm—his right. A steel hook projected from his left sleeve. Even there, in the depths of French Equatorial Africa, any Bando or Shari native could have told you that this man was Armless O'Neil.

Armless O'Neil. He inhaled, and looked across the swamp. Only a scant fifty meters of it were visible before the footway disappeared among bulbous-trunked trees, dead and dying beneath tons of parasitic vines. Here and there, at widely spaced intervals, an opening in the vast sponge of leaves let through a long-slanting ray of sunshine.

"*Bondele* tired. *Bondele fobwa* tired!" Gongomed chanted.

"*Bondeles* never get tired," O'Neil growled from the side of his mouth not scissored on the cigarette. "White man like *n'koi,*" he said wearily. "White man never get tired."

It was the first principle of all white men in the tropics never to show weakness before a native. After fifteen years on the seething black-and-brown belt that extends from Boma to Port Moresby along the beltline of the globe, it was the only white man's standard that O'Neil still paid consistent homage to. That, and his pants, and the pistol strapped around his waist.

His statement brought no response, not even from Bobolongonga, his gargantuan black man from Katanga, so O'Neil repeated in a sharper tone,

"White man never get tired!"

"*Ay-ya, Allah!*" chanted Bobolongonga. He was a magnificent black, large as any two of these skinny Banda porters, and made to seem larger than he really was by the flowing, gray kuftan that clothed him. "*Allah humma! Bonde-humma!*" he chanted pointing at Armless O'Neil with practiced magnificence. "Hear him, our *bondele* who strikes down even the rhino with his mighty hook! Hear him, our great *bondele* who will soon fork over to this humble servant eighteen months back wages so I may return a man of wealth to my two faithful wives in Katanga."

O'Neil's lips were still set and saturnine around the blue-paper cigarette as he chose to ignore the reference to Bobolongonga's back wages. It was not eighteen months, anyway. It was only sixteen months, if one considered the bribe O'Neil had been obliged to pay that thieving French-Arab jailer in Fort Campell to win Bobolongonga's freedom after his most recent excursion among the fleshpots. Bobolongonga had been bringing up the subject of back wages a trifle too frequently of late, and one of these days O'Neil would have to straighten him out, literally, with a blow of his hook. But not this evening, with heat hanging oppressively beneath the bush ebonies.

O'Neil drew a fly whisk from his belt, signaled with it, getting the natives strung out in their proper order. There were twenty-one of them, carrying a mixed cargo of copal gum and scrivelo tusks, no more than two-thirds of a load to each one, for the trading had not been brisk. More and more the camel caravans had been coming down from El Fasher, beating the colonial taxes, bleeding the country.

He gave them a last scrutiny, and slapped the fly whisk against his boot, starting the safari.

THE POLE crossing was tricky, especially for a white man whose boots are not suited to it as are the long toes of a native. The poles kept sinking, coming up slippery from muck and green scum. Here and there, at one side or the other, O'Neil could see the marks where the white man had fallen and then recovered himself.

He couldn't help speculating. He'd never expected to run across another white man in this forgotten corner of the jungle, this shortcut route between the Shinko and Mombu that he'd taken to beat the greater rains of March.

"*Kay-abba!*" the *capito* boy shouted again, balancing himself and pointing across weed and muck. "Mighty *bondele* fall again."

"Keep going!" O'Neil growled. He kept his face set along grim lines until the natives had turned from watching him, then his lips softened a trifle. Little by little even these black boys of the deep bush were getting to suspect that white men were not gods after all.

The saplings ended, and a path slanted up through shoulder-high cane grass and orchilla. Beyond was a small clearing where the brightness of sunshine still held.

A n'gila monkey swung overhead, clinging by tail and arm, chattering. Something about the sound of the little animal was an alarm. O'Neil shouted, warning the men ahead of him. He started forward. A gun exploded. Close, but humidity, heat and the surrounding vegetation closed on it, giving it a flat sound.

The bullet ripped past, cutting cane grass, making a noise like tearing paper.

The *capito* boy screamed and plunged face down. He wasn't hit. The bullet was wild at O'Neil's right. The other blacks were down an instant later. All except Bobolongonga. He was huge and conspicuous in his gray kuftan and white topi, trying to strip a Lebel rifle from its sling across his shoulder.

"Down!" O'Neil barked.

There was a second explosion three or four seconds after the first. Bobolongonga spun as though hit. He caught himself on one knee, lowering his head below the cane grass, and spent some time running a forefinger through the successive holes that the bullet had torn through the kuftan's folds.

He saw O'Neil, spoke. "Behold, O *bwana!* See for yourself how thy servant hath sacrificed his costly garment in thy service—"

O'Neil spoke through his teeth, telling him to be quiet. He drew the automatic from its latched-down holster. It was one of those big, forward-heavy Mausers, the chrome-plated type that had filtered down from the desert country after the German invasion. A man can never be certain of a gun in that country where twenty generations of fungus can grow across metal surfaces in a single day. O'Neil examined it, decided it was all right, rose to a crouch and made it up the path, past prone porters, guided by a slight, grayish puff of cordite smoke that had risen and lay suspended just over the grass tips.

No dampness here. The footpath became hard-baked, reddish earth. Orchilla played out, and there was only the cane grass with the path like a canyon cutting through it. It curved, and his boys were hidden behind him. He kept moving, studying the earth, avoiding twigs that might crack beneath his weight. Close now.

The sharp odor of burnt cordite was strong in his nostrils. He paused, listened.

Seconds passed. It seemed like half a minute. He could hear the jingle of copper leg bracelets as some of the porters sought better places to hide. Then there were other sounds—the whisper of grass leaves across someone's clothing, the repeated, quick, wheezing noise of a man's breath.

The man was moving forward through the cane grass.

O'Neil was on one knee, Mauser held slightly angled toward the sky. The man was close—so close they could have reached hands and touched, but the grass was a solid, green wall, hiding them.

THE MAN came in view with unexpected suddenness. He'd stumbled, and now he was lurching forward. O'Neil started to pull the trigger, realized at the final instant that the man was not deliberately springing on him.

He had no chance to check himself from squeezing the trigger. He angled the gun upward, and it pounded, sending its bullet over the man's head.

The man saw O'Neil, tried to check himself. He twisted over as though the bullet had struck him, then he fell on his side, one arm extended, elbow on O'Neil's right foot.

He'd had an automatic pistol in his hand. The fall jarred it from his fingers. It struck the stiff cane grass and fell to the pathway, reflecting gunmetal blue. The fellow raised himself on one hand, groped for it. His hand went from side to side in rapid, futile movements.

"Let it go!" O'Neil said.

The man turned half over. He was looking at the Mauser, at O'Neil's face. His eyes were pale and off focus. His hand touched the automatic, fingers closed on the butt. O'Neil stepped, pinning the man's wrist beneath his instep. He pressed down until his weight forced the man's fingers to open. He picked up the gun. It was a Browning from the Belgian factory. He put it in his hip pocket. Then he stepped back and had his first good look at the man.

He was short and moderately heavy. Forty or forty-five. His skin was reddish dark from years of the tropics; his eyes seemed to lack the ability to focus. The erratic movements of his hands and a flush along his neck showed that he was suffering from fever.

The man hissed something in Dutch or German.

"Talk English," said O'Neil.

"Yah. Don't—shoot." His eyes had finally concentrated on the Mauser.

"I should blast your insides out for those bush-bullets you turned loose."

"No. No, *Herr….*" He pushed himself to a sitting position, kept licking his dry lips. It took him a while to understand that O'Neil was not going to kill him. Then his eyes came to focus on O'Neil's hook arm.

"*Herr* O'Neil!" he said.

O'Neil hadn't expected to be called by name. He had a good memory for faces, and this fellow seemed to be a stranger. He looked again, eyes narrowed, wondering where they'd met before.

"Forgiff me, O'Neil. I did not know. Thank Gott I did not kill you. You see—mitout glasses—"

The glasses! O'Neil knew then. "You're Otto Hein."

"*Yah!* Otto Hein… Otto Hein… Otto…." He kept repeating his name, trying to stagger to his feet. Fever and fatigue acted like a drug, encasing his brain.

"Why'd you open up on me?" O'Neil asked.

"*Yah.* I think. Maybe you come… for me…."

"What are you running away from?"

Hein blinked his watery, near-sighted eyes. He was half blind without his glasses. "Nothing. I do not run. I—"

"What are you doing here, without a safari?"

"Safari. I come—from Bangui. My safari. Black swine. They run. Rob and run. They would haff kill me."

The man was lying. He was on the jump for some reason. O'Neil could read the fear that still twisted his face.

Bobolongonga had stalked up with the Lebel across his arm. He swung it down, thrust it forward, pressed the muzzle to Hein's temple. Hein trembled, sank to his knees. Bobolongonga said, "*Bwana!* I will now kill this infidel eater of pork—"

"Get your gun away!" O'Neil said.

Bobolongonga moved it a few degrees. "But see what the Christian's bullet has done to my costly robe! How will I buy another, this poor servant, who hath owing to him a chief's ransom in back wages—"

"Get the uniform can."

Bobolongonga withdrew, grumbling, to do his bidding.

The uniform can was a metal box, large as a small hand-trunk, painted aluminum. O'Neil unlocked it, found a bottle of sulfa tablets.

"Been drinking swamp water?" he asked.

"*Yah.*"

O'NEIL SHRUGGED. Some men will live through anything, and maybe Hein was one of them. He opened a canteen and held it to Hein's lips until he'd swallowed the tablet. Then he ordered the natives to build a *tepoi* so they could carry the sick *bondele* down to the Bahi Kuru.

Hein. O'Neil stood looking at his flabby atabrine-yellow face while the native boys went to work. He'd known him in Boma, and again at Albertville, two-thirds the distance across Africa. He'd been a diamond grader in Kimberley—a trusted employee until one day when some grade-one canary yellows turned up in a shipment of industrials and that had been his finish with the Monopoly. Since then he'd tried his hand at many things—copper, latex, palm nuts.

He was lying on his back. There was a fat billy-bag strapped to his shoulders, making a big hump over which he had to lie. His eyes were closed, and he seemed to be asleep. O'Neil knelt and started to unstrap the billy-bag. Hein moved suddenly, waking from his moment of fevered sleep. He rolled, came to a crouch, hand darting to the empty holster.

"*Nein!*" he hissed. "You will not try to take it, *Herr* O'Neil!"

O'Neil watched with slitted, curious eyes. Then he let a laugh jolt his shoulders. "What the hell do I want of your billy-bag? If you want to sleep with your spine bent like a Shari bow, I suppose it's your business."

"You want it, like the rest—" He cut off with a jerk.

"Like who?"

Hein ignored the question. He drew his lips back, showing the tips of his small, yellowish teeth. "You will keep your hands from it, *Herr!*"

O'Neil kept looking down at him, his face the old, bronzed mask. He was thinking that there was something important in the billy-bag, and that Hein was a fool for calling his attention to it.

He said, "I don't give a damn what's inside it." He slapped his hand to the Mauser in its latched-down holster. "But you're dumb as an ass if you think I wouldn't take it if I wanted to."

"No. You would not kill me. The gendarmes…."

"I don't think the gendarmes have ever been through this way."

Hein remained crouched, thinking it over. He knew it was true, that here, in this deep jungle O'Neil could do as he pleased.

He laughed. It wasn't a good laugh, not the careless one he attempted. "Ach! Der billy-bag. Nothing. Personal papers. A few francs. You are not one to be interested in a few francs. Nothing to kill poor Hein for. *Nein.* You are not small jungle tramp. You are Armless O'Neil, famous Yankee soldier of fortune."

Still crouching, eyes on O'Neil, he unfastened the straps of the billy-bag. It was canvas, a foot by a foot-and-a-half in size, and perhaps eight inches thick, filled to capacity, locked by a small combination padlock.

After removing the sack, he didn't let it out of his hands, though he allowed O'Neil to touch it, place it on the earth beneath his head for a pillow.

It took half an hour to fashion a *tepoi* from bamboo poles and blanket, and until late twilight to reach a ravine where fresh water flowed down to the Bahi Kuru, a slow, silty stream that tunnelled through jungle toward the Ubangi.

THEY CAMPED there for two days while O'Neil treated him with sulfa and lime-water tonic. Then his temperature subsided and he was well enough to crawl shaky-legged from the hammock and ask for *schnapps.*

O'Neil found a flat bottle of English whisky and pulled the cork. Hein drank and shuddered ague from his bones.

"So. You haff been generous mit poor Hein. In jungle you pick him up, give him *schnapps,* medicines, your own hammock, yah. You haff saved mine life, and after I would maybe haff shot you mit pistol."

"You're a white man, aren't you?"

O'Neil didn't pretend to any charity. In the jungle, one white man has to stick with another. That was the only reason he'd done anything for Hein. He'd never liked nor trusted the man. He cut Hein off at two drinks and put the bottle back.

"Yah. White man. But me, Hein, I am forever grateful. Never will I be able to repay."

"Not even with the billy-bag?"

"You joke! You think Hein is fool, watching the billy-bag. *Yah*-so. You are right. Man mit fever. It is nothing. Like your own uniform can. It was not I did not trust you. Only fever, and the pictures fever makes in man's brain." He was trying hard to appear contemptuous of the thing's value, but he still kept it close to him. He hesitated, thinking over what he was going to say. Now that the fever was gone, a dead sallowness had come to his face, and the combination with his pale eyes was not pleasant. "I owe you explanation, *yah?*"

"You don't owe me anything."

"I owe you truth of why I am here, so far from Bangui. After my bullets you think I am on run from gendarmes, *yah?*"

O'Neil felt for a cigarette. He had none. He was down to inyorka tobacco—vile, native stuff which he was forced to roll himself. He twisted up a cigarette, started to light it from some coals that lingered in the fire.

"Permit me!" Hein worked the combination of the padlock which closed the billy-bag, drew out a folder of Spanish matches—the kind that are made like miniature tallow candles with a dab of chemical at both ends so each can be lighted twice. He was using the matches only as a gesture to prove that there was really nothing secret in the bag.

"So. I owe you the truth, *Herr* O'Neil. I am now in palm-nut business. Buying, selling. Independent. You understand. Now, after two years mit Barkolo Vegetable Oils am I on mine own. But this year is business bad. Perhaps I will be bankrupt. It is not goot at mine age, O'Neil, that man is broke, as you Yankees say, in jungle. So, I haff one chance to save mineself. Perhaps, if I can reach Bakoville before rains, then catch upriver steamboat to Cotes Nord, and native villages of N'bimwa. You understand? *Yah.* So I must move fast. Ahead of other buyers. So I take this cross-country, by old Arab slave trail, through country of pigmy and black cannibal to Bakoville."

O'Neil's eyes narrowed as he watched the man through rising tobacco smoke. "You mean you're headed to *Bakoville?*"

"This iss not the way?"

O'Neil laughed smoke from his lungs, spat at the inyorka's vile taste. "It *could* be the way. It could be the way to Bakoville, or El Nahas, or 'Dorwung. Or it could be the way to hell."

"It iss way to Bakoville!"

"Sure. If you're man enough to make it."

"I am man enough to make it, *Herr* O'Neil!"

O'Neil looked at him, something like a smile twisting the corners of his hard-cut mouth. After almost twenty years of the tropics, a man should learn the folly of judging anyone by his physical appearances. Hein was soft looking, with flesh that seemed as though it would hold an impression like putty, but often it's guts more than physique that takes a man through.

"All right," he said, "so you're man enough. Do you know the way?"

Otto Hein relaxed from his stiffened attitude. "Perhaps—not. Because now, *Herr* O'Neil, I do not need to know der way, for you will guide me."

The billy bag was still unlocked. He reached inside, drew out a flat leather money folder, opened it, pulled out a thick packet of French Colonial notes, counted almost half of them out.

"Fifty thousand francs, *Herr* O'Neil." He was smiling while his little, pale eyes tried to read O'Neil's expression. "Come. None of your Yankee poker faces on old Hein! You are not 'in the bucks' like Yankee say. *Nein.* Mit fifty thousand francs could man buy whole safari load of ivory, copal gum. So. I giff you money now. Cash, as you say, on barrelhead. Fifty thousand francs—five hundred Yankee dollars. But wait! Yet haff you not heard all from Hein! For you, fifty thousand more when you lead me in sight of Bakoville. Now what iss it you say to old Hein?"

O'Neil laughed, the movement of his lips shaking ash from the inyorka cigarette.

"What is there to say? We go to Bakoville!"

Chapter 2

HEIN HAD been lying, of course. Only a fool would go cross country from Bangui to Bakoville in hopes of catching a steamboat to the upper villages, and Hein was not a fool. But there was no lie about the money. It was there, fifty thousand francs of it, making a good, thick packet between O'Neil's fingers. So he threw the cigarette away, got up, and commenced putting the safari in order to travel.

They crossed the river on a raft of silk-cotton saplings lashed with *ngogi* vine, took a deep-trampled elephant trail that angled cross-country to a region of forested hills. There, true to O'Neil's mental geometry, they struck the thousand-year-old trail of the Saharah slave traders.

That portion of the trip required two days, with Hein spending most of his time in the *tepoi,* carried on the shoulders of four blacks. It was easier going along the slave trail, through jungle clearings where nut-palms and wild coffees sometimes grew, and he spent more and more of his time afoot, and after two more days the *tepoi* was abandoned altogether.

On the fifth day from the Bahi Kuru they reached a village of tiny, pointed huts surrounded by cassava and yam potatoes where natives first hid and threatened with poison arrows, and then crept out to jabber a mongrel mixture of Bantu and Shari, and stare at the white men, perhaps the first they'd ever seen.

O'Neil had some cheap French jewelry left from his northern trading expedition, which he exchanged for bananas and casava meal before taking the descending trail through the swamps of *Ulu.*

Rains had not commenced, and the heat of the dry season had been unusually severe, leaving a four-inch crust over bottomless muck. The crust supported them, vibrating like a drum head to their passage. It took from dawn until siesta to cross, then the slave trail curved south, heading toward the ancient rendezvous of the Basira chieftains, where even to that day the black Arab merchants of the north traded salt of far-away Bhar Ghazal for the black maidens who would be returned, bound wrist to wrist in human chains, to stand naked on the auction blocks of Azben, Tintumma and Wadeai.

It took a day to make the next five kilometers, following elephant trails, hacking their way with brush machetes. There was a river—vast, apparently stagnant, without movement. The Luleba or the Na-ulu. No one has ever really determined the courses of some of these streams, large as the upper Mississippi, which wind through the vast sinkhole of central Africa.

There was another trail, a footpath from north-west which took them to a pigmy village where a suspension bridge had been built across the stream.

It was a miracle of engineering, a single, bamboo-slatted footway, slung from the top of a huge mahogany tree, descending, bent by its own weight, almost to the surface of the water, then swinging up again, diminishing, becoming a mere thread in the high distance.

A toll was charged. O'Neil paid with trinkets and a few copper coins. Then, with burdens lashed to their backs, the black boys ascended the tree by successive ladders to a landing on its high, swaying top, and they went, one man at a time, between waist-high guide ropes.

Two pigmies, skinny fellows muscular and quick as 'gila monkeys were at work near the center of the span, plaiting new strands of a type of sisal in one of the old ropes, a process that had gone on for many centuries, making the bridge continually renew itself, like the human body, so that it would remain, a source of revenue to their grandchildren as it had been to their fathers.

There was a second village of pigmies at the far side, and there the chief, a withered old man weighted by copper ornaments, emerged from a mud and thatch hut to lift a hand in greeting and jabber a mixture of many tongues, the speech he'd picked up through living a lifetime at this jungle crossroads.

"Mengtabba?" O'Neil asked.

THE CHIEFTAIN cackled *"ay-ya!"* and made the sign of danger with his fingers. O'Neil understood. These pigmies, and the savage Mengtabba tribesmen farther along had long cooperated to their mutual profit. He paid over more coins, ornaments, added a roll of copper wire.

"Enough," he said.

"Na-toohi!" raged the chieftain. He jerked a poisoned dart from his belt and leaped up and down, jangling copper bracelets, lifting the dart high as O'Neil's shoulder.

O'Neil growled at him and added a bottle of brilliant purple ink-paste for tatooing, and then a small bag of salt.

"Enough!" O'Neil cried, slapping palm on pistol.

Thus the bargain was reached. The chief, satisfied with his booty, grinned, showing betel-blackened teeth.

"Enough."

He brought an earthen jug of arrack wine as a gesture of good will, and after spending siesta in the village, O'Neil led on across hummocky cassava fields. A message drum was thud-thudding behind them, telling the Mengtabba that gifts had been received, and that the *bondele* should pass and live. The drum paused, and another picked it up in the distance, and after that still another, so far away that only the louder notes were audible.

The Mengtabba villages were at distances of ten, twenty, twenty-five kilometers, and true to the pygmy bargain the safari passed through without an assegai spear being lifted against it.

They were tall men, arrogant, somewhat lighter skinned than most natives of Bantu blood. In two of the villages, impromptu dances were organized, but O'Neil kept going, and it was a relief when the Mengtabba country was left behind.

For a day's travel the footpath tunnelled through vegetation so solid that the sun's rays were glimpsed not once in an hour, then there was a village on high stilts occupying the weeded silt-flats of a river where canoes and paddle boys were secured for the remaining half-day journey to Bakoville.

"Bakoville!" O'Neil gestured with his hook at a line of docks and rusting metal storehouses. "Bakoville, the metropolis of Bahi Kuru." He turned and watched Hein climb to the canoe dock beside him. The billy-bag was still locked, strapped to his shoulders. "You're forgetting something, aren't you?"

Even with the malaria dormant in his bloodstream, it took his eyes a long time to focus. *"Yah.* But I have not forgotten." O'Neil had given him back his Browning automatic, and he had a habit of standing with palm resting on its butt. *"Yah, mine freund.* Hein remembers. You will always find that Hein has goot memory. I say, at Bakoville, another fifty thousand francs."

"All right then, I'll take it."

He shook his head. *"Nein.* The fifty thousand I have been thinking over."

O'Neil looked him up and down. The cool scrutiny took him a couple of seconds, then he laughed, cynically, letting it jerk his broad shoulders.

"The hell you have!"

"Yah." He nodded, still placid, smiling. O'Neil made a move toward him, but Hein raised his hand, asking attention for what he had to say. "Wait! Did I not once say you would guide me to

Bakoville? Und iss it not so? Und now I say you will not collect other fifty thousand francs, should you not listen also?"

"All right, keep talking."

"Yah." He flung an arm up, indicating the part of Bakoville one could see, and a great deal more of it hidden by palms and bokongu trees. "There are here, in Bakoville, certain people—how should I say it?—certain people who would not wish Hein to go to upriver villages und buy palm nuts. So. I would like to leave Bakoville alive. Like you. *Nicht war?*"

"Sure."

"So, you will see to it I am alive to leave."

"And *then* you'll pay me the fifty thousand?"

"No. I will pay you *one hundred* thousand. One hundred thousand Colonial francs. But wait! Not *Colonials de France,* but much better. An order for the *Colonials de Belgium.*" He stripped the billy-bag from his shoulders, got down on one knee, worked the combination, once again drew out the money folder. He unzipped a new compartment and took out two pieces of stiff, peach-colored paper. They were filled out in violet ink by a checkwriting machine and bore the imprint of the Banque du Kongo Belge, Leopoldville. A rubber stamp had placed the words *"Atteste de"* diagonally across the backs, and underneath someone had scrawled his signature. They were certified checks.

Hein rose to one knee and crouched forward, the untrimmed nail of his thumb indicating the amount for which they were drawn, each for exactly one hundred thousand Belgian francs.

"You see? Each of them for more than one thousand Yankee dollars! It makes your ivory und copal gum cargo look small, *nein?*"

Sight of the certified checks softened O'Neil. He grinned and said, "You have me right where you want me, don't you?"

Hein chuckled, put the checks back, locked the billy-bag. *"Yah.* Now they are useless to you. Even mit poor Hein dead, they are useless. Mitout signature—mitout endorsement. So. Only when I leave will I endorse one to you." He kept laughing, shaking the unhealthful fat that made up his jowls. *"Yah,* mit money always can be made Yankee goot fellow. For Yankee—money. For Frenchman—women. For English—cool verandah and sundowner while world burns."

"And for the German?"

"Ach—mine poor people. So—little. Beer, sausage. Hear me, O'Neil!—you could lead me over the edge of hell mit one goot, cold bottle Vassheimer beer mit *mettwurst* sausage."

O'NEIL PAID off the paddle boys and led the way across the canoe dock to an elevated sidewalk. There was a hundred meters of the walk, its high stilts lifting it above an area of cracked, whitish clay which later would become a muddy lagoon when the river raised from the greater spring rains.

The town was all around them then, but still no sign of it through giant mahoganies, bokongus and palms. The sidewalk ended, there was a cobble path along rising ground, and the trees opened up giving a view of some palm nut storehouses with sheet-metal sides and thick, thatch roofs.

O'Neil left the safari in a fenced-off area provided for the purpose by the Franconi Company; then, accompanied by Hein with his locked billy-bag, and Bobolongonga, erect despite his fifty-kilo load of uniform can and baggage, he went on, around a government compound to the town's main street.

The street was almost a hundred meters across, with groves of raffia palms and cape jasmines growing down its middle. There were signs that a lorry had used it at one time or another, hauling supplies to the d'Alouette diamond mine in the high hinterland, but the street had never been laid out with motor transport in mind, and footways of cobblestones crossed and re-crossed it.

Most of the buildings were sawed hardwood with thick, thatch roofs, although one, the offices of Franconi Soap, was white stucco topped by green tile. Overhead were some wireless towers, and through an open window one could hear the peep-peep of a message coming in on the Continental code. There was a two-story rest house built in the conventional double-verandah design, some trade stores, and a considerable variety of less substantial places—the souks of tall, bold-faced Arabs from Khartoum dealing in salt and religious amulets atop their counters and opium beneath, and smaller, darker men, Hindus from Zanzibar, with their usual assortments of brindle cotton and slum jewelry.

A path struck diagonally across the wide street, taking them to the rest house.

It was still quite light in the open although the sun had dropped beyond the bokongu trees, but beneath the lower verandah of the rest house it was twilight.

A native boy was curled up on a piece of palm matting sound asleep, and O'Neil almost stepped on him. He stopped, looked around. He'd been there once, long before, but it took him a while to remember the plan of the house. There was a stairway somewhere at the left that would take them to the second story; straight ahead was the door to a hot little lounge that nobody ever used and had become the home of ghekkos, thatch snakes and other assorted fauna that like to cohabit with man in those latitudes; and around a corner to his right was the bar where Portugee DeSilva used vile cognac in concocting sundowners that were warm as a man's blood.

HE WALKED on, turned the corner. A glassless window looked in on the bar. Everything was exactly the same as O'Neil remembered it. There were the round okumé-wood tables, turned black from the sweat-greasy forearms of men, the dark stained bar with its empty decanters and fungus-etched mirror behind it, the peddle organ from Saxony covered with spiderwebs and dust like gray veils at the back of a tiny alcove stage. A petrol lamp was already burning over the bar, and beneath it stood Portugee DeSilva, lean and leathery. The seven or eight years had changed him no more than it would a mummy.

He turned, having heard the scrape of feet, and peered at the window. It was covered by bronze screen, and evidently the reflection of the petrol lamp kept him from seeing O'Neil's face.

"Eh?" he said. He wore small, crescent shaped earrings set with diamonds, and the diamonds kept sending needle-shafts of reflection as he turned his head from one side to another, trying to make his protruding eyeballs pierce the gloom.

O'Neil started as though to answer. Then his gaze fell on Hein.

Hein had flattened himself to the wall. In the half darkness his skin turned the hue of one who'd bled to death. The Browning was drawn from its holster. He commenced lifting it as though to aim through the window.

O'Neil seized his wrist, forced his hand down.

"Put it away."

Hein licked his lips several times and said, *"Yah."* O'Neil had to take the gun from him and put it away in the man's holster himself. Then Hein whispered, "You see him, *Herr* Yankee?"

O'Neil thought he meant the Portugee. Then he realized that Hein's gaze had never been near the bar. He'd been looking at a man who was seated at one of the okumé-wood tables.

Chapter 3

HE WAS A raw-boned man with strong lips and deep-set eyes. He sat in a rattan chair, leaning back, but that position did not prevent his forearms from being planted on the table. He had a thick, white cheroot in his mouth, and the way his lips were pressed around it made them seem a trifle too large for the rest of his face.

O'Neil saw him, and made a little, involuntary start. Then he smiled a little. There were few of these jungle tramps that he did not recognize. And this particular one wasn't the kind a person ever forgot.

Runkhammer. That was his name—Runkhammer, though perhaps not ten other men on the continent knew it. To most he was simply "The Hammer."

"What?" The Hammer asked in a great, raw voice that exactly matched his appearance. "What did you say, Portugee?"

"Someone…." DeSilva lifted his angular shoulders. "I think perhaps somebody came. A guest. Customer."

The Hammer laughed. DeSilva bumped the bar, making some glasses tinkle, and there was the illusion that the man's laugh had caused it. It was that kind of a laugh.

"Customer!" The Hammer shouted. His lips moved far out with the word, still holding the white cheroot. "Here in this sinkhole of *schnapps* you call a salon? You still look for customers here, you old fool? You will die without a customer—except for me, and LecKurti, and fat Schmaltz from the radio shack. You would be dead of starvation long ago if we did not pay for your slop, *Senhor* Portugee!"

DeSilva looked at a tab. "You owe me exactly—eight hundred francs."

The Hammer heard him, but it was a slow process for rage to take over his face. His lips stiffened, eyes protruded, the muscles corded like pythons beneath his sweaty white shirt. He lifted his arm, smashed fist and forearm to the table making it jump and raise dust from the dirt-clotted mattings that covered the floor.

"You would starve without my patronage, *Senhor*!"

The barkeeper gave no sign of hearing. The Hammer bellowed, "Listen, swine!

Did you hear me say you would starve without me?"

"By you I am owed eight hundred francs," Portugee said wearily.

Runkhammer had come half erect from the strength with which he had punished the table. He remained that way, his legs bent and spread wide showing their muscles which were on the scale of a percheron stallion's, then he took a couple of deep breaths and relaxed. Exertion and anger had brought droplets of perspiration along his hairline. He swabbed them off with a massive, hairy forearm and sat down. His weight made the rattan chair sag to one side.

He said, "It is true I owe you the eight hundred francs. Eight hundred and twenty-five, including your charge for the glass of cognac you will bring me now."

Portugee poured from a long-necked bottle, mixed it with water *sa-tengah* after the Eastern manner, and carried it over with a slap-slapping sound of his tennis shoes.

"No hard feelings," the big man growled. He took the glass. It was a medium sized tall glass but it almost disappeared when his hand closed around it. "I know of no man in the Congo I would rather favor with my account, old chappie."

He spoke the last words with the accent of a British colonial, though for the most part his inflection was not British nor anything else. It was the type of English one finds spoken by that globe-trotter class to whom all tongues are familiar.

THE HAMMER. O'Neil had run onto him three or four times in the past, and they'd had cognac together. He remembered one evening in particular, down in Mozambique when they sat on the hot, airless terrace of the Hotel Covilha and the Hammer had propositioned him in the matter of high-jacking some Arab *dhows* that were delivering crude opium from British mandate for reshipment inside bales of sisal, all with the help, or at least without the hindrance, of certain Portuguese officials who were getting their usual percentage. The Hammer had been somewhat drunker than usual that night, and O'Neil had learned some things about him. He learned his real name, Runkhammer, and that he'd once been an officer in the British army of India. He was born there, his father a British official, his mother daughter of a Portuguese exporter from Goa. There was some other blood in his veins, too; a person could tell that by the peculiar, flecked brown of his eyes, but

Runkhammer wasn't the sort of man you ever hinted it to.

He'd left the British army after what was politely called *an unfortunate incident*. Later, O'Neil had heard the story of how he'd locked himself in a room with three Sikh non-coms and beat them to death with his fists after some trouble concerning a half-caste woman.

Anger rose easily in the Hammer, and it left easily. Now he was seated leaning back in the same position as when O'Neil first saw him. There was less cross-light and the rays of the petrol lamp struck his face more sharply, revealing the extremely close-clipped moustache on his lip. He'd grown that since O'Neil saw him last.

O'Neil moved from the window and once again looked at Hein.

"He's the one who's out to get you?" he asked.

"The Hammer? Who knows? I—"

"If you want me to keep you alive, it'd be a good idea to let me know."

"So. Perhaps. Und perhaps others. The world iss full of men who cut throats for a hundred-franc note."

"Who else is gunning for you?"

"How would I know? The world iss full—"

"You said that before!" O'Neil growled from the side of his mouth. He started away, motioning for Hein and Bobolongonga to follow, took them up the rotting verandah stairs, found a spot where parasitic vines hung in heavy masses making shadow deep as night. "Stay here!"

Bobolongonga's hand was beneath his kuftan, on the hilt of his machete, and O'Neil knew that Hein would stay there all right.

He went downstairs, inside the bar, walked to the Hammer's table.

The Hammer sat for a while, looking up at O'Neil's face with fierce, deep-set eyes. Then he saw the hook and lunged to his feet. The cognac glass was in his hand. He squeezed down on it, and a portion of the rim snapped off. He cursed, flung the glass in one direction, seized the heavy okumé table and hurled it in another.

"Sweet name of hell! You! Armless O'Neil!" He was grinning, teeth clamped on the white cheroot. Then as suddenly as it had appeared, the grin turned to a scowl. "I should strangle you, you Yankee green-guts, you *bowane*. You piece of camel's dung. You—"

"Mind your tongue, Runkhammer, or I'll split that skull of yours with my hook."

The Hammer turned and spat. "I have a

thick skull. There have been those who have tried to split it, here and there, as I have traveled along. It does not split easily. Right-o?" He had a way of cutting his words off like a Hungarian or other mid-European, but every so often he'd drop that "right-o" just to prove he was British. "A thick skull—good in this country. It keeps out the heat, it wears well, it keeps the memory of old things inside a long time. They tried to arrest me, those pigs of the Colonial police, the day after you left Mozambique."

"I didn't squeal on you in Mozambique," O'Neil grunted as though not giving a particular damn whether the Hammer believed him or not.

O'NEIL WALKED over, caught the upended table with his hook, brought it back on four legs. He found a chair and sat down. Then he repeated. "No, I didn't squeal on you in Mozambique. If you want to know how the Colonial Police got hold of your plan I'll tell you—it was because you get too drunk and talk too loud."

The Hammer laughed and sat down across the table from him. His hand was running blood from the broken cognac glass. It was the first he'd noticed. He wiped the cut back and forth across a leg of his sweaty white pants.

"Right-o. I guess Armless O'Neil never loved gendarmes."

O'Neil shrugged. He rapped with his hook and called for cognac. When Portugee approached, carrying a bottle of cheap Morocco, O'Neil cursed him. After much rattling among bottles, Portugee padded over with a battle of Haute Lavaur. He stood, clutching it with both hands,

"Five hundred francs! Before I break the seal…."

O'Neil flung out a thousand-franc note with the carelessness which is born of bottomless supply, and Portugee, after examining it against the light walked backward, bowing and groveling, all the way to his money drawer.

"Hah!" cried the Hammer, holding the bottle to admire its French label. With the bottle still in the man's fingers, O'Neil swung his hook, neatly chopping its neck off. It pleased the Hammer who roared approval. "French brandy, after the pig swill he has been serving *me,* his best customer! You must forgive me for calling you green-gutted, O'Neil. Had I known you were in the big dollars I would only have called you a piece of camel's dung."

They poured cognac and drank. It was the first decent liquor O'Neil had tasted after months of dehydrating in the heat of dry season, and he was in no hurry coming to the point. He had three from the bottle, then said,

"What do you know about Otto Hein?"

"Hein? Hein?" It took several seconds for the name to register on the Hammer's brain. Then he slammed the table with fist and forearm. "Hein, the near-sighted one!" He started to say some more, and then stopped abruptly, merely naming Hein a vile word.

O'Neil waited. To kill time he rolled a cigarette, lighted it. His eyes never left the Hammer's truculent face. He said, "Yes, Otto Hein. Tell me about Hein."

"What should I tell you about him?"

"Why do you want to kill him?"

The Hammer spat. "Why should I want to stick that fat little pig?" Now, after his first lurch of surprise, the Hammer would like to pretend that Hein meant nothing to him, that he was not even curious, but he was not a good actor. He chuckled and said, "Tell me, chappie-lad, where is this Hein you talk about?"

"Why do you want to kill him?"

"Don't answer me one question by asking another!"

He roared the words, but there was no sign of O'Neil's even hearing him. He leaned back in the chair, cigarette in his lips, and the blue smoke drifting up made his coppery ugly face look like an idol of Buddha with incense burning before it.

"Answer!" the Hammer shouted. "Answer, damn you, before I tramp your ribs in." He was suddenly up on his feet.

O'Neil merely sat and watched. Sight of him infuriated Runkhammer still more. There was a half-filled cognac glass in his fingers. He flung it, and it shattered against one of the bamboo slats of the wall.

O'Neil said, "Sit down or I'll put you down."

Runkhammer swept the table from his way, lunged forward, one long arm reaching for O'Neil's shirt. O'Neil remained as he was for still another second. He let the man get hold of him, jerk him forward, then he brought the hook around and up, backarm, in a smashing arc.

IT CONNECTED along the Hammer's jaw and skull. His fingers let go O'Neil's shirt. He reeled, tripped over the heels of his *veldtschoen.* There was a chair behind him. It fell. He trampled over it. It tangled

around his feet, and he kicked it to a mass of useless rungs. By that time he'd regained his balance. His eyes roved and came to rest on O'Neil who was standing, stuffing the front of his shirt back in his trousers.

O'Neil said, "Why is Hein afraid of you?"

The Hammer muttered something. He rubbed jaw and scalp where the hook had landed. Here and there blood was oozing, and his fingers mixed it with oily sweat and smeared it across his vast face.

"Ha! Hein. You still talk about Hein. Why is Hein afraid of the Hammer!" He commenced to laugh. He laughed in a series of rolling shouts, laughed with fists lifted on bent arms, muscles flexed, head reared back. "Why should he not be afraid of the Hammer? Because I hate his green guts and would strangle him with this one hand."

He thrust his hand out, closed the fingers slowly. His heavy lips were flared out in a gleeful-savage smile, his eyes were bright, imagining those fingers were actually strangling the life out of the German. "Like this I would strangle him, O'Neil. Until his face turned black, and his eyes popped out and hung like white marbles on two strings, until his tongue was too thick for his mouth…."

"Why?" O'Neil barked.

"Hah!" Runkhammer made a movement of revulsion as though throwing the man's carcass away. He stepped back, grimacing, pulling his pants high and tight around his thighs. "Why is it one white man kills another in this rotten country? For women, for money, for revenge. Or maybe it is because I do not like the mouse-color of his eyes."

O'Neil knew that he wasn't going to get the truth from Runkhammer, and he had no intention of telling him that Hein was waiting in the shadows outside.

"Sit down," he growled, kicking a chair over for Runkhammer. "You just strangled a man. You're tired. You need a drink."

"Right-o!" Despite the blow he'd taken, Runkhammer had recovered his temper. He sat down, poured cognac, watched as O'Neil left him and walked to the bar.

"Guest book," O'Neil said to Portugee. The old, mildewed book opened to the right place, and O'Neil signed his name in stub pencil, *"O'Neil, Bangui, Dept. Chari, F.E.A."* He snapped it shut and said, "Two rooms."

"Two, *Senhor?*"

"Two."

"As you say; the payment will be in advance."

O'Neil wasn't in a mood for haggling.

He simply tossed over five hundred francs, saying there'd be an equal amount waiting in the morning provided he liked the rooms. The Portugee jingled a little brass bell, awakening the black boy who'd been asleep on the verandah floor. O'Neil knew without looking around that Runkhammer had followed and was looking down at the back of his head.

"*Two* rooms?" Runkhammer asked. He was grinning, showing his powerful, shell-white teeth.

"Sure. One bed for myself and one for my pet cobra. I always like to give men a fifty-fifty chance when they come around after dark to run a machete through me."

"If I wanted to kill you," the Hammer rumbled, "I would kill you now."

O'Neil took the two big, brass keys and followed the gangling houseboy outside and up the verandah stairs.

Chapter 4

THE SUN was down, but there was a bright, violet glow through the mists that rose from the jungle and, finding its way along the upper verandah, the glow caught reflection along the blued barrel of an automatic.

"Put it away!" O'Neil said.

"*Yah,*" Hein whispered. "You were talking to him?"

"Why's he after you?"

"You told him I vas here?"

"I didn't tell him a damned thing." Hein had picked up a leech off the vines, and now he was trying to pull it free from the flesh of his neck. O'Neil watched until he was through. It was one of those bull-dog leeches that hurt like a hot needle when they're pulled loose, but Hein made no show of feeling. He could take pain all right. "How long do I have to keep you alive?"

"Why do you say it like so, *Herr?*"

"Because I don't like the job if the Hammer's gunning for you."

"Until—tomorrow. *Yah,* until steamboat upriver."

O'Neil took him to one of the rooms. The door was already unlocked. He stepped inside. It was almost completely dark, with only a few pale slats of light coming through the half-shut jalousies. O'Neil closed them the rest of the way, pumped up the petrol lamp, got its mantle to hissing. It gave a good, white light.

He looked around. The room was like all rooms in all jungle hotels. The walls were woven bamboo. Overhead was a dusty net designed to catch ghekkos and snakes that are forever dropping from thatch roofs. Mattings covered the floor. They were new-woven of that year's palm, and still gave off a sweet, pitchy odor. An iron bed stood in the middle of the room, surrounded by mosquito net. O'Neil walked to the windows, examined them. No glass. Only jalousies, bronze screen, and a couple of heavy, teak-wood bars to delay the entrance of prowlers. There was a second door in the back of the room. Latch-locked on the inside. He opened it. It led to a disused hall smelling of dust and dryrot.

He came back inside. "Stay here," he said to Hein. "Keep the door locked. I'll check on that steamboat."

He stood on the verandah, listening to Hein drop the bar in place. Bobolongonga was nearby, a huge, gray shadow in his kuftan.

"Don't let anybody in."

"No, Master. Were it the Prophet himself I would send him back to paradise on his foam-white camel." Bobolongonga drew hilt-half of a huge machete from beneath the robe. "Behold, O *bwana m'kumbwa,* how brave is your servant Bobolongonga. Behold how he risks his neck for thee, even though he hath not five Yankee bucks to his name, being without his wages since hell was covered with ice as the prophets of thy land say it, Master."

O'Neil grinned in the dark. "You're a great guy, Bobo."

"Aye, but goeth not off half-cocked. Behold, that Hammer is strong as two men and he would wring thy neck off like a rooster's at the fetish house. Preserve thyself, O Master, for if thou should kick the bucket, who then would pay me my back wages so I could return a man of wealth to the two wives who have awaited lo the five years in Katanga?"

O'Neil still grinned, but there was no sign of it in his voice when he named the big black man the child of an unwed goat, and promised to split his skull like a ripe durian nut if he mentioned money again. "Did I not just empty a purse of gold into the laps of those thieving Colonials at Campell to free you from their monkey-house?"

Actually, O'Neil had bribed the jailer only to the extent of six dollars, American, which was something less than half his fine, had it been paid, but the amount had grown through telling until Bobolongonga pictured himself as having been rescued from the chemin de fer gang by the treasure of Solomon.

O'Neil went down the stairs; saw the Hammer inside examining Portugee's guest book; walked quietly down the cobblestone path, losing himself among shadowy palms and cape jasmines that grew down the center of the street.

THERE WAS a light burning inside the Franconi Company offices, and a small, old Frenchman was seated in the breeze of an automatic punkha, working on a set of books. O'Neil went in, spoke French, inquiring about the steamboat.

The Frenchman climbed down and got ice cubes from a noisy little American refrigerator and mixed two sundowners of *schnapps* and Brazzaville water before making any move toward answering. Then he said, "Yesterday, there was the steamboat *Frioul.*"

"It went upriver?"

"No, *Monsieur.* Not at this early season. The mudbars, you understand. Not fit for crocodiles is the river before mid-March."

"There'll be no boat for the upriver till then?"

The Frenchman shrugged and tinkled the ice of his sundowner. Then, instead of answering, he cupped his hands and shouted, "Schmaltz!"

The name was familiar. O'Neil remembered the Hammer mentioning it to Portugee as one of his three customers: Schmaltz "from the radio shack." There was a shuffle of feet and a fat Dutchman came in. He was about twenty-five, though his flesh made him seem older.

"*Mynheer!*" he said, looking at the sundowners, letting his little, pointed tongue flick along his lips, but the Frenchman didn't invite him to join them.

He asked, "Any boats expected from upriver?"

"The *Frioul* only yesterday—"

"Of course," the Frenchman cried impatiently. "But answer my question."

"No boat," Schmaltz muttered.

So Hein had been lying about the upriver steamboat! O'Neil left two sundowners later. Lights were burning here and there in the rest house. He glanced in the bar. The Hammer was gone. He climbed to the verandah, walked down its dark length, back again. There was movement among vines and he spun, half drawing his Mauser pistol before recognizing Bobolongonga.

"No trouble?"

Bobolongonga signed in the negative.

The light was still burning in Hein's room. O'Neil listened at the door a few seconds, then rapped. No answer. He called, "Hein! Open up. It's O'Neil."

There was still no answer. He listened a while, turned and looked up at Bobolongonga.

"What the hell?"

"He is still there, *bwana!*" the big black cried defensively. "It must be he is still there. No one come. No sound. Nothing."

O'Neil didn't try to force his way through that door. There was the second entrance leading from the disused hall.

It was close and still warm in the hall. O'Neil lighted a match and nursed its flame as he walked to the door. Locked. He rammed with his shoulder, and the rusted lock screws gave way, spilling him inside.

The petrol lamp was hissing, fluttering, hissing again. It was either out of fuel or pressure. No one in the room. He looked for the billy-bag. Gone, of course. He cursed. The German had gone, and O'Neil would have the fifty thousand francs owing him forever.

O'Neil inquired downstairs. One of the houseboys had seen the near-sighted *bwana* headed cross-street toward the Company building. He'd seen nothing of a billy-bag.

O'Neil crossed once more. Frenchman on his old stool. He circled to the low-roofed building that housed the company wireless station. A light inside, but bamboo shutters cut off his view. He listened. A radio was bringing in repeated crashes of static with a dance band far in the background. No one there. Schmaltz had gone away, leaving the set turned on.

He went inside. The wireless control panel was lighted, humming softly with the gain turned down. Static was coming over a sprawling conglomeration of equipment Schmaltz had evidently strung together himself. O'Neil glanced in an ash tray, and experienced the shock of finding exactly what he expected to find—one of those wax-wicked Spanish matches burned at both ends. He'd been there then—Hein.

O'Neil went back outside where Bobolongonga waited.

"He was not there?"

"No."

"Ay-ya, Allah! He hath gone, leaving thee flat on thy financial fanny, as the wise of thy country sayeth. Who now will pay me my back wages, O *Allah?"*

IT WOULD be useless, trying to trace Hein through the jungle night. O'Neil went back, noticed the lamp in Hein's room had run dry and gone out. He didn't bother to knock. He went to his own room, rang for a houseboy, ordered supper. Then he stripped, poured water from the pitcher over his head, stood with arms aloft while Bobolongonga rubbed him dry with a piece of native-weave. The bath put him in better spirits. A long cognac *sa-tengah* and a fresh supply of cigarettes completed the job.

He stretched out in a siesta chair while the houseboy set table for him. Slowly, apparently without the least rancor, he cursed Otto Hein in English, French, Arabic and Congoese.

He ate lamb and rice, yellow from saffron, two tiny hen's eggs, a mango and banana salad, some of the milky, half-fermented papaya juice that is universally taken along the equator for *"bondele stomach."* the prevalent liver complaint. His meal was topped off by a tiny cup of coffee made after the Arabian method, bitter, syrupy and cold.

He sat back, feet still up, smoking another cigarette.

Someone was climbing the verandah stairs. No sound—just the movement of a man's weight, telegraphing itself across the long, termite eaten supports of the building. O'Neil sat quite still, letting the cigarette burn down in his fingers. Movement gone now. There should have been footsteps, the sound of a door opening, closing. There were none of those things.

He pressed out the cigarette coal, stepped out to the verandah. Cool now, with breeze moving from upriver carrying odors of jasmine and decay, rustling the leaves of raffia palms whose tops were almost level with the verandah roof. Somewhere in the native village hidden by jungle came the inevitable nightly thud-thud of fetish drums.

He felt a tremble of footsteps again—but that was only Bobolongonga following him.

Something creaked. Metal on metal. A poor hinge, fungus coated, long without oil.

"Stay there," O'Neil said, indicating Hein's verandah door.

Bobolongonga lifted fingers in salute to show that he had heard. O'Neil walked on, turned at the corner to look back. Bobolongonga had already lost himself in vine shadow.

He reached the central hall. Still dark, hot, musty-smelling. This time he did not strike a match. Light came from somewhere. It was hard to tell. A quick glow, appearing and disappearing, like that phosphorescent witches'-fire one sees in the jungle at night.

He realized what it was—the door to Hein's room was slightly ajar and someone was moving the rays of an electric torch around.

The light was gone. He found the door, touched it. It swung to his fingers, making the grating-creaking noise. He moved inside. The air was filled with odors—drying palm nuts, the gassy odor left when the petrol lamp failed, and the sweat-odor of men.

The room was completely dark. Not even a hint of light through closed jalousies. He moved on a step. There'd been one of those long siesta chairs between the door and the bed. He groped for it. It was not where he expected. He drew up, struck by the feeling that a man was only a short reach away. The Mauser butt felt good to his hand.

Someone moved, weight telegraphing itself across the floor. O'Neil fell back, reached the wall. He tried to recall the features of the room—position of netting, bed, furnishings. He wanted to circle, reach the door, lift the bar and thus give access to Bobolongonga if he needed him.

He took three steps. Someone moved close ahead of him. He tried to step aside, but the rattan siesta chair was there to block his way.

He caught himself, made an attempt to circle the chair's foot. It sat at a different angle than he supposed and he tripped, half fell, catching himself with hand and one knee on the footrest.

A man muttered a curse of surprise and something swung, making a current of air over O'Neil's head.

He knew the voice—Runkhammer.

O'NEIL TURNED and crouched with an instinctive feel of the man's position. His hook came up and around, but Runkhammer was a little closer than he expected, and the hook caught in the fabric of his shirt. O'Neil ripped back to free it. It made Runkhammer stagger forward, and O'Neil met him with the sharp impact of his fist.

It connected with Runkhammer's jaw, but it lacked the stunning impact that comes from timing. O'Neil got himself free of the chair and backed away. He drew the Mauser.

"I have you covered!" he said, and moved aside.

A gun flashed, and there was a vacuum sound of rushing air. No other report. The gun was fitted with a silencer. O'Neil might have killed him at such close range, aiming at the flash. He checked his trigger finger. There was another man in the room. Revealing his position might be suicide.

He was crouched by the chair on one knee. That other man was ramming furniture in the dark, pawing his way. Bobolongonga had heard commotion outside and was banging at the door.

"Hammer!" a man hissed. *"Eh, vous—"*

The man had a nasal sound. French, or one of those mixed races of North Africa to whom the French tongue has become native.

The floor creaked beneath Hammer's weight as he moved away, and the man said "Hammer!" more loudly.

"Don't say my name, you loose-tongued son of an ass!"

"You have killed him?"

"Perhaps." Runkhammer was already in the hall. He said, "Come, before that black raises the gendarmes."

The door gave with a sharp splinter of panels beneath Bobolongonga's shoulder. He was silhouetted for a second in dim reflected moonlight. Machete steel gleamed in his hand. He moved on, huge in his gray kuftan, and was blended with the room's darkness.

"Bwana!"

"I'm all right."

"They have not killed you?"

"I don't think so." He stood up. "Close the door."

He could hear Bobolongonga breathing through his nostrils. The big negro found the door, lifted it back on sprung hinges. O'Neil scratched a match. There was a candle in the dusty holder. He lighted it. The room was upset, mattress turned upside down, part of the wall mat torn away.

"They were searching, *bwana?*"

"Looking for the billy-bag."

"Ha-a!" said Bobolongonga. His tone made O'Neil spin around and watch him. He walked to the wall and pulled out one of the segments of woven bamboo, reached far down, and came out with it—the billy-bag. He grinned, flashing teeth like a row of piano keys. "Is not your Bobolongonga a good servant, Master?"

O'Neil grinned and made a mental note about paying some of the big fellow's wages after all. The padlock was still intact, holding the bag shut. He inserted his hook, ripped it free, dumped the bag out on the table.

It contained a leather portmanteau and some clothing. There was a name in gold on the portmanteau—Dr. Morrison Keane.

He opened the portmanteau. Some letters were addressed to Dr. Morrison Keane, National University, Dublin; others to Keane in Boma and in Brazzaville. He laid them aside and looked further. A square manila envelope contained an explorer's permit signed by the Governor-General. Other envelopes contained maps to the Khaba Hills region. There was a cardboard box held shut by rubber bands. It contained blue clay. Just that—fine, blue clay.

He sat down and rubbed some of the clay against his palm. It was ordinary stuff, the sort you'd find by drying out the mud of any swamp. He put it back and examined the letters. Dr. Keane was evidently a scientist—but where he was, or what Otto Hein was doing with his portmanteau O'Neil had no way of knowing.

Hein's money folder was there. O'Neil took from it the fifty thousand that was owing him and returned the billy-bag to its hiding place. Then he went outside with Bobolongonga.

There was little excitement. Only some legionnaires shouting and playing high dice for drinks at the bar. He went to his room, slept.

HE AWOKE almost immediately with someone shouting in French through his screen door. It was one of the local gendarmes.

"I am sorry, *Monsieur*, but there has been white man murdered." He barked it in a way which showed he was not in truth sorry at all, but happy over the incident which gave him the opportunity of commanding a white man. The gendarme was mulatto. "You will hurry, *Monsieur!*"

"I'll take my own damned time," O'Neil growled back and sat on the bed to strap on his hook.

"Bowels of a pig!" Bobolongonga said to the gendarme. "Thou essence of camel's dung!"

"Keep your mouth shut," said O'Neil. He stood and lighted the petrol lamp. By that time he could see other men outside—lesser gendarmes negroes in tunics, shorts, kepis but no shoes.

O'Neil opened the door and motioned the gendarme inside. He wore the chevrons of a sergeant of Colonials.

"Who was murdered?" O'Neil asked, knowing damned well who it would be.

"The white man. *Monsieur* Hein."

"Shot?"

"As *Monsieur* says—shot."

O'Neil sat down and gestured for Bobolon-

gonga to pour from the cognac bottle. The gendarme watched while he tossed it down.

"When you las' see Hein?" he asked.

"Sundown."

"You come Bakoville together?"

"Yes."

"You quarrel las' night? You—"

O'Neil flung the glass. It struck the bamboo-weave wall and bounded without breaking. He cursed and said, "Stop trying to be subtle. It's bad enough to see a native wear pants without hearing him be *subtle*. You know what the word means? No? Well no *ku-yap*. Just ask me if I killed him." He shouted, "Ask me!"

"You kill-em?"

"No."

The gendarme had evidently expected O'Neil to say "Yes." His face drooped and his eyes grew large and round. O'Neil saw his expression and laughed. He lighted a cigarette and laughed some more. Then the laugh ended and there seemed to be a bad taste in his mouth.

"Where is he?"

"The *bondele?* White man?"

"Of course, you ass."

"On—lower verandah."

"Where did you find him?"

"In garden." He pointed outside with his lower lip, native style. "By thick frangapani bush." Then he asked, "You sure you don' do it?"

"Damned sure."

O'Neil went below with the three gendarmes following. Hein's body was stretched out atop a table of amber, African teak, and there were a dozen assorted mulattos and black men staring at him. He'd been stripped to the waist. The bullet had entered his back, glanced and emerged just beneath the collar bone on the left side. His mouth was open, and there were bits of loam and dead leaves beneath his lower teeth. By that O'Neil knew he'd been on the run when the bullet got him. No telling what calibre, but it must have been a .30 Luger or one with similar authority. He'd heard no report. Hein had been killed elsewhere and carried to the garden, or the gun had been equipped with a silencer. The silencer was it, of course. Runkhammer's gun had been fitted with one.

O'NEIL DIDN'T touch the body. He'd been around enough dead men, Allah knew, but he'd never got over the feeling of revulsion on touching one. "You were born to be a poet," Tommy Huston used to tell him. There was a jackass laugh for you—Armless O'Neil a poet.

The gendarme was talking to him—"You no shoot? You maybe know *bondele* who have pistol with silencer?"

O'Neil looked at him through the smoke of his cigarette. The native was smarter than O'Neil had given him credit for being. He acknowledged that by grinning and offering him a cigarette. The gendarme was flattered and took one.

A white man arrived. He was narrow-faced and big nosed, dressed in stiff-starched whites. Generoux, the District Commissaire. He shook hands with O'Neil, and they called each other by name.

"Know who killed him?" Generoux asked, hooking his thumb at the body.

A laugh jolted O'Neil's shoulders. "You aren't even as clever as your gendarmes."

"I'm not trying to be clever. There's no need in being clever. Hein was the one man who could be shot with impunity. His name was up in Bangui."

"What was he wanted for?"

"Murder."

"Of Dr. Morrison Keane?"

"He told you?"

"I can't be bushed-in with a fever case for two days without learning some of the things that are on his conscience."

O'Neil didn't mention finding Keane's name in the billy-bag.

"Robbery, too?" O'Neil asked.

"There was something apparently quite valuable inside a portmanteau. You didn't see anything of that when you were bushed in with him?"

"He had a billy-bag. Locked. I'm no snooper."

"Where is it now?"

"Ask the man that killed him."

"And that's not you." Generoux gave the impression of not caring a damn whether it was O'Neil or not. "You had too good a chance to croak him in the jungle. You wouldn't bring him here to do it."

Generoux invited O'Neil to the Government House for a cognac. They had two. It took the better part of an hour. Then O'Neil went back to the rest house. The light was still burning in his room. Bobolongonga was inside, sitting on the floor, his big form shadowed against the screen. O'Neil could read things from his posture. In this instance, he knew there was a visitor. He drew his Mauser, snapped off the safety, stepped inside. There, sitting in the siesta chair, was a girl.

Chapter 5

SHE WAS one of the most lovely girls O'Neil had ever seen.

"Don't move," he said. "Don't say anything. Just sit there a second and let me look at you."

How long had it been since O'Neil had seen a girl like her?—a white girl with brown hair that had no trace of the darker bloods in it; a girl with blue eyes, and skin that still had the blush and white that soon departs under the influence of heat and quinine. It brought pain, a dull knife of regret, looking at her, thinking of the things he'd tossed aside in coming here, to the tropics, and staying even after he knew what they always did to a white man.

"Can I move now?" she said.

Her voice was exactly the way it should be, controlled, soft, with a metallic aloofness in it.

"Sure." O'Neil was his old self again. He sheathd the Mauser and walked to the cognac bottle. "Drink?"

"No."

"Suit yourself." He poured one with his back turned. It wasn't the way he wanted to act toward a girl like her. He did it to let her know what kind of a man he was, and it helped him to remember, too. He was Armless O'Neil, jungle tramp, and she was a long way south of that line where the Ten Commandments can be expected to operate.

"It's French cognac," he said.

"I didn't come here to drink with you."

"What *did* you come here for?"

She didn't answer that. Not immediately. He looked at her. His gaze wasn't essentially different from the one an Arab slave dealer would give any recent acquisition. She was rather short, and her body had the sort of curves that did something for the white skirt and blouse she wore.

She let him look for a while and then spoke, "Tell your boy to leave, do you mind?"

"No, I wouldn't mind." In fact, he rather liked the idea. He thumbed Bobolongonga from the door, and the big native obeyed with ponderous reluctance. He lurked just outside, peering through the screen, so O'Neil closed the bamboo jalousies. He hooked the door, too. He turned around and found himself staring into the muzzle of an automatic pistol.

IT WASN'T a large gun. It looked like a toy after a person grew used to a Mauser, but it threw a 7.65 M.M. slug by the looks of it, and 7.65 was quite sufficient.

"Now I need another drink," O'Neil said.

She watched him walk to the bottle. He poured one and turned with it in his fingers. He wanted to be doing something with his hand. She didn't want to shoot him, but he could tell how tight her nerves were drawn, and while his hand was high and occupied she'd have time to settle down a little.

He walked back to the middle of the room. Her nostrils flared a little each time she breathed, and there was a tiny nervous tremble to her eyelids. The safety was off, and her finger was riding the trigger.

"Be careful of that thing," he said. "You'll touch it off, and then what'd you have? One hundred and eighty pounds of dead man. Sister, what in the name of hell would you do with all that dead man?"

She snapped the safety on. The sound of it startled her. She was crouched forward, bent over the gun. The hand that held it was pressed against her bosom and he could see the little, jiggling movements that marked the quick beat of her heart.

"I didn't come here to kill you," she whispered. "I only wanted to ask you some questions."

"Ask!"

"You were with Hein?"

"Sure. My boys carried him when he was down with fever. He paid me to bring him here to Bakoville. Promised me a lot more if I got him out alive—but I didn't. He's dead." He drank half the cognac and grinned. "Sister, maybe you better take it from there."

"He was carrying a package."

"He had a billy-bag on his back and he kept it locked."

"Where is it?"

"Maybe you'd better ask the man who killed him."

"*He* didn't get it."

"Now how would a sweet little girl like yourself know that?"

"I saw his body. He was shot in the back. He had a mouthful of dirt. He was running away."

She noticed things.

"Who are you?" he asked.

"I'm—Kerry Keane."

Keane! The name "Dr. Morrison Keane" flashed back to him. It was the name gold-stamped on the portmanteau that Hein had been carrying in his billy-bag.

O'Neil said the name. "Dr. Morrison Keane—any relation?"

"My father."

"What was Hein doing with his portmanteau?"

"Then you did know!"

"Of course. I lie like the rug peddlers of Damascus."

"Get it!—the portmanteau."

"All right. But I haven't got it *here.*"

"You're lying. It's in this room." Her thumb was on the safety. There was a thick-padded Arabian pillow fallen to the floor. He picked it up, pressed it against the gun muzzle. She tensed and snapped off the safety. He thought for a moment she was going to fire.

"Go ahead. Shoot, if it'll make you feel better. There's nothing like kapok stuffing to stop bullet lead."

She started to twist the gun aside. He was ready for that. His hook came up, caught the gun by its trigger guard. It bucked against her finger and discharged, sending a streak of burning powder toward the far wall. The gun fell to the floor. He picked it up. At the same instant Bobolongonga crashed through the hooked door and stood blinking at them.

"It's nothing," O'Neil said. He glanced at the gun, snapped the safety back, and handed it to her. "Put it in your handbag where it belongs."

SHE WAS frightened and pale. The feel of the gun seemed to revolt her—it was as though she were holding a snake.

"I might have killed you!" she whispered.

"You and half the people in Africa."

A gendarme arrived, having heard the shot. O'Neil met him, told him he'd been cleaning his gun, sent him away. Then he walked to Hein's room. The billy-bag was still there, between the walls. He brought it back, tossed it on the table.

She opened it and looked at its contents—the clothing, the map, the box of finely divided clay.

He was watching her expression. "Maybe it isn't all there."

"Yes, it's all here." She met his eyes. "You're puzzled?"

"It's none of my business."

"But I want to tell you."

Suddenly she was almost pleading with him. He knew how it was—it's hard to be alone anywhere, worst of all in a jungle hole like Bakoville. You have to trust somebody.

"My father. You heard? He is dead. Murdered. Outside Bangui. Hein did it."

"Maybe you'd better start at the beginning."

She sat down and started talking, rapidly. It had started when the National University, Dublin, sent one of its staff, Dr. Patrick McCrady, to the Khaba Hills of French Equatorial Africa to search certain Mesozoic strata for signs of prehistoric life. It was a routine assignment, one of the University's never-ending investigations which have made its departments of zoology and geology famous throughout the civilized world. At least it had seemed routine at the start. Six months almost to the hour after McCrady's departure from Dublin, Keane received a radiogram from him saying that he had made a discovery of such amazing proportions that the original project must be abandoned. Would Dr. Keane immediately fly to Brazzaville where he, McCrady, would met him and reveal the full particulars? There had been no hint of the nature of his discovery, but nevertheless Keane had laid everything aside to come.

"Alone?" O'Neil asked.

"Father and I. I am—*was* his secretary."

"Is it his policy to fly over the world when some subordinate in his department asks him to?"

"Dr. McCrady was not really a *subordinate*. He had an international reputation in his field."

"And so you came to Brazzaville. Was Dr. McCrady waiting for you there?"

"I thought you knew. Dr. McCrady was murdered. Here. In this very hotel. We waited in Brazzaville for two weeks before the Governor-General finally got through on the wireless. It was then we found out."

"And your father decided he'd come on to Bakoville."

"Not immediately. The gendarmes at Division headquarters in Bangui were holding McCrady's effects, so we went there." She pointed to the things on the table. "We found these. Clothes, the map, his permit, and the box of blue clay. You see the box it was in? One of those moisture-resisting specimen boxes. He'd sealed it, but the gendarmes in Bakoville had broken it open. Anyway, all it contained was the clay. Dust. We analyzed it—but it was nothing." She opened the box and let some of the clay sift through her fingers. "What do you make of it?"

O'Neil shrugged. "What happened next?—in Bangui?"

"Hein. That awful, near-sighted man. He came to us. To my father. He pretended to know something about McCrady's murder. He told us so many things—lies. He seemed to think there was some great secret contained in the things the gendarmes had sent out. Something that would tell McCrady's secret. He wanted to join our *expedition* as he called it. He even offered money. Finally my father called the gendarmes and he left."

"And he came back."

"He told you?"

"No. I just knew Hein."

"Yes, he came back. He tried to rob our rooms. Father fought him in the dark. Father decided to leave for Bakoville, but he didn't want Hein to know. He led him to believe he was taking a safari across the *soudan* to the Khabas. He intended to circle back and take the steamboat at a concession wharf near the Boma. I was to hire a petrol launch and meet him there. I waited, but my father did not come. I went back to Bangui. That same day his black boys brought him in—dead. He'd been dead for four days. I cannot tell you how—"

"Never mind," growled O'Neil. "Don't think about it." He knew how those black boys would bring a body in—bones and tendons, after the flesh had been eaten away in a termite mound. It was the only way, Congo climate being what it is.

"Hein had murdered him?"

She nodded. "They found him run through by an assegai spear. In his tent—at night. But the portmanteau was gone, and his *capito* boy was gone. I suppose Hein hired him."

"And then he killed the *capito*. Hein was alone when I found him."

"I tried to tell the gendarmes. They wouldn't listen. Even the Commissaire! He gave me champagne and tried to hold my hand—"

"The swine."

O'Neil didn't blame the Commissaire. The girl was lovely.

She said, "So I left. There was no steamboat. I hired a petrol launch as far as the Graviston Pontoons, and some paddle boys from there."

"How was McCrady murdered?"

"A knife. They found him in his room—at this very hotel."

SHE SAT, looking up at him, her lips parted a little. She needed his help but she wasn't the type who would ask it.

O'Neil said, "McCrady had a safari—was it a large one?"

"I don't know. Maybe thirty or forty men."

"He set out from here?"

"Yes." She was watching him. "You've thought of something?"

He shrugged. "How about McCrady's radiogram. *Exactly* what did it say?"

She took the portmateau and led O'Neil around the verandah to her room. She unlocked the door, went in, found a bit of folded, bluish paper.

AMAZING DISCOVERY IN SWAMPS OF MOKWANDU FORCES POSTPONEMENT OF ORIGINAL PROJECT. PRESENT MEDIUM RENDERS FULL EXPLANATION INADVISABLE. FLY IMMEDIATELY TO BRAZZAVILLE WHERE I WILL MEET YOU

MCCRADY

He read it through, then his eyes went back and rested on the words "Swamps of Mokwandu."

"Does it tell you something?" she asked.

"What are the Swamps of Mokwandu?"

"I don't know. We looked for them on the maps. There was no such place."

O'Neil knew that the word *mokwandu* meant "wise old one" in the Lusaba dialect, thus it was probable that Mokwandu was not a place name, but the name of a man, one who had guided the Doctor to the swamps.

He handed the wireless message back and walked to the door. "You still have that automatic," he grinned.

"You're going…"

"I'm going to find out who *Mokwandu* is."

Chapter 6

HE STEPPED outside, closed the door, waited until he heard the sound of her bolting it. Bobolongonga was in the near shadow.

"There is then a treasure, O Master? There is then a secret of treasure in that box of blue clay?"

"You're damned right. Gold and gems and thousand-franc notes tied in bundles like Egyptian tobacco."

"Praise Allah, then when this adventure is ended I will collect my back wages and return like a sultan to my faithful wives who have wept for me these five years in Katanga."

They went down verandah stairs into the cool tropic night. A dim light burned in the wireless shack. O'Neil tried the screen. Locked. He slid his hook through the mesh, found the bolt, jerked it free.

"Stay here," he said to Bobolongonga and went inside.

Schmaltz wasn't in the room. The transmitter was off, but it still radiated the smell of warm plastic insulation. O'Neil went on through the inside door, scratched a

match. Its flame revealed a short length of hall. A black boy was sleeping on a pallet. He sat up, the whites of his eyes surprised into prominence. He started to speak, but O'Neil silenced him.

"Schmaltz?" he hissed. "Take me."

"Yes, *bwana*."

The boy led O'Neil to a door, pulled it open. A voice from inside startled the silence. Schmaltz. "Dombe! Is that you, Dombe?"

O'Neil groped his way toward the sound, touched the mosquito netting. Schmaltz was crawling out of bed. They collided in the dark. He was holding a gun. O'Neil instinctively grabbed it, wrenched it from his hand. Schmaltz must have been sleeping on it, for its steel was blood-warm.

Schmaltz started back and there was the sound of his shoulder striking the bamboo-weave wall. He moved aside. Momentarily his heavy body was revealed against moon-strips that entered through the slats of the jalousies.

"Take it easy," O'Neil growled.

Schmaltz stopped, whispered, *"Yah."*

He stood quite still, wheezing from excitement and exertion.

"Come along," O'Neil said, turning to the lighted transmitter room.

THERE WAS no fight in Schmaltz. He stood with the night-light shining on him. He was naked save for crumpled white shorts. Sweat ran down both sides of his neck, joined on his hairless chest and made a single, crooked stream down the middle of his belly. His colorless eyes were still frightened, still watching O'Neil.

"You knew Dr. McCrady," O'Neil said.

"I'm only *nederig* wireless operator. I'm—"

"You sent a radiogram for McCrady. Then you kept a copy of it and showed it to somebody." O'Neil spoke in a flat voice, not asking, just stating the facts as though he knew quite well already. "You showed it to Hammer." He waited for Schmaltz to answer, then raised his voice and repeated, "You showed it to the Hammer."

"Yah, to Mynheer Hammer," Schmaltz whispered.

"And to Otto Hein. You showed it to Hein, too."

"Listen to me, *Mynheer*. I meant nothing. No harm. The Hammer—he was mit *Mynheer* Dokter on expedition to Khaba Hills, so of course when he comes to ask see radiogram…."

"Of course." O'Neil's eyes narrowed, but there was no other sign of learning that the

Hammer had accompanied Dr. McCrady. "So you showed it to him, and then you got curious about it yourself, and showed it to your friend, Otto Hein."

"Yah."

"You showed the message to Hein, and he went to Bangui so he'd get first chance at Dr. Keane. He killed Dr. Keane, did you know that?"

Schmaltz didn't answer. He looked sick, like one stricken by dysentery.

"They could put you on The Island for twenty years for being accomplice in it. Do you realize that?"

"Yah."

"Tell me what else you know."

"I know nothings. Nothings, *Mynheer. Gott* be mine judge—"

"Who killed McCrady?"

"I do not know."

"Who killed Hein tonight?"

"I do not know!" he wept.

He was probably telling the truth. O'Neil looked at the gun he'd taken from him. A Luger. He pulled the clip and thumbed its cartridges to the floor, handed it back.

"So the Hammer was along on McCrady's expedition," he said softly.

"Yah. And LecKurti. Gito was *capito* boy. Lobiste, Koto-lewa. Some more *Negers*. You could find them in the village, *Mynheer*."

O'NEIL TOLD him to go back to bed and went outside. Bobolongonga was there, waiting. They made a circle of town and found a gloomy jungle footpath leading to the native village.

Fetish drums had been thudding the nightly dance, but they'd stopped about an hour ago. No moon. There was a grayish hint of dawn in the sky, and when the trail emerged from jungle they could see the central clearing with dome-shaped fetish-houses and pointed thatch huts blending into the shadows of towering okumé trees. A fire, died to a heap of coals, cast ruddy glow on three tree-trunk drums, thick as a hippo's body, standing on wooden X supports.

There was no one around. O'Neil crossed the clearing, sat crosslegged on the ground, nodded at the drums and told Bobolongonga to call Gito, the boy Schmaltz had named as the expedition's *capito*.

Bobolongonga commenced slapping one of the huge drums with the palms of his hands, raising a sound like low thunder that rose and fell forming the "tongue" that has meaning to a black man's ear. The village was awake, listening, O'Neil could sense that, but for a long time no one stirred. At last a form appeared—a squat, bowlegged native walking warily across the clearing.

Bobolongonga stopped and spoke to him, "You Gito?"

The man made an affirmative sign, and Bobolongonga motioned at the darkness where O'Neil sat. *"Bwana m'kumbwa!"* he intoned.

Gito stopped abruptly. His eyes showed white in his vast, cacao-brown face. He hadn't expected a white man. O'Neil had a hunch he'd not have answered the drum had he known a white man was waiting. He started to back away, but O'Neil stopped him with a commanding gesture.

"Bwana-baminga," he said, calling himself a friend.

"Baminga," Gito repeated.

He'd turned a trifle, and O'Neil had a better look at him. He was about forty, ugly at best, covered by milk-white tatooing and tribal welts until he was grotesque.

"You were *capito* boy for McCrady," O'Neil said, speaking the Congo jargon.

Gito signed, "Yes."

"You know of Mokwandu swamp?"

He signed, "No."

O'Neil studied his face. It was a mask of welts and tatooing.

"You know a *man* named Mokwandu?"

Gito took a quick breath. He'd have lied then, and said "no," but the expression of O'Neil's eyes stopped him.

"I know Mokwandu," he breathed.

"Mokwandu guided McCrady to the swamps. The swamps of Blue Clay."

"To the swamp of the damned. Perhaps to swamp of Gorah, the Monster Fetish." Gito rolled his eyes to show terror. "Those were his people, *bwana.* Those of the monster fetish."

"And from there *Bwana* McCrady brought the box of blue clay?"

"I do not know, *bwana.* Me only poor black boy. Me only—"

"You will take me to this Mokwandu." O'Neil drew copper franc pieces from his pocket and jingled them. "You will guide me to Mokwandu—to the swamp of the Monster Fetish. Tomorrow after siesta you will start to guide me."

DAWN HAD changed from a gray to rose color when they returned to the rest house verandah. A light still burned in the girl's room. O'Neil rapped, called her name.

"Kerry! Kerry Keane!"

No answer. He listened, ear close to the tilted bamboo slats of the door. There was a slight, creaking sound, like someone's weight turning on a stretched canvas bed. O'Neil seized the latch and started to shoulder his way through, but the door was unlocked. He paused just inside. The room seemed to be empty. Then he saw the girl's form inside the gray-white film of mosquito netting that circled the bed.

He whipped the netting aside, looked down on her. She was tied, arms at her sides, bare feet lashed to the foot of the bed. A gag was drawn tightly around her mouth. Her eyes stared up at him. Her shirt had been torn from one arm and brutal red welts extended across the soft flesh of her shoulder.

O'Neil drew a folding machete, opened the blade with his teeth, cut the bonds with quick movements. It took her a few seconds to get her muscles to moving.

"The Hammer," O'Neil hissed. He grabbed her shoulders, lifted her to a sitting position. "Was it the Hammer?"

"I don't know. They rapped. I thought it was you. I opened the door a little. It was a houseboy with a pitcher of water. I reached to take it and suddenly they were inside. A white man. A big white man. And another with him. A hook-nosed Moor. I don't know their names. They took the automatic from me. I tried to fight them. It was no use. They wanted the portmanteau."

"And they got it?"

She nodded.

O'Neil cursed himself for leaving her alone. "What good was it to them?" he asked. "Why would a box of blue clay and those few government maps be valuable? You haven't told me everything!"

"I have!"

O'Neil bit down on his anger.

"You screened diamonds out of that blue clay, didn't you?"

"I've told you—everything!" She almost sobbed the words. She was sitting, her legs drawn under her. He could see three circular red marks on the flesh of her forearm.

"They tortured you!" he said.

"Yes." She covered her eyes and sobbed. "I'm sorry. I didn't mean to tell them. They pressed lighted cigarettes into my arm and I couldn't stand it. It hurt so I couldn't think—"

"Sure, kid." O'Neil sat down and put his arm around her. "I know how it is. It's not easy when they start putting the pain on. What did you tell them?"

"About—you. That you'd gone to look for a man named Mokwandu."

THE HAMMER and his partner, LecKurti, had been gone a couple of hours. Kerry couldn't be sure. Every hour had seemed like five, lying bound and gagged. O'Neil did not go to the gendarmes. He left Bobolongonga with her, examined the loads in his Mauser, and walked to the mud and grass *rendeval* hut where the Hammer lived with his current wife, a coal-black Bouracho girl.

It was the girl who met him in the door. She was young and soon to be a mother. She stood, naked save for a calico loin cloth and a dozen-odd pounds of copper bracelets, looking at him with frightened eyes.

"He not here," she whispered. *"Bwana* Hammer, he go."

O'Neil went inside as she backed in front of him. The hut consisted of a single, circular room with six windows. Strings of long, cucumber-shaped papayas hung from the bamboo rafters. Some white man's clothes were on a peg. No sign of the Hammer.

O'Neil said, "He went on trip. Khaba Hills. To Swamps of Mokwandu."

She didn't know, or was too frightened to tell. O'Neil returned to the rest house. The sun was turning jungle mists a flaming violet. Bobolongonga sat crosslegged in front of Kerry Keane's door, asleep. O'Neil didn't awaken him. He went to his room, lay down, smoked a cigarette. He awoke an hour later with sun shining hot through the jalousies and the half-burned cigarette dead in his fingers.

He sent for water, stood with arms high while a houseboy bathed him. He ate and sent Bobolongonga to the village for Gito. In half an hour Bobolongonga returned with word that Gito had disappeared. The Hammer had taken him.

Nothing could be done while the heat of day hung over jungle and town like a dense, damp blanket. He rested until late afternoon then hunted out his safari. Two of the boys had deserted, taking their guns with them in place of their wages, but the rest were ready enough to travel. He laid in supplies—bully beef, kaffir meat, ammunition. It was twilight and the blacks were lined up for final inspection when Kerry Keane arrived. She was dressed in short-boots, trousers and bush-jacket, carrying a trail machete and an Enfield rifle.

She had a right to go if she wanted to, so O'Neil did not object. "It'll be hell out there," he said, jerking his head north at the jungle.

"Yes," she answered. "I've been in the jungle before. I know."

Chapter 7

THEY LEFT at dawn. A crew of Bouracho boys paddled them upriver to the old Sauvage Concession, a rubber plantation now abandoned and trampled by herds of roving elephants. From Sauvage they went overland, following a footpath that burrowed through jungle. They reached a river on the fourth day—a nameless stream, quarter-mile wide and apparently stagnant. They crossed on a raft of silk cottons and the footpath took them on through cane and spear grass high as the back of an elephant. Next day one of the porters died suddenly, without apparent reason. Perhaps it was a mamba's bite, perhaps a blow-gun dart that had delivered its deadly prick and dropped out of sight in the grass. The other porters, terrified, commenced chanting the words of Nyamo, charm of the unseen death, but O'Neil, fearing danger, drove them on with blows and curses until the Khaba Hills rose through night-mists to the north-east.

Next morning, an hour on their way, a two-toned message drum broke the insect-drone of the jungle.

O'Neil listened, and asked Bobolongonga what natives they were. The big black man rolled his eyes ominously and said, "The tribe of Telebiste. Worshipers of the Black Fetish."

O'Neil was not an entire stranger to the country. He'd heard of the Telebiste, but up to now had avoided crossing their domain. The safe way would have meant a swing around the Khaba Hills in the region of Dr. McCrady's old camp, but the short way was directly on, and it was his one chance of reaching Mokwandu before the Hammer. He camped the safari, unlocked the uniform can, took two glass tubes of chemical from the medicine compartment. The chemical was sal ammoniac, a remedy for jungle cough. The tubes were sealed and afterwards dipped in wax as double precaution against dampness that would make the chemical quickly disintegrate into its component gasses.

"Stay here!" he said to the others.

After fifty strides a turn in the footpath hid the safari from sight. He was alone then, save for the monkeys that swung in the vines above, looking down with pinched faces—and save for the native eyes that watched, unseen, from the dense green walls of the path.

An odor of fires burning thatch came to his nostrils, so he knew the village was close.

He passed a hummocky little cassava patch, some voodoo spirit poles with tufts of chicken feathers and human hair dangling—each tuft taken from a different sacrifice. More drums were beating—booming drums of hippo and elephant hide that shook the footpath beneath him. The jungle opened quite suddenly, and the village was in sight.

It was not a big village. Domelike, palm-bundle huts made two crooked rows, one on each side of the footpath. The old stench of filth and spoiled meat was there—the stench he'd learned to associate with native settlements from Zululand to Soudan. Warriors in groups of four and five were coming towards him, dancing to the drum rhythm, swinging iron-pointed assegai spears overhead with intricate, jerky movements.

Some of them danced close, threatening his throat and heart with their spears, but O'Neil strode on, his face contemptuous, eyes on the ceremonial fire that had just been kindled before the voodoo hut.

A witch doctor with a mask that made him look half head stood in the hut entrance, waiting. Whether the tribe had a chief or not, this fetisher was head man. It was generally that way.

O'NEIL PAUSED a scant four strides from the fetisher and let one tube of sal ammoniac fall. He ground it to bits with his boot heel and stepped back. A wisp of smoke curled up as the jungle's dense humidity acted on it. The smoke increased. It became a billow, and during its final seconds the chemical reaction was almost explosive. He could see not a foot in front of him. Natives were shouting, retreating. Finally the smoke drifted away, and he could see the fetisher still facing him. O'Neil handed him the second tube and said in the Shari dialect. "To my brother master of spirits I give this devil's smoke to do with as he wishes, but I will have a favor in return."

The fetisher's fingers closed on the tube. Its contents would some day allow him to perform a similar miracle and make him great among fetishers. "The favor is yours, O *bonde!*"

"I search for a man named Mokwandu."

"I know no man named Mokwandu."

"I look for his tribe, the tribe of the Gorah fetish—the Fetish of Monsters."

The fetisher turned, swinging his huge mask, and pointed with an arm that emerged from the mask's left ear. Afterward, when O'Neil brought up his safari, the fetisher furnished four warriors who guided them

a half-dozen kilometers to the edge of a swamp. Beyond that they refused to venture, speaking in awed tones of the Gorah. O'Neil sent them back and took siesta. He started again when the heat of afternoon was spent, following an ancient footway of springpole saplings laid across the mire.

Towards nightfall they reached higher ground, a reef of bluish clay with a half-overgrown footpath along its middle. Animals were abundant, and he knew that meant many islands. Hippos occupied the deeper water where there was hint of river current; there were monkeys and parrots by the thousands, and a dozen times he had glimpses of ugly blue-faced baboons that would have been worth a small fortune if a man could get them alive to the zoos.

There were other creatures, too. The slimy, crawling ones. Crocodiles, with their bony armor and teeth that could saw a man in half, and once a three-foot lizard with dwarfed blow-wings like some prehistoric monster slid along the path and wriggled from sight in the sea of herbage.

TWO OF the porters had deserted at siesta, but the rest stayed close, fearing the journey back as much as the one ahead. At night they camped on an island. It was black dark. Occasionally a deep, booming sound came across the water. One always hears such swamp sounds at night, but this night it seemed louder, more ghostly and ominous. One of the porters, an adherent of the Sabata fetish, improvised a drum of an empty sugar can and chanted a long incantation, flattering and appeasing the evil spirits. It seemed to settle the blacks a trifle—even Bobolongonga, despite his conversion to Islam.

The Sabata fetisher finally stopped. No swamp-booming now. Silence and darkness were complete. There was a breathless quality to the air, then the tip of a dead *ule* tree commenced to glow with witches'-fire, a swamp phenomena that often precedes electrical storm.

The storm came—first a roar of high tree tops, then thunder, lightning and the deluge, a dense flood of water. It stopped abruptly. The air was still close and oppressive. Then came a new sound—a slow thud, heavy, so heavy it shook the tiny island. It was like the tread of a giant.

The Sabata fetisher commenced wailing, frenziedly slapping hands on his tin-can drum.

"Be quiet!" O'Neil said.

He'd drawn his Mauser. He didn't remember doing it—the gun was simply there, in his hand. Without reasoning his action he snapped off the safety, pulled its trigger. Gunflame and explosion ripped the dark. Natives cried a wild "aya-ya." At the same instant he could hear and feel the impact of heavy feet on swamp earth, and there was a trumpeting animal cry. The great cats of the jungle sometimes cry in a similar manner—but this was no cat. It was a beast unfamiliar to O'Neil's ears. A tree splintered with a crash like near lightning. Next second came a mighty splash—and soon after, silence.

O'Neil crouched, gun still in his hand, he could hear the breathing of natives behind him. The girl was close. After a long wait, little waves slap-slapped along the muddy shore. It had taken all that time for them to reach him. The thing, whatever it was, had not been close.

O'Neil pulled himself erect, laughed. The sound, coming after a long, tense silence, had a surprising impact—like one jeering in a cathedral.

He said, "You think it's the Gorah—the Monster of the fetish." He spat, or made the sound of spitting. "You cowards of the tribe of Banda! I, your *bwana,* will walk by myself into the darkness and challenge this Gorah fetish. I, your *bwana,* will show you how strong is the gri-gri of my people!"

He took an electric torch from the uniform can and started away. Someone was following. Kerry Keane.

"Then you know what it is?" she whispered.

"Perhaps it *was* the Gorah."

He heard her inhale quickly. "Why not?" he asked. "There are more things in this jungle than a white man has ever put on photographic film or inside the texts of that university of yours."

She had hold of his arm. Her voice was almost pleading. "But no *monsters!*"

O'Neil laughed and kept following the path, with the electric beam showing the way. After a hundred meters they found the tree that had been snapped. It was a foot-thick *ule,* shattered ten feet above the ground. Beneath were signs of some heavy creature, but rain-wet herbage and the swamp water had kept the actual tracks from showing.

"Elephant," she said.

"All right," O'Neil grinned. "Elephant. That's good enough to tell the natives."

There were no further signs of the creature, and by daylight the whole thing seemed preposterous. Next day there was nothing out of the ordinary, and on the following morning they found a canoe dock where a dozen boats were tied. A footpath led through jungle.

A message drum commenced thudding. They'd been discovered even sooner than O'Neil had expected.

Chapter 8

O'NEIL STRODE on, leading his safari, looking neither to right nor left. Black men watched from the wall of jungle at each side of the path, some so close he might have touched them with an extended rifle barrel, but nothing except an occasional leaf tremble hinted at their presence.

The jungle commenced breaking up into little clearings. There were hills, yellow-green with savannah grass, with groves of wild coffee and monkey-bread trees at their tops. A stream muttered in the overgrown depths of a steep ravine, and a system of wooden waterwheels had been installed to lift water to the yam fields during dry season.

At a low ridge O'Neil paused. A village lay before him. He looked back. Natives had emerged from the jungle in a dozen spots, their assegai spears flashing in the late-morning sun.

He went on, leading the safari across hummocky cassava fields to the village.

Women and children lined the path, jabbering an unfamiliar variety of Shari. He noticed that the women wore bark cloth and raffia rather than calico. The village was beyond the reach of even the wandering black-Arab traders. Native warriors, most of them carrying keen-pointed assegais, stayed near their hut doorways refusing to display curiosity at O'Neil, or even Kerry who was perhaps the first white girl they had ever seen.

He walked straight on, erect, the Mauser undrawn but fully in sight, slapping his thigh, his hook arm reflecting the late-morning sun. Here, as in the Telebiste village, the head fetisher was waiting. He was unmasked, skinny, spidery. Barbs of ivory had been thrust through the lobes of his ears, a copper ring was in his nose, tufts of goat hair had been passed through the skin of his chest, and he was tattooed with strange figures resembling prehistoric reptiles. He was naked save for skeins of cowrie shells dangling below his withered belly.

As O'Neil approached the man, a special guard of assegai experts emerged from one of the huts and ranged themselves to stop him at a distance of a dozen paces.

O'Neil made the Shari sign of "friend," but the fetisher made no move to order his guardsmen back. O'Neil swung his hook, smashing the closest assegais to one side. He expected them to retreat and let him through, but instead their leader made a darting movement with his spear and its point burned like a hot wire as it snagged flesh beneath O'Neil's arm, pinning him.

"Abba-ta!" he was given the command to halt.

"Sure." O'Neil stood poker faced, the point still holding, pressed through a ribbon of skin and flesh. He looked over at the fetisher. "Tell your swine to take his assegai back before I sink my hook through his skull! Is this the way you treat one who comes in friendship?"

The fetisher signaled, and the guardsman reluctantly withdrew the point of his assegai.

"Speak! Why do you come?"

"I look for Mokwandu."

The fetisher exhaled. The sound was like wind across dry leaves. He was smiling a trifle, showing black, file-pointed teeth. "We have expected you. *You,* the *bonde,* who would come back to see Mokwandu. Come then and I will show Mokwandu to you."

THE FETISHER walked up the hard-packed pathway. A row of spring-poles were set in the ground and each was bowed over, supporting portions of a skeleton—generally the skull, spinal column, and rib case, pelvis and legs, but neither arms nor feet. The bones had been drilled near the joints and tied together by twisted goat's hair. He paused at the closest one, a skeleton still an unbleached yellow, grabbed the spine and gave it a jerk which sent it off on a wild dance at the end of the bowed-over spring-pole.

"Mokwandu!" he hissed at O'Neil. "Speak to Mokwandu. Mokwandu, who was friend of *bonde.* Friend of white man. Mokwandu the traitor who would sell to white man the tracks of the fetish!" Then the fetisher turned to his guardsmen, uttered a sharp command. It was an order to take O'Neil prisoner.

O'Neil instinctively reached for his Mauser. A heavy-pointed assegai struck him aside the head. He was down in the reddish dust. It took a while for the buzzing to leave his ears. He sat up. His Mauser was gone. One of the blacks was looking at it, turning it in his hand. He saw Kerry Keane held by two guardsmen. She was twisting back and forth, teeth set, sobbing from the futility of her effort.

O'Neil made it to his feet. He groped for support. Assegai points surrounded him, aimed at his heart.

A man laughed. A white man. He spun around and saw the Hammer walking towards him. The hook-nosed Moor, LecKurti lurked in the shadowed doorway of the fetish hut, watching.

"So, you got here at last. What the hell, O'Neil?—you used to be a fast traveler. But of course you brought the girl. For me, I suppose. It's good to have friends in this country. But I never expected you to be this kind to poor, lonely Runkhammer."

He was speaking to O'Neil, but all the while he walked toward Kerry Keane. She'd stopped struggling against her black captors. The Hammer stood over her for a few seconds, then he reached to pinch her chin between thumb and forefinger. She twisted aside and he laughed.

"Ho! You are the spitfire yet. Like that time in the rest house. I treated you like a lady then. I only tied you up and left you. But now you have followed me here. To this jungle." He thrust his face down, close to hers. "Know what that means? No gendarmes here. Only the law of fang and claw. Here the strong man takes what he wants. Maybe you're what I want."

Thorns had torn her brown shirt in many places. He reached, seized a bit of the frayed material, ripped it free revealing her shoulder. O'Neil smashed assegais aside with his hook, and before the guards could stop him he'd covered the distance. Runkhammer whirled to face him. He saw the hook start for his head and tossed up a forearm to catch it. The hook cut the flesh of his arm just above the elbow. He howled and fell back a step, dragging at his Luger pistol. Assegai-men rushed O'Neil, hauled him back, two of them on each arm. The Hammer followed, balancing the Luger in his hand. He swung the barrel to O'Neil's head.

It struck, and things spun across his eyes. He'd have fallen but the guards still held him. The gun struck again and again, driving him ever deeper into the black chasm of unconsciousness.

HE CAME to with pain like a white-hot iron in his head and neck. He was aware that considerable time had passed. He forced himself to a sitting position. Bobolongonga's voice was close—

"Aye-aye-Allah! Behold this hook-armed *bondele* and the potful of trouble he hath dragged me into. Hear me, *Allah!* Free me from the prison of the unbelievers and I will return repentant on hands and knees asking forgiveness of my two wives in Katanga."

O'Neil cursed him. His tongue seemed rough and thick. His hair was stiff, matted with drying blood. Sight was returning to him. They'd locked him in a hut, or rather a stockade of pointed hardwood posts with a frame of palm mats laid over the top for shade. Sun slatted through, falling bright yellow on the thatch-strewn ground. The air was oppressive with heat and the fly-drone of midday. No drums. Occasionally he could hear the rattle of leg bracelets as a guard walked outside.

"How long have I been here?" O'Neil asked.

"Perhaps for one white man's hour."

"What did they do with her—Kerry?"

"In another prison room, Master."

There was no water, and O'Neil's thirst became more intense as the hours of afternoon passed. Finally, a scrawny arm bearing slave brands appeared beneath the door and thrust a couple of halved papaya inside. They were ripe and watery. Eating one quenched his thirst. Twilight came, and with it the thud of voodoo drums, an odor of fires. He'd dozed off and was awakened by sound of the door being unbarred.

He sat up and saw Runkhammer grinning down at him.

"No hard feelings, O'Neil?"

O'Neil called him a suitable name and asked what he wanted.

"Now, chappie-boy! White men and all that, what-ho?" After thus reaffirming his identity as an Englishman, he paused just inside the door, right hand near the butt of his Luger. "I got no reason to love you, O'Neil, and after that business in Mozambique, but I'm a forgivin' chap. Aye, that I am, or I'd have caved your skull in out there this morning."

"What do you want?" O'Neil growled.

"Well, maybe I *do* want something. I'd like to help myself, along with you, and the girl, and your whole damned safari. You're all in a bit of a tight spot, you know, with these black fellows sharpening their meat hooks—"

"What do you want?"

"Just what you think." He lowered to his heels, hand still near the Luger. "I got that damned portmanteau in Brazzaville, but what with the gendarmes and this and

that I didn't have too much time to search it. Now, in it was a box of blue clay, and I've been a bit curious about it. Mokwandu wouldn't tell, and maybe I was a bit too quick with a stranglehold—"

"You killed Mokwandu!"

"I started it, and the black boys finished it. I'll admit maybe it was a mistake." He narrowed his eyes. "Oh come, now, chappie! Don't try to fool old Runkhammer. You know what the blue clay was about, and things being what they are you'd better tell. I'm friend-*bondele* here, you know, and you're just *Monsieur* Camel-dung as far as they're concerned. So you better dance my step." His eyes were intent on O'Neil's. "Now tell me all about the blue clay, chappie."

O'Neil thought it over. He let a laugh jerk his shoulders. "Sure. I'm in no shape to argue. You got here first, and you did all right. As for the blue clay—haven't you ever seen *blue ground* before?"

The implication of O'Neil's words slowly registered. "You mean there's *diamonds* in it?"

"You've been in Kimberley, haven't you?"

"But there was nothing—"

"There was before Doc Keane screened them out."

It was not a good lie. It was just the best one that O'Neil could manufacture at the moment. Actually, the stuff bore little resemblance to the blue ground that held the diamonds of Kimberley.

"Where did it come from?" The Hammer asked.

"Think I'd be fool enough to tell you that? Get me out of here, Runkhammer. Me, and Bobo, and the girl. We'll lead you to it."

Runkhammer made a violent gesture, spat. "You liar! That stuff is nothing but dried swamp earth. You took out whatever Doctor McCrady had, and substituted that worthless clay. Tell me what was in the box—*when you got it from Hein?"*

"Just what you found."

The Hammer's face became flushed and the veins stood out at his temples. He started to lunge forward, stopped himself.

"So you'd rather not tell me. You'd rather let the girl die. She along with the rest of you. You know how they do with a long-haired one, these Gorahs? They bend a sapling over and tie it to their hair. It half lifts them off the ground, that sapling. *Half* lifts them, O'Neil. But *just her head* won't keep that sapling bowed over. Not after the fetisher gets busy with his machete." He crouched forward and spoke in a raw whisper. "It's something to watch, that machete dance.

There she'll be with the sapling tied to her hair and her white throat stretched out and there'll be that fetisher capering around with his machete, making a swing a minute, and nobody ever knowing which one it'll be that does the business. Not even the fetisher. It's something to watch, O'Neil. Something to wait for—that machete swing that'll turn the sapling loose with the head atop it, switching around forty feet high—"

O'Neil lunged at him. Runkhammer roared laughter.

"Maybe you'll talk when that machete dance starts, O'Neil. But it'll be too late. Too late to do anything."

He was outside with assegai-men blocking O'Neil's way. They rammed the door shut. O'Neil crouched, peered through timbers....

Chapter 9

THERE WAS another prison but fifty or sixty paces away. Something was doing over there. Natives kept passing, blocking his view. A dance had started. Sound of the chanting came to his ears—weird, rising and falling, keeping time with the drums. Jungle darkness was settling swiftly. They were leading someone from the hut. It was still a moment before he caught her silhouette against one of the fires, but he already knew it was the girl, Kerry Keane.

O'Neil was long accustomed to the savagery of the jungle, but Runkhammer's description of the machete dance was still in his mind, and the thought of Kerry Keane being its victim made nausea spread through him. He cursed and hurled his shoulder against the door. Assegai-men laughed and jabbered outside. One of them, still laughing, spat a stream of betel at him through the crack.

More guardsmen were coming. O'Neil could hear a conversation outside. Then the door opened. A massive fellow, unusual for a Shari, stood looking at him. He was evidently some sort of a chief, for his body was almost covered by copper bracelets and ivory beads. He pointed to O'Neil and Bobolongonga, signaled to bring them out.

A shout went up at sight of O'Neil. Natives with oiled bodies danced around the fire. Movement and shifting firelight mixed with the heavy boom of the drums gave the scene a nightmare quality.

He turned then and saw her.

She was tied, wrists to ankles. It prevented her standing, but a hardwood springpole had been set in the ground a dozen strides behind her and bowed far over, its top fastened to her hair, and the power of it lifted her partly from the ground, stretched her neck full length, revealed her soft throat to the fire.

The guardsmen backed O'Neil and Bobolongonga to some carved spirit-posts and bound them there, arms behind them, tight to the posts.

Bobolongonga kept chanting to himself—the Arab words of prayer. Minutes passed as the drums increased their tempo. A brass gong sounded. It was a signal, and eight hooded figures emerged from the fetish hut.

All except one of them crouched near the fire, bending to the dance rhythm. The other kept moving with little, scraping steps, swinging the raffia-leaf robe that covered him from hood to feet.

He kept going until a scant three steps separated him from the girl. Then he whipped a long machete from beneath the raffia robe, flourished it, the blade flashing firelight, and swung it in a horizontal arc at the girl's throat.

O'Neil steadied himself, forced himself to think calmly. His arms were bound—or rather, his arm and the hook. He might pull the stump of his left arm free, but it would gain him nothing. He moved the hook up and down. Fungus had long ago pitted the steel. It worked like a rude file. One of the thongs parted. Feel of it brought sudden elation. Other thongs still held, but if one could be cut, all of them could.

An assegai-man was looking at him. He stopped, The assegai-man took a step towards him. O'Neil looked straight ahead. Something was going on near the largest fetish hut. Its huge, side doors were king dragged open.

The assegai-man turned with the others to watch. O'Neil was poker-faced, but he could feel the trickle of perspiration down his cheek.

SOME HUGE thing was dragging itself from the door. It resembled a gigantic salamander. It was twelve or fourteen feet high at the shoulders, it had short front legs, a serpentlike neck, a tiny head. From the open, fanged mouth, smoke emerged.

Drums were at a frenzy. Warriors danced themselves into a wild hypnotism. It came closer, and the fire reflected from it. Its scaly side was a greenish-brownish hue, its belly the color of a python's. It seemed impossible that a group of natives in this unfrequented hole of the black continent could have conceived and constructed such a thing.

After covering half the distance across the dancing area the thing wheeled itself around, ponderously but with excellent synchronization. There must have been at least four men inside, furnishing locomotion and operating the fire that fed smoke to its mouth, but they moved as though controlled by a single set of nerves.

It went toward Kerry, lowered its head, and for a second she was almost obscured by the smoke from its mouth and nostrils. Then it turned and made its way toward O'Neil.

All eyes were on the monster now. O'Neil sawed with his hook and felt the thongs part one after another.

He waited. It seemed to take a long time for the monster to get there. Its head slowly bent. O'Neil, knowing he could break free, forced himself to a rigid posture. The smoke poured over him. It was heavy with the stench of burning hair. He set himself, then twisted, lunged forward.

He was free. The men operating the creature tried to get the head up. His hook arm swung. It ripped through gum-cured skin. He jerked it forward and over to the ground.

Men were screaming inside, trying to extricate themselves. There were crashing, ripping sounds as the hollow monster collapsed. The skin was hardened with gum, stretched over an intricate frame of bamboo. The firepot inside it had spilled. The skin caught and blazed as though dipped in kerosene. Guardsmen, terrified, trampled over one another.

O'Neil spun, located Bobolongonga. He was rocking the post but still captive.

Three or four of the guards were converging. One drove his assegai. O'Neil hooked it from his way. It flipped free of the man's hand. O'Neil seized it, smashed another native from his way, reached Bobolongonga's side. He swung the assegai, using its head like an axe, cutting him free.

The monster was now a mass of flame. Its heat drove other guardsmen back. A pot of burning pitch had rolled to the ground. It was part of the mechanism that supplied smoke to the monster's mouth. O'Neil snatched it up, hurled it. It made a high, flaming arc and spilled fire across the thatch roof of the fetish house.

There had been no rain for twenty-four hours, and the thatch had been dried by sun until it was almost explosive. In seconds it became a gigantic torch.

Natives stampeded to escape the blinding intensity of the heat. For the moment there was no one near the girl. Then, apparently from nowhere, the head fetisher dashed into sight.

The machete was in his hand. O'Neil shouted at him. He ran, but the distance was too great. No chance of heading the fetisher off. O'Neil set himself, hurled the assegai.

IT WAS long range. A man had to be lucky. The fellow's machete was high, the girl's throat white in firelight. The assegai arched down and smashed its heavy copper head through the bony box of his chest, went on taking the shaft with it. The fetisher dropped his machete and clawed. He went on over backward, the assegai point sticking in earth. For a second he was still up, propped by the assegai, then he slid down its smooth shaft and was lifeless on the hard-hammered ground.

The fetish hut seemed to explode at the same instant. Big thatch houses often do that when explosive gasses get trapped inside. The air was filled with flying fragments of burning wood. O'Neil ran on, blinded, hunting his way.

He ran into someone. Bobolongonga.

"You have her?"

"No, *bwana.*"

He kept going. Through dark and smoke the skeleton forms of blazing huts kept looming before him.

He had no real memory of finding his way from the village. He seemed to have been walking in a dream, and then suddenly awakened. Bobolongonga was still beside him. He stopped.

"We have to go back. Kerry—"

"This way, *bwana.* I strangled it out of an Unbeliever, a native. He took her this way, *bwana.* That swine, Runkhammer, and that slave of a swine, LecKurti."

Strength flowed quickly through O'Neil's body once the raw smoke and heat of the burning village were behind. He ran. A black shouted to him in the Mengbattu tongue. It was one of the boys from his safari. There were others. They'd find their way all right. He left them behind, found the black shadow of the jungle footpath.

He could see nothing, but that did not force him to slow his pace. He guided himself by instinct—or by the slight echo that his movements made, echoing from treetrunks and deadfalls.

A sound like a woman's scream came to his ears. He couldn't be sure. He kept going. Fatigue was like opium spreading through his muscles.

Bobolongonga wheezed behind him, *"Bwana,* stop—"

He cursed the big black through his teeth, thinking he was going to quit. The next second he'd plunged knee-deep into swamp water. The canoe dock was there. Through a rift in the jungle a shaft of moonlight picked out the Gorah design on one of the boats.

"The canoe, *bwana!"* Bobolongonga said.

He seized one of them, dragged it through mud to the water. The swamp poured like a geyser through a hole that been chopped in its bottom. They looked at others. Runkhammer had gotten here first.

Chapter 10

BOBOLONGONGA COMMENCED stuffing a hole with the rags of his kuftan. "No use," O'Neil said. "We'll have to take it on foot."

"In darkness, with mire thirty feet deep—"

O'Neil was already gone. He waded, found the narrow strip of land they'd followed in approaching the village that morning. It seemed different by night. He drove on, alternately knee-deep in muck, ripped by jungle. He heard a splashing sound—the sound of paddles. At his right, through a veil of parasitic vines.

There were some narrows here, but farther on the swamp would widen and split into a maze of arms. It was his final chance.

He tore through the vines. They were twisted like serpents, thick as his arm. He clambered, balanced, went on. He was in the open with water beneath. Water, and the shadow movement of a canoe.

A huge *swamp-bokongu* stood nearby. He took off his boots, climbed the trunk, clinging with toes and fingers, repeatedly driving his hook, pulling himself with it.

It was easier going after the first branches. He climbed higher and higher to the *bokongu's* remote top.

Wind was blowing there. He had an impression of the roof of the jungle, rolling away in successive billows, its green looking grayish by moonlight.

He caught a vine with his hook, sprang into the abyss, swung, crashed amid branches and vines of a second tree. He twisted his hook loose and grabbed for support. Found a branch. Wide projecting, thick as his thigh. He climbed out on it. He was far over the water, and there was movement—the canoe, almost directly below.

He leaped. For a second he seemed poised in mid-air with air rushing around him. Then the water sprang toward him. He struck, went deep, popped up with the side of the canoe striking his shoulder.

He swung his hook. It sank in soft, silk-cotton wood. He pulled himself up, sprawled over the side.

LecKurti was there. The rangy, hook-nosed Moor. A rifle was in his hands. O'Neil drove upward from his crouched position, hooked the gun from his hands. It spun, caught a flash of moonlight, splashed and disappeared. The canoe pitched, making LecKurti lose balance. He backpedaled, tripped over Kerry's prone form, and collided with the Hammer.

The Hammer's gun was drawn. It exploded as LecKurti rammed him. The bullet smashed LecKurti through the middle of his belly. He gasped and doubled over, turned, pitched, over the edge. He was threshing water….

The Hammer tried to bring his gun around but O'Neil had covered the distance. He chopped with his hook and the gun splashed to the bilge water in the canoe's bottom.

THE COLLECTION OF
HARDEN BAYLE
BERTON E. COOK

FOR A second they faced each other, standing in the swaying canoe. The Hammer swung a massive, right-hand blow.

It was not a punch—rather a sweep designed to send O'Neil flying from the canoe.

O'Neil parried it and smashed a right of his own.

He'd have followed with the hook, but the Hammer expected it. He seized the hook arm, twisted it behind O'Neil in a hammerlock.

The man was far heavier, taller than O'Neil, and now he was in position to make weight and height count. He braced his legs to the sides of the canoe, reared straight, dragging the hook with him. It was as though O'Neil's shoulder bone were being torn from flesh.

The Hammer was poised there, above. Then he hurled himself down with crushing force.

O'Neil had already sensed his purpose He moved at the last possible instant—not back, as Runkhammer had expected, but forward, beneath. It made the hammerlock slip free. He was under, Runkhammer high above. He could have thrown him overboard. Instead he turned and drove him head down to the canoe bottom.

It would have killed a lesser man. The Hammer had brute bone and brain that was practically impervious to shock.

He was down only half a second. He rolled, came to one knee. His hands roved the bottom, closed on a waterlogged paddle. He came, massive and powerful as a gorilla, and the paddle was a club in his hands.

O'Neil's closeness saved him. He took the shock of it across arm, and shoulder, and the side of his head. His hook swung up and around, smashing the Hammer's skull.

The Hammer was standing, but stunned by the hook. He reeled back. The paddle was still in his hands. He swung it back, braced himself, legs wide, and drove like one swinging a sledge.

O'Neil was inside as the swing started. His hook came up, the point sank itself through skin and flesh beneath Runkhammer's jaw bone. The paddle dropped from Runkhammer's hands. He tore at the hook, writhing like some great fish brought to gaff. O'Neil set himself, twisted, bent double. The hook dragged Runkhammer off his feet, sent him belly foremost to the water.

He splashed, sank. He came up threshing. He was shoulder-deep. O'Neil expected him to come ploughing back. He didn't. Fear had at last taken form in his brain.

He turned, waded, swam. His strength was not like the ordinary man's. Weeds tangled him. He kept going in spite of them. But the water became deeper, the weeds like a huge net. In the dark, O'Neil could hear his threshing movements for a long time. At last there was silence. The Hammer was done for.

No sign of LecKurti. Even without that bullet in his guts he'd have had little enough chance in the dark swamp.

O'Neil turned, looked at Kerry Keane. She was conscious, staring at him. Her hands and feet were tied. He had no machete, and it took several minutes to untie the knots. Bobolongonga was shouting his name from the jungle shore.

"Here!" growled O'Neil.

"Aye-aye-Allah! Praise thy golden city that my *bwana* lives!"

Bobolongonga waded and swam to the canoe, climbed over the side.

For a while they were content to rest. Later, O'Neil discovered Runkhammer's duffle bag, opened it and found a supply of clothing and tinned bully beef. They ate, tapped a milkvine for drinking water. About midnight they set out, Bobolongonga in the stern, swinging a paddle, guiding the canoe in a winding course through swamp channels. O'Neil sat amidships. Kerry was asleep beside him.

As though by accident, her head had fallen on his chest. O'Neil did not stir for fear of waking her.

He looked at her face revealed by reflected moonlight. She was twenty, and he was getting toward the repentant side of thirty-five; she was young and fresh with a decent life ahead of her, while O'Neil was only a jungle tramp. There was only one thing for him to do. He'd take her to Brazzaville and leave her. Then he'd come back with a safari of fighting men. Some of those Niams. There's nothing as tough as a Niam with a machete-sword in his sash and a Magnum rifle in his hands. Yes, he'd say good-bye to her and come back, to this swamp, to the big thing Doc McCrady had run onto. Because now O'Neil knew what it was. Now he knew the meaning of that box of clay. He'd suspected ever since the head fetisher told him that Mokwandu had been killed for selling the "tracks of the fetish." And he'd been certain after seeing that reconstructed monster.

MOKWANDU HAD led Dr. McCrady to the swamp and showed him the footprints of one of the monsters pressed in clay. McCrady had waited for the clay to dry, and had lifted the print, after the manner of geologists preserving any fossil, and had packed it in a specimen box. River dampness had later caused it to crumble and become nothing but the meaningless blue clay that other men had wondered about.

So that was the way of it, and O'Neil was the only white man left in all creation that knew the secret.

So he'd be back. One of those monsters would be worth a fortune on the outside. Or even the skin of one! O'Neil could almost feel the money, the thick sheafs of currency, the musty, green smell of it. He could imagine himself in a siesta chair with the white waves of Miami brushing the sand at his feet, or at Monte Carlo listening to the click-click of an ivory ball. And through it all, in his dreaming, Kerry Keane was beside him.

Bobolongonga had stopped to rest. For a while he was hunched over, head between his knees, asleep. Dawn sent streaks of light through parasitic vines. O'Neil noticed that Kerry's eyes were open. He expected her to move away when she discovered that her head was on his chest, but instead she wriggled closer, smiling.

"You *do* care for me!" she whispered.

"Sure."

O'Neil knew how it was with her. He wasn't fooling himself. It was one thing here, in this jungle, with her needing him, and quite another thing when they were safely to civilization.

She went back to sleep, and O'Neil closed his own eyes. He imagined it was not now, but twelve or thirteen years ago, before the tropics with its malaria and quinine and bad cognac had taken him down the one-way skids; imagined he was young, like her, and the world was breaking, like the dawn, in flames of red, yellow and violet before him.

Bobolongonga awoke. He blinked, saw the man and woman, and a grin spread across his vast countenance.

"Praise thy green turban he has found her, O *Allah!*" he said, facing east with the Moslem salute. "Praise thy glory that thou hast sent a wife for my *bwana's* tent at last. And now perhaps will his heart of stone see the justice of my plea for back wages. Now will he have pity on me, his faithful servant. For is not my longing twice as great as his, O Allah, having not *one,* but *two* wives waiting in Katanga?" ◣◥

THE WHITE PERIL

by Frederick Nebel

D STRYKER drew up before his spruce log trapping shack as the swift Labrador night was closing in. He unstrapped his oval-shaped rackets, pushed open the door and booted it shut behind him. Little icicles hung at the corners of his wide mouth, and frozen ridges of rheum were under his eyes. For it was November, and the long cold had come to stay.

"Hello there, Keepee, old scout," he called to a tall Indian who stood by the sheet-iron stove, mixing fresh bannocks.

Keepee, which is Cree for "make haste," said, without looking up, " 'Lo."

Stryker, a whale of a man, shrugged out of his deerskin *koolutik* and hung it on a peg near the stove. They were not Labrador men, these two; their native habitat was many miles westward, beyond Hudson Bay, way over in the Saskatchewan River country. But furs run mighty fast along the Koksoak, and the Barren Lands produce no finer black foxes. Stryker, an Old Company "freeman," had seen wealth in the Labrador while still with the Company, and when he resigned he had persuaded Keepee, an old friend, to join him and try their luck there.

He was saying: "Say, Keepee, there's a blackie snooping around that deadfall you made. Bet we'll nab him before the week's out. Three prime marten today and a beauty silver. Some running, eh?"

"Um."

Stryker bathed his face with snow while the Indian set out the supper. The cabin was small, barely clearing Stryker's head. It was patched with earth and moss, which subsequently had been treated with water, so that a layer of ice covered it and checked the bitter winds that were always howling down from Ungava Bay.

Stryker was just about to sit down to a steaming meal when the door whipped open and a fur-swathed man pitched to the floor, clawing at the boards. Keepee closed the door. Stryker bent down and turned the man over, and gave a little gasp when he saw the stranger was white. There are not many white men in the Labrador wilds.

"That brandy!" snapped Stryker, at the same time tearing open the man's furs.

Keepee brought a black bottle from the larder and put it to the man's lips. Stryker went outside and came back with an armful of snow, bathed the man's feet and hands and face. The nose was in critical condition, and he pressed it in his cold hand instead of using snow, for at a certain state of frost-bite snow will tear the skin.

The man began to mutter unintelligible things. He stirred; his hands writhed. His red-rimmed eyes opened, and in them was an appeal that beckoned Stryker to lean closer.

"Letter… pocket… Kuglictuk… go… life depends… name o' God…."

A rattle choked the words in his throat. His eyes glared for a moment, then became glazed and expressionless. A sigh fluttered from his blackened lips. Then he lay very still.

STRYKER ROSE, a little awed, then bowed his head for a brief moment. After which he bent down again and rummaged in the dead man's pockets. He found a little note-book, a sort of diary, bearing the name, "Harry P. Kavanagh." He scanned the entries made under various dates, from which he learned that a certain sloop had put out from Fort Churchill in hopes of making Whale River Post before the freeze-up. Things had gone wrong. The sloop had been wrecked by floe ice. The writer claimed to be the only survivor. He didn't know the country. He was without food.

"I guess that about tells the story," muttered Stryker grimly. "Now he said something about a letter and a life and for me to go some place. Let's see. Oh, yes! Kuglictuk, he said. That's a river."

After further searching he found an envelope bearing one word—"Jack." He paused before breaking the seal, then finally tore it open and read:

"Dear Jack:

Everything is all right. The beast disappeared into the Barrens almost a year ago, and no one has seen him since. I am count-ing the days till I see you. Harry was always a good boy, and he volunteered to go and find you, and both our hearts are broken while you are away...."

There were two pages of maternal sentiment, written in fine script, and signed, "Mother."

Stryker folded them after two perusals and sat down to think. There were two roads open to him. He could disregard the letter, continue with his trap-lines and bury the late Harry P. Kavanagh when the spring thaw came. On the other hand, he could take his dog-team, mush to Fort Chimo and then start east for the white, barren tundra that lies between there and the Kuglictuk River. If he chose the latter he would face death and starvation, and after it all was over he would return to the Saskatchewan with empty pockets.

A man named Jack was apparently in hiding. It is bad for a white man to stay in the Labrador alone. And Ed Stryker was of the brotherhood of the wilds. So he said to Keepee:

"Old scout, I'm pulling out to-morrow. Got a little job. You go right ahead with the trapping and make yourself rich. I may get back to nab a few more furs and I may not. When you got all the furs you want leg it to Chimo and I'll meet you there when it's over. I'll have to take the team, but I'll leave most of the provisions with you and stock up at the Post. You can have my traps, too. I don't know what this letter's all about, but this chum who just died tried to tell me to carry on, and I'm obliging him."

Keepee, having finished his meal despite the newly dead, mumbled:

"Want me help? Me go dam' quick, betcha."

"No, Keepee. I know you're a good sort. But this is a whim of mine. I brought you over here and I want to see you get something out of it. Maybe I'll try next year; maybe, as I said, I'll get back in time to run the traps again. Anyhow, I'm going, for some chum's struck a streak of bad luck and I'm going to lend a hand."

Keepee understood his white companion, and he pressed the subject no further.

In the morning, when it was still dark, they drove the six wolf-dogs out of the lean-to in the rear and then brought out the twelve-foot *komatik,* a sturdy Eskimo sled which Stryker had purchased at Fort Chimo. Quickly it was loaded with grub, blankets and sealskin robes, and some blackies which Stryker intended to sell at the Post. Then they shook hands, the white man and the red, and their hearts were in their palms.

"Luck, Ed," murmured the Indian, then waved his hand skyward. *"Kisse-Manito* watch um."

"Thanks, Keepee. I'll see you later at Chimo."

"At Chimo. Good."

The thirty-five-foot walrus-hide whip snaked out and ended with a sharp report, and the big wolf-dogs lunged ahead, passed through a growth of stunted larch and tamarack and then struck the Koksoak River, heading north.

Chapter 2

THEY FOUND good going down the Koksoak. The dogs were in fine fettle, and Stryker reeled off fifty miles the first day. At dusk of the second, when a cold moon hung over the frozen world, Stryker trotted into Fort Chimo at the head of his outfit and went directly to the H.B.C. store.

Flemming, the acting factor, looked up from a copy of "Pil-grim's Progress" and said:

"Hello, Stryker. What brings you up here already? Thought you were holed up for the winter."

They shook.

"Strange things happen," laughed Stryker. "Chap blew into my shack and cashed in. Had a letter on him. Asked me to find somebody named Jack."

Briefly he related the whole affair, showed Flemming the letter and asked for a guide.

"A guide?" echoed the factor. "I wish I could, but every Indian and husky's off to the traps. Seems you've struck bad luck to begin with. Why not take a run over to Revillon's?"

"H'm. Might as well try. Thanks. See you again."

Monsieur De Loge, the agent at the Revillon Freres Post, was a genial man. He said after Stryker had given him details:

"Ah, *m'sieu,* I should lak to help you ver' much, but you will see by glancing about dat no one ees here. It ees a bad time, dis, to secure guides. De traps, you know. Meantime, howevaire, you will be my guest? De table is ready."

After a splendid meal with monsieur *le facteur* Stryker went out to a clump of scrub spruce and fed his dogs. He had suspected all along that a guide would be unavailable, and now that the fact was thrust upon him he was a little undecided just what to do. He knew very little about the Ungava, and for a stranger to get stranded in the white peril of snow and ice and low temperatures, is suicide.

He went back to the French post. A lone Eskimo had just arrived from the east, and on his *komatik* was a dog that had been unable to stand the toil of trail and trace. The Eskimo's dark face glistened with a layer of ice, and his sealskin *netsek* was caked with hoar frost.

De Loge greeted him.

"Ah, Chevik, a bad trail, *oui?*"

Chevik grunted and threw open his skins.

"Chevik, me frien'," proceeded De Loge. "M'sieu Stryker, here, desires a guide to de Kuglictuk. It ees a mission of great importance. *M'sieu* desires to find some one by de name of Jack, who is white."

Chevik's eyes narrowed. He shot a quick look at Stryker, then at De Loge. Then he stuffed his pipe and moved away toward the stove.

"Say, Chevik, what do you say about that?" called Stryker. "Good pay, Chevik."

Chevik, holding a match to his pipe, looked up and straight into Stryker's eyes. Stryker saw hatred in that gaze. The whole face, with its pulpy mouth, its slanting forehead and flat nose, emanated danger. With a faint sneer, Chevik continued to light his pipe, then drew his skins about him and went outside.

"Now what do you know about that!" exclaimed Stryker softly.

De Loge said:

"He would be a good guide, too. Speaks ver' good English, unlak de Eskimo. A great fighter, *m'sieu,* and marvelous wit' de knife. Hence his name, Chevik, which means de knife. Ah—he dislaks you, howevaire."

"That's putting it mild," laughed Stryker. "He *hates* me. Why, I don't know."

Flemming managed to find sleeping quarters for him that night in a cabin that was also shared by one of the assistants. He was worn out from the day's hard traveling, and he turned in early. But he lay awake a long time, figuring things out, and before he finally closed his eyes he had decided that, guide or no guide, he would leave next day for the Kuglictuk.

He awoke some minutes later to find a dark, fur-swathed form standing in the doorway. For a long moment the stranger did not move, but Stryker felt that a pair of eyes were regarding him, despite the thick gloom. Cautiously he slipped his hand toward the stool beside his bed, where lay his belt and revolver.

Then the stranger moved. Instinctively Stryker dodged to one side. A knife whizzed across the room, grazed his cheek and stuck in the wall behind his head. With that he dived for his revolver, but the door slammed shut and the stranger was gone. Gun in hand, Stryker jumped to the door, hurled it open and swung his gun low for immediate action. But only a sharp wind and the cold night sky greeted him, and farther away the yellow square of light that marked the H.B.C. store. He thought of dressing and going over to tell Flemming and his assistant, but changed his mind.

In the morning he said nothing about the attack. He went over to see the agent at Revillon's and discovered that Chevik had departed more than two hours before. Stryker was almost positive that it was Chevik who had thrown the knife, and he felt that he would cross Chevik's trail before long.

WHEN HE announced his intention of proceeding alone Flemming threw up his hands. De Loge, a bit of a humorist, wanted to know what kind of flowers should be put on the grave. But between them they mapped out a course and gave him hints on the country, for they were wise in the ways of the Labrador.

Daylight was almost complete when, his *komatik* loaded with a month's provisions, he pulled out of Fort Chimo. As he put the Koksoak farther and farther behind him the timber died away, until finally nothing but bare, ragged hills swept away toward the horizon and the frosty air hung like gauze all about him. It was the land of *Torngak,* the Death Spirit of the Eskimo; but Stryker was entering it unafraid.

That night he took some wood from his *komatik,* built a little fire, ate bannock, pork, and beans cooked in seal oil. He cut blocks of snow and raised a snow wall against the wind. He went to sleep huddled in his blankets and robes. Some time after midnight he was startled awake by a big form that was bending over him. With a sharp oath he tried to heave himself up; but a mittened hand smashed him between the eyes, and things spun around and then went black.

When he awoke he was sitting against his *komatik.* On the other side of the fire sat Chevik, the Knife, regarding him impassively, with a rifle resting across his knee.

"Don't move," grunted the Eskimo. Stryker was cramming tobacco into his pipe.

"What's the idea of the big grudge you've got against me, Chevik? I'd like to be your friend."

Chevik sneered. "Me your en'my. Me kill you—you don't go back Chimo."

"You will, eh? Well, let me tell you something, Chevik, I'm bound for the Kuglictuk. See? I'm turning back for no damned husky, either. The factor at Chimo knows I'm over this way, and De Loge saw that look you gave me. If I don't get back he'll tell the Mounties, and he'll tell 'em about you."

Chevik frowned darkly and nursed his pipe.

"Me kill," he muttered thickly. Stryker got up. Chevik rose also, his gun still leveled, his eyes beady. They locked gazes. Then Stryker, shrugging his shoulders, bent down by the fire, looking for a fagot with which to light his pipe—or so it seemed. He pulled out a flaming stick of tamarack, held it to his pipe, then with a rapid movement flipped it up so that it struck Chevik across the forehead.

Snarling, the Eskimo hurtled backward. At the same time his gun boomed and the shot buzzed over Stryker's head. But Stryker cleared the fire in a mighty leap and bore Chevik down upon the snow. The Eskimo lost his gun in the mix-up and met Stryker with his short, powerful arms. Still locked, they struggled to their feet, reeling, staggering about the fire, while the wolf-dogs looked on with eager eyes. For they understood.

In a break Chevik whipped out a short, broad knife, crouched, then dived at Stryker with animal-like ferocity. It was a downward thrust, and it carried all the Eskimo's weight behind it, so that when he missed he toppled over and buried the knife hilt-deep in the frozen snow. With a mad little laugh Stryker was upon him and lifted him up with such force that he ripped away the stout hide collar. His next blow caught Chevik on the Adam's apple and he jack-knifed to the snow and writhed, struggling for his breath.

When he tottered to his feet Stryker had a gun on him.

"Where's your outfit?" he snapped.

Chevik nodded toward the gloom sullenly.

"Lead me to it," said Stryker.

Chevik started off and half an hour later brought up before his campfire. Stryker bound him hand and foot, piled more wood on the fire, then said:

"It'll take you about five hours to work loose. The fire'll burn till then. After this don't go fooling around with strangers. Good night."

Chapter 3

AT NOON of the following day Stryker crossed the Whale River a hundred miles south of Whale River Post, one of the loneliest stations in all the Ungava. Chevik had not yet put in an appearance, although this did not cause Stryker to relax his vigilance, which he maintained night and day for the next two days. After passing the Whale and then the Mukalik, he headed northeast and at last came to the headwaters of the Kuglictuk. Flemming and De Loge had given him good instructions, and he knew that without the map they had supplied he would never have reached the river.

Desolation was all about him; stark, naked hills, fading into the cold film that always hangs over the Labrador, with here and there a wind-blown tree, and the frozen waterway winding silently to the distant Ungava Bay.

"It's a hell of a country for a man to live," he said aloud. "I wonder what the devil drove that there Jack fellow up this way."

He made a fire and put up his Eskimo *tupik* (tent), banking it with blocks of ice. Later a high wind worked across the tundra and snow began to drive down, pattering on the *tupik* like buckshot. The dogs crouched down on the lee side of the shelter. The wind became a howling maelstrom, hurling the snow madly before it, so that in short time the fire was beaten out and Stryker huddled deep in his robes.

He drowsed despite the bedlam. He was sound asleep when a man cautiously pulled aside the flap of his tent and looked in, then, satisfied that Stryker was sleeping, bent down and cracked him over the head with the butt of his rifle.

Stryker jerked awake, still able to see.

"Chevik—damn you!" he burst out.

The Eskimo chuckled.

"Me come. Me kill. Not with knife. Not with gun. Me let *Torngek* kill. Take dogs, grub, gun. You starve, freeze."

"You dirty—"

His words were cut short by another blow on the head. He passed out completely. Chevik chuckled, then began to tear down the *tupik*. Then he piled it on the sled along with the robes, lined up the dogs and drove off into the white cloud of the blizzard.

When Stryker came to his face was covered with snow. His shelter was gone. Only one 4-point blanket remained with him, and the awful cold was gnawing into his bones. He struggled to his feet, drawing the blanket about him, cursing deep in his throat. Everything was gone, even his ax, with which he might have built a snow wall. No food, no rifle, no robes—nothing.

"God!" he whispered.

He kept up a brisk pace to prevent his blood from freezing. He kept it up when the storm died and the dim dawn broke bleak and gray and cold, with all around him swells of virgin snow—and nothing more.

He figured he was about fifty miles from the mouth of the Kuglictuk. If he followed it to the sea and then struck west he might by chance strike Whale River Post, which was almost another fifty miles away. But then his snow-shoes were gone! How can a man trek through the Labrador without them?

He cursed the Labrador and every Eskimo in it. And he cursed himself for having penetrated it. He had a little tobacco and a dozen matches. He made a fire and had for breakfast one pipeful of tobacco.

Sinking knee-deep in the fresh snow, he began to follow the river northward. Perhaps that mysterious Jack was holed up somewhere along it. Perhaps he would meet a friendly Indian or Eskimo.

Three hours later, as he topped a barren ridge, he saw far ahead several wisps of smoke rising. His heart missed several beats and he gave a glad little cry. He summoned every bit of strength he possessed, until he rounded a bend in the river and saw on the west bank a settlement of three shacks and several *tupiks*. He tottered up to the largest of the cabins, pushed open the door and rocked in.

SMOKE HUNG heavily in the low room. There was a sheet iron stove in the center, and sitting about this were three men. Two were French *voyageurs,* and the saucy clothes they wore suggested the country west of Hudson Bay. The third man was big and thick-chested, freshly shaven, with a hard jaw and a hard, cold eye.

"Hello," called Stryker. "I'm a stranger over this way. Had a team but some blasted husky banged me over the head and ran off with every thing I had."

The *voyageurs* looked at each other sharply. The big man spat deftly out of the side of his mouth and said:

"Don't say! This is no tourist country anyhow, stranger. What brings you up this way?"

"Do I look like a tourist?" shot back Stryker crisply.

"Well, I didn't mean it that way." He winked at one of his companions. Then: "Sit down. What's the news?" At that moment the door opened and a young woman entered clad in sealskins. Stryker eyed her for a long minute, marveled at the beauty of her dark eyes.

The big man interrupted. "My name's Delevan. What did you say about that husky?"

"Oh, yes," said Stryker, and gave his own name.

The woman passed to the rear of the room. Stryker went on:

"Well, as I said, the fellow robbed me. Didn't like me since he saw me at Fort Chimo. I'm over here looking for some one whose front name is Jack."

The girl gave a little cry. Delevan fixed her with a threatening look. She turned away, trembling, and disappeared behind a curtain which separated part of the cabin.

"Yes, Jack's the name," continued Stryker. "I was running a trapline over on the Koksoak when a chap blew into my shack, gave me a letter, mentioned this river and then died. The name on the letter is Jack; that's all."

"Let's have it," said Delevan.

"I'm sorry, chum, but it's only for Jack."

Delevan glowered. "Oh, you don't say? All right, then. Well, there's no Jack around this camp, so you might as well move on. Who'd you say was the man died?"

"I didn't say, but it was a chap named Kavanagh."

"Kavanagh!" Delevan half rose from the chair, his eyes wide.

A choked sob issued from behind the curtain. Delevan snapped to his feet and went behind. Stryker could not hear what he said, but he noted the low, menacing tone of his voice. Then Delevan came out again, his face a little flushed.

"Stranger, there's a cabin next door you can share with Paul and Rex, here. Show him, Rex," he said to one of the Frenchmen.

A little perplexed at the way things were going, Stryker followed Rex to the little shack. It had but one room; and robes on the floor served for bunks.

"You expect to go on soon, *m'sieu?*" purred Rex, his dark eyes sparkling.

"As soon as I get a guide. I'd like to run up against that husky that swiped my outfit. Crack team that was. I'd break his greasy neck." Rex chuckled liquidly.

"Good luck to you, *m'sieu,*" he said, and sauntered out.

And Stryker did not fail to get the sinister note in his voice.

Chapter 4

REX AND Paul came into the cabin later, and the latter made supper. Stryker, sitting beside the little stove, told himself that both of them bore the earmarks of the devil. Rex was always chuckling, and Paul, as though understanding its meaning, would wink back and then favor Stryker with a wide, ingratiating smile. And Stryker was charged with a desire to get up and knock the fellow for a row of stumps. He bided his time, however, for he felt that he was on a warm trail, that Delevan and his henchmen knew something about Jack, and that the girl would be prevented from telling what she knew.

He tried to stay awake that night. He lay on one side of the stove, while Rex and Paul lay on the other side, and he damned the luck that had left him without a gun. But try as he would, his eyes refused to stay open. He fell into sound slumber.

Later on he awoke with a start and tried to cry out, but found a dirty piece of hide across his mouth. Then a bag was pulled over his head and tied about his neck. Hoarse whispers floated to him. Rough hands picked him up; and then he felt the bitter cold against his body, and he knew he had been carried from the cabin.

Five minutes later his captors halted. More whispers… a brief, rasping argument… silence. He knew that something terrible was going to happen. He struggled frantically. And then he felt himself released. A moment later an icy shock went through his body and his blood seemed to congeal instantly.

He was in the cold waters of the Kuglictuk!

He struck out. His feet touched the river bottom, and he guessed the water was no more than eight feet deep. He sprang up in an attempt to grasp the edge of the hole through which he had been dropped. His head bumped against the ice. He tried again, and this time his frozen hands caught onto the rim of the hole, but his fast dying strength was not sufficient to haul his body clear. With a groan he started to sink again.

Then, magically, he felt himself being drawn up. His body was too numb to sense contact, but he knew that he was clear of the water, that some one was carrying him across the ice. Already his clothing was frozen stiff as a board.

He heard a door slam. He felt a new warmth. Then his clothes were being torn off. Brandy was thrown down his throat. Deft hands were massaging and slapping his purple flesh. He could see nothing. He was in a semi-stupor, and he could only hear; and by and by he began to feel.

Warm, soft Hudson Bay blankets were wrapped around him. He was lying on a pile of robes. His eyes opened, but he saw through a haze. The red stove looked like a big evil eye. Several short, squat figures hovered near him. Another shot of brandy was poured between his lips. Things cleared. He was in a cabin. A round, swarthy face was near his own.

"Better?" a voice inquired.

He squinted, and as his vision became perfect he gave a little start. *The man bending over him, administering to him, was Chevik, the Knife!*

"You!" he choked.

The Eskimo raised a hand in warning. "No noise. You better soon."

An hour later Stryker sat up. His vitality was remarkable, and anyhow a bath in frozen water is not so bad as it often is supposed, provided expert attention is given immediately. He looked around for Chevik. The Eskimo was gone, but another squatted stolidly by the stove.

"Chevik?" asked Stryker.

The Eskimo made signs which Stryker took as indicating that Chevik had gone out and would return shortly. He found his pipe and found some tobacco on the table. Then he searched for the letter and the notebook which had been in an inner pocket. His clothes, hanging by the stove, were still wet, and both letter and book had been removed.

"Delevan's work!" he muttered bitterly.

The door whipped open. Chevik waddled in, regarded Stryker studiously for a moment, then went to the rear of the shack and came back with dry clothes.

"Put on," he said shortly.

"Say, did Delevan and his gang heave me in the river?" Stryker asked.

Chevik nodded.

Stryker proceeded:

"Tell me what it's all about, will you? First you try to kill me, then Delevan tries his luck, and then you come along and save me. Dammit, what makes me so blasted important anyhow? And where does the lady fit in?"

Chevik pointed to the fresh clothes.

"Put on—dam' quick." He went to the door and looked out, then closed it quietly.

"Dam' quick!" he repeated.

While he dressed, Chevik went out. Ten minutes later he re-entered, only to pause in the doorway and jerk his thumb over his shoulder. Stryker followed him outside. His old dog-team was there, and he saw that his *komatik* had been replenished with provisions. Chevik handed him the walrus hide whip.

"Go north," he said. "Turn west mouth river, reach Whale River. Go!"

"What's the idea?"

"Go. Delevan kill."

"Who sent you?"

"White woman."

Stryker thought over this. "What is she here?"

"Delevan's wife."

Stryker spat sharply. "But that letter. Delevan stole a letter from me. I want it."

"Go!"

"Damned if I will! Who the hell does Delevan think he is? I'm going to get that letter. Where's my rifle?"

Chevik pointed to the *komatik*. Stryker snatched up the rifle. Chevik grasped his arm.

"White woman say go. Delevan kill."

Stryker tore the Eskimo's hand away.

"No, Chevik, old chum. I'm indebted to you for saving my life. But I'm looking for somebody, and I've got a hunch this is the end of the trail. I'm going over there to Delevan's cabin and talk cold turkey to that bum. Hands off, Chevik!"

Chapter 5

CHEVIK'S CABIN was only a quarter of a mile from the one in which Stryker first had met Delevan. When he left the Eskimo he trotted briskly along on the hard surface of the snow, topped a rise and then swung down toward the river, where he could see the lighted cabins. He drew up before the large cabin and put his ear to the door. He heard a loud guffaw, then the unmistakable, fiendish chuckle of Rex. He held his rifle tightly, then banged open the door, entered and kicked it shut with his heel.

Delevan and his two henchmen were sitting at the table with a bottle of whiskey between them. Delevan was the first to look up. His face froze. Rex almost toppled over. Paul crushed the glass of whiskey which he was about to raise to his lips. The room was deathly still.

"Not a move!" snapped Stryker. Then: "You, Delevan, out with that letter and book you swiped. Quick! Don't look at me like a damned fool! Show some life!" His voice rang with command.

Delevan, his mouth twitching, fumbled in his shirt pocket and brought out the letter and then the notebook. The two Frenchmen had overcome their momentary paralysis and were now eyeing Stryker craftily. Tension was high in the low room.

Stryker said: "Get up, the three of you. Put your guns on the table and line up against the wall."

Delevan, now sullen with rage, obeyed reluctantly. Rex and Paul followed their chief's example. As they backed against the wall Rex's hand rested lightly on his right hip.

"You, Rex, take that knife out of your sash," lashed out Stryker. "Something tells me you're not going to live long. Out with it!"

With a sneer the Frenchman pulled a knife from his sash and threw it upon the table. As Stryker stepped forward to gather up the letter and book, the curtains in the rear parted and the mystery woman stepped out. There was a big revolver in her hand.

"Back!" she warned Stryker coolly.

With a nasty laugh Delevan, thinking he had the better of the break, lunged toward the table for his knife.

"You too—back. All of you," said the woman.

Delevan snarled, "You brat!"

Stryker said, "What the devil!"

"Back!" warned Delevan's wife.

Perplexed, angry, yet marveling at the girl's cool nerve, Stryker held his peace. She picked up the letter and the book, then smiled across at Stryker.

"You'd better keep your gun on these fellows," she told him.

"But those—they're mine, madam."

Without another word she disappeared behind the curtains. A moment later she came out dressed for the trail. For a brief instant Stryker was undecided whether to detain her or keep his gun on the three others. But that brief instant, the split-second's relaxation, gave Rex time to dive for the table, snatch up his revolver and drop behind it. The next moment his gun blazed. Simultaneously Delevan and Paul jumped for their weapons. Stryker's gun boomed twice wildly. The girl was tugging at his arm.

"Come! Out!" she screamed.

"I'll not let these dirty—"

"Fool! Come!"

SHE HALF-DRAGGED him through the door and began to run off toward Chevik's cabin, yelling for Stryker to follow her. He was taking her advice a little against his will, for he felt that he had more than one score to settle with Delevan and the two Frenchmen. And his blood was up. And he was ripe for anything short of murder.

"I wish you'd let me—" he started to say.

"Never mind. It's only started," panted the girl. "You'll get all the fight you want."

Delevan and his henchmen were already on the trail. Half a dozen huskies came tumbling out of the smaller shacks and took up the pursuit, and the frosty night was shattered with rifle fire and mad oaths.

Stryker and the girl reached the cabin and burst in. Chevik and the other Eskimo were sitting by the stove, half asleep. The door was bolted.

The girl said: "Chevik, Tuktoluk, quick! Big fight!"

The Eskimos grunted, yawned and picked up their rifles. The girl took a handful of shells from her pocket and placed them on the table. Stryker loaded his rifle to capacity. The grimy oil lamp was extinguished, and the heavy table was braced against the door.

The pursuers arrived, and Delevan's voice boomed:

"Open that damned door! Open, d'you hear?"

"Go 'way; you make me laugh," shot back Stryker.

"I do, eh? All right, you pup, you'll laugh the other way when I'm finished with you."

"That's cheap talk, Delevan. Let's see what you can do."

Delevan swore and fired, but the door was of stout spruce and merely absorbed the lead. Then the attackers hurled themselves against it *en masse,* and it shivered but gave no hint of breaking down.

"I want my wife!" bawled Delevan furiously.

"You don't say!" replied the girl. "Try and get me, then." She was cool as ice.

There was a lull. Then there were sounds on the low roof, the crunch of many feet, and after that came the ring of an ax. Stryker stood so close to the girl he could look into her eyes.

"They're going to chop through," he muttered.

"Yes," she said, and let her hand fall upon his arm.

He thrilled.

"But we'll win through," he grated out.

"Yes—we will," she said.

The ax was still pounding away. The roof was straining and snapping. Then the ax stopped, and several men began to jump up and down. The roof strained more and more until finally the middle of it caved in and a deluge of snow and men crashed to the floor. Chevik caught Paul neatly across the back of the neck with a wielded gun and reduced their number by one. But more dropped through and guns and knives were swung with murderous ferocity.

Stryker, having killed one of the attacking Eskimos, swung open the door and led the fight out into the open with the girl beside him. Chevik, his face bleeding, rolled out after them, and close on his heels came Tuktoluk, shooting back as he ran. Delevan's gang, falling over one another, burst out in hot pursuit, their guns flaming, with Delevan himself, a gun in each hand and red murder in his eyes, at the fore.

Stryker reached the settlement of three cabins and drew the girl down with him beside the nearest. Chevik and Tuktoluk rocked up behind him and threw themselves to the snow. The attackers came up over the ridge, and as they swung down toward the cabins Stryker bowled over one of them with two fast shots. Chevik wounded another but did not put him out of the fight.

The attackers drew up and dropped to the snow, taking potshots at the cabins. The Northern Lights grew brighter, flinging their ghostly banners across the white tundra. The attackers, realizing they were too much in the open, retreated and worked away toward the river, but Tuktoluk dropped one of them and the girl's shot made another stagger until a companion helped him along.

Chapter 6

"ABOUT SIX left," observed Stryker.

The girl started to say something; but at that moment a gun was poked in the air, and from it fluttered a piece of white cloth.

Stryker yelled, "Come on up, only one, and have your say!"

It was Rex who came forward over the little ridge that concealed the others, holding the flag of truce before him.

"Well?" snapped Stryker.

"M'sieu," began the man, "we have no desire to murder you. M'sieu Delevan says to let his wife go and call t'ings off. It ees bad policy, *m'sieu,* to steal another man's wife."

Stryker looked at the girl. "Did you hear that? I'm here to help you out. I'm not interfering; but Delevan tried to murder me, and it seems he's none too good to you. I'll fight this thing out as you say. If you go over to him or not, he's got to settle with me for other things."

He paused. He was not a man to mince words. That is why he asked: "Do you love him?"

She shuddered, "No. But I'd better—"

"That's all. You were going to say you'd better go over to save me." To Rex, "Tell Delevan to go to the devil."

The Frenchman did not move. He regarded Stryker with a strange twinkle in his eyes.

Then something happened. There was a rush from the rear. At the same time Rex swung his gun butt to hip. Stryker, sensing immediately that the others had crept around while Rex was offering a truce, swung his rifle in a short arc and broke the Frenchman's jaw.

He whirled around and found the girl in his arms. She whispered:

"There's one bullet in my gun. I'll keep it for myself."

Scarcely without knowing what he did he kissed her, then pushed her behind him and fired his gun point blank at an Eskimo that was just about to brain him. The husky went down with a scream. Chevik and Tuktoluk were at close quarters with four others, and Delevan was lunging wolfishly toward Stryker.

Stryker, his rifle empty, advanced to meet him. They both swung at the same time. The rifles crashed in mid-career, broke, and the two men grappled. Delevan broke away and came back with a mighty fist that grazed Stryker's jaw and turned him completely around. Following up, Delevan caught him behind the ear with a short but terrific jab that sent him head first to the snow. But Stryker was a hard man and quick for his size. He was up and at Delevan, and everything he had was behind his blows.

It was furious, the way they mixed it, and before many minutes both were spitting blood, and their hide mittens were soggy with it.

Tuktoluk went down with a smashed skull even as Chevik broke one opponent's neck. The other three piled on him and, fighting to the last, he went down. As one of the huskies raised his knife to stab him, the girl, with a little cry, swung her revolver about and fired with her last shot—the shot she was going to save for herself. The husky dropped across the groaning Chevik.

The other two rushed at the girl and overpowered her, then began to carry her off, each striving to tear her from the other. With a mad snarl one let her go, whipped up his knife and buried it in the other's back. Then, cackling, he picked her up and disappeared behind one of the cabins. A little later he mushed out behind a *komatik* and a four-dog team, and the girl was strapped to the *komatik.*

Stryker and Delevan, struggling to the death, did not see this. Now they were down on the snow, locked in each other's arms, kicking, biting, cursing, with one and then the other on top. They carried the fight over the little ridge and right down to the river. Then they were up again and out upon the frozen waterway, slugging, taking and giving, streaming blood.

"Delevan," ground out Stryker, "this is the last fight you'll ever do. I'm going to pound you to death."

Delevan spat out a tooth. "D'you think so? G'on, you pup; the wolves 'll get you before morning."

They closed and rocked farther out upon the river. They neared a hole cut in the ice which apparently had been used for fishing. Delevan had Stryker by the nose and was trying to twist it off, and with the intense pain the latter's knees buckled as he tried to tear away. Then they went down in a heap, with Stryker underneath. Frantically Delevan pulled a long, slim knife from inside his sealskin coat and raised it high above his head.

Chevik was tottering and reeling down toward the waterway. He saw Delevan draw his knife. Chevik, the cleverest Eskimo with a knife in all the Labrador, hesitated for a split second. Then he fingered his own knife gingerly, gauged the distance with a calculating eye and threw it. It sang eerily through the air, struck Delevan point first in the side of the neck. His throat rattled. He heaved to one side, lost his balance and plunged through the hole in the ice to the bitter waters of the Kuglictuk.

Panting, Stryker struggled up and lunged toward the shore. He fell upon Chevik,

grasped his hand and pressed it till the Eskimo winced.

"Thanks, Chevik! God—thanks, old chum!" Then, "Where's the white woman?"

"Gone. I see go. Man take."

The two badly mutilated men stumbled to Chevik's cabin, lashed out the dogs and followed the trail made by the abductor.

Chapter 7

THE DAWN broke gray and leaden above the winter-locked Labrador. Stryker was running up beside his lead-dog. Chevik was trotting behind the *komatik* and cracking the whip. Men and dogs were covered with hoar frost.

Rounding a bend in the river, Stryker raised his hand, and Chevik called the dogs to a halt. Up ahead, on the west bank, was the smoke of a camp-fire, and Stryker could make out two figures beside it.

"It's them," he said.

He rummaged in his equipage and found a revolver, then continued at breakneck speed. Immediately there was a stir in the camp. One of the figures bundled the other upon the *komatik,* swung out the dogs and began to drive madly northward.

But Stryker had a powerful team, and in short time he was within pistol shot of the kidnapper. He fired. Missed. The other, without stopping, turned and returned fire. The shot went wild. Stryker stopped, took careful aim and shot again. This time the man stumbled, tried to grasp the gee-bar of his *komatik,* missed and sprawled headlong on the snow.

He was dead when Stryker drew up. A hundred feet farther on the team had stopped. He found the girl trying to struggle from her thongs. When she saw him she stopped struggling and lapsed into a coma.

Chevik made a fire. Strong tea revived the girl, and when she came to she found herself in Stryker's arms. And she did not seem to care.

"Thank God you came," she said with a shudder. "That beast of an Eskimo…."

"Yes, I understand," nodded Stryker. "I may as well tell you now that the whole gang is cleaned out, including your husband. He was about to stick a knife in me when Chevik, here, pitched his own knife and hit the bull's eye. Delevan is now at the bottom of the river. This husky back here was the last of the pack."

"Good Chevik," she murmured. Then: "And my husband dead? It might sound cruel, but I'm glad. And—and thanks for bringing that letter. Poor Harry, he had to die."

Stryker, looked puzzled. "Letter? Harry?"

"Yes. You see, I am Jack. Funny name for a girl, isn't it?"

Stryker was stunned. "You—Jack?"

"Yes. Harry Kavanagh was my brother. It's hard to say why I ever married Pete Delevan. It happened two years ago. But I haven't lived with him for one day. He was a beast. My folks didn't believe in divorce, so what could I do? I told him to stay away from me, but he wouldn't. He hounded me wherever I went.

"My father used to run a trading post in the Labrador, and when he gave it up and came home he brought his servant, Chevik, with him. It was Chevik who helped me get away. He knew the Labrador well, and I asked him if he would bring me here and help me to hide. He did. He's faithful, Chevik is.

"He'd never seen Delevan, so when you asked him to guide you over this way he suspected you were the man. He told me about that meeting at Fort Chimo, how he had left you to starve and all that. Then when I told him that while he was at Chimo Delevan had tracked me with the aid of two villainous Frenchmen, he was very sorry. Delevan had whiskey, and with it he bribed most of the Eskimos; but Chevik and his brother, Tuktoluk, remained loyal, although they gave Delevan to believe otherwise.

"When you came in and told Delevan whom you were after, he threatened to kill you if I revealed my identity. I figured he would try to kill you anyhow, so I set Chevik to watch him. And Chevik saved you from drowning. I—I guess I've caused you an awful lot of trouble, Mr. Stryker."

"Mister? My front name's Ed."

"Well, Ed, then."

And she smiled up into his bruised face.

"No trouble at all, Jack," he lied nobly. "Just a little excitement."

Chapter 8

ONE DAY, as the sun was making its brief appearance above the southern bulge of the earth, Monsieur De Loge, of Revillons, went over to pay a visit to his rival and friend, Donald Flemming, acting factor of the H.B.C. Post at Fort Chimo.

He said, "M'sieu, I wonder if dat daredevil, M'sieu Stryker, has found himself a grave out dere near de Kuglictuk, or if he ees safe."

"It's hard to say, Mr. De Loge," returned Flemming. "He's an old-timer on the trail, you know, and maybe he's pulled through. Let's hope so anyway. But between you and me, I'd be damned if I'd take that trip for some mysterious person named Jack."

"It ees youth, I s'pose, m'sieu. Youth ees afraid of nodding."

The conversation was interrupted by a commotion just outside the door. There was a boisterous laugh, the snarl of a dog, and then the sound of a woman's voice.

The door swung open. De Loge stared, speechless. Flemming dropped his pipe. Ed Stryker, his face and *koolutik* sparkling with frost, rocked in with his arm around a very charming young lady.

"Hello, De Loge—Flemming," called Stryker. "How's everything?"

De Loge jumped to his feet and wrung Stryker's hand, and Flemming, his face beaming now, was close behind. Then they looked at the girl.

"This is Jack," laughed Stryker.

After that the factors argued at length as to who should act as host to Ed Stryker and the girl he had brought out of the wilds. They compromised. Stryker went with De Loge. Jack stayed with Flemming.

But first Stryker asked:

"Listen, Flemming. Pst! Is the missioner at the Post?"

Jack blushed. Stryker felt a little uneasy. Chevik shoved his head in the door and blinked. And the two factors looked at each other knowingly. ◀▩▶

SPY AGAINST EUROPE

by H. Bedford-Jones

WHEN JOHN Barnes stepped aboard the Imperial Airways plane at Croyden field, he was taking his life in his hand, and knew it. When he stepped out of the plane at Le Bourget and got into the bus headed for downtown Paris, Death was chuckling at his ear. His one chance was that nobody suspected what he was doing.

Back in London, just before he left, the American ambassador had made things quite clear.

"It's a new deal all around, Barnes, at home and abroad. We're fighting these Europeans with their own weapons for a change. Remember, you've no earthly connection with Washington! You and the other chaps in the game are taking your chances—long chances, Barnes. You're devoting your time, money, and lives to a cause. You'll have no reward except the satisfaction of serving your country. If you're caught—goodnight!"

"Thanks," Barnes said laconically. "Instructions?"

The ambassador handed him an envelope. "Here. Chew up the paper and destroy it before you land at Le Bourget. This assassination of King Boris and the other in Marseilles has turned things upside down; vital information is en route to us, and it must reach Washington at once. There's a leak in the Paris embassy; we can't trust it. If you can get the message here—well, it's up to you."

Aboard the plane, Barnes memorized his instructions. With them he found a list of eight secret agents who had been caught and killed within the past month. None were Americans, but the grim significance of this list was obvious. Barnes knew Europe. He had lived abroad for several years. He had been in business in Paris. Level-eyed, quiet, seldom losing his head, Barnes was no Herculean figure; that was how he got results. Few people suspected his capabilities.

That other men, like himself, were unofficially serving their country, that he had been drawn into a free-lance game against all Europe, was great news. As the bus headed along the cobbled, ugly streets of Paris slipped past. Barnes stared out at them unseeing, his mind active, racing.

A new deal, now! America, unofficially, was taking a hand in the game. The very thought held a tang of adventure. No dirty spy stuff; that was barred. Europe was back in prewar days now. Intrigue, suspicion, assassination, war trembling on every frontier; a secret, merciless war going on beneath the surface. Barnes had caught echoes of it here and there; he knew what he was heading into. A new deal, eh? Yes, European diplomacy was going to get a hot jolt.

His primary instructions were simple. He was to go to the Hotel Dupont in the Rue du Selz and there await from Sheldon

some word, which might come in an hour or a week. Sheldon was trying to get out of Belgrade, which was no easy matter. If he reached Paris alive, he would no doubt be trailed and shadowed.

"Then it's my job to get the information, whatever it is, out of France," Barnes reflected. "But the Dupont! Why pick on that joint, of all places?"

He knew the Hotel Dupont by reputation, which was bad. The little downtown hostelry was no better than a house of assignation. To anyone who knew Paris, the place had an evil stench. However, orders were orders.

Upon reaching the bus terminal at the Crillon, Barnes picked up his one small bag, which was little more than a brief-case, and set out afoot for his destination. He did not know Sheldon; a former newspaper correspondent, who had become the mainspring of America's new initiative against the massed intrigues of Europe. He had a full description of Sheldon, however, and could not mistake his man.

Barnes sauntered along the narrow little Rue du Selz. Gone were the old gay dollar-grabbing days when tourists had flooded Paris. Now the shops looked dingier, the prices were down, only French faces appeared in the streets. Paris was still staggering under depression and the resentment of unpaid national debts.

There was the old Dupont. A mere entry way between two store fronts. Pushing into the place, Barnes found himself in a narrow little hall; a desk on one side, an elevator on the other, a flight of stairs in the rear. At the desk was a man, swarthy, sharp-eyed, who folded up a newspaper and rose.

"Good morning," Barnes greeted him in French. "I'd like a room, a double room. It's just possible that I shall have company later. With bath."

The other beamed. "All things can be arranged, *m'sieu*. A fine chamber on the third is vacant. Fifty francs."

Barnes protested this price, which was presently cut to forty. He filled out the police registration slip; as instructed in his orders, he gave the name of John Smithson. The police, he knew, would not bother to check up on his identity unless some trouble arose. And if this happened, Barnes intended to be gone before his real name could be involved and his passport impounded.

As he was finishing with the various blanks on the paper, a young woman descended the stairs and came to the desk, leaving her key. Barnes glanced up and thrilled to the sight of her face; dark and lovely, with eyes to hold a man in dreams. Those eyes dwelt upon him for an instant, and he fancied that a startled flame rose in them. Then she was gone out the doorway to the street.

"You are lucky, *m'sieu!*" and the greasy proprietor winked at Barnes. "*M'amselle* Nicolas is also on the third—eh, eh, what is this? *Tiens, tiens!* Smeethson—name of a little black dog! *M'sieu,* there was a gentleman here inquiring for one of this name, not twenty minutes ago. He would soon return, he said."

"When he returns, send him straight up to my room, if you please."

The other nodded and opened the elevator door. Barnes was taken up to the third—which, in America, would be the fourth. The ground floor is not counted in France. His room was comfortable enough. It had one window opening on a little iron balcony, and a makeshift bathroom, with all plumbing exposed, the pipes running along the wall.

Left alone, Barnes lit a cigarette and went to the window, which looked out on a court. Probably there were not twenty rooms in this whole "hotel," which was merely a slice from some ancient building, refinished and painted liberally.

"This is a devil of a hole in which to do any waiting," he mused. "But, since it must have been Sheldon who asked for me, I'll not have long to wait. I wonder why that girl gave me such a queer look? Nicolas, eh? Names mean nothing. She was a beauty, all right."

It was past noon; no wonder he felt hungry. A house telephone was on the wall. Barnes gave the proprietor a ring and ordered a meal. Then he began to pace up and down the room. Just what was he in for, anyway? He had not the least idea. Even the ambassador had not known.

ONLY SHELDON knew just what was up, it seemed. With a shrug, Barnes dismissed his pondering, threw open the window for air, and was tempted to step out on the balcony. He refrained, however. Best not to show himself there.

A waiter arrived with a folding table, spread out an excellent luncheon, and departed with his pay. Barnes drew up a chair, poured some wine, and pitched into his meal. He was nervous and uneasy. He had the distinct feel of something about to happen. His usual calm, his cheerful audacity, was darkened; his high spirits were dulled.

Suddenly came a sharp rap at the door. Before he could respond, the knob was turned.

The door opened and closed again, to admit a man. It was Sheldon; thin, red-haired, with a big nose. A man of forty. He looked at Barnes and grinned.

"Hello! So you got here, eh? I'm Sheldon. Had your description."

Barnes reached for the other's hand, eagerly.

"Barnes is the name—as you seem to know. Join me?"

"You bet. Grub looks good; I'm famished. Got here this morning and have been imagining things ever since. How soon can you clear out for London?"

"In five minutes."

Sheldon dropped into a chair, his back to the open window, and seized on a glass of wine.

"Not quite so fast, but almost, is necessary. You know what's up?"

"I know nothing," Barnes replied. The other was eating as he spoke.

"Hell of a mess. This murder of King Boris has precipitated no end of trouble; we don't know if it means war or what. I had to come via Germany, and couldn't get out. Barely got a plane before the Nazi pincers closed down. I expected they'd have spies waiting to meet me here, but nothing so far. Boy, I've got the goods!"

His blue eyes gleamed exultantly. From his pocket he drew a small but heavy brown envelope, most impressively sealed, which he tossed at Barnes.

"This is a fake, in case you're caught. It's a good fake, too." From his wrist he unbuckled a watch, which he passed over likewise. "Here's the real stuff; get it to the ambassador in London at all costs."

"This watch?" queried Barnes.

"Exactly. Never mind explanations; the less you know, the less you'll give away."

"Right," said Barnes. He gave Sheldon his own watch and buckled on the one given him; it was not running, he observed.

"We've got a hell of a big strike," Sheldon ejaculated between bites. "The lowdown straight out of Belgrade—secret treaties with Italy and so on. The less you know the better, I suppose."

"Who's against us in this deal?"

"Everybody," snapped Sheldon. "We've got what nobody else has, and what they're all after. Me, I'm all shot to pieces. My nerve's gone."

"Any special instructions?" Barnes demanded, pocketing the sealed envelope. Sheldon gave him a shrewd look.

"Yes. This is no kindergarten game we're in. These birds have their countries back of 'em; you and I don't. When you've been in it as long as I have, your nerves will go, too. Suspect everybody! And remember, murder is nothing in this business. They're on to me, all right, but let's hope you've not been spotted. I'll let 'em follow me, while you get across the Channel in a hurry."

"Right. How did you come to pick on this hotel?" queried Barnes.

"I know the chap who runs it; he's part-way straight. There's a hell of a fine girl here—the Nicolas girl. She's been working for Bulgaria, but somebody double-crossed her and I hear she's in Italian pay now. I believe she's in Rome at present."

"She was here when I entered," Barnes said. "The man at the desk called her by name. Very pretty, with dark eyes."

"What the devil! Then somebody lied to me—as usual," Sheldon exclaimed. "No matter. I've not slept for two nights. Lock the door, will you? I was warned they'd try to murder me; I haven't felt safe until now." Barnes went to the door and shot the bolt.

"Wouldn't you be safer in a big hotel like the Lutetia?"

"Nope. They probably know already that I'm here. You'd better be moving. Spare no expense; you may need this, take it." He flung on the table a big wad of various European currencies. "Get out to Le Bourget and hire a special plane; an English one."

"Thanks." Pocketing the money, Barnes began to pack up his few belongings. He went into the bathroom, getting his toilet things. "Who's your danger from?"

"All directions," came the voice of Sheldon. "We're safe enough from the English; they're not interested this time. Boy, with this information we can blow all the others high, wide and handsome! All these double-crossing rats!"

"Hope so." Barnes was packing his toilet articles. "Finish up the grub. I'll get some more at Le Bourget. The room's paid for, by the way."

A grunt from the other room made response.

Swiftly, Barnes repacked. He was in the game at last; elation filled him, all his depression was gone. Now he was alert, eager, tense.

Another half hour and he would be at the air field, then swiftly winging back to England!

"When I reach London, I'll send a wire, so you can take it easy," he called. Sheldon made no response. When he finished his packing, Barnes carried his little bag out into the other room. Then, abruptly, he came to a dead stop.

Sheldon had fallen over sideways in the chair, his head lolling. From the back of his neck protruded the haft of a long, heavy knife.

At this instant came a harsh, determined pounding on the door.

"In the name of the law, m'sieu!" came a stentorian voice. "Open!"

Chapter 2

BARNES GLANCED swiftly about. Sheldon was dead; murdered a moment ago. One glance at that horribly lolling head told the tale. By whom? The room was empty. Ah—the open window, the balcony! Someone had been outside there—

And, in a flash, Barnes knew that this same balcony was his one hope of escape. He knew what threatened him and his precious burden. Let him be caught, accused of this crime, let the French have any handle by which to detain him, and his mission was ruined. It was his job to get through with that information—at all costs!

His hesitation lasted no more than ten seconds. His bag bore nothing to reveal his identity; he dropped it beside the dead Sheldon and darted to the window. There, to his surprise he found that the balcony was not merely confined to his own window, but ran around all the windows of the courtyard. Thus, anyone could go from one room to the others of this same floor. The balcony was now empty, however.

"Made to order for hotel rats, diplomats and assassins!" Barnes thought grimly. A tremendous burst of hammering came from the door of his room. He stepped outside.

To tell whence the assassin had come, was impossible; the rooms to the left, however, would be closer to the stairway. Barnes turned left at a venture. A low cross-bar of iron, over which he stepped, and he was at the adjoining window. Closed and locked. He passed on. At the next, he found the door-like sash also closed. A splintering crash came from behind, a burst of voices; his room had been entered. A moment more, and he would be discovered here.

The window sagged under his hand. He pushed, threw his weight against it; the double sash flew open, and he staggered into the room.

To his vast relief, the chamber proved to be empty.

He closed and fastened the window again, then glanced around. The room was smaller than his own. Women's clothes were in sight. Could it be possible?

Was this the room of the Nicolas girl, which was on his own floor? With a shrug, he dismissed the thought, and stood listening.

The tumult of feet and voices continued. Realization of his own predicament grew upon Barnes with acute force. Smithson would certainly be accused of the murder. Should he walk downstairs now, at once, daring everything? Audacity, always audacity! So thinking, Barnes went to the door and reached for the knob.

At this instant, a key was inserted from the outside.

A laugh, a man's laugh, came clearly to him. The door was unlocked and thrown open, thrown back against Barnes as he slipped aside. It momentarily concealed his figure.

"Very well, I have kept my promise," said a woman's cool, poised voice. "You are in my room. Now clear out—and do it fast!"

"Bah! Don't play the fine lady with me. Shut the door and be sensible," said the man, in a light and bantering tone. "What's all the commotion about?"

"I don't know and don't care," the woman replied. "Get out!"

A laugh, a heavy thudding slap—then the door was slammed shut and locked.

Against it stood the Nicolas girl, flushed, angry. For an instant she did not realize the presence of Barnes, who thus stood revealed. Then her eyes dilated in evident fear. Pallor flashed into her face. She shrank back a little against the door.

"So I was right!" she murmured in English. "When I saw you downstairs, I should have taken warning. I guessed that you must be the man—"

"Apparently you made a very good guess," Barnes said coolly. He was not the person to miss so obvious a cue. Next instant she drew herself up, her dark eyes ablaze.

"You dare not, you dare not touch me!" she exclaimed. "There are police in the building now; at a scream from me, they will come!

"What's more, Sheldon should be here at any moment; Sheldon, do you understand? This is France, my friend, and not Russia."

Barnes was startled. "So it is, Miss Nicolas. What is Sheldon to you?"

"Nothing. He is a friend, and an honest man. No assassin like yourself!"

"Be sensible. I've no intention of harming you," and Barnes smiled faintly. He was badly shaken by what had taken place. Above all, he was conscious of the hatred and fear straining in her eyes.

"Liar! You are trying to trick me, eh?" she said scornfully. "As though I didn't know they were sending you! As though I haven't been watching every day, every hour! Only, I expected it would be Borescu. Come, who are you?"

Barnes produced and lit a cigarette, with assumed composure.

HE WAS fascinated by her beauty—a perilous beauty. After what Sheldon had told him, he knew her for one of those magnificently alluring women who play an old, old game in Europe. What cause they serve, whose pay they take, to whom their reports go, remains obscure; except when one of them is stood against a wall and shot. And not bad women, either. Sheldon had said this was a fine girl, and Barnes could well believe it. Character and brains, not loose morals, are needed to play such a game as hers.

"You just mentioned a Rumanian name with which I am not familiar," Barnes said.

"Borescu? The murderer? Well, never mind evasion. Just who are you?"

"If I told you that," Barnes replied calmly, "you'd know far too much. In plain words, I'm not the person you take me for. I was hiding in this room."

"Nonsense. You even know my name."

"Certainly. Sheldon told me about you. He thought you were in Italy."

"Sheldon!" Her lovely eyes dilated again. "Then he is here?"

"Ten minutes ago, yes. He was murdered, two rooms from here."

Her features tightened; a flame of swift, passionate anger leaped in her eyes.

She believed in him, but she betrayed no shock, no grief. Evidently Sheldon had been nothing to her—nothing more than a friend.

"He was an honest man, that American. And you killed him?"

"No," said Barnes. "Why go into all this business of explaining? It takes too much time, and you'd not believe me anyway."

She regarded him steadily for a moment, and made a sudden gesture.

"I believe you. I may be a fool, but I know when a man tells me the truth. So I made a mistake, and you say he is dead; who are you, what are you doing here?"

"Trying to get out into the street unseen." Barnes smiled in his shy, whimsical manner.

"Ah, I knew he would fail!" she muttered, then collected herself. "Yes, yes, you are right not to trust me. We can trust no one. That is our punishment for thefts, lies, seductions, murders. And it is called patriotism—bah! Well, I knew Sheldon; he was a good friend. Now I must go to London. And you? Where do you go?"

"To London also," Barnes repeated. "I hope to hire a plane."

Her eyes narrowed, then she broke into a quick smile. "I see! Then you are completing Sheldon's errand! Good; we shall go to London together. Aren't you afraid I might try to rob you?"

"Yes."

So lovely, so charming was her smile, that Barnes was astonished once more.

"Oh, I like you! Suspect everyone, eh? Sheldon would have told you that. He told me he expected to meet someone here. Well," and she turned quickly aside, to show a small automatic pistol in her hand, "if I wished to rob you, I could do so. Come along! Let's get out of here before I get knifed in the back! That's Borescu's specialty."

"What's that?" Barnes started slightly. His eyes hardened. "His specialty! It was a knife in the back, thrown from the open window, that killed poor Sheldon! If I thought the murderer—but no. I can't remain here, or delay."

She laid her hand on his arm, looked steadily into his face.

"My friend, I know men; that's my business. I believe you, I like you. What you have just said, proves that Borescu must be here somewhere. Well, I am afraid; I confess it. Certain people have sworn to kill me, and here in this place I'm out of my depth. Give me three minutes, and we'll leave together. Agreed?"

Barnes nodded, and lit a fresh cigarette.

Without more ado, she set to work throwing her things into a bag; the art of light travel was clearly an old story to her. A curtain across one corner of the room provided a closet. She stepped behind this curtain, and he caught a flash of her bare arms above it. She was changing her clothes there.

Barnes looked away. Something at the window caught his eye, a moving object outside and clearly visible through the lace coverings of the sash. A hand and arm, moving across from beside the window, clutching at the knob of the sash and trying to open it.

Then the arm was drawn back. The window had opened a trifle.

Barnes quietly went to the window. Someone was outside on the balcony, waiting and listening. He got behind the slightly opened sash and waited. Miss Nicolas was humming a soft, gay tune.

She had come out from behind the curtain, and was closing her bag.

The hand appeared again. The window-sash was pushed inward. The figure of a man came swiftly into sight; a small man, crouched there, balanced, peering forward into the room. His arm swung up, and a knife was in his hand.

Barnes slammed the sash full against him, all his weight upon it.

THERE WAS a crash and tinkle of broken glass, a wild exclamation. The assassin was hurled back against the ancient iron railing of the balcony. It broke under his weight. From the courtyard echoed up a frantic scream, that ceased abruptly.

Barnes found the girl at his side, staring at the broken window, the empty balcony.

"It was he, Borescu!" she breathed. "I saw his face as he fell—"

"Get going," snapped Barnes. "Hear those shouts? It's my one chance to get out, while everyone's around his body. Step on it, girl! I hope the murdering devil is done for!"

He darted to the door. She caught her bag up and joined him; the stairs lay before them, empty. They hurried down together.

A moment later they reached the first floor landing. The stairs were still empty. But below, in the narrow hallway that served as entrance, stood two agents of police. Barnes knew that they were stopping all egress from the hotel. At this instant a burst of frantic voices from the courtyard alarmed the two agents; they swung around, broke into a run, and disappeared. Evidently the body of Borescu was causing a terrific commotion on all sides.

Next moment, Barnes stepped out into the street, holding the girl's bag. She took his arm, very calmly.

"The death of that assassin will make you a hero, my friend."

"Forget it," Barnes broke in curtly. He motioned to a taxicab that swerved in to the curb. "We're well out of a bad mess. Now, I'm going to put you into this cab. You go to Le Bourget, and if I don't show up in half an hour, play your own game."

"What?" Dismay rose in her eyes. "Do we not go together?"

"Not much."

The girl turned to him swiftly. "I don't know your name, but I owe you much," she said earnestly. "Believe me, I shall not forget. I understand; you wish to part with me now, and perhaps you are right. But in London, if you need aid, telephone Charing Cross three eleven and ask for Nicolas. I always pay my debts. Good-bye, my friend!"

And, to the utter astonishment of Barnes, she flung her arms about him and kissed him twice on the lips. Then she caught the bag from his hand and was gone into the cab.

"Le Bourget!" came her voice. "Quickly!"

The chauffeur grinned delightedly at the staring, dumfounded Barnes, and the taxicab went whirring away.

"Whew! What a flame of a girl she is!" thought the American. He signaled another cab. "Going by air, is she? Well, she's welcome. It occurs to me that, with so darned much dirty work going on, this airport is the one place in Paris that's liable to be unhealthy. That's where poor Sheldon slipped up. He came by air, and they knew it, and this knife artist was waiting for him."

He stepped into his cab, ordering the driver to the Hotel Terminus.

With this grim sequence of events at the Hotel Dupont, Barnes had abruptly changed his entire course of campaign. Air was the quickest system of transport, but for this very reason was also the most dangerous. Let the Nicolas girl go by air if she were fool enough to do so! Not he.

Barnes wanted to reach London alive. And dinned into his brain was the determination to accomplish his mission—at all costs.

His taxicab drew up before the dingy old pile of the Hotel Terminus, that once famous but of late rather notorious hostelry beside the Gare St. Lazare. Barnes left the cab, went straight into the hotel, and at the desk he secured a twenty-franc room, for which he paid in advance. He filled out the police registry slip in his proper name, displayed his passport, and was then shown to his room. He explained that his luggage would arrive later.

After five minutes he left his room and descended to the café.

Here he secured a sidewalk table and ordered a sandwich. It was twelve forty. At one ten, as he knew, a train left for Havre, an express that would reach there before dinner time. The question now in the mind of Barnes was whether he had thrown off any possible trailers. Even if not, he still had another string to his bow.

That evening the regular English line left Havre for Southampton, which it reached early in the morning. Altogether the slowest, safest and most comfortable route between Paris and London. Nobody in a hurry would dream of taking it.

At the next table, he observed a jovial fat man who had an expansive gold-toothed smile and a half bald pate. This gentleman settled himself with an aperitif and a copy of *L'Echo de Paris,* and absorbed himself in the news. Barnes idly read the side of the folded paper that was toward him. But he watched the time as well.

One o'clock precisely. Barnes rose, flung down a note to pay the waiter, and then passed into the hotel by the front entrance.

He passed out at the side entrance immediately after. Heading straight into the station, he bought his Havre ticket, passed the gates, and lingered on the train platform to buy newspapers and magazines from the pushcart there. Preliminary toots of the engine, the calls and whistles of the guards, rang out. The train began to move. Barnes hopped aboard.

There was no crowd. Barnes presently found a first-class compartment that was empty, and esconced himself in it comfortably. He lit a cigarette, opened a newspaper, and patted the breast pocket in which the brown envelope reposed. Then he suddenly dropped the newspaper and reached into his pocket.

The brown envelope was not there. Gone!

Chapter 3

IN THE other breast pocket, Barnes found his passport and papers intact, of course. He thought back, swiftly.

True, that brown envelope had been a trifle large for his pocket; but who could have seen it? Who could have taken it? Certainly it had not dropped out. Suddenly he recollected how Miss Nicolas had flung her arms about his neck and kissed him with warm gratitude. At this, his eyes twinkled.

The smart little skirt! She had pulled the job off neatly. At thought of those impulsive kisses, and her quick getaway, his lips twitched amusedly.

"Much good it may do her!" he reflected. "If she did put one over on me, she hasn't gained much by her agility. And to think of her handing me all that line of talk, then calmly picking my pocket! So she's working for Italy, eh? Looks as though Sheldon had told her too much, friend or no friend."

The information that he carried was obviously of interest in more than one quarter. Everybody in the business was out to hijack him, apparently, and there were no rules in the game, as he had been warned. He had just saved the Nicolas girl's life, and she turned around and picked his pocket.

The guard came through, verified the first-class ticket of Barnes, and punched it. Five minutes later, a figure darkened the compartment door, opened it, and entered.

"With your permission, *m'sieu?* Thank you."

Barnes nodded. Then he took a second look at the man who settled down on the opposite seat—a look of incredulity, of startled recognition. Here was the fat man of the Hotel Terminus café!

The other met his look and smiled, showing the gold teeth.

"We have met before—ah, I remember! *M'sieu* was at the next table in the café, of course!" the fat man said cordially. "*M'sieu* is an American, yes? One observes the shoes, naturally. And the first-class travel. Me, I slip in after the guard has gone through, and it costs me nothing. But perhaps *m'sieu* does not speak French?"

Barnes shrugged. From the very slight accent, he took the man to be a German.

"Afraid I don't understand you, mister," he returned with a nasal drawl. "Don't mind me. I'll take a nap as we ride."

With this he pulled his hat over his eyes, laid back his head, and to all appearance dropped off to sleep. It was no trick to open his lids very slightly—enough to let him look down his nose at the fat, half-bald man opposite.

Barnes was by no means certain whether this might not be a mere coincidence. The fat man sighed, laid aside his hat, and mopped his shining dome. Then he took from his pocket a newspaper, folded in the French fashion, and began to peruse it attentively. The newspaper was the same *Echo* he had been reading at the café table.

It was folded in exactly the same way, he was reading precisely the same story, now as then.

That settled his doubts. And after a little he observed that the fat man, while pretending to read, was in reality furtively studying him.

Presently a man came past in the corridor. The fat gentleman glanced up, and behind the folded newspaper his hand made a gesture. The man outside nodded and passed on. At this, Barnes concluded that things were threatening to grow uncomfortably warm. He opened his eyes, looked at the fat man, and smiled.

"Just how many of you are there aboard?" he asked in French.

Without the least astonishment, the fat man laid aside his newspaper.

"Ah! You Americans are brusque and to the point, eh?"

His broad features fairly radiated jovial good humor as he spoke. And suddenly Barnes perceived how fearfully dangerous such a man might be. With a nod, the other went on in fluent English:

"I am glad to find you frank; one can do business with such a person." The little eyes bored shrewdly into Barnes. "You are no fool, Mr. Barnes. You are a wise man, I see."

"Eh?" Barnes started. "How the devil do you know my name?"

The fat man burst into a hearty, roly-poly sort of laugh.

"Oh, that is a mere detail! When you arrived this morning from London, we received you, without ostentation, of course. We knew of your coming, my friend. In the little hotel, out of the little hotel again, with that charming young lady! You see, I am quite frank. Now, would it please you to talk business? You are an American, and you know the value of money."

Barnes lifted his brows slightly; this was frankness with a vengeance! So his very coming had been known from the start. "Undoubtedly, money has value," he agreed. This fellow must have the prevalent European notion that all Americans would sell their souls for money. "You, however, have the advantage of me."

"Ah, a thousand apologies! My name, Mr. Barnes, is Rothstern. Let us see, now. Would a hundred thousand francs interest you? I am naming my highest figure. I warn you."

A glitter came into the eye of Barnes. "A hundred thousand francs? It certainly would, if I could get hold of it. That all depends on how it could be earned."

"Very easily. I ask only a few moments to look over the papers Mr. Sheldon confided to you. No one will know; the hundred thousand francs is ready."

THE EYES of Barnes widened in very real astonishment for an instant—astonishment that any secret agent could be so obtuse, so blundering. Still, this was evidently the nature of Rothstern himself. Barnes shook his head gloomily.

"Just my cursed luck," he muttered. "No harm in letting you see the papers, if I had them. I discovered it not five minutes ago."

"Discovered what?"

"The envelope's gone," Barnes said, with a dejected air. "All those business memoranda are gone! The girl you mentioned—she kissed me when we parted. No one else could have taken the envelope. A hundred thousand francs lost!"

The little eyes bit into him like gimlets.

"Come, come! You think to fool old Rothstern with such a story? It is true that she kissed you goodby. But to tell me—"

Barnes angrily broke in upon him.

"You don't believe me? Wake up to yourself. Good heavens—a hundred thousand francs just to look over those business agreements Sheldon made? Why, it would be like finding money!" His voice was shrill, impetuous, dismayed. "And now the envelope's gone! If you doubt my word, look for yourself. I've no luggage, search me!" And Barnes began to tumble things out of his pocket. "It was a brown envelope, sealed with red wax. I haven't got it, I tell you; it's gone! She must have taken it."

The fat features became grimly intent and appraising. The vehemence of Barnes was impressive. His agitation, his intense chagrin, his boyish excitement, could scarcely be doubted. Rothstern nodded again.

"So! You tell me such a story and expect me to believe it? Well, it is true that you could not hide the envelope, unless you put it behind your seat-cushions there.

"The brown envelope; yes, that is the one. You will let me see in your pockets, my friend?"

Barnes threw out his hands. "Of course; frisk me if you like. I tell you she got it; and she was going to London by air, too!"

"She is not such a fool," grunted Rothstern. Evidently he had come to the conclusion that Barnes was very much of a fool. "Will you kindly stand up—"

Barnes leaped to his feet. He had been in doubt as to his own course, but now it was plain enough. Rothstern had swallowed the bait of the brown envelope, and so had the girl. What had threatened to become a tragedy aboard the Havre Express, was now turning into comedy or even farce.

So the American made not the least protest as Rothstern swiftly searched him. He seemed quite as anxious as the other man to find the envelope, and even turned out his shoes at the grumbling demand. He carried no papers except his passport and a few personal letters, and it was obviously impossible for him to have concealed that brown envelope anywhere, without the flimsiest search turning it up.

"There are still the seat-cushions," Rothstern said, desisting at last from the search. Barnes, who had put on his shoes again, swore heartily.

"Look all you please. I'm going to the diner for a bottle of beer. But see here! I've told you what became of the envelope and where it is. I should get something for that, at least."

"Swine head!" the other grunted in German, then grinned. "All right, that is true. Here is a hundred francs, my friend."

Barnes took the banknote and walked out.

Not for nothing had he played his cards so carefully. Now Rothstern knew him as a mercenary American more than willing to betray his trust for a few dollars. Others would learn of it. The character so craftily established might, at some future time, prove invaluable to him.

BARNES WAS still sitting in the diner, lingering over his bottle of beer when the train entered Rouen. Exclamations of astonishment came from the waiters when it became evident that the non-stop express was, for once, halting. They peered out of the windows, and so did Barnes.

For the merest moment, the train halted and then rolled on once more. A smile touched the lips of Barnes as he saw three figures hurriedly crossing the platform to the station—the fat shape of Rothstern, and two other men. Barnes raised his glass.

"To your health, my friend!" he murmured under his breath. "At least the first round goes to the despised American amateur. And the first, let us hope, will be the last so far as you're concerned. You're at liberty to trail the girl, who can take care of herself and give you a headache to boot."

Presently he returned to his compartment, and for the remainder of the journey perused his magazines and newspapers undisturbed. That is to say, from without. As the train was nearing Havre, a very serious disturbance arose in his brain.

He was turning the pages of an illustrated French weekly, when the face of Miss Nicolas suddenly looked out at him. No doubt about it—the same! But it was the line of text below her picture that widened his eyes: "Mlle. Marie Nicolas, fiancée of the Grand Duke Alexis."

Alexis! That rascally old roué of a Russian exile, notorious all over the world for his rascality—about to marry this girl! The thing was preposterous.

"Still, it's none of my business," and Barnes shrugged. "Damned shame, though. That sprig of nobility has been in more scandals and dirty messes than most, which is saying a lot. Well, better forget about it. Maybe it's not true. Even if it is, it's nothing to me."

So he dismissed the matter, a little scornfully, as one does when any charming member of the opposite sex becomes involved in the wrong way.

When the train pulled into Havre, he found himself with time to burn; the boat for Southampton would not leave until nine that night. He strolled about the old streets of the port section, and came at length to the long quays where the English boat and the little ferries for Deauville and Trouville lay berthed by the sheds of the customs inspectors. He stopped in at a nearby café and dined at his ease.

Later he sauntered on to the Southampton boat-shed. Taking nothing for granted now, he stood about smoking and narrowly watching the few people in sight. Freight was being sent aboard, and a number of cars returning from Continental trips. Barnes half expected to catch sight of the huge Rothstern again. Nothing would have astonished him by this time.

However, his critical eye discerned nobody who was in the least way suspicious. He purchased his ticket at last. With some jests upon his lack of any baggage, he passed through the customs shed and went up the gangplank. His passport had been looked over and returned without question, which argued that the Paris police might be looking for Smithson, but were not looking for John Barnes.

A steward led him to the cabin which he had engaged for his exclusive use. It was one of the de luxe cabins on the upper deck. He paused before it, as the steward unlocked the door and switched on the lights. Then he was aware of a voice coming from the adjoining cabin.

"No, no!" It was a low, tense voice, which brought Barnes around like a shot. The window of this next cabin, almost at his elbow, was a trifle open. "No, no! I tell you it is impossible! It would be murder!"

It was the voice of Miss Nicolas.

Chapter 4

BARNES QUIETLY tipped his steward and dismissed the man. Then he switched off his cabin lights and stepped outside again. His feet made no sound on the resilient decking. Hereabouts all was deserted; few of these more expensive cabins were used, unless there happened to be a crowd aboard.

Barnes stood poised, waiting, outside that adjoining cabin window. That girl here—why, it was incredible! Or was it? Now he recalled what Rothstern had said about her going by air to London—"she would be no such fool." But how the devil could she have reached Havre, when she had not come on the express? By air, of course; or even by auto. She had let him think she was going to Le Bourget. Perhaps she, too, had figured this slower channel crossing as the safest.

In this, however, she had been far wrong. Barnes listened, then caught his breath. The man's voice that he heard was cold, suave, deadly. An English voice, assuredly.

"Don't try to charm me, you little fool; and they said you were smart! You flew to Deauville to lose yourself in the casino crowds, you caught the ferry over here, slipped aboard—and here I am. And do you know why? Because Rothstern was too cursed clever for you. He telephoned me to look out for you here. Come along; we know you have it. Turn it over or I'll squeeze your pretty little throat still tighter. I'd like to squeeze the life out of you as well! Damn you!"

There was an incoherent, strangling sound, a cough.

"I—I haven't got it!" the girl's voice gasped.

"You lie. We know all about it. You took it from him when you kissed him good-bye."

Barnes turned, and rapped sharply at the door of the cabin. There was an instant of startled silence. Then the man's voice made response.

"Who is it? What do you want?"

"Beg pardon, sir; it's the steward." Barnes made no effort to disguise his voice. He knew the girl was sharp enough to recognize it. "Shall I close your window, sir?"

A suppressed oath. "No! Go away!"

"Very good, sir."

Barnes tried the cabin door. It proved to be locked.

"Confound you, I told you to clear out!"

At this moment a shadow drifted across the deck. It became a man, who closed in upon Barnes and touched his arm, and spoke quietly.

"Here's half a crown for you, steward. You'd best get below decks and leave off bothering passengers who want nothing."

"Oh, thank you very much, sir!"

In the dim radiance reflected from the lights on the quay, Barnes made out a man of about his own height. So there were two of them! He took the proffered coin and turned away. Then he pivoted sharply, abruptly, and his left slammed home in a brutally low body-blow.

There was a gasping groan; the shadowy figure collapsed like a punctured balloon.

Barnes stooped swiftly. He caught hold of the limp figure, dragged it into his own cabin doorway, then inside, and stepped out again. He closed and locked the door. As he did so, the door of the adjoining cabin was flung violently open.

"What's going on out here?" It was the man's voice. "Stacey! Where are you?"

Barnes laughed softly, and stepped into the shaft of light, and down it full into the doorway.

"I'm afraid Stacey has gone on a long journey," he said lightly, whimsically. "At least, the police seem very glad to have hold of him."

HE PRODUCED a cigarette and lit it, but his eyes missed nothing. This staring man was tall, bony-featured, wide of shoulder. The face was powerful, lean-jawed, ugly. At the back of the cabin, one arm flung out against the upper berth, stood Miss Nicolas. Her hair and dress were disordered; one hand was at her throat, her wide eyes were upon Barnes.

"Who the devil are you?" snapped the Englishman.

Barnes waved his cigarette airily.

"A competitor, my friend, a competitor. Now, Miss Nicolas, hand over the brown envelope, if you please. You know me. My men are below and on the quay. The envelope you took from the American—quickly! Otherwise, you go to jail and this gentleman will follow his friend Stacey. At once, if you please!"

The crisp authority of Barnes' voice, his air of easy assurance, and the disappearance of Stacey, all seemed to cause the dark Englishman inexpressible alarm. He took a step backward, one hand flitting toward his armpit. Barnes merely regarded him with a smile, and the hand dropped. This man was dealing with the unknown; he was beaten.

"My friend," Barnes said pleasantly to him, with a glance at his wrist-watch, "you have exactly five minutes to get off the ship and the quay. As you know, it is a contravention of the French law to carry weapons. Get out, and do it fast. Now, Miss Nicolas, hand over the envelope."

The girl awoke. Her hand went to her bosom; she produced the envelope, now folded and crumpled.

With a subdued oath, the dark Englishman strode past Barnes, and was gone. Barnes swung the door shut. He took a quick step forward and caught the brown envelope from the girl's hand. He glanced at it, then gave her a quizzical look.

"Seals unbroken! Upon my word, you've wasted a lot of time," he said coolly. "And for a young lady so quick with her pistol where I was concerned, you were certainly meek enough when that rascal choked you."

She pointed to the floor. Her pistol lay there. Quick color rushed into her cheeks.

"You don't know him; Truxon is a devil!" she gasped out. "Oh, are you real? It can't be—it's impossible! How did you get here?"

Barnes perceived that she was close to hysterics.

"My dear Marie, you're scarcely the bold bad woman of fiction," he observed, with his warm and twinkling smile. "Upon my word, the more I see of you, the better I like you. Now, tell me why you took the envelope from me, in the first place. Second, why you didn't open it?"

The girl stooped, picked her pistol from the floor, and tossed it into the lower berth. She patted her hair into place, glanced at her torn dress. Barnes began to see that there must have been quite a struggle here before he happened on the scene.

"I owed Sheldon a good turn," she said, and looked him in the face with a hint of frowning wonder in her eyes. "I wanted to help him; and you seemed such a simpleton. You said you were going by air; only a fool would do that, when the air ports are so carefully watched. Why should I open it? I meant to deliver it—"

She broke off abruptly. The quiet smile of Barnes brought a flame of anger into her dark eyes.

"For whom are you working, Marie?"

"None of your business; so you don't believe me? Oh, what a fool you are—no, no." She checked herself abruptly. "No; it's you who made a fool out of me. You're clever; good lord, who'd have thought it of you? Walking in here like this! I owe you everything, yes; but you've made a fool out of me—"

"And you can't forgive it?" Barnes chuckled. "Calm down; keep your head. Nobody's a fool, I'm afraid. It's entirely due to me that Rothstern trapped you here. But who was this Englishman who just walked out?"

"Truxon, of course."

"I honestly hate to corroborate your idea of my simpletonian quality—but who may Truxon be?"

"Still playing innocent, are you?" she said, with an air of scorn.

"If I weren't as innocent as a lamb, I might be in your shoes. You seem to be petrified with terror of everything around you. Borescu puts you in a sweat. This Truxon shows up and you bleat frantically—"

She became white with fury. Barnes paused, listening.

"I take it from the context that Truxon is working with friend Rothstern; yet he's apparently an Englishman. It's too complex for my simple brain. But am I correct in thinking that we're off at last?"

She nodded slightly, as though in relief. Excited voices were sounding faintly from the quay, winches had ceased rattling, and now the ship shuddered to the reverberation of her deep whistle.

"Tell me!" broke out the girl abruptly. "You must know that Truxon and Stacey were broken, smashed, fired out of the English service last year—and lucky they got no worse. But where is Stacey? I know he was watching while Truxon was in here. You had no men, no police—that was all bluff."

"Of course." Barnes started suddenly. "What the devil! I locked Stacey in my cabin. I'd better turn him loose and get rid of him—"

As he strode outside, he was thinking that after all he had learned everything he needed to know—except what he most wanted to know. The girl hesitated, then switched off her cabin lights and followed him.

BARNES FOUND his own cabin door ajar, the room empty. Stacey, obviously, had come to himself and escaped.

"The bird's flown—good!" he exclaimed.

Together in silence, they sauntered to the rail and stood watching the arc-lights of the quays float past and recede, the duller lights of the town blending in a mass and falling away, as the ship pointed out for the Seine estuary. Then Barnes was aware of her quiet voice beside him. She was herself again, composed and poised.

"I can't figure you out. Are you really as new in this work as you appear?"

"You flatter me." Barnes laughed a little. "Question for question. Are you really going to marry the Grand Duke Alexis?"

She gave no evidence of surprise at the question.

"Certainly not. He thought I was, of course; on his part, he was merely after my money. It was all part of the Bulgarian affair, which is quite off the boards by now. But you haven't answered my question."

"My own question ought to answer it. I wish that I knew more about you. Then you are Bulgarian?"

"Heavens, no!" She broke into a short, amused laugh. "I'm an American, silly! Because my father had various electrical concessions over here I began to handle some deals for him, then I gradually worked into the game. It's not a nice game, at times, but I've made a place for myself. I just came from Rome. They made me a very flattering offer there, and it really tempted me."

"Tell me the truth," Barnes urged her quietly. "For whom are you working?"

"You wouldn't know the truth when you heard it," she said bitterly. "At the moment I'm working for no one, and tonight I'm a very humble and defeated person."

Barnes shrugged lightly in the darkness. So she would not come through and be frank! Yet the story that she told had fascinating possibilities; he almost believed it. He found himself liking her strangely, perilously. He liked her very weakness in the face of danger; too efficient a woman loses her most enchanting heritage.

"Yes, I'm new to the business," he said musingly. "So new, that I didn't even take it very seriously, I'm afraid, until—well, poor Sheldon's murder jerked me awake. Well, that's past; it's all over now. We're off for England, and all's well."

"You're optimistic," she said ironically. "You're taking up this business seriously?"

"I hope so."

"For whom, then? Who pays you?"

After information, was she? He laughed to himself. She would not believe the truth.

"Nobody. If some of us put ourselves, our money, our ability, at the service of our country, can anything in the way of money pay us?"

"I know; that's what Sheldon said," she replied in a low voice, to his astonishment. "Oh, I do wish you'd been in it before now! There are so many unsettled things a man like you should have handled, that were frightfully messed up by our diplomatists! Let's hope the new deal extends far and lasts long. Well, I wonder where Rothstern is now?"

"Probably in Paris, gnashing his teeth."

She laughed. "Not he! This business is a gamble; that's why I like it. There are no personalities; if you lose, take it like a sport and try again. But this Truxon is plain bad; so is Stacey. They're hired mercenaries, dishonored men, rascals, working today for the brownshirts, tomorrow for France. So you think we've left all trouble behind, eh?"

Barnes pointed back at the flashing lighthouse.

"There's the answer. Thank you for the 'we.' It's flattering."

"Your optimism is incorrigible. Well, comrade, goodnight and pleasant dreams!"

"Same to you. If you need me, call; I'm in the adjoining cabin."

He liked her firm, quick handshake. In fact, he warned himself frankly, he liked her altogether too much.

IN HIS own cabin, he found no traces of his late captive. How Stacey escaped from the locked cabin was a mystery, but it was significant.

"They're a tricky, fly lot, all this crowd of

comic-opera assassins," Barnes reflected as he prepared for bed. "Keep one step ahead of 'em and you've got them cinched; that's the recipe. Hand 'em a new deal and they don't know what to make of it. So Marie didn't break into the envelope, eh? Just trying to help out a poor benighted countryman, eh? That's a good line, but I'd hate to trust her very far. Ten to one she's guessed that the brown envelope is a fake. Queer that Sheldon would do so much talking to her; he wasn't the kind to shoot off his mouth without a reason."

So pondering, he fell asleep with the envelope under his pillow.

An insistent hammering at his door finally aroused him to sunlight and the voice of a steward. The boat was docked, everyone was being turned out; and as he had left no call for breakfast, Barnes was just out of luck on this head.

He examined his effects; everything was intact, and there had evidently been no intruders. Dressing hurriedly, Barnes stepped outside and knocked at the adjoining door. No answer. He tried the door and flung it wide open. To his astonishment there was no indication of occupancy; even the berths were made up. Yet the girl had been in this cabin. Seeing the steward pass, Barnes summoned him. To his inquiry, the steward gave him a blank look.

"No, sir, that cabin was not occupied. You had the only one on this deck, sir."

"What? When you brought me up here last night, people were talking in there!"

"Yes, sir, a gentleman did have the cabin engaged, but he went ashore again before we left Havre."

Barnes made his way to the reception sheds. Who had lied to him, and why? He had certainly accompanied her to that cabin after their stroll on deck. Had Truxon engaged it, then? Perhaps; she might have had an entirely different cabin, and had said nothing about it. Yes, she had a shrewd little head and no mistake. Trusted nobody. She was as sharp as a whip—and what a good liar! Besides, he reflected, a fat tip to the steward would have caused that individual to lie fast and hard about the cabin being unoccupied.

The customs and passport formalities were quickly settled. Finding that he had ten minutes to spare before the boat-train departed for London, Barnes dashed into the refreshment counter for a bite to eat.

He was gulping his coffee down when there came a quick, lithe step behind him. He sensed her presence and swung around.

Yes, she was there at his elbow, her eyes glinting with dark lights of danger.

"You! Well, I thought you'd skipped out!"

"You would think so," she said in a low voice, not without its touch of scorn. Despite everything, then, she still thought him something of a simpleton.

"I'm in debt to you, and I pay my debts," she went on under her breath. "Truxon went ashore at Havre. He flew across ahead of us. Now there's a small army of the worst rascals in Europe out to get you. Half a dozen of them are planted on the boat-train. They'll stop at nothing, and you'll never reach London alive."

"Whew!" Barnes whistled softly. "Looks as though we needed the good old interference play, eh?"

"Come along with me," she said, not asking him, but as though giving him the order. "I have a car and a chauffeur waiting. Hurry! We can drive up to London before the train gets there, and they'll not suspect. Come on."

She turned and was gone, giving him no chance to argue or question. Barnes followed her swiftly. In a flash he perceived that she had pitched upon the one chance to get through without trouble. He caught up with her at the station entrance.

"What about an appeal to the police?"

The question was rather inane and he knew it. She merely gave him one disdainful look, and went on to where a Daimler was drawn up. A chauffeur in whipcord held open the door. She entered; Barnes followed her in. The door slammed. The chauffeur slipped under the wheel on the right side, and next minute the car thrummed away and shot out like an arrow.

"By all means, this beats the train!" exclaimed Barnes, as they flashed through the streets of Southampton at top speed. To his astonishment, she flung him a look of sheer anger.

"You'd fall for anything, wouldn't you?" she snapped. "And I thought you were smart in spite of appearances!"

Barnes, mystified, blinked at her. Then sudden comprehension rushed upon him. Had she trapped him, after all?

He had no time to think, to speak. Even as he realized what must have happened, how easily he must have walked into her trap, the brakes squealed. The car turned a corner, ground to a halt, and a man from the curb leaped on the running-board. Next instant he was in the car, as it went on again. Barnes looked into a pistol.

"Keep your hands on your knees," snapped the stranger. "Sure he's the right one, Marie?"

"Yes," she said calmly.

Chapter 5

BARNES LOOKED at the man, who occupied the jump-seat facing him and the girl. The stranger was dark, grave, intent; he meant business. Barnes turned to Miss Nicolas.

"I congratulate you," he said coolly. "I rather fancied that your confidences of last night were—shall I say, a little too frank to be real?"

"You would," she rejoined cuttingly. The reiteration of this phrase got under the skin of Barnes, brought a flush to his cheeks; her scorn of him bit deeply.

"Was there any truth at all in your recent story about Truxon being here?"

"Yes," she said.

Silence fell. The car rushed on. They were out of the city now, following a surfaced but narrow road at tremendous speed. The chauffeur was expert. He avoided other vehicles in the swiftly-jerking, abrupt English fashion that always brought the heart of Barnes into his mouth; he could never get used to English driving.

"Well," and Barnes turned to the girl again, with the whimsical smile which seemed to anger her, "my eagerness in leaping to your aid would appear to have been wasted, eh?"

"You seem to have a lot to learn," she returned, level-eyed and coolly poised again.

"Undoubtedly. You don't seem overjoyed at the success of your strategem."

Color came into her cheeks. "I hoped you'd have too much sense to fall for it."

"You really are an excellent liar, you know."

"Call me an actress and be less insulting."

"Insulting? Not a bit of it. I think you're splendid!" Barnes said warmly. She bit her lip, and her dark eyes flamed at him.

"Will you hand over what you carry, Mr. Barnes? Or must we use other measures?"

Barnes shrugged. "I have no choice. You've got me."

With a sigh, he drew the brown envelope from his pocket and handed it to her. She seized it impatiently—and flung it through the open window of the car.

"Simpleton! There's nothing but blank paper in that envelope. No more trickery, if you please! Hand over the real message!"

Barnes broke into a laugh of such genuine amusement that it brought confusion to her features.

"So you didn't waste your time after all, Marie?" he exclaimed. "Blank paper, eh? But that blank paper held secret writing, my dear—"

"It did not," she exclaimed flatly. At this instant, as the Daimler roared along the twisting, narrow lane between the English hedgerows, the chauffeur uttered a sharp cry and slammed on his brakes. They were around a sharp curve, and here the road was blocked. Two cars had halted, the drivers were talking together. The horn of the Daimler blared at them.

"Look out!" cried the girl suddenly. "Look out—"

Her partner, on the jump-seat, flung open the door and leaped out. There was a shot, and he staggered, then fell forward on his face. Several men had appeared from the hedge on either side of the road. They ran at the Daimler, pistols in their hands. The girl made an impulsive movement to rise, but Barnes swept her back with his arm.

"Quiet," he said calmly. "There's Truxon. Keep your head."

Truxon, indeed, coming forward to the side of the Daimler, while another man held the chauffeur covered and helpless. Truxon; lean, dark, savage of face, and there at the roadside was the man Stacey. The girl murmured his name. Barnes looked out at him with interest. A rather weak, vicious sort of face; this fellow Stacey had none of his friend Truxon's vigorous be-damned-to-you hardness.

"Good morning to you," said Truxon, unsmiling, lean, narrow-eyed, looking in at the two of them over his pistol. "Will you step along with me, or must I use force?"

"Just a minute," interposed Barnes. "I'm rather anxious to get up to London. If money will talk—"

"Nothing will talk except what I'm after—and you know what that is," Truxon said, meeting his gaze inflexibly. "Which of you has it, I don't know; you'll both come along. Yes or no?"

BARNES GLANCED at Miss Nicolas. She was white, her eyes desperate; obviously, this man Truxon inspired her with actual terror. She nodded and rose. Barnes followed her out of the car. Truxon, with a word of direction, piloted them over to one of the two waiting cars and got in with them. He told the man under the wheel to wait, and sat there with his pistol covering Barnes.

The other men flung themselves on the Daimler, beginning a minute search of the car. The partner of Miss Nicolas was lifted

and placed inside; whether he were dead or wounded, Barnes could not tell.

A warning cry arose. Another car was coming along the road from Southampton. Truxon flung a command at Stacey, who walked back along the road and met it when it stopped. After a moment Stacey came along to the car in which the three sat, and was holding the brown envelope. He handed it to Truxon, with a grin.

"This was thrown out of their car a few miles back," he said.

"All right. Come along with us. Tell them, if they find nothing, to separate and let the Daimler go. That fellow is only shot in the leg. They can tie him up a bit."

Stacey fulfilled his errand, came back, and got in with them. Truxon flung an order at the driver, and the car moved off.

Barnes took the hand of the girl beside him, and patted it.

"Cheer up, Marie; you made a good try for it—"

"Shut up!" snapped Truxon. "Talk when you're asked, not until, unless you want a crack over the head."

Barnes nodded and kept quiet. He began to understand the paralysis of the girl before this man, whose lean, hard savagery held something inhuman. None the less, after a moment, he ventured to speak again, this time directly to Truxon.

"I'm apparently the person you want. You have me. Is it necessary to bother this young lady?"

Truxon grinned at him. "And let her go with the message, eh? Don't come anything like that. Either one or the other of you has it; and I'll get it. Now shut up."

The car swerved abruptly out of the surfaced road and turned into a lane. This ended at a pleasant old house, green trees about it, a low wall encircling the whole place. The gates stood wide ajar. The car swept in and halted directly before the house door. Truxon got out.

"Come along," he said, waiting, his pistol ready.

Barnes alighted, gave Miss Nicolas his hand, and caught a pressure from her fingers as she followed. Stacey came last. All four went into the house. The driver of the car left it where it was, and went around to the back of the house.

Truxon led his guests into a reception room, where an iron-jawed, elderly woman stood waiting. He nodded to her.

"All right, Wiggins; stand by. You two, sit down."

He tore at the brown envelope and brought to light a wad of blank paper sheets. He glanced at them, and handed them to Stacey.

"As I thought, a ruse. Just to make sure, have them tested at once for any secret writing. Marie, hand over that little pistol you don't know how to use. Quickly!"

The girl fumbled in her hand-bag. Wiggins, the hard-faced woman, came to her and caught the pistol out of her hand. Truxon nodded.

"Take her along, Wiggins, and go over her. Lock her in the east bedroom until I'm ready to talk with her. Report to me as soon as you've searched her. Run along, Marie; no protests, or I'll send Stacey to lend a hand with the search."

Stacey grinned at this. The girl flashed him a glance of contempt, then without a word accompanied Wiggins out of the room. Truxon turned to Barnes.

"All right. Will you hand over the paper we want, or not?"

"Paper?" repeated Barnes, with a puzzled air. "My dear fellow, that envelope was the only thing I have in the way of papers, upon my word! Surely you'll believe me?"

"Absolutely," said Truxon, with his mirthless grin. He handed over his pistol to Stacey. "Your job is to watch him every minute. Don't bungle it. Evidently there was nothing in the car. I doubt if she'll have anything. He's our meat."

Truxon went over to the door, that opened into the hall, and closed it. He came back and looked at Barnes.

"All right. Strip."

BARNES OBEYED without any useless protest. Realizing the prominence of the wrist-watch if he were naked, he tossed it on top of his shirt, finished stripping, then retrieved his cigarette case and took out a cigarette. Truxon snatched it from his hand, split it open, found only tobacco, and, with a grunt, handed him a cigarette and a match from his own case. Barnes lit the cigarette with a mild word of thanks.

Truxon slit every cigarette in the case of Barnes, examined the case narrowly, then examined Barnes from hair to toe-nails. He worked rapidly and in silence, but with obvious efficiency, while Stacey lolled in a chair and held the pistol. Upon a couch nearby lay a long dressing-gown of silk, obviously made ready in advance. When he had finished with the person of Barnes, Truxon picked this up and gave it to him.

"Thanks," Barnes said as he got into the

silken gown. "I must say that your foresight in all directions is admirable."

Truxon paid no attention, but fell upon the clothes at one side. Every garment was examined minutely. The shoes bore the brunt of this, their heels and soles being slit; satisfied that they held nothing, Truxon bade his prisoner put them on again, and went on with his search. There remained his money, including the roll of notes Sheldon had given him, and the articles from his pockets. These Truxon put on a table, and sat down to his job.

The passport covers were slit and inspected. The pen and pencil were opened up. The larger coins were tested for hollow cavities. The paper money was held to the light and scrutinized under a magnifying glass, note by note.

Barnes waited, smoking, in silence. The wrist-watch, he had already guessed from its being out of order, was merely a hollow bluff enclosing the message. He tried to keep his mind off it, lest Truxon catch the mental wave. His personal letters came next. Truxon glanced over these, then tossed them through the air to Stacey.

"Have these looked over with the blank paper. Under the postage stamps, remember. I don't think we'll find anything there, but neglect nothing."

Truxon picked up the wrist-watch. He looked it over, examined the strap with care, then pried off the back of the case. He pried off a second and inner back. Like many cheap European watches, this consisted of small round works contained in a square case. Over the works, Truxon held the magnifying glass, scrutinized them and then the lids and the whole watch with care.

Then, with a shake of the head, he snapped on the two back lids.

Barnes pressed out his cigarette in an ash tray. Nothing in the watch after all, then. No message. What the devil did it mean?

Chapter 6

THERE CAME a sharp rapping at the door. Truxon rose, betraying no disappointment, and waved his hand at the clothes and other things.

"Take whatever you want, except the clothes," he said to Barnes, carelessly. "You'll not need them for a bit."

Stacey chuckled evilly at these words. Truxon strode to the door and opened it to show Wiggins outside.

"Nothing, sir," she reported. "I've locked

PAT SAVAGE

SIX SCARLET SCORPIONS

When a man so anemic that he could be a vampire's victim comes to Patricia Savage for rescue, the impetuous girl can't say no. Excitement is her meat and danger her dessert.

Accompanied by Doc Savage aide, Monk Mayfair, Pat finds herself in the worst danger of her life. Wanted for murder, hounded by the minions of a weird mystery figure calling himself Chief Standing Scorpion, narrowly evading the hordes of the Vinegarroon tribe, the bronze-skinned golden girl battles her way to a sinister secret cached in an ancient ruin.

From the oilfields of Oklahoma to the forbidding Ozark Mountains, the trail of scorpionic doom winds. Will Pat Savage's first great adventure also be her last?

$24.95 softcover / $34.95 hardcover

ALTUS PRESS · THE NAME IN PULP PUBLICATIONS

her in there, but of course she can break out by the windows and get to the front entrance-roof."

"It'll do for the present," Truxon said. "I'll attend to her after a bit."

Barnes was standing at the table, stuffing the money, passport and other things into his dressing-gown pockets. Suddenly he was conscious that Truxon, from the door, was eying him keenly. Oh, clever Truxon! Just in time, Barnes was aware of the trap. He picked up the wrist-watch, looked at it, tossed it aside, pocketed his cigarette case. Then, as an after-thought, he took up the watch and negligently stuffed it into a pocket with the money.

Truxon came over to him.

"Barnes, I'm going to have that message," he said with calm, impersonal detachment. "It is now on your person. The chief terms of any secret Jugo-Slav entente wouldn't require much space. Well, you can imagine the next stage. I trust you'll not make things unpleasant for us? Here's your chance to hand it over."

Barnes looked at him, wide-eyed.

"The next stage? Oh, come, come! Surely you don't hint at medieval methods?"

"If I must, I'll burn it out of you inch by inch," Truxon said quietly. "Yes or no?"

Barnes merely shrugged.

"Come along," Truxon ordered curtly. "Stacey, follow on. We'll leave him in safety while you go over those papers."

Barnes knew now that he was a lost man; Truxon meant those words to the letter. And, when he had again picked up his possessions, he did exactly what Truxon had meant him to do.

He naturally would make sure of whatever held the hidden message. Somehow, of course, the secret must lie concealed in that wrist-watch.

He followed Truxon out into the hall, with Stacey at his heels. A stairway went to the upper floor of the house. Truxon strode on past this staircase, flung open a door underneath it, and disclosed a corresponding stairs that led down into the cellar. He turned a light switch and started down.

"Come on," he ordered.

Barnes followed him. On the second step, the American caught his toe, stumbled, and to save himself from falling, put out a hand to the wall. From the corner of his eye, he saw Stacey directly behind him and above.

Now, in a split second, Barnes acted. He caught Stacey's pistol-wrist and jerked at the man with all his strength, bending low as he did so. Caught off guard, Stacey was instantly unbalanced. The pistol exploded, drawing a sharp, agonized cry from Truxon below; probably the bullet struck him. Then Barnes had literally pulled Stacey over his head and sent him hurtling down through space, to crash into Truxon's figure.

With one leap, Barnes was back, catching at the door. He swung it shut, found a bolt, and shot it. Then, gathering up the dressing-gown about his knees, he dashed for the open front door and that car that still stood outside.

He was out of the house now, under the entrance portico, jumping for the car. As he reached it, a sudden laugh of exultation broke from him. The ignition key was still in the lock!

There was a crash, a tinkle of bursting glass. Barnes swung open the car door and glanced back. He saw Miss Nicolas scrambling from a window to the portico roof just above, and at the same instant, a pistol exploded somewhere. The bullet whined past his head and pinged off the side of the car.

Barnes leaped in, turned the key, and started the engine. As it roared, another bullet burst the windshield in his very face. The engine roared, and he reached for the gearshift lever. The girl was hanging from the edge of the roof. She came down with a rush, dropped, was up again.

The car moved. Miss Nicolas, panting, came scrambling in beside him, slamming the car door, sinking down breathless. The car pointed out for the open gates. Another bullet came crashing through, and another—

Barnes fell over sideways. He knew that the girl's hand had caught at the steering wheel, her other hand opening up the throttle. He slumped down, falling into darkness.

"Looks like—you win," he muttered, and then went to sleep.

WHEN BARNES opened his eyes and looked up, he blinked in astonishment.

He remembered everything very clearly, up to a certain point. But he could not credit his own eyes. For there, standing beside his bed and smiling down at him, was Marie Nicolas—and with her, the ambassador!

"Welcome back, Barnes," said the ambassador quietly. "Glad to hear you're not badly off after all. I must say you've accomplished something new to London—coming to an embassy in a dressing-gown! You know Miss Nicolas, I think?"

"Too well," said Barnes faintly.

"Well, man—the message?" The ambassador pulled up a chair. "Did you bring it through? Miss Nicolas is one of us. She thought she could handle things better than you could; she was going to bring you safe on from Southampton despite yourself. Where is it? Didn't Sheldon give you a wrist-watch for me?"

"Oh—that!" Barnes gulped hard. "My dressing-gown pocket—"

On a nearby chair lay the silk dressing-gown. The girl snatched it up. From its pockets she tumbled everything out on the bed. With a swift exclamation, the ambassador pounced upon the wrist-watch.

"Thank heaven!"

One of us! One of us! Barnes could only lie there, staring at Miss Nicolas, those words burning into him. One of us!

Drawing out a penknife, the ambassador pried the crystal from the watch. With the blade, he carefully broke off the two hands. He then lifted up the cardboard face inscribed with hours and minutes. This came clear; beneath were several thin slices of paper. He detached these, then sprang to his feet.

"Excuse me, please. I'll have these decoded instantly."

Barnes found himself alone with Miss Nicolas. She sank down on the edge of the bed and met his gaze, a little color rising in her cheeks.

"Oh, don't look at me like that!" she broke out. "I'm supposed to be in Italian pay; yes, I'm really one of you, as he said. I should have told you, perhaps; but I dared not. Sheldon knew; he warned me not to let a soul suspect the truth. I really do some work for Italy, you know. I'm an utter fool. I've made a mess of everything. And you— oh, how you tricked us all! You, with your innocence, your naïve cantrap, your pretended childishness; a Sphinx, that's what you are! A rascal!"

She laughed a little as she looked down at him, a hidden tenderness in her eyes. But Barnes blinked suddenly. His face changed. He came to one elbow.

"What an idea!" he exclaimed. "My dear Marie, you've done something—upon my word! No, no; never mind now. Later on, perhaps. The Sphinx! The Sphinx! Exactly the thing!"

And, forgetting her, forgetting all else, he stared up at the ceiling with a glow of eagerness lighting his face.

Made in United States
North Haven, CT
10 February 2023

32286334R00057